CW01217018

THE STORM
BENEATH THE WORLD
CHILDREN OF CORRUPTION #1

Other Books by Michael R. Fletcher

Black Stone Heart (The Obsidian Path #1)
She Dreams in Blood (The Obsidian Path #2)
An End to Sorrow (The Obsidian Path #3)

Beyond Redemption (Manifest Delusions #1)
The Mirror's Truth (Manifest Delusions #2)
A War to End All (Manifest Delusions #3 w/ Clayton W. Snyder)

Smoke and Stone (City of Sacrifice #1)
Ash and Bones (City of Sacrifice #2)
Sin and Sorrow (City of Sacrifice #3)

Swarm and Steel (Manifest Delusions Standalone)
Norylska Groans (w/ Clayton W. Snyder)
Ghosts of Tomorrow
In the Shadow of Their Dying (w/ Anna Smith Spark)
The Millennial Manifesto
A Collection of Obsessions

Coming Soon…
The River of Days (Children of Corruption #2)
Descent to Azakmar (The Driftland Dragons #1)
Dust of the Dead (A Novel of the Listening World)

THE STORM BENEATH THE WORLD

This is mostly a work of fiction. Names, characters, weird insect people, businesses, events, and incidents are the products of the author's demented imagination. Any resemblance to actual insects, living or dead, or actual events is probably coincidental. Except for the bugs living on sentient floating islands in the upper atmosphere of a gas giant. That happened.

Copyright © 2024 by Michael R. Fletcher

All rights reserved. No part of this publication may be reproduced, distributed, eaten, smoked, snorted, or transmitted in any form or by any means, including photocopying, recording, semaphore, smoke signal, mime, or other electronic or mechanical methods, without the prior written permission of the publisher (who is unstable at the best of times and let's be real, these ain't them), except in the case of brief quotations embodied in critical reviews (hopefully not *too* critical) and certain other non-commercial uses permitted by copyright law.
And let me be perfectly clear on this one: Using this novel to train your so-called AI is forbidden.

THE STORM BENEATH THE WORLD

For Carrie Chi Lough, First Reader.

# Ashkaro – Female

AHK TAY KYM

Blessed is she who never discovers her talent.
—The Redemption

Shadow blanketed the family estate, robbing the world of colour. Leaning back on her four hind legs, Ahk watched the majestic skerry descend, graceful despite its size. Mother said this one had several structures mounted on the arch of its back with room enough for twenty ashkaro. The silhouetted creature, all writhing tentacles from this angle, grew in detail as it reached the landing dock. A questing limb ending in a jagged maw reminiscent of those carnivorous plants in the wilder jungles, found one of the mooring pylons. Barbed spikes caught in wood and the skerry tilted as it pulled itself toward the dock. On the far side, another arm found the opposing pylon, righting the massive beast.

Ahk gasped in wonder. *It's beautiful!*

Infatuated with the play of light and the infinite hues of the world, she studied the skerry's shimmering carapace. A thousand shades of yellow and gold glowed lustrous, its underbelly darkening to something not far from the green of her own exoskeleton. Where the skerry's translucent shell ended, the remaining tentacles swayed in the morning breeze. The balloon creature hung suspended in the air as if by magic, losing altitude with maddening patience. Out of Ahk's sight, somewhere on its back, a crew guided the creature toward the Kym family landing pad.

It was rare to see skerry here, the platform more commonly a roost for the flitting tramea the family used to deliver messages. She loved watching the riders bring the vicious four-winged predators toward the dock in a mad, plummeting spiral as if tumbling out of control, only slowing their descent at the last possible moment. They'd dismount like heroes from the stories, dip a respectful nod to Ahk even though she was a child, and rush to report to Mother. Father said they were showing off, that such aerial acrobatics were dangerous and unnecessary. Mother said males couldn't understand such things. Ahk suspected both were right, but it was still a beautiful sight.

More of the skerry's tentacles reached for pylons with serpentine elegance. Finding purchase, they coiled tight like they meant to crush the towering poles or tear them from the ground. Once anchored, the massive beast pulled itself down until it hovered a few strides above the landing pad. Born in the endless skies, such creatures never truly landed. Family staff dashed forward pushing a wheeled staircase until it connected with the skerry's side. It all looked horribly precarious, the wooden structure wavering until the crew riding in the gondola mounted on the creature's back attached it there.

Grandmother Kym owned several skerry and a fleet of nimble tramea for flying patrols over the family's more leeward farms, but this was the largest Ahk had ever seen. She rode in one once when Mother took her to the capital to be introduced to the extended family. As the firstborn female and heir to the Kym family holdings, it was important everyone get a chance to meet her. That was ages ago, and Ahk couldn't remember much beyond how disappointed she'd been that they wouldn't let her out of the gondola. She'd wanted to look over the edge of the skerry's carapace and see the world below.

"It'll be like seeing what the gods see," she'd explained to Mother, only to be hushed and receive yet another confusing lesson about blasphemy.

She'd been a small child then, empty of responsibilities, with nothing more important than playing with her friends. Now, the grownups kept using words like 'young adult' and talking about how she needed to learn to accept responsibility without actually giving her any. Even the children of the household staff, most of them dulls or lower ranked brights, had more responsibility than Ahk. Bon, a dull boy her age, oversaw weeding her mother's sprawling flower gardens. When Ahk complained, Mother said, 'Ahk Tay Kym, that is dull work and beneath you.' Ahk argued that dull work was better than no work and Mother gave her a list of chores so unimportant they weren't even assigned to the staff.

After that, she snuck out each morning after her lessons to help Bon weed. It was nice working in the rich soil, brilliant flowers filling her thoughts with a peaceful hum of pleasure. At least until Father caught her and turned Ahk over to Mother. Annoyed, the Kym matriarch declared Ahk ready for weapons training even though she was a year shy of the standard age. Knowing it was purest bribery changed nothing. While Ahk glowed with pride at the opportunity, that feeling paled in comparison to watching the play of light change how various flowers looked.

"Ahk Tay Kym," said Bon, approaching from behind.

His carapace a muted brown with undertones of earthy orange, he stood a full head taller than Ahk. When they were out of antennae range of others, he called her by her first name, as she instructed. Where others might overhear, he was careful to use her full name.

"Bon," she said, tipping an antenna toward him in greeting.

His craft arms crossed over his chest, his raptorial arms hung loose, a dirt-caked shovel in one raptorial claw.

Antennae bent respectfully away, so as to display no untoward interest, Bon offered a slight bow.

As children, they'd been best friends. Now, each meeting felt more awkward than the last. Where she was being groomed for great things—serving with the Queen's Wing and eventually taking Mother's place as matriarch of the family—Bon would never be more than a gardener. Much as she hated to admit it, perhaps her mother was right: Brights and dulls could never be friends.

"You won't get in trouble for leaving the field?" Ahk asked, scanning the gathered ashkaro for Mother.

Bon's upper wings gave a casual flick. If he got caught neglecting his duties again, there'd be trouble.

Not sure what to say, Ahk said, "Come to see us off?"

"Only you."

Previously, she'd seen his every emotion in the twitch and wave of his antennae. She still caught hints of what was going on inside the boy, but he was becoming increasingly difficult to read. For the most part, he rarely showed anything more than polite deference.

A few months back Ahk made the mistake of trying to talk to her mother about it. Mother said Bon was 'old family dull' and knew his place. Frustratingly vague, as always. Of course, she would never say such a thing beyond the walls of her home. In public, everyone was equal, and, dull or bright, the colour of one's carapace didn't matter. She funded scholarships for gifted dulls too poor to attend the better schools. She gave speeches at the local university applauding the dull students of whom she was a patron, promising them positions within the family business should they graduate with sufficiently high grades.

In private, Mother bemoaned the inability of even the smartest dull to follow the simplest order.

"We'll be back in two weeks," Ahk said to fill the awkward silence.

"Then I look forward to a very quiet couple of weeks," Bon answered, antennae showing a hint of humour. "Mot said you were going to the edge of the world."

"Dull stupidity," she grumbled, feeling bad when Bon looked hurt. "Sorry. Look, the Nysh Queendom isn't the world. The islands are like that skerry," she explained, gesturing toward the floating creature, "but so much bigger it's impossible to imagine. We ashkaro live on their backs, forever travelling the river of days."

She'd read stories of islands populated by the banished Corrupt and marauding pirates. There were savage, feral islands where ashkaro had reverted to their hive roots and the queen ruled over mindless drones, warriors, and workers. It was too big for even a bright to truly understand. What chance did an uneducated dull have?

"The cottage is near the edge of the island," Ahk added. "Mother promised we'd go see it."

Bon's wings shivered in excitement. "You'll get to see Kratosh, the storm beneath the world," he said, voice soft. Darting a quick look to make sure no one had noticed them talking, he added, "Will you tell me about it when you get back?" An antenna bent toward her and then flicked guiltily back into place.

"I will."

"You're very good at describing things," he said. "I like to close my eyes and lose myself in your words. The colours. Every subtle shading. It's like I'm there. Like you somehow transport me." One main eye glanced in her direction before again focussing on the skerry. "It's how I'll get to be there with you."

"I'll tell you every detail," Ahk promised.

Mother won't like that.

The older Ahk got, the more Mother disapproved of her spending time with the dull boy. Or any of the one-name dull staff, for that matter. Ahk's little sister, Rayt, spent most of her time playing with a dull girl the same age and no one cared, but if Ahk spent more than a moment chatting with Bon, her mother appeared as if by magic and assigned them both chores. Usually on opposite sides of the estate.

Bon's antennae twitched, suddenly betraying nervous energy.

"What?" she demanded. "Spit it out."

Reaching into the front pocket of his earth-stained smock with a craft claw, he withdrew a wooden figurine. He kept it hidden from sight.

"What is that?" she asked. "Did you make it?"

He nodded.

"Show me."

They might be friends, but Bon was a dull fieldclaw and Ahk was heir to the Kym family business. He couldn't help but obey. Bon lifted his claw, opening it to display the figurine. Plucking it from his grip, she leaned forward, squinting to take in the exquisite detail. Carved and painted, it depicted a bright female. The veins in the upper wings were meticulously captured. The antennae, whisps of thin wood that looked like they'd snap if she breathed on them, expressed exuberant humour. Its carapace, painted a thousand shimmering hues of green, glowed with lustrous health. Breathtaking, it somehow captured the sleek deadliness of an ashkaro female in mid-hunt.

"It's beautiful," she gasped, and both sets of Bon's wings folded tight to his back. "It's…" Enthralled by the interplay of light and colour, she recognized that green. "It's me?"

Except eight times more beautiful and perfect than she could ever be.

This was a totem of worship, a creation of incredible skill and dedication.

Fear thrummed through Ahk. "Where did you find it?"

"I made it."

She'd already known that was the case yet prayed otherwise.

"Ahk Tay Kym," her mother bellowed from the front porch of the main house. The use of her full name spelled trouble. "Get back in here and finish packing this instant!"

"Tell no one," Ahk whispered, jamming the figurine into the front pocket of her smock. She cringed, feeling one of the delicate antennas snap off in protest at the harsh treatment, and saw Bon's grimace of pain. "Tell no one."

Then she fled. Mind racing, trying to fit this into her boring world where nothing ever happened, she dashed past her mother, heading for her rooms. Mother said something that she didn't hear.

Bon is a Corrupt.

Only someone cursed could make something so perfect and beautiful.

The dull discovered his talent and, instead of reporting it to the church so he could get the help he needed, he hid it. Until now. Until Ahk was leaving. Judging from the craftsmanship, he'd been practicing for some time. Was this why he'd become so sloppy in completing his chores? How far lost was he? Without guidance from the Redemption, he'd fall to the lure of his talent, and spend more and more time practicing until the addiction took him. Unable to care for himself, he'd carve ever more detailed and exquisite works of art until he starved to death.

Small clues, ignored for not being part of something she recognized, suddenly painted a terrible picture. Lately, he'd been dirtier than she remembered. As a fieldclaw, he'd always worked in the soil and so she hadn't paid attention. In the past months, his already dull carapace had gone from a clean matte brown to stained and scuffed. She'd teased him about it but assumed he was dirtier because he now worked more difficult jobs.

Ducking into the safety of her room, Ahk closed the door behind her. She stood dazed, antennae twitching in panicked confusion.

What should I do?

She knew what she was *supposed* to do: report Bon to Pol Mek Nan, the family's Redemption priest.

She'll take care of him. She'll... Ahk cursed silently.

The Redemption would take him away. His talent wasn't dangerous, so they wouldn't banish him to a Corrupt island, but he would be sent to the leeward desert. He'd spend the rest of his life living among the Corrupt, never to return. She'd never see him again.

The polite knock of house staff sounded on her bedroom door.

"Enter."

The door swung open revealing Vaz Wen's pale red carapace. No matter how she might buff it, it would never shine.

The head of the maids bowed. "Ahk Tay Kym, your mother sent me. The family is boarding now."

"I have to finish packing," Ahk said, realizing the clothes she'd previously laid out were gone. She'd been too distracted to notice.

"It's all taken care of," said Vaz, antennae dipping in apologetic correction.

Of course, it had. Mother only called her in to get her away from Bon without having to be rude to the boy.

Numbly thanking Vaz, Ahk headed to the waiting skerry.

The household staff and groundskeepers gathered to see the family off. Scanning the crowd, Ahk saw no sign of Bon. Had he left to work on the next figurine?

Why carve me?

She worried she knew the answer.

THE STORM BENEATH THE WORLD

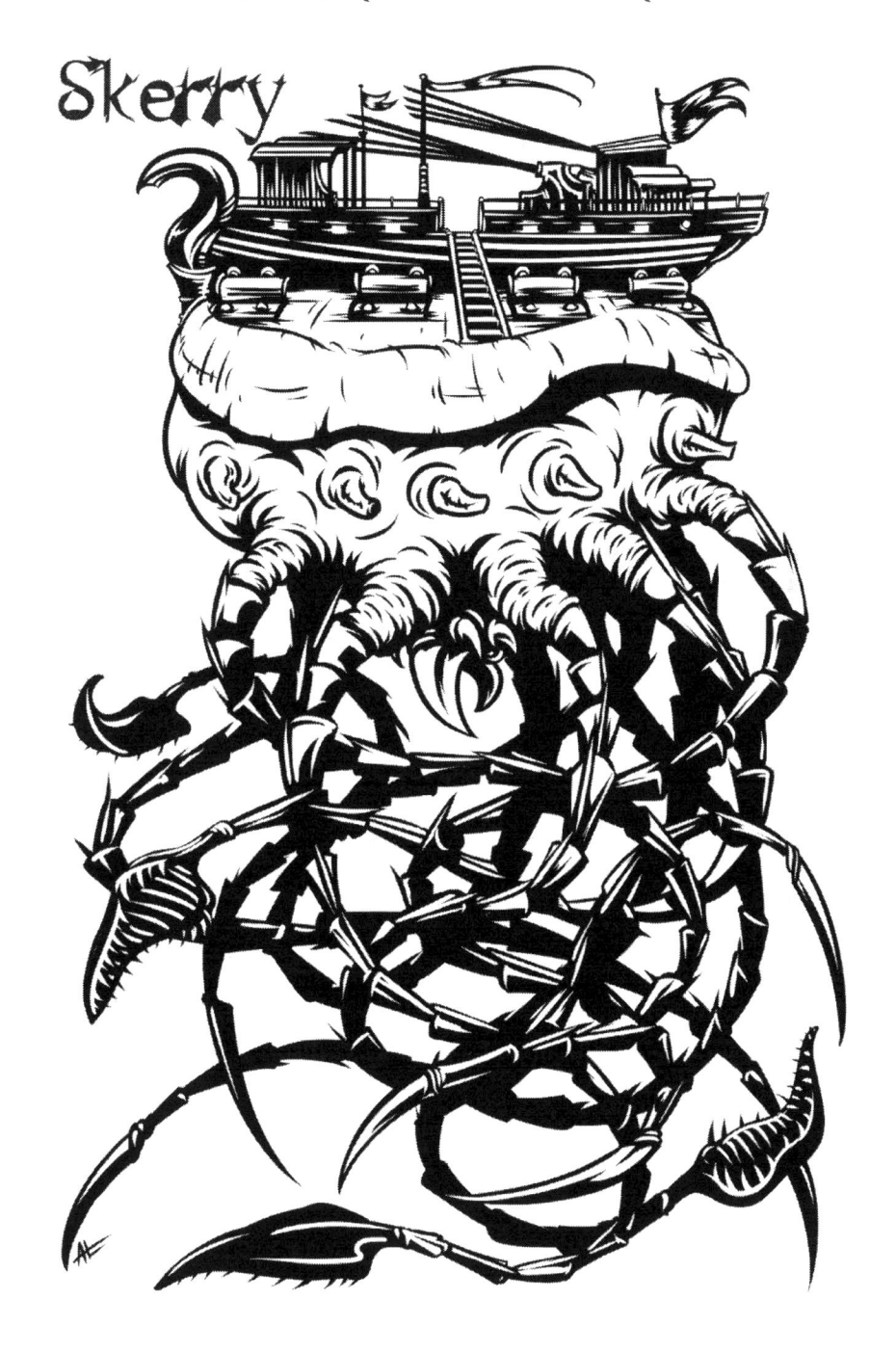

Skerry

JOH

The Sisters of the Storm are the military wing of Queen Yil's Church of the Storm. Trained in every form of stealth, combat, and infiltration, they are spies and assassins. It has been theorized that in the Nysh Queendom one in eight families has been infected by the Mad Queen's rhetoric and now harbours dissenters. More troubling are the rumours that the Sisters of the Storm have begun training the Corrupt instead of banishing them.

—*A History of the Mad Queen,* by Chuo Sdai Rhaj Een

Hanging in the frayed webbing of his hammock, Joh woke to the dim light before the morning's truth. The night's chill still claimed the air, tightening the joints and spiracles through which he breathed. Pale sand dusted his dull carapace, sticking in every groove and joint. Even here, somewhere between the leeward desert and the lush forests of the windward side of the island, coarse grit got in everything. Every root and grub tasted like sand; every sip of water left his mouth coated with dust.

With a groan, Joh straightened all eight limbs. Shaking them, he shed sand onto the floor. "Dad?"

No one answered.

Pushing himself upright, he saw his father's empty hammock. Either he'd risen early to make the trek from farm-to-farm begging for work, or more likely, he found work yesterday and spent the evening drinking his earnings at the Dripping Trough. If he wasn't in too rough shape, he might leave to seek employment from wherever he slept rather than returning home. Unless he had money left and felt guilty, in which case he might return with a treat for Joh. Maybe even sugar water. More likely, he'd return angry and hollowed out by whatever poisons he ingested in search of an escape and smack his son around before collapsing into his hammock.

Stretching again and shaking out the last of the sand, Joh left the shared bedroom. The shack's main room was as he'd left it the night before. He saw no sign of his father's typical clumsy stumbling. Constructed of branches, leaves, and thick mud, the hut was intended more as somewhere to hide from the dry daytime heat than protection from the night's chill. Gaps in the leeward wall showed a smear of golden light as the gods made ready to rise as they did each morning.

Padding into the kitchen area on four stiff legs, wings still twitching and fluttering from the cold, he hunted through the food baskets for something to eat. Dried puffer flies, little better than husks. They weren't too bad if you soaked them in water. He'd saved these in hopes they might distract his father's anger. Searching the makeshift counter, an unsteady affair of crates propping up a warped slab of wood, he spotted the water bucket. Glancing within, he saw half a claw's depth of stale, brackish water.

His antennae sagged.

Better to leave it. If his father returned and there was no water, he'd be mean and angry. He'd be worse than that if he was still bent from whatever he got into overnight.

I should suggest he'd do better if he stopped drinking.

So many mornings he thought that, just like so many nights he lay curled beneath his father's rage, protecting his sensitive antennae and the vulnerable joints of his craft arms, thinking he should propose father find some other outlet for his anger.

But he never did.

Some things you just didn't do. Some lines were not to be crossed. Father might be a hollowed wreck of an ashkaro, but he was all Joh had. He was family, and respecting family was an important part of the path to redemption.

Still, it was tempting.

Exiting the shack, Joh turned to face leeward, toward the growing brightness of the rising gods. The ever-present wind pushed him from behind as if urging him to set off into the desert.

"There's nothing there," Joh told the wind. "Nothing but sand and death and the Corrupt."

The wind didn't care.

Here, on the edge of the desert, some hardy plants still clung stubbornly to life. Stunted trees, bent and gnarled like an old ashkaro dull, littered the arid landscape, their cracked leaves rustling in the breeze. As he watched, a leaf surrendered to the inevitable and gave up on life. Twisting and dancing in celebration of its short-lived freedom, it rode the wind, racing off toward the rising gods.

After the leaf disappeared, Joh made his way to the sheltered garden plot at the side of the shack. Not too far into the desert, the soil retained enough moisture for a few of the tougher plants to grow. Nothing thrived out here, but life found a way. Father told him the deep desert was dead, endless dunes littered with the desiccated husks of those foolish enough to wander there. Sometimes he wove tales of strange creatures from the island's earliest days, back before the gods gifted the ashkaro with intelligence, elevating them beyond the hive. He said there were sun-bleached remains of massive and strange invertebrate monsters so huge you could walk within the walls they created. Having seen the little invertebrates scampering among the scrubs, Joh shuddered at the thought. Disgusting and squishy, the creatures were repellent in every way, the stuff of nightmares.

It never rained here, but some mornings Joh found dew clinging to the larger plants. Licking the drops, grateful for the moisture, he collected those leaves ready for harvesting. Not quite a meal, it might blunt his father's hunger enough to improve his mood. For all the priests rambled on about falling to the lure of the Corruption, and the brutal addiction that came with discovering one's talent, they blithely accepted the other addictions plaguing ashkaro life.

Can self-pity be an addiction?

Could that be his father's talent?

And then there was his dad's endless thirst for honey beer and his willingness to ingest anything that might alter his mental state or perceptions. Sometimes, it seemed like as long as your addiction made you miserable and was only harmful to yourself and your family, the priests of the Redemption didn't much care. It was only those talents that made you happy when you used them that the Redemption hated.

Being such a useless drunk that your wife abandoned you and your son was fine. The Redemption saw no sin there. But should you discover that people tended to follow your advice, and then use that to make life better for them, that was foulest blasphemy!

Tucking the broad leaves under a raptorial arm, Joh jumped to the well, all four wings pumping to make the distance. Leaning forward, he peered into the dark depths of the brick-lined hole. The well had already been here, long abandoned, when the family made their final leeward move, chasing ever scarcer employment. Mom said the old well was good luck, and that this was the perfect place to make their permanent home. There was a farm village called Landon not too far windward with a school Joh could attend, and a Redemption church. There was a score of farms within walking distance where father could find work, and she'd use the fibrous plants growing on the property to weave baskets for the locals.

Less than a year later, she was gone.

After that, father drank more, stayed out later and later trying to chase away whatever haunted him.

Damp mud sat at the bottom of the well. It'd be another day or two before enough moisture soaked out of the ground to make it worth lowering the bucket.

Nibbling the corner of one leaf, Joh returned to the hut, piling what was left in one of the food baskets. He stopped, attention locked on the container, main eyes and antennae focussed while his secondary eyes kept watch on the entrance. Weaved tight with a combination of skill and effort, it was all that remained of his mother. When she sold the first baskets in town, the local priest, a bright female named Shel San Qun, came from Landon to visit. Everyone knew she was investigating to see if the baskets had been constructed with talent, or if they were simply the result of dedication and years of practice. After watching mother work for an entire morning, Shel San Qun welcomed them to the community and left. Good as she was at weaving, the arduous task brought her no real pleasure and left her craft claws scraped and scuffed.

She used to—

A trilled whistle of greeting sounded from outside and Joh froze.

THE STORM BENEATH THE WORLD

Lost in thought, he hadn't heard anyone approach. It wasn't father, that much he knew. It might be someone bringing father home. That was bad, likely meant he'd been violent and maybe even spent the night sleeping it off in the church. There'd be fines to pay, apologies to make under Shel San Qun's watchful eye. Father would be angry and embarrassed despite it being his own choices and actions that caused it. If it was Constable Ghen Dai, Joh might be able to convince the elderly female to let father off with a stern talking to and maybe an order to stay out of the Dripping Trough for a few days. If Shel San Qun brought father home, Joh would remain quiet and subservient as was proper for a dull male. The Constable might be the law out here, the Queen's representative, but everyone bent before the will of the Redemption. The priests watched everything and everyone, examining every choice and action with a judging eye. Even Ghen Dai bowed low to Shel San Qun, her wings tight and controlled, antennae bent back in respectful obeisance.

The trilled whistle of greeting, tinged with polite deference, sounded again.

Too timid to be a priest, Joh decided.

It wasn't the Constable either. Though only a two-name dull, she'd never show such courtesy to a one-name dull household.

Is there anyone you'd be happy to find standing at the front door?

There wasn't.

Joh's wings gave an indecisive flutter of dark amusement. If he didn't answer the door, whoever it was might decide this rundown shack was abandoned and wander in to explore. Being caught inside with a stranger left him feeling more vulnerable than meeting one at the threshold.

Pushing the door open, Joh remained within.

Still low on the leeward horizon, Alatash, the glowing city of the gods, source of all light and warmth, continued its ascent. Forever hidden from the eyes of their undeserving children, the gods lived above the clouds.

Joh muttered a quick prayer of thanks, lifting all four arms in supplication, in case it was Shel San Qun. One could never be too pious in the presence of the Redemption.

THE STORM BENEATH THE WORLD

Two scruffy whites stood outside, bleached carapaces cracked and weathered from years in the arid desert air. The male, a hulking brute whose limbs showed many thickenings where his exoskeleton had been damaged, wore the faded vest of the Queen's Wagoneers. The female, slightly taller than Joh, who was unusually small for his age, shivered uncontrollably.

He recognized the tremors. His father showed the first signs of fenrik leaf addiction, wings sometimes twitching.

If he doesn't stop, by the end of the year, he'll be just like her.

The big male crossed scarred raptorial arms and bowed as if he stood before a bright female rather than a dull male child. Joh saw no hint of mockery.

"Greetings," said the male, body language showing nothing but deepest respect. "We are two veterans travelling windward in search of employment."

Dehydrated by the desert air, their pale carapaces doomed them. It was hard enough for Father to find work; no one would hire a white. At best, folks would assume they were of such low standing they'd be too stupid to follow the simplest instruction. At worst, people would think them banished Corrupt trying to sneak back into civilized society.

"We have no work here," said Joh. "Our garden is small. And we have no money with which to pay you," he added, hoping to forestall any thought of robbery.

The female twitched. The male's nod of glum acceptance sent a twinge of guilt through Joh for assuming the worst.

"Could we bother you for a sip of water?" the male asked. "I see you have a well. We would happily work for it. Perhaps I could weed your garden in return for a cup?" Reaching out, he placed a gentle craft claw on the female's shoulder, stilling the shivers.

"The well is mud," said Joh. "Sorry."

The male sagged, massive and yet cut low by a few simple words.

You have to help them.

Knowing this would earn him a thrashing, Joh said, "I have a small amount of water inside. The two of you could share it."

The male perked up, antennae straightening. "We'd be grateful. We could—"

"No need," said Joh. Charity wasn't charity if you asked for something in return. "Sit in the shade of the hut and I'll bring the water." An odd thrill of pleasure shivered his wings as the two ashkaro did as he suggested.

Careful, he cautioned. Sometimes it slipped out, unbidden and unplanned.

Ducking back into the shack, he fetched the cup and brought it to the two crouching in the shade. He offered it first to the female and she spasmed, staring at the cup with something between horror and desperate hope.

"Please," said the male, "allow me. Kash has the shakes bad today."

"Fenrik leaf?" asked Joh, and the male's antennae nodded agreement. "My father—" He stopped, unwilling to say more. Instead, he passed the cup.

With surprising care, the big brute fed sips of water to his companion, fussing over her, and making sure no drop was wasted. Only when her shakes receded did he allow himself a taste.

"You can finish it," said Joh.

"You have more?"

"Soon I'll be able to get more from the well." It wasn't quite a lie, but he didn't want the whites to feel guilty. They needed it more than he and father.

Bowing low in gratitude, the male fed the rest to Kash, taking none for himself.

"I'm not sure there's much work around here," Joh said. He didn't want to hurt them but hoped to save them some pain and disappointment. "There's a church in Landon, the nearest town," he added so they knew to be wary. They might not be Corrupt, but if they were, that knowledge would surely turn them back.

The Redemption's holy purpose was saving the ashkaro, ensuring every soul had the chance to earn forgiveness. Up to a point. Refuse to obey the laws and there were worse punishments than the slow desiccating death of the desert.

Or at least that's what his father said. 'Better behave, or the priests will drag you to the edge of the world and feed you to the storm.

THE STORM BENEATH THE WORLD

Katlipok will devour your soul. You'll never be born again!'

All the gods in Alatash forbid father ever learns my secret.

Dad might be a drunk and a fenrik leaf addict, but he was a pious drunk and addict. He even claimed to have made a pilgrimage to the edge to see the storm back before he met Mom.

The big male carefully returned the empty cup to Joh, offering it with both craft claws. "We have to try," he said, looking windward. "I have to try."

Forever curious, Joh had too many questions: Were they both military veterans, and if so, how did they end up in the desert? Were they Corrupt? What were their talents? Were they dangerous? The two dulls looked old, though it was difficult to judge age in a white. Had they fought in wars? Who had they fought? Were they spies from the Yil Queendom come to preach subversion?

You could suggest they tell you.

Crushing his curiosity, Joh accepted the cup. Father would be angry if he thought Joh drank it all, leaving him none. He'd be livid if he discovered his son gave it to vagrant whites.

The brights look down on us. They think we're stupid. We, in turn, sneer at the whites. Who do they get to look down on?

Holding the cup in one of his craft claws, Joh crouched in the dwindling shade, watching the two whites walk windward. The female stumbled often, her limbs refusing to cooperate. The male kept her upright. By the time they were gone, the gods had risen high enough to banish the last shadows. And still Joh stared windward, a strange feeling scraping at his nerves. Something between soul-deep sadness and an appreciation for the white male's loyalty to his mate even though she was in the final stage of her addiction. Within weeks she'd become immobilized, limbs incapable of synching. If the male could supply more leaf and feed her, she might last another month. Otherwise, it was a race between starvation and withdrawal to see which killed her first.

Another emotion scratched at the inside of his carapace, trying to break free. This dusty place with its mud well wasn't so different than death. He wanted to leave, to *move*. The Nysh Queendom was massive beyond understanding. Mom had told him about forests, towering trees growing so close together an ashkaro couldn't walk between them. On the windward side of the island, she said, even a dull's carapace might shine with health. Fields of crops reaching to the horizon. Green grass and wet air. Lakes and ponds. Hundreds of thousands of ashkaro living in massive cities. It beggared comprehension. The population of Landon, the only sizeable settlement he'd ever known, numbered maybe three hundred. He'd seen skerry pass by overhead but couldn't imagine riding one. He'd heard tales of daring pilots mounted on tramea, riding the swift predators into battle. The few he'd seen were haggard and feral.

I'll never see any of that.

This middle ground between the lush life of the windward side and the leeward desert was a hell worse than Kratosh if only because it was his life. Not that he didn't believe in the gods in Alatash and the Queen of the Storm.

A dull life for a dull boy.

Shel San Qun preached acceptance of one's lot. Every ashkaro was born into the life they were supposed to lead. Abandoned by his mother, his father a fenrick addict, this was his.

This was what he deserved. Such things couldn't be changed.

We are born to our fate.

A dry breeze whispered through husked leaves. Dust swirled in miniature funnels, dancing like tiny wind demons, and then fell dead and still. Nothing moved and no insects sang.

A quiet hell.

The passing whites were likely the sum-total of the excitement he'd see for the next few hundred days. Though perhaps the beating father would give him when he got home might surpass it.

Probably not.

Everywhere is better than here.

Travel leeward and there were the desert cities where the Redemption banished the Corrupt deemed safe enough to remain on the island. Joh tried to imagine a city populated by ashkaro who had discovered their talent. What wonders were possible? Buildings designed by Corrupt architects and built by the Corrupt talented in such things. How could such a place be less interesting than a crumbling shack and mud well?

Out in the true desert were storms, parched winds clawing the land, colossal whirlwinds of scouring sand. Unknown monsters lurked beneath the dunes or coasted invisible in the clouds above.

Sometimes huge shadows swept by their shack and Dad screamed at Joh to run for cover or cower beneath one of the stunted trees, hiding from whatever prowled the sky. Sometimes larger shapes blotted the light of the gods. Nothing ever came of it, and he rarely saw anything more dangerous than flying rafak snakes. Even then, they were usually juveniles, too small to eat an ashkaro.

After spending a few hours making a half-hearted attempt at weeding the garden—though, truth be told, the weeds fared no better than the crops—Joh retreated indoors. He felt as dry as the garden soil.

Propping the door open, he crouched in the shade.

A bright light beyond the clouds, Alatash fell toward the windward horizon. Indistinct shadows grew long and still his father failed to return.

Joh waited until the insects and animals of the night raised their voices in predatory chorus before closing the door. There were things out there more dangerous than whites begging for water. Sand snakes, segmented and silent, hunted the dunes for prey. Though he was too large for most to swallow whole, many could kill with their venomous bites and stings. Some planted eggs in their paralyzed victim, their offspring devouring it from within until they were large enough to claw their way free. Dad claimed the poor bastard was awake and alive through the entire process—which sometimes took weeks. Recently, Joh had begun to doubt some of the things his father said. Sometimes Dad's antennae suggested muted humour during such grotesque stories. While Joh might no longer believe everything, he still didn't want to die feeding a nest of writhing baby rafak.

Tramea hunted at night. The wild ones were usually too small to carry away even a runt like Joh, but some grew to be terrifyingly large, easily capable of plucking a full-grown male from the ground. Even scarier were the soft, mud-like creatures Mom said had internal skeletons called *bones* rather than exoskeletons. Most fled squeaking if Joh came near. Some, however, got very quiet and very scary, their disgusting wet mouths full of protruding bits of their internal bones like a mockery of the natural laws. Back before Mom left, one chased him home. After that, he decided to avoid them.

Dark followed Alatash's descent, claiming the world as the gods sank from sight.

Still no sign of his father.

Joh ate one of the slugs he collected earlier, spitting the sandy grit. His vest would have tasted better.

Wish you hadn't given away the last of the water now, don't you? he thought, imagining his father's voice.

Thirsty as he was, he felt no regret. Though, if the well still showed nothing but mud tomorrow, that might change.

WEX JEL

The gods of Alatash lifted the ashkaro above the beasts, ending the days of hive. First, the queens became sentient. Then, with the passing generations, her guards, warriors, workers, and even the male drones, became self-aware.

The gods showered their children with gifts: They tamed the colossal islands floating in the river of days so we might live upon them. They taught us to wield simple tools and later craft our own. They taught us to mine compacted clay from the backs of the ancient islands and they taught us to fire those bricks so we might construct temples to their glory. Finally, well-pleased with their work, the gods gifted their children with talents so we might one day ascend to join them in Alatash.

But the god Katlipok grew jealous and twisted those talents, perverting them so they devoured those who dared use their gift. In a rage, the other gods banished Katlipok to Kratosh and she became the Queen of the Storm.

—The Redemption

Deserts are so boring!

With Mom and Dad pulling a double in the brickworks factory, Wex wandered the three-room home they shared, fidgety and impatient. As a shift manager, her mother earned enough they never went hungry and had the luxury of spare water for bathing. Where the carapaces of many of Wex's friends were already fading, hers remained a healthy matte brown shot with green stripes. Like everything, however, there were two sides to the leaf. Being able to occasionally spritz herself with water meant Wex's exoskeleton remained healthy. Dull as she was, that greatly improved her marriage prospects. Unfortunately, Mom was already talking about an arranged marriage to the son of one of her superiors, a two-name bright whose family long ago fell from grace. Wex met the boy once at a casual lunch that was anything but casual and found him nice but tediously docile. As Mom so often liked to remind her, out here in the desert, the pickings were slim.

Worse than that, as a dull with a healthy carapace, she didn't fit in anywhere. The other dulls, all slowly fading as the desert sun bleached their carapaces, looked upon her as if she'd sold some part of her soul. No matter how she cared for her exoskeleton, buffing and polishing, brights never saw her as anything more than another dull.

Returning to the main room, which served as kitchen, dining, and socializing area, Wex ate a few damp slugs, enjoying the crunchy texture.

Dad, a general labourer at the same brickworks, should be home first. That wouldn't be for several hours, longer than she could pace the shack stalking imaginary prey.

So bored!

She'd learned never to say such things aloud; doing so invariably resulted in chores.

Wex's antennae twitched, searching for movement. A little jumping arachn or webling. Anything! Her raptorial arms reached for nothing, barbed spines ready to trap her next meal, and retracted empty. Mom said it was because Wex neared hunting age, that time when females went a little crazy and got into all sorts of trouble. Dad grumbled about having a feral tramea in the house who was always hungry and looking at everything like she meant to tear it apart.

'Girls will be girls,' Mom said. 'You've got to stay out of the way until they get it out of their system.'

Back in the main room, Wex ate several more grubs, her stomach complaining it wanted something bigger.

Meat. Real meat.

Though she'd never hunted, she craved the thrill of the chase. The idea of stalking something with the intent to kill and devour it was tantalizing. Pitting oneself against the wild. The ultimate test, Mom called it, though Dad always shook his head and grumbled about how you could take the female out of the hunt but not the hunt out of the female. Truth was, he was proud of Mom's past, even if she didn't talk much of her time in the Queen's Claw.

I bet she fought pirate islands!

That, she decided was a fun idea. Maybe some of the neighbourhood kids would join her in a game of Queen's Claw versus Pirates.

Anxious to be moving, she left the shack, slamming the door behind her.

An eternal dome of cloud blanketed the sky in every direction. From somewhere beyond that wall, a single source of light illuminated the queendom. The clouds were so high! She read once that no skerry or tramea-mounted Queen's Claw had come anywhere near reaching them.

How shiny would Alatash have to be for its light to make it here?

In a moment of amused blasphemy, she imagined gods stumbling around, squinting through their claws, blinded by their own brightness, and laughed.

The arid breeze felt like a reminder of mortality, a constant air of desiccating death. Every day hundreds of exoskeletons of small creatures blew into Brickworks #7 to litter the streets. Sometimes the soldiers who patrolled the desert found the empty shells of ashkaro who got lost in sandstorms or were devoured by wild tramea or poisoned by winged rafak snakes. They always carried them back to town so the carapace might be seen to by the Redemption.

Chad, the white who cleaned the streets of Brickworks #7 in a futile attempt to keep them free of sand, stood nearby, leaning against his two brooms. A jump leg idly scratched at the back of a steering leg as he studied the street he just swept. Unnoticed, Wex watched him watch sand blow across the lane, undoing his efforts.

"Makes you think, doesn't it?" she called, more to be friendly than out of a desire for conversation.

Chad moved with the cautious patience of an elderly male. Recognizing Wex, he nodded deferential respect beyond anything she deserved. "Huntress Wex Jel, a beautiful morning to you. And no, it doesn't."

Chad always used outdated formal modes of address. Particularly when conversing with children, whom he always talked to as if they were court royalty, no matter their carapace.

"But you have to see it's a pointless task," she said. "I mean, the very street you're currently sweeping has already got sand on it."

Chad leaned heavier on the broom, glancing at the street. "Yes. And yet, no."

Was the question too tricky for his desiccated white mind?

With nothing else to do, and seeing no other children on the street, Wex asked, "How so?"

"Perception," he answered. Noting her confusion, he added, "The town council think they hire me to sweep the streets."

Wex's antennae straightened in surprise. "I'd say most people think that."

Chad twitched one wing to say, *This may be true, and yet...* "People think what people think, but just because they think something doesn't make it true. When you are the subject of their thoughts, it's what *you* think that matters."

Oh gods, an individualist.

The town priest said that while the ashkaro had evolved beyond hive, they were still social creatures. She said some ashkaro took it too far, focussing selfishly on themselves. The sermons were hard to follow and seemed to suggest that while it was okay to be an individual, you shouldn't be *too much* of one. When Wex tried to ask how much individuality was acceptable, her mother shushed her.

Curious despite herself, Wex asked, "If that's why the council hired you, doesn't that suggest it's your job?"

"Most definitely, wise huntress."

"But, there's a but."

"But there's always a but," he agreed. "The council thinks my job is sweeping streets. I think my job is getting paid." Releasing one of the brooms and letting it lean against his thorax, he waved a craft claw at the sand. "And so, I don't think about the futility. In fact, there's probably a life lesson there."

Life lesson from a white male? This should be good.

One main eye watching Wex, the other checked to see no one noticed him slacking off, he said, "Futility is a bad thing, right?"

"Right," she agreed. "No one wants to do something pointless."

"But if the sand didn't undo my work, someday I'd be out of a job. Futility keeps me employed. Anyway, as I said, sweeping isn't why I sweep."

"Getting paid is."

"A most sharp huntress! And getting paid is never futile."

"Where's the life lesson?" Wex asked.

"What life lesson?"

With a courtly bow, Chad wandered off, once again lazily pushing his brooms before him.

"Now what?" Wex asked the empty street.

Scanning her surroundings, she searched for inspiration. The so-called downtown core of Brickworks #7 consisted of a score of neat clay brick homes clustered around the mammoth factory, itself constructed of the same bricks. Thick smoke vomited from all six chimneys, the clay ovens hard at work.

Did they make those here before the factory was built, or make them elsewhere and cart them here?

Those houses close to the factory—some, two or three stories tall—belonged to the brights who owned and ran the brickworks. Usually they were uninhabited, a few staff left to dust and maintain the property.

Beyond the clean and tidy homes of the wealthy brights lay fifty some-odd shacks, most built of wood and mud. A few bent and exhausted ashkaro coming off their shift, carapaces coated in clay dust and stained black from smoke, staggered toward their homes. Several more, slightly cleaner though no less tired, shuffled toward the factory.

Neither group looked happy.

Is that it?

Though ancient and faded white from the dry desert air, Chad was cleaner, less bent from his efforts, and arguably happier than any of them.

Not so dumb, perhaps.

What did it mean if an old white was the smartest ashkaro she knew?

She watched the two groups pass in the street, barely

acknowledging each other. Was that her future? As a two-name female, she'd likely land a job much like her mother's. Though Mom came home less dirty than Dad, who worked feeding the endlessly voracious ovens, she seemed no happier. When the brights who owned the brickworks visited, they rarely entered the factory. Mostly, they lounged under broad parasols sipping drinks as their employees sprayed them with water pumped from private wells. When they got bored, they'd gather up their hunting bows and long spears and wander into the desert to stalk tramea. They'd return bragging of their successes, not bothering to haul the carcasses back despite all the dull families scraping a subsistence living on grubs and leaves.

That's it! I'll go hunting!

Wex looked back toward the shack. She could duck inside and get Mom's bow and arrows. Every ashkaro who did military service retired with their weapons and gear, the quality of which was beyond anything a dull could afford. It was, Mom said, because service to the queendom never truly ended. If the Mad Queen Yil invaded when Mom was on her deathbed, Mom would rise, grab her weapons, and go to war.

She'll be angry if she finds out.

And even angrier if Wex damaged them.

That said, if she killed something big enough to feed the family, everyone would be so happy to eat something besides slugs the transgression would be ignored. Or at least the punishment minimal.

And if you don't bring home dinner?

Turning her back on Brickworks #7, Wex headed out into the desert. First, she'd find a rock capable of holding an edge. Then she'd search for a stick of a decent length and turn it into a crude spear. Maybe it was Chad calling her huntress, but this sounded more fun and a lot less dangerous than touching Mom's military gear.

Stick and stone, she'd hunt like ashkaro did in the days of hive.

SHAN WYN VAL NUL NYSH

In days long past savage ashkaro burned their dead.
 The Redemption tells us that the souls of those who burn are incinerated, never to be reborn. The souls of those thrown to the storm are claimed by Katlipok, also never to be reborn. If fire destroys souls, what happened to the souls of all those ancient ashkaro? Will the river of days eventually run out of ashkaro, or are new souls being made? And if so, where are they coming from?
 Are the gods in Alatash—who the Redemption tell us abandoned their creations—making new souls?

—Awar Dun Nih Yhir, Philosopher

After a brutal game of rush that ended with Nin Arl Zon being carted off the field on a stretcher, Shan's team returned to the locker room in high spirits. Wax candles lined the clay brick walls, lighting the room a golden yellow and filling it with the scent of honey. When Shan first joined the team his family worried that he might have discovered his talent, so earnestly did he throw himself into the game. After sitting in on a few practice sessions, the family priest assured Shan's mother the boy was 'overly exuberant.' Shan was less sure. He never felt quite so alive as when playing.

Overly exuberant.

Such a casual dismissal of his effort, as if he could never do anything important.

When a female became intent about something, they said she was 'making an important contribution,' or 'doing serious work.' When a male did the same, it was 'look how cute he is when he's trying to focus.'

"Did you hear Nin's leg break?" crowed Styr Alm Nib Tys. "That's going to leave a thickening!"

Shan winced. He hadn't meant to hit Nin that hard, but with it being the last game of the season and the school's pride at stake, he'd been entirely fixated on winning.

The splash of blood when the leg snapped and the sight of Nin's splintered exoskeleton, blue ichor gushing through the cracks, turned Shan's gut.

"I hope he's all right," he said, careful not to sound too caring. There were limits to how much concern one should show for a lower-caste bright.

Styr waved it away with a craft claw. "You get in the way of the queen's nephew, you get stomped. Anyway, it's all part of the game."

While true, Shan still felt a pang of guilt. Rush was a rough sport, dating back to the days of hive when males had to show their worth to earn a place in the colony. Though simple on the surface—get the wicker ball across the enemy's goal line—it was surprisingly difficult, with a near infinite number of strategies and plays. When Shan's coach and teammates visited for game-plan sessions Mom inevitably took a moment to belittle their efforts. She'd mutter about how adorable it was watching males strategizing how to get a ball over a line.

There were few rules to the game. Weapons were forbidden, and the ball had to cross the line intact. Crushing an opponent so the ball he carried was ruined was fair game. It wasn't Shan's fault Nin hadn't seen his mighty wing-assisted jump.

He should have been paying attention!

Stripping off their jerseys, the team, all bright males of the best families, entered the showers. Those few who weren't too dirty finished in minutes, towelling off their carapaces and heading to class. Shan, caked in dirt and Nin's blood, was the last to finish. He always was. Returning to the locker room, he found it empty, the way he liked it. Life as the queen's nephew was a careful balance between poised perfection, carapace polished to a gleaming shine, and making it look effortless. As such, he'd built a reputation for striding into every class late, even when he didn't need the extra time to buff out some smudge.

With nothing scheduled for the next period, Shan took his time, working his carapace until he achieved a mirrored gloss of golden fire. Once he had the school vest, rich burgundy on a shimmering grey with his family crest prominently displayed, sitting to best effect in the centre of his thorax, he left the locker room to look for lunch.

Distracted checking the lay of his wings, he didn't see Nyk Arl Zon, Nin's older sister, until the door closed behind him. Slowing to a halt, Shan checked the hall, finding it empty. With no other sports scheduled today, no one would enter the building until tomorrow.

Small, sleek, and deadly, Nyk focussed all six eyes and both antennae on Shan. "Well, if it isn't the golden shit," she drawled.

Shan took an awkward step back and she followed with predatory grace.

"I'm sorry about your brother," he mumbled. "It's…it's part of the game. He should have—"

"You're twice his size," said Nyk, which wasn't true, though he was twice her size. Not that it mattered. "You did it on purpose," she finished.

"I didn't!"

She skittered forward, barbed arms reaching teasingly for him. If it was any other female in any other place at any other time, it would have been incredibly sexy. Instead, he was torn between curling into a ball and screaming for help or being submissive in the hopes she wouldn't kill him.

Shan backed away.

"You're almost too pretty to hurt," she said, matching his retreat.

He looked down at her in fear. Being bigger wasn't worth much when your opponent was twice as fast and had the best combat schooling available to a wealthy bright family. From the viciously sharp tibia to the gripping tarsi to the barbed arms, every part of Nyk was a weapon. Long ago, males like Shan would have lumbered about the hive building and repairing. Nyk would have been a hunter or a warrior. Over and over his teachers drilled into him that fighting a trained bright female was suicide. To make her point clear to the others, his elderly unarmed-combat instructor took great pleasure in humiliating him in front of the class, cooing about how something so pretty could never be dangerous. In all the time he sparred with her, he hadn't once landed a solid blow.

THE STORM BENEATH THE WORLD

"I think," said Nyk, "I'll do to you what you did to my brother." Antennae flicking in cruel humour, she added, "It's just part of the game."

Fleeing would be pointless. She'd catch him before he reached the first door.

Shan stood his ground. *Bluff your way out of this.* "What, exactly, do you think will happen here?" he demanded, fighting to keep his voice calm. "How do you see this ending? You *know* who I am. You think—"

"Lovely as you are," said Nyk, "you're the youngest son. Your sister told me you're failing half your classes and barely passing the rest. Pretty, and pretty dumb."

Shan tried to make himself bigger to hide the fear. Of *course* his older sister was friends with Nyk. He imagined them laughing about his grades, making fun of how long he spent each morning caring for his carapace.

"Your sister says you're an embarrassment," said Nyk. "I might not have your name, but my family owns the largest, most fertile farm island in the queendom. I'll take my slap on the tarsi if it means I get to watch you carried out on a stretcher like you watched my little brother."

She wasn't wrong. Last time Mom saw his grades, she shook her head in disappointment and grumbled about how she'd have to find him an advantageous marriage, preferably to someone either dim-witted or shallow and blinded by his beauty. Even his older brothers treated him like an idiot. If no one ever trusted him with real responsibility, how was he supposed to prove himself?

Nyk crouched, legs braced and ready to pounce.

Call for help.

If he was loud enough, maybe someone would hear and come to investigate. Maybe they'd get here before she broke him. He turned one main eye toward the door, praying it would swing open as someone return to fetch something they'd forgotten in the locker room.

Please.

Screaming for help would be the coward's way.

But that wasn't the problem; limbs locked rigid in terror, Shan couldn't move.

"I didn't mean—"

THE STORM BENEATH THE WORLD

Faster than eye or antennae, Nyk lashed out with a claw, leaving a long gouge in his carapace. She'd been careful not to puncture, and he felt no pain as he stared at the appalling damage.

"Not so brave without your gang of moron males, are you?" Her wings fluttered in excitement, claws clicking. "I'm going to—"

A stutter of sparks lit the air between them.

Nyk shook her head as if trying to dislodge the vision. Main eyes suddenly focussing on Shan's antennae, she hesitated.

Did she do that?

By all the gods of Alatash, had he been cornered by a deranged Corrupt?

Nyk swept Shan's front legs out from under him, crashing him to the floor. Kicking and flailing, he tried to fight, hoping to startle her with unexpected ferocity. She stomped on his head, leaving him dazed, and pinned him effortlessly. Both craft arms bent the wrong way, the feel of grinding exoskeleton reverberating through his entire body, he became still and compliant.

Scream. Call for help. Do whatever she wants.

Anything to avoid permanent damage.

"Just let it happen," Nyk whispered, wrenching one arm until he whimpered in pain. "Let it happen or I'll break them both."

"Stop. *Please.*"

A gouged carapace was one thing, but torn joints often healed badly, leaving the victim limping and crippled.

"I'm sorry," he begged. "I can make it right. My family has money."

"You can't make it right, you vacuous *trophy.*" She leaned closer. "But *I* can."

Shan screamed when she gave his right craft arm a vicious twist. A bright flash lit the dim hall, and her weight was gone. Rolling to his feet, he rubbed at the tender joint and turned to find her staring at him with rapt and terrifying attention.

"That was you," she said, retreating. Gone was the predatory grace, replaced by a deep and ancient horror.

"No."

"Corrupt," she hissed.

THE STORM BENEATH THE WORLD

I can't be Corrupt, I'm a Nysh!

Nyk backed away another step. "I'm going to tell." Mandibles clicking in ferocious glee, she added, "This is even better! The Redemption will banish you!"

More sparks stuttered between them, brighter and hotter. The air stank like burnt grass.

The Redemption would take him from his family. They'd ship him off to a Corrupt island. He'd lose everything, his beautiful carapace drying and cracking until it became white and disgusting.

Mom will disown me.

"I'll tell them you attacked me, that you're dangerous!" She grabbed a candle off the wall. "Maybe I'll light a few fires, say you lost control."

Nothing was more terrifying than a Corrupt with a talent for fire loose in Nysh city. He knew immediately what would happen. He'd be considered too dangerous to transport. He'd never see an island because they'd kill him to protect queen and city.

Seeing the set of her arms and antennae, he knew Nyk had already decided. Maybe she was playing with him before, teasing, wanting only to smell his fear and hear him beg. He was the queen's nephew after all. Now, however, she saw a way to get her revenge.

Why does she hate me?

Ashkaro got hurt playing rush all the time. The version females played was eight times more dangerous!

One main eye on Shan, the other watched as she raised the candle to the wall. The clay darkened. "Goodbye, *Corrupt*," she said, turning away.

The fear of having a limb broken was nothing compared to the panic he felt now.

They'll put a spike through my brain.

Sometimes, if a dangerous Corrupt was captured and sedated enough to be harmless, the Queen's Keepers would hold a public execution. Mom took him to one when he was small. The Keepers pulled the dazed and stumbling ashkaro onto a stage erected in the heart of the city. It had been a bright female, maybe not of Shan's caste, but a three-name at the least. A dull male in the blood-blue robes of an executioner stood behind her, a long fire-hardened bone spear clutched in all four claws. The Keepers held the female helpless as the monstrous dull pushed the tip of the spear into the joint at the base of her skull, where the carapace overlapped to allow movement. It hadn't been fast. Bit by bit, he eased the spear in, angling it upward. The Corrupt shivered, her body locked and vibrating, until the tip of the spear poked through one of her eyes. When she finally went limp, the executioner withdrew the spear with that same calm patience. Much to his mother's disgust, Shan had puked.

He didn't puke now, though he wanted to.

Stop her. Offer her something. Yourself! Anything!

Helpless, he panicked.

Harsh sheets of white fire lit the hall. Nyk screamed in fear and agony and then hissed, steam escaping her joints, as she boiled from within. Clay brick walls browned and cracked, mortar crumbling. A trophy case of ancient wood burst into flames, generations of carved awards and faded fabric ribbons igniting in an instant.

Shan wailed in terror, imagining the bone spear slowly pushing through the back of his skull.

Fire. Raging heat and flame. Roiling chaos.

By all the gods of Alatash it felt good! The harder he pushed, the brighter he burned, the better it felt.

Shan lost himself in euphoric bliss.

THE STORM BENEATH THE WORLD

Ashkaro Female and Male

AHK TAY KYM

Upon discovering one's talent, it is critical to report immediately to the Redemption. If caught early enough, before the Corrupt succumb to the lure, it is possible to break the addiction. Waiting beyond a few weeks inevitably dooms them to a cursed life and eventual death.

—The Redemption

Exiting her home, Ahk Tay Kym headed toward the landing platform where the moored skerry waited. The wheeled steps had been bolted to the ground for stability, the top end lashed to the floating beast's hard upper shell.

Whatever he felt, Bon was a dull and a fieldclaw working for her family. He couldn't possibly have imagined they might have a future together.

He should know better!

Even if Ahk thought of him that way—and she didn't—Mother would never allow it. She had plans for her daughter and marrying into anything less than a fourth name would be seen as failure.

Reaching the foot of the mobile staircase, she leaned back to take in the colossal size of the skerry. Most of it was inflated balloon armoured in translucent carapace. The beast's organs and brain—what little of that there was—were all located in its undercarriage, hidden among the silken black tangle of smaller tentacles. She once read that some philosophers believed skerry were baby islands. It was almost impossible to fathom that the entirety of the Nysh Queendom, from the leeward desert to the lush windward jungles, was balanced on the back of an overgrown skerry.

"Hurry, now," Mother called from the top of the staircase before disappearing.

Ahk climbed the steps, scanning the gathered crowd for Bon as she went.

Nothing.

Not wanting to risk her mother's curiosity, she gave up as she reached the top.

Leaving the wheeled staircase, she found the structure awaiting her larger than expected. Mother used words like gondola, which left her thinking it was some crude and simplistic hut. It wasn't. Though small compared to the sprawling family homestead, it looked like a well-appointed cottage. Entering, she discovered signs with directions pointing to all the important rooms. 'Steerage' was located at the skerry's front, though what defined front and back for an oblong balloon capable of travelling in any direction remained a mystery. Skimming the signs, she saw there was a single kitchen, two dining rooms, and separate wings for family, staff, and crew.

Knowing Mother would want to be where things were happening, Ahk headed to the steerage. She found the Kym Matriarch standing at the helm, raptorial arms resting on an ornate wheel with decoratively carved spokes.

Bon could carve that better.

Would he make each spoke a depiction of me? Ahk pushed the thought away.

The captain, a bright female Ahk didn't recognize, stood behind Mother, back straight, both wings folded tight and respectful, awaiting the order to take over.

She'll be waiting a while.

Mother liked being in control, and a chance to pilot a skerry this big was a rare occurrence.

One of her mother's antennae flicked in Ahk's direction. Descended from a long line of hunters dating back to the hive queens, as father liked to brag, her spatial awareness was both impressive and annoying to a child trying to sneak treats.

"Come," said Mother, one main eye watching the ground ahead, the other scanning the sky.

THE STORM BENEATH THE WORLD

The captain nodded in greeting and stepped back to make room as Ahk crossed the cabin to stand at her mother's side. Looking out the steerage windows, Ahk saw little more than the skerry's back. Beyond that lay the manicured gardens circling the estate, fieldclaws taking advantage of the event to lean against hoes and shovels and watch the departure. The family homestead below was invisible, hidden by the giant beast.

"How do you land something like this?" Ahk asked. "I can't see what's underneath us."

"Steering something this big is a bit of a joke," Mother admitted. "If it decides to wander off, there's little we can do to stop it. Luckily, they're smart enough to be somewhat trainable and generally remain content to go where directed. As for landing, you get it close enough to the mooring pylons that the tentacles can reach them and give it the order. Then, it grabs the pylons and pulls you in."

"What happens if it decides not to?"

Mother's smaller upper wings gave an amused flutter. "Then you end up wherever it wants to go. It's rare. Most skerry prefer to stay near one of the larger islands, but sometimes they float off into the river of days and anyone unlucky enough to be caught onboard is never seen again."

Ahk had seen plays about that. Lost brights battling rogue pirate islands or feral hives. Strange monsters and the thrill of the unknown. She once saw a play about a research skerry that passed through the northern stormwall and found an alien reality on the far side. The Redemption shut it down the next day.

Torn by the fear of losing everything and everyone she'd ever known and the romantic notion of exploring the river of days, Ahk asked, "Do you think the skerry are heading to another island when they leave, or are they wandering off into the nothing at random?"

Both ideas were scary. Foreign islands with strange ashkaro. The Yil Queendom was close enough there was some limited trade, though she'd overheard Mother talking about growing tensions as the two islands appeared to be heading toward each other. There were countless other islands; no one knew how many. And there were predators out beyond the islands, things big enough to kill and devour even a skerry as large as this one.

"I had a teacher," Mother said, attention on the view, "who believed skerry communicate with each other in a way we can neither detect nor comprehend. She thought they could talk to islands as well, and when they set out into the nothing, they know exactly where they're going."

A tremor ran through the floorboards and the scene beyond the edge of the skerry shifted to one side.

"Matriarch Kym," said the captain, seeing her chance to politely interrupt. "*A Slow and Gentle Descent into Dark* has released the mooring pylons. All tentacles are loose."

Mother's wings showed satisfaction. "Good." Gripping the wheel with her stronger raptorial arms, she leaned back with all her weight.

Slowly, the wheel tilted, stopping after it moved the width of a craft claw. For a moment, nothing happened. Then, Ahk's stomach lurched as the great skerry rose with majestic grace. Little changed at first, the horizon beyond the curve of the creature's back dropping away with excruciating leisure.

"At this rate," Ahk said, "It'll take half a day to clear the trees at the edge of the property."

Mother shot her a look somewhere between annoyance and amusement. "Would you rather walk?"

Ahk dipped her antennae in feigned contrition.

Mother laughed, shaking her head. "We'll start forward once we've cleared the local obstacles. I once saw an impatient captain head off too early. The skerry's tentacles latched onto a wagon and an outhouse. Tore the latter right out of the ground. What a mess! Sufficed to say, she lost her command after that."

Ahk pretended to patiently enjoy the view and then gave up the impossible charade, roving the steerage cabin in search of something interesting or dangerous. The crew, always politely deferential, kept her away from anything too fascinating, answering her questions in clipped military tones. Except for the steward, a bright male, the rest were bright females. Ahk resisted the temptation to ask why. Saying all ashkaro were equal while making it clear with their actions that it was not true was typical adult behaviour. She mentioned her observation to Mother once.

THE STORM BENEATH THE WORLD

After a long and torturous explanation of history, biological imperatives, and a detour into how ancient hive roles influenced modern sociobiological institutions, Mother became angry and sent her to bed.

Judging from the cuticle thickening around old wounds and the scuffed and scarred appearance of their carapaces, most of the females had seen active duty. The male, gleaming exoskeleton buffed to a flawless shine, looked like he hadn't seen anything more dangerous than an overcooked lunch.

"Ahk," said Mother, the captain still waiting behind her, all four claws crossed over her thorax, "would you like to steer?"

"Kratosh, yes!" Ahk bounced over the nearest desk, using her wings to extend the jump.

"Don't swear, dear, and what have I told you about wing-assisted jumps indoors?"

"Sorry, Mother."

The scolding was more for decorum and the benefit of the crew; her mother wasn't angry. Stepping aside, she left the wheel unattended and Ahk hurried to take her place before anyone had the chance to protest or change their mind. She gripped the wheel with all four claws, unsure what to do.

"Push against the wheel," Mother instructed. "That will give *A Slow and Gentle Descent into Dark* the signal to begin forward movement. Skerry are lazy beasts and she'll happily hover here for the next month if we don't give her a little prodding."

Ahk pushed and nothing happened.

"Harder," said Mother. "Push with all your weight.

Bracing with all four legs, claws digging into the wood of the floor, she leaned against the wheel. Slowly, slowly, it tilted forward.

And still nothing happened.

"It's not moving," complained Ahk.

"*A Slow and Gentle Descent into Dark* is no nimble tramea," Mother said. "She takes her time."

A shudder, so subtle Ahk wondered if she imagined it, ran through the floor. The false horizon of the skerry's back dipped a fraction of a degree and the horizon began to move.

"At least the *Slow and Gentle* part is right," said Ahk. "I could walk faster than this."

"It will gain speed over the next few days," said Mother. "While there are faster modes of transport—"

"So many faster modes," mumbled Ahk.

"—none are more civilized. If you walked to the windward edge from here, you'd arrive dirty and exhausted. Instead, we'll enjoy a few days of relaxation and arrive refreshed." Mother turned both antennae toward Ahk. "When we've gained a little more height, we'll go up to the observation deck. The view is stunning."

Glancing out the forward window, Ahk saw the ground falling away with increasing speed. Though hardly fast, they were already higher than she'd ever been.

"Will I be able to see the leeward desert?" she asked.

"No, child." Mother's antennae, still tilted toward her eldest daughter, showed amusement. "We're much too far away for that."

Still gripping the spoked wheel with all four claws, Ahk gave it an experimental turn, checking over her shoulder to see if Mother or the captain reacted. When Mother gave an affirmative nod, she turned the wheel farther. The distant horizon tilted a degree as the skerry banked in that direction.

"How long would it take to turn a complete circle?" Ahk asked.

"About an hour," answered Mother. "Skerry aren't built for aerial acrobatics."

"And how does the wheel work?"

At a glance from the Kym Matriarch, the captain answered, "It's attached to an intricate pulley system below us. Turning the wheel pulls long ropes attached to spears driven into the skerry near its forward sensory organs. When it feels pressure from a spear on one side, it turns in that direction."

Ahk released the wheel, suddenly feeling guilty. "Spears? Won't that hurt?"

"Only if you turned the wheel a great many times," said the captain. "We've been training *A Slow and Gentle Descent into Dark* since she was small. She's an old and wise beast now, attentive and receptive to command. We'd only turn the wheel that much in an emergency, and, assuming everyone is doing their job, that will never happen."

THE STORM BENEATH THE WORLD

Ahk asked, "How old is *A Slow and Gentle?*"

The captain looked thoughtful, antennae stilling. "Somewhere between five and seven hundred years. She'll live five thousand more before she becomes too big to be pilotable. At that point we'll free her, and she'll live many countless thousands more, free to wander where she wills."

The numbers were too vast to comprehend. Male ashkaro rarely lived more than forty years. Females might live eighty, with some few reaching the ripe old age of ninety. Only queens lived longer, with the oldest on record living to an impossible three hundred.

Thinking of Bon's blasphemous questions, Ahk asked, "Is it true that skerry are baby islands?"

The captains' antennae wavered with doubt. "I've worked this skerry for twenty years. First as a forward observer, then as ship's second before finally becoming captain. She has not noticeably grown in that time. For a skerry to reach the size of an island like Nysh would take millions of years."

That sounded like the cautious kind of 'no' adults used when they were pretending to be open minded. Like a 'probably not' that meant 'absolutely no way.'

"The captain will take over now," said Mother, clasping her craft claws over her upper thorax and offering the captain a polite bow. "Thank Captain Bhrad Pah Dok for her time."

Ahk bowed lower than her mother had, twitching in surprise as her craft claws grazed the figurine she'd stuffed into the pocket there. "Uh…Th-thank you Captain Bhrad Pah Dok," she stuttered.

"Come," said Mother. "Let's visit the observation deck."

She left quickly, walking with that deadly grace that caused Father's jumping legs to twitch. Pretending not to notice the teasing covert looks her parents shared had long grown tiresome. These days, she curled her antennae away in mock disgust at their flirtatious behaviour and stomped loudly from the room.

"What's in your pocket?" Mother asked as they followed the signs to the nearest stairs.

Oh no. "Nothing."

"Ahk Tay Kym, you are going to have to learn to control your wings and antennae better if you are going to start lying."

Kratosh! she cursed. Mother was perceptive in a way Father never managed. Ahk could lie to him all day and he accepted everything as if he couldn't imagine her so much as bending a truth.

"Sorry." Ahk concentrated on keeping her antennae loose and bored. "It's nothing."

"Better, but you're still lying. It is quite obviously *something*."

"How did you know?" Ahk asked, hoping to distract her into a discourse on reading body language and all the other exciting things she'd learned during her years of military service.

Mother wasn't having it. "I guessed. Now what is it?"

"Nothing much. Just something Bon gave me."

"A going away present?"

"Kind of." She tried to hide her grimace. She should have said something more definitive, leaving less room for more questions.

"Hiding it to save him from trouble is commendable, but the boy should know his place. Show it to me."

"It's really—" Seeing the determined set of mother's antennae, Ahk surrendered to the inevitable. "Just a little carving," she said, drawing it from the pocket but keeping it concealed in her craft claw.

Her mother held out an open claw.

She'll never let this go.

Ahk gave her the figurine.

Mother's wings stilled, locked tight and tense. Her antennae flicked, reaching in every direction, checking no one loitered nearby. Keeping the carving cupped in her claw, she lifted it, studying the incredible detail.

"It's you," she said. "The craftsmanship is excellent."

It was beyond excellent, but Ahk knew better than to say that. "I had no idea he—"

"Too good to be the work of someone his age."

"Maybe he stole—"

Mother silenced her with a look. "The boy has discovered his talent."

"It's just a carving! It's harmless!"

Her mother shook her head, looking disappointed. "My fault for not noticing sooner. He's been lax with his chores. I'd assumed he'd met a female and was distracted. Males his age are useless." She gazed sadly at the figurine. "I guess I was partly right," she said, one main eye turning to Ahk. "He has been distracted by a female."

Confused, Ahk said, "I barely see him now."

"That's because he spends all his time making things like this. I bet there are hundreds of figurines hidden in his room." She sighed, lower wings sagging. "I'll send word to Pol Mek Nan when we land."

"But he's not hurting anyone," begged Ahk. "Pol will send him away. He'll be banished to the desert!"

"We have to help him," said Mother. "If we don't, he'll spend more and more time carving ever more detailed and beautiful figurines until he starves. Pol will make sure he gets the help he needs. Bon is young. If they can break his fixation, he might still live a normal life."

"Normal?" demanded Ahk. "Even if they don't send him away, he'll be an outcast. No family will hire him."

At least no family worth working for.

Mother stroked Ahk's upper wings, calming their agitated twitching. "He's Corrupt."

And that was it. There could be no arguing with her mother and no arguing with the Redemption. She'd read about ashkaro falling to the lure, but never dreamed someone she knew would discover their gods-given talent. Finding the singular skill that brought true bliss was the foulest curse. That the gods would do this to a good ashkaro like Bon seemed unreasonably cruel.

"Pol will take care of him?" Ahk asked.

"She will," her mother promised. "As you said, his is not a dangerous talent. He won't be sent to a Corrupt island, probably not even to the desert. If he can get his talent under control, resist the lure, he'll be assigned to one of the leeward Redemption-run farms where they can watch over him." She pulled Ahk into a tight hug. "He'll be fine. They'll take care of him."

Mother passed the figurine from a craft claw to a stronger raptorial claw and gripped it tight. The wood groaned under the strain and then crumbled apart. She spilled the splinters onto the floor.

Ahk stared, unable to pull her attention from the ruined beauty.

THE STORM BENEATH THE WORLD

Why destroy it?

By the time she returned home, Bon would be gone. No one would ever speak his name again. Some other dull would do his job and all the times they'd played together as children were worth nothing.

Her heart broke at the thought.

He was my friend.

"Come," Mother said. "We're flying over some of the lushest farmland in all Nysh. It's a beautiful view."

Mother was right.

Beyond the eternal dome of swirling blue green cloud, Alatash tracked its stately path. Each morning the gods' city rose on the leeward side of the island, traversed the firmament, and sank below the windward edge.

Despite the intricate plays of light, Ahk couldn't bring herself to appreciate the beauty.

From up here, the island of Nysh looked like a quilted blanket, each octagon's colour determined by the crops growing there.

Standing atop the gondola mounted on the skerry's back, Ahk turned in a circle.

Mother's right, I can't see the desert from here.

"Is that the edge of the island?" she asked, pointing windward.

"No, dear. That's the horizon. We won't see the edge for six more days."

"But we will see it?"

The Kym Matriarch rested a craft claw on Ahk's slim shoulder. "We'll walk right to it so you can look down and see the storm beneath the world."

Skirrak

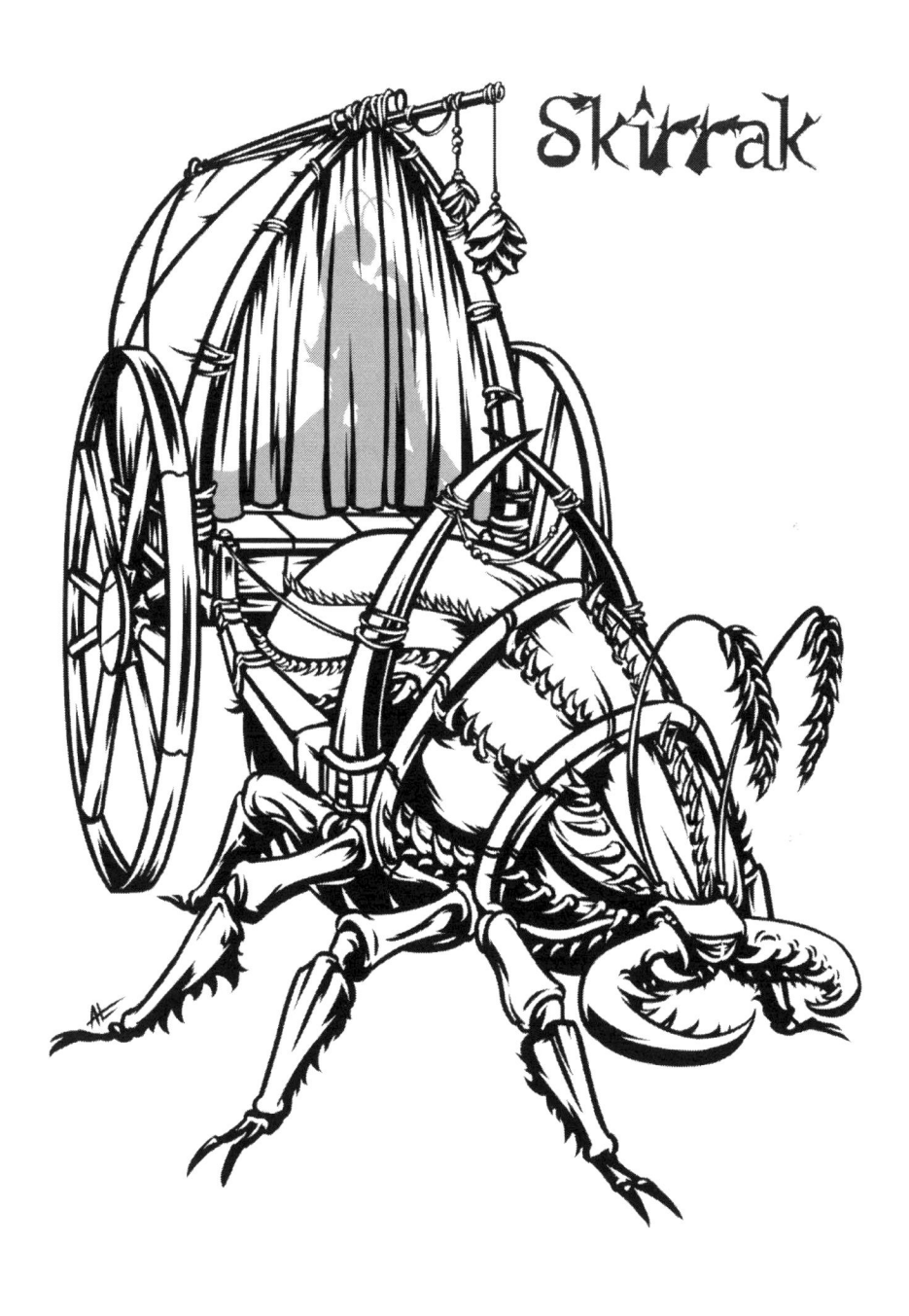

JOH

When the skerry dispatched to haul the banished to Kyar—a Corrupt island in the vicinity of Nysh—failed to return, a second skerry was sent. This one, escorted by a full complement of tramea-mounted Queen's Wing, is now one month overdue.

—Officer Wen Ban Zji, The Queen's Wing.

Early the next morning Joh woke to a sharp rapping on the door. Constructed of hollow reeds bound by fibrous plant twine, it rattled noisily in its crooked frame. For a terrified instant he thought his father was returning, too bent by whatever he'd ingested to figure out the simple latch. The knock sounded again, calm, but insistent.

Not Dad.

Not the polite whistle of the two whites either.

Clambering from his hammock, wings tucked, he stood, uncertain. Alatash had yet to rise, leaving the room gloomy. Antennae searching the air, he found no trace of his father. It was unusual for him to be gone so long.

"Blessed be," said a male voice in the cultured tones of a bright. "Siblings we are under the light of Alatash."

Joh's antennae drooped. Male priests were rare, but not unheard of. "May we someday be worthy of redemption," he answered, repeating the words Shel San Qun demanded of her congregation.

"May I enter?"

Polite, but a formality at best. No one refused a priest—even a male one—ever.

"Of course," Joh answered. "Enter and be welcome."

THE STORM BENEATH THE WORLD

Abandoning the illusory safety of the sleeping room, Joh flipped the latch on the door, pushing it open. He retreated to allow the priest—a dull male with a carapace of muted brown—entry. Cracks and scars marred the male's exoskeleton, worse even than the two whites who passed through the previous day. If not for the priest's vest, Joh would have thought him another vagrant.

The priest remained at the entrance, studying the interior before turning his attention on Joh. "Greetings, sibling. Your name?"

Crossing all four arms, Joh bowed. "Joh."

Stained with dust and much patched, the male's vest looked like those of any priest. A strange symbol embroidered in a faded blue that might have once been the deep cerulean of fresh blood, adorned the centre of his thorax.

Noting his attention, the priest said, "I am a member of the Defiled."

"Oh," said Joh, nodding understanding though he hadn't a clue what that meant.

"We serve the queen in many different capacities, depending on our talents. I hunt the Corrupt."

"Oh," repeated Joh, careful not to allow his antennae to betray his sudden rush of fear. He knew exactly what that meant.

The priest entered the home like he owned it, stalking into the eating area and glancing in every basket. His carapace might be dull, but he moved like a bright, utterly confident in his existence.

"Water?" the priest asked.

"Sorry," said Joh, wondering if there was a polite way to ask a priest their name or if even the thought of such temerity might be blasphemous. "Haven't checked the well this morning," he added. "Was sleeping." He winced, realizing it might sound like he was upset at being woken so early. "Was time to get up anyway." Did that sound worse?

The priest grunted his disappointment. "It will be a long and dusty ride."

Ride? "Sorry," Joh repeated.

Abandoning his search, the priest turned both antennae and all six eyes on Joh. Uncomfortable being the subject of such scrutiny, Joh ducked his head, antennae bent away, meek and subservient. As predators, it was rare for ashkaro to focus like that on anything they weren't planning on killing. Joh shrank from the priest, trying to bend himself into the smallest, least threatening shape possible.

"I've been rude," said the priest. "My name is Rel, and I have a very rare talent."

Joh twitched in fear, too scared to move. Defiled. It suddenly made sense. This male dull was Corrupt, one of the few who turned their curse to the service of queen and Redemption.

"It's not dangerous," said the priest, failing to alleviate Joh's fears. "In fact, in any other job, it would be useless. I'd be banished to the desert." His upper wings gave a fluttering shrug. "And not to teach."

"Teach?" Joh's voice cracked.

"I'm an instructor at Amphazar, a school in the heart of the desert."

He'd known there were towns and cities, most based around clay mines and brick-baking factories. It made sense, he guessed, that there'd be schools for the dull children as well. There was one in Landon run by Shel San Qun but after Mom left his father stopped sending him.

The priest's antennae finally relaxed the intensity of their scrutiny, though it did nothing to ease Joh's tension. "I teach Corrupt children to control their talents so they might serve the queen. Finding those children is my talent." His antennae made a show of testing the air. "I can sniff out the Corruption."

Fear thrummed through Joh. "Oh." He glanced toward the door. "And your talent led you here?"

"It did."

"They left yesterday," said Joh.

The priest's antennae straightened in surprise, then flicked about, searching the small shack. "They?"

"The two whites from the desert. They stopped for water and headed windward when they left."

"I came from windward."

"Then I'm surprised you didn't see them," Joh said. "I wondered if they were Corrupt. Your talent must have scented them." And then, more daring, he suggested, "If you head windward now, you should be able to catch them." Bliss shivered his wings, and he stilled them. If the priest saw the reaction, he'd know Joh had used his talent.

The priest's antennae leaned toward the door, uncertain. "You're sure?"

"I'm sure they went windward. I watched them until they were out of sight. Not much else to do here." He gave a small shrug of his own. "Maybe they left the road?"

For a moment the priest hesitated, torn between rushing after his new prey and staying to further question the boy. "Two?"

"Male and female, from the desert."

Decision made, the priest headed out the door. Joh followed, curious. Outside, an open carriage large enough to hold a dozen ashkaro adults awaited. Two huge skirrak were harnessed to the carriage, the eight-legged beasts nosing through the half-dead plant life at their feet in search of roots and grubs. Heavily armoured carapaces of green reflected the first light of the rising gods.

Distracted and muttering to himself, the priest jumped to the driver's seat with a flutter of thin, ancient wings. With a snap of the reins, he set the two skirrak into motion, the carriage lumbering along behind them.

Making his own wing-assisted jump, Joh caught up to the carriage, jogging along beside it. The old dull gave him an inquisitive look, one distracted antenna turning toward him.

"You really travel the queendom looking for Corrupt?" Joh asked, matching the skirrak's pace.

"I do."

"You take them back to the school where you teach?" He hesitated, then added, "*All* of them?"

"Not all. Only a special few."

Joh hid his disappointment. A leeward-born dull was never going to be one of a 'very special few.'

"Well," he said, slowing to let the wagon move past him, "good luck finding them. I suggest you keep going north if you don't find them in town. You should probably hurry!"

Two suggestions in a row and he stumbled, lost in crashing waves of euphoria.

The dull priest nodded farewell and snapped the reins. The skirrak trudged faster and he snapped them again.

Joh watched him leave.

A dull priest! I had no idea that was possible.

Shel San Qun preached equality in her church in Landon, but no one believed her. Not really. Not out here where you could go months without seeing a bright other than the priest.

Were it not for the wagon and skirrak, he'd have believed the old ashkaro a raving Corrupt broken by the dry air. Even with the ample evidence it was hard to believe the dull wasn't crazy.

He came here, so he wasn't lying about his talent.

With the gods rising and still no sign of father, Joh made another tour of the garden and surrounding crops and weeds, searching for slugs and worms. Anything with a hint of moisture. Finding a couple of scrawny wrigglers, he brought them inside to save for later.

He spent the rest of the day hiding from the sun, constantly checking the horizon.

Why would the Redemption have a school for Corrupt in the middle of the desert?

The priest hadn't hesitated to tell Joh about it, so it wasn't a matter of secrecy. He didn't even have to ask prodding questions like he usually did when trying to pry information from reticent adults.

They train Corrupt to serve the queen.

It made sense. The priests were training the Corrupt to serve the queen in dangerous situations. Even that old priest with his otherwise useless talent rode from danger to danger. He seemed harmless enough, but likely had hidden weapons. Maybe he lied about his talent.

If they're training Corrupt, then they're going to want the ones with the most powerful and deadly talents.

Some might willingly go, tempted by regular meals and the promise of shelter. Thirst growing, Joh shook off the desire to chase after the dull priest.

He said his name was Rel.

One syllable, no family name worth mentioning. A simple dull name.

Rel wouldn't take him to some fancy school in the desert. There'd be no escaping his father. Instead, Joh would be shipped off to some clay mine or brickworks factory to work until he died, carapace white and flaking. Unless, that is, they decided he was dangerous and threw him to the storm or whatever they did with the scary Corrupt.

The gods' home traversed the sky above, marking the passing of the day. The relentless dry wind stole moisture from every breath. Life slowed and withered. A sluggish rafak, wings barely keeping the flying snake airborne, plucked a desiccated worm from the ground. Sucking out what little meat it could, the beast discarded the empty shell and went in search of shade. And still Joh's father failed to return.

What if he doesn't come back?

Should he follow the priest into town to look for his father?

Tomorrow, Joh decided.

He'd give the priest time to search Landon and move on. Hopefully the whites had already left and would draw him windward.

Another day passed, the well still mud. He weeded the garden, finding little to do, and searched for more slugs. When the uncaring gods once again sank toward the windward horizon, he retired inside, looking for things to tidy so Father would have nothing to complain about. He dusted and swept the sand out the door. After checking the weaves on the baskets and tightening a few, he ate two of the drier slugs, saving the plump ones for his father.

He sat in the dark, listening to the world beyond the shack. A dry wind rattled the walls, whistled through every crack. The distant cry of a feral tramea was answered by another, closer call.

Alone, he listened.

Alone, he contemplated a life without his father.

Who would hire a runt of a dull male?

No one. Unemployed, he'd starve.

Unless I use my talent to suggest people hire me.

Though, if he was going to do that, why not simply suggest they give him whatever he needed?

A new sound reached him, a rattling clatter of wooden wheels.

Joh's antennae sagged. *He's returned.*

Standing, he threw open the door as the priest's wagon came to a shuddering, dust-raising halt.

Rel studied Joh from the driver's seat. "That was well done."

Joh said nothing.

"But you overstepped. Your last suggestion that I hurry kept nagging me as I raced windward. I needed to rush and yet didn't know why. You have an interesting talent but are crude and untutored in its use."

"You're mistaken," said Joh. "You should probably leave." A thrill of fear and pleasure thrummed through his carapace.

About to snap the reins and set his skirrak into motion, the priest flinched. "Won't work now that I know what you're doing. Come with me, and we'll teach you how to use your talent. Serve your queen."

"And if I refuse?"

"Yours is a potentially dangerous talent," answered Rel.

"Ah."

They'd send him to an island populated by Corrupt. Not a great place for a weak and unusually small dull male.

Suggest he go away. Tell him to forget he ever saw you.

"I would like a chance to serve the queen," Joh said, unsure if he lied. "But what about my father? He'll be worried when he comes home and I'm not here."

Rel looked toward the distant town of Landon, his wings giving a small shiver of sadness. "No. He won't."

Won't worry or won't come home?

He wanted to ask and didn't want to know.

"You father struck Constable Ghen Dai," Rel said. "She killed him."

Joh saw it all too clearly: his father, drunk and belligerent. Ghen Dai, no doubt annoyed at having to once again deal with his behaviour, trying to send him home.

He's dead?

Just the other day Joh had thought about suggesting to his father that he stop his self-destructive behaviour.

I could have saved him.

But according to the Redemption, that would have been wrong.

I wanted to feel more. Guilt. Shame. Sadness. Any emotion that might mean he wasn't a soulless monster.

There's nothing for me here.

If he stayed, he'd have no choice but use his talent or starve.

He'd see what this school offered. Couldn't be worse than the life he had here. If he didn't like it, he'd suggest to someone less prepared than Rel that he be allowed to leave.

Joh made a wing-assisted hop to land beside the priest. Making himself comfortable on the bench he said, "Is the school nice?"

Rel gave a rueful flick of his upper wings. "The air is very dry, but you're fed every day. There's water brought in, so the teachers and students don't dry out. Can't serve the queen if you look like a white."

Interesting. They want us to be able to blend in.

Regular meals sounded promising too.

"My talent is neither powerful nor dangerous," said Joh. "I don't see how it could be useful."

Turning all six eyes on the youth, Rel examined him. "Your talent might not be much now, but with the right training I suspect you'll be terrifying."

Me? Terrifying?

He rather liked the sound of that.

WEX JEL

Much like the river of days, ashkaro souls are eternal, living and dying over and over, moving ever closer to the time of Redemption. Unlike Queen Yil's Church of the Storm, who throw blasphemers from the island to feed their foul god, Katlipok, the Redemption seeks to save every soul. Even those who fall to the lure are worthy of Redemption.

—The Redemption

Leaving Brickworks #7 behind, Wex walked deeper into the desert as Alatash crossed the mid-point of the sky and began its slow descent toward the windward horizon. With hours left in the day, she had plenty of time to fashion a spear and kill something. Truth be told, she didn't much care if her hunt was successful. Aimlessly wandering the desert was more fun than prowling the shack until she lost her mind.

Hiking over rolling hills of dead earth and compacted sand, her path weaved between tufts of sharp vegetation clinging desperately to life. It reminded her of Mom's lectures on the dangers of the desert: 'It may seem quiet and dead,' Mom said, 'but it's teaming with life and all too deadly.'

Wex snorted. "Teaming with life?"

So far, she hadn't seen anything but a tiny winged rafak snake too small to be worth killing. Not that she'd had much of a chance. Barbed tail flicking and stabbing in panicked threat, it fled from sight in an instant. There were supposed to be bigger rafak deep in the desert, flying in perfect silence, dropping from above to strike their victim.

Wex looked up. Roiling swirls of leaf-green clouds darkened to a deep emerald near the leeward horizon. Warmer colours owned the windward sky, burnt orange and twists of red.

No flying snakes.

Cresting another dune, she spotted a stunted forest of johak trees. More stubborn than hardy, they stood bent and forever at the edge of death. If she was going to find a stick anywhere, this was it. Heading into the valley, Wex entered the sparse thicket, the dry crunch of husked insects beneath her claws.

In one of her rare moods, Mom once talked about patrolling a forest of towering trees on the edge of the island. A grunt in the Queen's Army at the time, she manned a watchtower with a dozen other dulls and a single bright officer. The officer lived at the top of the tower and spent her days searching the sky through a hollowed wood tube with finely crafted lenses that allowed her to see farther than was normally possible. Mom said it was the best four years of her life, damp grass underfoot, the air always wet. There was something humbling about walking to the edge of the island and looking down into the roiling storm below. Sometimes, she said, one of the island's colossal tentacles would swing into view and crush your understanding of scale. In all the time Mom was stationed there, she never saw pirates or raiders, and nothing ever happened. 'You can't appreciate boredom,' she often said, 'until you've fought for your life.'

Finding a stick twice her height that didn't crumble the moment Ahk touched it took most of an hour. She studied it, turning the wood in her craft claws. Not as straight as she wanted, she felt unbothered by the failure.

Break it in two. Make stab sticks.

Out here, rocks were easier to find. Once she had both stick and stone, Wex sat under the largest of the johak trees. Hunched like a terrifying nightmare, it was four times her height. Though not offering much in the way of shade, its roots ran deep. The sparse leaves were an easy source of water. Snapping the tip off the nearest, she sucked out the damp spongy interior until the wound congealed.

Wex studied her stick. Mom said the best wood for weapons—and everything else—came from the windward forests where the rainfall and deeper soil meant trees grew straight and tall. Having never seen anything other than johak thickets, Wex had difficulty picturing it. But this stick felt good. Except for a bend in the centre, it was almost straight. Grabbing each end with a raptorial claw, she pushed a craft claw against the middle. It broke easily, making a dry splintering sound.

Shorter, it'll be stronger.

She hoped she was right.

After shuffling about and kicking a few twigs and clods of hard dirt away to make her spot more comfortable, she set to work. Finding a second stone, she used it to knap the first, giving it an edge which she then used to sharpen both sticks. Knowing she wasn't making weapons likely to survive their first conflict, she wasted no time making them pretty. Crude and utilitarian, barbarically simple, they felt right in her claws.

Stab sticks complete, Wex stood. Though not perfect, she enjoyed the small accomplishment.

Swinging one stick, she made a stabbing motion with the other. It felt awkward.

How do you fight with these?

For the next hour she shuffled about the thicket, attacking trees, and experimenting with different grip combinations. Held in her craft claws, the sticks were a blur but lacked power. In her raptorial claws, she was better able to put her weight behind attacks, but at the cost of finesse. With more experimentation she discovered a combination of craft and raptorial claws worked best, giving her both the power and control she wanted.

"I knew I heard the clumsy stumbling of a dull mud-grub!"

Startled, Wex spun, sticks raised in what felt like a defensive posture. Two young brights stood atop the nearest dune, looking down upon her. Close to her own age, they wore sheathed weapons. The more colourful of the two, carapace a rainbow cascade of purples, had a gorgeous set of military stab sticks hanging at her side. The other, a more muted green, carried a wood bow and quiver of hunting arrows.

Wex recognized the daughter of one of Brickworks #7's upper managers. "Cayr Rie Chi Lo," she said. "I didn't hear you coming."

This couldn't be coincidence. They must have followed her from town.

THE STORM BENEATH THE WORLD

"Dull is as dull does," said Cayr, purples shimmering in the light of Alatash. "I can't remember your name."

They'd met in town a dozen times and been introduced at least twice.

"My name is—"

"You misunderstand," said Cayr. "I can't remember because I don't care." She glanced at her green friend. "This mud thinks she's a warrior."

The green laughed, a cruel bark of derision.

"So," said Cayr, drawing her own finely crafted stab sticks, "let's see how good a warrior a mud can be."

Wex's antennae bent away from the bright, her upper wings fluttering nervously. She retreated, letting her arms fall to her sides. Though not yet of military age, Cayr's family would have provided combat training from the moment she could grip a weapon. Compared to Wex's twigs, her stab sticks would be unbreakable.

"I'm not a warrior," said Wex. "Cayr, I came—"

"We're not *friends*, mud. Use my full name."

"Cayr Rie Chi Lo, I came out to hunt."

Cayr shot her friend a look of feigned confusion. "I thought muds only ate grubs." Looking back to Wex she said, "Look under any leaf and there's dinner for the whole family!" Spinning the sticks in nimble claws, all four arms working in perfect synchronicity, she advanced down the hill. "I was watching. You move well."

"I—"

"For a clumsy mud. Let's spar." Stab sticks twirled, gleaming wood mesmerizing.

"I should go home," said Wex, edging sideways.

Cayr moved to block her. "Just a couple of passes." An inquisitive antenna straightened. "I see the way you stare at my sticks. Beautiful, aren't they?" She held one out as if in offering.

Wex knew better. "I'm going home now."

"Tell you what," said Cayr. "Three passes. If you so much as touch me with your twigs, these are yours."

Looking from her pathetic sticks to Cayr's polished weapons, Wex knew a hunger having nothing to do with food. She *needed* them.

How hard can it be to hit her once?

"I just have to touch you?" Wex asked.

"And they're yours," agreed Cayr. "I swear to you upon Queen Nysh. If I'm lying, may I die banished and alone and in shame." She glanced at her friend. "Shef Wal Gan, here, is my witness."

Shef nodded with solemn finality, accepting the duty assigned by the higher caste Cayr.

"And if you win?" Wex asked, looking for the loophole.

"Thrashing you will be payment enough."

Getting wacked a few times was entirely worth the chance to own those beautiful weapons. Mom would ask awkward questions, but that was a problem for later.

Lifting her sticks into what she hoped was a ready position, Wex said, "Three passes."

Cayr lost all hint of jocular humour, crouching as she stalked her victim. It was like the spoiled child disappeared, suddenly replaced by a killer schooled in the deadly arts, a four-name bright groomed for command.

Kratosh! Wex retreated. Was it too late to change her mind?

Cayr skittered forward, all six eyes and both antennae locked on her prey. Held in her craft claws, the sticks no longer danced in showy display. Her stronger raptorial arms reached wide and forward, ready to deflect an attack. All four legs spread, she made a low target, prepared to pounce in any direction.

Just touch her.

Cayr would dart forward, and rain blows down upon Wex. Wex would tap her useless stick against her opponent's carapace. She didn't need to hurt the bright; the slightest contact, and she won.

Cayr leapt forward and then bounced overtop Wex with a powerful wing-assisted jump. Unprepared and waiting for her chance to strike, Wex found herself face-first in the hard sand, head ringing from the kick it received.

Limbs tangled, Wex rolled away, scrambling to stand. Legs unsteady, she turned to find Cayr waiting patiently, antennae making a show of studying her surroundings as if bored.

"That wasn't fair!" said Wex.

THE STORM BENEATH THE WORLD

"Why not? Just because I hold stab sticks doesn't mean they're my only weapon. Let's call this lesson number one, little mud warrior. If you have a weapon, your enemy will expect you to use it. Never be predictable. You ready?"

Despite the growing pain in her head, a thrill ran through Wex. She wouldn't fall for that trick again.

She'll use the sticks this time.

Cayr went from bored to attacking without transition.

One of Wex's sticks shattered in an explosion of splinters and she screamed in agony, retreating. Her left craft claw hung limp, the joint damaged.

"Oh," said Cayr. "That's lesson number two: don't leave limbs where they can be easily hit. Keep moving."

Wex barely heard. She'd seen something in the bright's attack. Blindingly fast as Cayr was, there was a predictability in the way she moved that left a hole—a weakness—that Wex couldn't put words to. But it was there, she knew it in her blood.

You're trying to touch her when you should be trying to fight.

Knowing the punishment for striking a high caste bright, she'd held back.

You want those sticks?

She did. More than anything.

Then fight.

"When I finish here," Cayr said to the green, "let's get lunch. I'm hungry" Turning a dismissive antenna in Wex's direction, she said, "You ready, or would you like to beg off? Should I let her beg?" she asked her friend.

Shef Wal Gan fluttered an uncaring wing. "Maybe. If she goes belly down. If she *really* begs."

"You want to beg?" Cayr asked Wex.

Gripping her remaining stick, Wex said, "Let's do this."

Suddenly relaxed, empty of worry and fear, she awaited Cayr's attack.

The bright shuffled forward, lunging and feinting, probing Wex's defences and reactions.

Wex did nothing, didn't move or twitch.

"You don't seem ready," said Cayr.

With the last word Cayr lunged, one stick moving in a sweeping arc meant to distract, the other thrust forward in a brutal attack.

Calm.

Peaceful serenity.

Worry and fear fell away, all existence focussed on her opponent.

Motes of sand hung motionless in the light of Alatash.

With one raptorial arm, Wex knocked aside the attack. Combining the dexterity of a craft arm and the strength of a raptorial arm, she touched Cayr with her stick.

"There," said Wex, elation bubbling deep in her carapace. "I touched you."

Cayr Rie Chi Lo stood rigid as if appalled at the impropriety of a dull having the brazen audacity to make contact.

Then she fell dead, Wex's stick jammed perfectly through the shoulder joint and angled to impale her heart.

"You killed her!" screamed the green bright, backing away.

"Did I?" A body-shaking wave of pure pleasure filled Wex, left no room for thought. Not the best meal, not the cleanest cold water, was ever so perfect. Nothing touched that moment, light filling her soul as if the gods who abandoned Alatash had returned to forgive their creations. She struggled to put words to the feeling.

"I saw…a gap…a weakness."

Bliss faded, blown away by the wind of understanding.

"I killed her."

Looking up, Wex discovered herself alone with the corpse. Alatash sat lower on the horizon than she remembered.

The green bright was gone.

"I killed Cayr Rie Chi Lo."

It wouldn't matter that Cayr started it.

Mom would lose her job, and no one would ever hire her again.

Run away.

Maybe if everyone thought she'd gone feral, they wouldn't blame her family.

Hide the body.

Then it would be Wex's word against Shef Wal Gan's.

THE STORM BENEATH THE WORLD

No one would believe a dull over a bright.

Catch Shef and kill her. Hide both bodies.

Better, but it felt like she'd stood there a long time. Shef had an impossible head start, might already be back in Brickworks #7 telling everyone what happened.

Kill yourself.

No one would blame Mom. The crime would die with Wex.

She couldn't do it. The souls of suicides went to the storm. No chance of redemption. An eternity in Kratosh, tortured by Katlipok, the fallen god.

Wex went belly down in the sand and prayed.

Forgive me. Save my family. Over and over. *Forgive me. Save my family.*

Alatash, forever shrouded in cloud, sank below the windward horizon.

Save my family.

Wex lay in the dark, begging the uncaring gods.

Hours later she heard the clatter of wheels, the grunt of skirrak hauling a wagon through the sands.

"Here she is," said a male voice. "Joh, help her on board."

THE STORM BENEATH THE WORLD

THE STORM BENEATH THE WORLD

SHAN WYN VAL NUL NYSH

Rumours the Sisters of the Storm have infiltrated towns on the leeward edge of Nysh island have proven incorrect. More typical fear mongering to bolster budgets.
—Second Officer Kri Stil Mah Tar, The Queen's Claw

Shan dreamed of a boring sermon he once dozed through. 'Burn the body, burn the soul,' the family priest said. 'In the days of hive, we burned murderers.'

He remembered thinking that punishing murderers by murdering them *and* their souls seemed a tad ironic.

Sound first, the world returned in starts and stutters.

Yelling.

I'm tired.

It would feel great to curl up in a hammock out in the gardens and sleep.

Someone barked orders, others shouted reports and warnings.

Shan became aware of smells next. Baked clay, charred wood, and burnt meat.

Wide eyes stared and saw nothing, blurred shapes slowly coalescing. His antennae ached, felt like they'd been scraped raw.

"What?" Shan managed, struggling to focus.

A bright female in the uniform of a Nysh City Fire Department warden hurried past followed by half a dozen dull males staggering under the burden of water buckets. Someone stood before him, speaking.

"What?" repeated Shan, trying to make the sights and sounds make sense.

THE STORM BENEATH THE WORLD

It was a priest, though he didn't recognize the patch adorning the curve of her thorax. An adult bright, her flower-pink carapace looked soft, like she'd recently moulted.

"Are you calm?" the priest asked, glancing at someone standing behind Shan.

A Redemption priest? Here?

Fire. Burning. Screaming steam.

"Yes," Shan answered.

"Mostly true," the priest said, antennae giving a pleased quiver. "If you remain calm, Knek here won't kill you. Can you remain calm?"

Can I?

Quashing his fear he answered, "Yes."

"Mostly true," she repeated. Once again, her antennae showed pleasure as if she was enjoying this horrible moment.

Chancing a look over his shoulder, Shan saw a massive dull with a bone spear behind him. The spear had been stained the deep blue of blood, the tip glistening black. The Nysh City Fire Department dashed everywhere, shovelling sand, or tossing water on smouldering fires. Cracks ran through the smoke-stained brick walls.

Something caught his attention and he stared, unable to look away: the husked carapace of an ashkaro, seared and splintered. Empty.

I did that.

He had to get away. Could he burn this priest and her dull assistant and make his escape? Seeing as he had no idea how he'd done it the first time, and had completely lost control, he decided not to chance it.

"I'm calm," Shan said, to be sure they still thought he was.

"Less true than it was," said the priest. One antenna showed deepening concern while euphoric tremors ran through the other. "But not quite a lie. See you remain that way."

"Not quite lying?"

She looked at him like he was an idiot. "Now, we must leave before anyone asks the right questions."

"Right questions?"

"Who started this fire, and how." Her antennae bent toward Shan. "And how did you escape such a devastating blaze unharmed?" She made an impatient gesture with her craft claws. "Get up."

Shan stood. All four knees wobbled, threatening to dump him back to the floor.

"Come," she ordered. Turning, she headed off down the hall.

But I'm Shan Wyn Val Nul Nysh, nephew of the queen!

Knek prodded Shan in the back of the neck. Shan hurried after the priest, the big dumb dull following behind.

Everyone scampered from the priest's path, antennae nodding in subservient recognition.

Exiting the sports arena, the priest led Shan through busy streets. Even hidden behind an eternity of cloud, Alatash lit the world, its light feeling strangely harsh. Cobbled streets shone, the red clay bricks scrubbed every day by roving teams of dulls. Ashkaro hustled about their business, well-dressed brights ornamented in wealth, simply clad dulls bent under the burdens of their tools or hauling rickshaws. Tramea flitted overhead, their riders carrying private messages and express mail from city to city. In the distance, bloated skerry, tentacles gripping landing poles, surrounded the Main Station downtown. From here Shan couldn't see the ashkaro boarding to leave for distant locations, but for the first time he wanted to be one of them.

Taking the first left, the priest headed for the downtown core. "My name is Myosh Pok Tel," she said without breaking stride. "You are?"

"Shan Wyn Val Nul Nysh."

"Kratosh!" Myosh cursed. "Well, there's nothing for it now. We'll send word to your mother later." An antenna bent in Shan's direction. "How long have you known?"

"Known?"

"Your talent. How long have you been hiding it?"

"Hiding?" Shan stumbled, his legs refusing to work right. "I'm not Corrupt! I can't be!"

"Hmn," she grunted. A wave of bliss ran through the antenna leaning in Shan's direction. "Not lying. Just stupid."

"Hey!"

"When was the first time you saw sparks? When was your first full-fledged fire?"

Shan slowed in confusion, only to be shoved back into motion by the rude dull.

"Don't touch me!" Shan snapped, appalled by the treatment.

The dull showed no hint of apology.

"Answer my questions," said Myosh, "or Knek here will spike your brain."

Shan stumbled after the priest, the last tremors of that incredible joy still swirling through his thoughts, muddying everything. By all the gods of Alatash he wanted to feel that pleasure again. "That was the first time."

Myosh stopped suddenly and Shan crashed into her, retreating with mumbled apologies.

Main eyes and both antennae examining him she said, "That was the first time?"

He signalled the affirmative.

"Answer aloud," she commanded.

"That was the first."

"By Katlipok!" she swore. "I've never seen so much power so early. Usually…" She trailed off, looking around as if seeking guidance. "Knek, if he does anything, if the temperature changes or you feel the slightest bit warm, kill him."

Knek turned a single main eye on Shan.

"I'm not dangerous," whispered Shan, afraid to move. "I would never hurt anyone."

One of Myosh's antennae bent in sardonic amusement. "Whoever that burnt shell back there would beg to differ. Come."

She set off again, this time at a quicker pace.

Shan followed. Somehow, he'd killed Nyk, cooked her alive leaving only her husked carapace. Would they figure out who that was back in the hall?

Not right away.

All colour had been blasted from her exoskeleton.

Eventually her family would report Nyk missing. It was only a matter of time until the authorities figured out that Shan had killed Nyk Arl Zon, heir to the largest farm island in the queendom. They'd throw him to the storm. Was it somehow worse that he killed her accidentally, wielding his talent?

Much worse.

THE STORM BENEATH THE WORLD

A team of massive skirrak pulling an eight-wheeled wagon loaded with wood crates rumbled past, kicking up clouds of dust. Wearing the uniform of one of Shan's relatives, the dull driver looked bored but content.

Call for help. Demand assistance.

What could a stupid dull do? He'd probably offer to give them a ride to wherever Myosh was taking Shan.

"Most powerful talent I've ever seen," Myosh muttered to herself as Shan tagged along behind, "and it had to be a male. Couldn't have been a military-trained female," she grumbled. "Kratosh, even a dull female would have been better."

"I don't—"

Myosh silenced him with the flick of an antenna. "I'll give you sixteen days to show me you can maintain some control and resist the lure."

"I don't understand."

"Did it feel good?" the priest asked.

"No," said Shan, recalling the incredible pleasure.

"A lie," said Myosh. "*How* good did it feel?"

How did one answer a question like that? Shan had been with a couple of his sister's friends who'd briefly taken interest in him only to inexplicably lose it shortly after. Burning Nyk felt infinitely better.

"It was pleasurable," he answered. "Not the killing. I didn't mean to do that." His gut twisted at the thought of what he'd done. "But the fire felt good."

Myosh shot him a pitying look. "Even if you survive the next sixteen days, you are not cut out for what will follow." She looked away. "Too much power too fast. We'll see if you can go two weeks without a single spark."

By all that was holy in Alatash, Shan wanted to make sparks again *now*. A few little ones. Just a taste of that overwhelming ecstasy.

Sixteen days. I can do that.

"And if I make sparks?" he asked, dreading the answer.

Myosh glanced at Knek.

"Oh."

The priest gestured at the crest in the centre of her vestments. "I'm a Defiled. You know what that means?"

Though he mostly slept through the sermons at the Grand Temple of Redemption in the centre of Nysh City, he remembered the Defiled.

"Corrupt who use their talents to serve the queen until…" He swallowed, uncomfortable.

"Until they die or are banished to a Corrupt island."

Only the most holy and dedicated could be Defiled. It took a certain kind of selfless ashkaro to serve knowing they'd one day be cast aside, discarded and disgraced, no matter what they achieved.

She wants me to prove I can control my talent.

He understood. "You want me to be a Defiled."

"No, my pretty child," soothed the priest. "You hardly have the wit or personality for such a calling."

He hid the sting of her words. His flawless and near-reflective carapace, the height of ashkaro beauty, didn't make him shallow or stupid.

"You'll never be a Defiled," continued Myosh. "But if you survive the next weeks, you *might* be given a chance to serve your queen."

How could a Corrupt bright youth with a talent for uncontrolled raging infernos serve the queen? Did she need someone to light the many fireplaces and candles? He wasn't sure he could control it enough for such finesse.

Myosh turned again, this time into a narrow alley. Though she avoided the main pedestrian streets, he realized they were heading toward the Grand Temple of Redemption.

"I'll take you to Kaylamnel," the priest said.

"You're taking me to a flower?"

"No." She sighed. "The school is named after a flower. There, if you're extremely lucky and of much stronger character than you appear, you will learn to control your curse."

"The priests say the Corruption can never be controlled."

Myosh grunted annoyance. "Control is perhaps too strong a word. With training and perseverance," she shot him a look suggesting she thought him incapable of the latter, "one can slow the speed with which they succumb to the lure."

Shan followed Myosh through the streets of Nysh City. There

were no brights in these back alleys, only poor dulls loitering in the shadows. Most fled when they saw the priest. The Grand Temple of the Redemption, a massive and sprawling structure built of fired clay bricks, loomed close.

A few sparks. She won't notice.

Tired as he was, he craved the sight of those dancing lights. His craft claws twitched with need. A taste. One little flame where no one could see.

Can I resist making sparks for sixteen days?

He had to, or they'd spike his brain.

Fear, he decided, was a surprisingly good motivator.

Turning into another trash-strewn alley, Shan saw they'd approached the temple from the rear. Instead of entering through the grand hall and passing between the wood statues of long-dead queens, Myosh led him toward what looked like a servants' entrance.

Two bright females wearing the vestments of Redeemers, the church's military force, stood guard at the door. Armed with recurve bows of bone and wood easily capable of punching through the thickest carapace, long barbed spears, and sheathed serrated bone knives, they stepped forward to block the priest. Neither so much as glanced at Shan and Knek.

"State your business, *Defiled*," said the brighter of the two, a warrior with a glistening blue-black carapace the colour of old blood.

She moved with a deadly grace that made Shan's femorotibial joints weak to watch. In the days of hive, she'd have stalked the island hunting and killing, bringing back prey for her queen. This was the kind of female his father warned him about, the kind every male wanted to belong to. The other Redeemer, scarred carapace a shimmering blend of greens, remained at attention. One main eye watched Myosh, while the other studied the street beyond.

"I need to commandeer a tramea," Myosh announced.

"Defiled may not enter the temple. Why do you need a tramea?"

One of Myosh's antennae twitched in Shan's direction. "To get this pretty thing out of the city before he burns it all to ash."

Only now did the Redeemers focus on him, gazes lingering in predatory appreciation.

THE STORM BENEATH THE WORLD

"Very nice," said the blue-black Redeemer. "Would it not be simpler to kill him and be done?"

"It would," agreed the priest. "But he has potential unlike anything I've seen. And my orders come from the queen herself."

Examining Shan, the guards seemed doubtful. As if something so gorgeous could never be useful, no matter what his talent.

Finally shrugging, the blue-black Redeemer said, "I'll get you your tramea," and disappeared into the church.

"We're flying?" Shan asked.

Having lived his entire life in Nysh City, he'd never flown before. Everything a young male could want was here, within a short walk or slightly longer rickshaw ride. Why go elsewhere? Some families vacationed in the windward-most cities or rode skerry to resort islands if they were wealthy enough. Shan, however, loved the city. He loved the crush of ashkaro, the taverns and shops. Anything worth having could be found in Nysh City.

"No," said Myosh. "We're getting a tramea so we can walk. Idiot."

He ignored the rude barb. "Couldn't we take a skerry? More comfortable. Stocked bar. My family has several. I'm sure my mother—"

"Do you really think your mom will want to see you?"

"But..."

The Defiled priest was right. Mother would disown him the moment she found out he was Corrupt. He would be struck from the family ledger. It would be like he never existed. Even his father, who loved him, would never again speak his name.

Sorrow and shame bent Shan's antennae back until they lay flat.

"I need to get you out of the city fast," said Myosh, ignoring his pain. "Until we know you have some measure of control, you'll be quarantined."

Quarantined?

Horror froze his limbs. Only the foulest most dangerous criminals were separated from society! Even the Corrupt were sent to islands where there were other Corrupt. The idea of being entirely alone made having a spear jammed into your brain a tempting alternative.

"I can control it," said Shan.

"I know you believe that to be true. If I listen for it, I can tell when someone is lying; it's my talent. But you can mean well and still fail." She patted his head like he was a pet. "Let's be honest, when has a pampered thing like you been tested? When have you needed will power or inner strength?"

Never.

As a Nysh, however distant from the queen, life had always been easy.

My fire is useful, he reminded himself.

It was the only reason they hadn't immediately spiked him. That must mean at some point they'd want him to use his talent.

Shan supressed a shiver of pleasure at the thought.

"I can control it," he repeated.

He would, because someday they'd ask him to burn.

AHK TAY KYM

'It takes a Corrupt to catch a Corrupt' is purest garbage. The Defiled are an abomination and our continued use of them—no matter how controlled—is blasphemy.

—Shhu Jin Kal, Redemption Priest

For the entirety of her first day on *A Slow and Gentle Descent into Dark*, Ahk refused to leave the gondola railing. Enraptured, she stared down at the endless forests, farms, and towns passing beneath the skerry. Crew members stopped to check on her from time to time, asking if she was hungry or thirsty. She was both but didn't care, waving them away. By the time Mother came to bring her inside, Ahk's joints felt stiff, hunger gnawing at her insides.

"Just a moment longer?" Ahk asked, spotting the lights of a distant city.

With Alatash sinking below the windward horizon, the island came to life like sparkflies.

"No, dear," her mother said. "You haven't eaten all day." Dressed in a quilted vest, Mother huddled her arms tight to her thorax for warmth.

Looking for a reason to stay a moment longer, Ahk pointed out the lights. "What city is that?"

"That's Quant Tzo."

Damn. She'd hoped her mother might see this as an opportunity for education. "What's the population?"

Mother made an amused chuffing noise. "About fifty thousand. And before you ask, it's based around a university, which makes its main export knowledge."

"Is that where I'll go to school?"

"No. We'll have the best teachers brought in to teach you one-on-one. Now—"

"What will I study? I like art and painting, anything with light and colour. But for business—"

"I think you've already mastered the diplomatic arts of distraction, negotiation, and stalling. Time to come inside." Seeing Ahk was about to ask more questions, her mother added, "Now."

Knowing better than to push further, Ahk surrendered. Leading the way, she headed for the family's quarters.

"How does the skerry fly with all this stuff on its back?" she asked over her shoulder.

"You'll notice there are no clay bricks," mother answered. "Everything is hollow wood. Only the lightest materials are used. That said, we could sacrifice some comfort for speed, if needed. On a military skerry everything is utilitarian. No sprawling loungers or huge dining tables."

Ahk pushed open the door to the family wing and entered the hall, Mother following. The dining room was empty, a single covered plate on the table.

Pointing at it, her mother said, "Sit. Eat."

Ahk sat, lifting the cover from the plate, and breathing deep the scent of steamed fish and soft shoots of grass. Though the meal had long gone cold, her stomach gurgled in anticipation as she devoured one of the leaves.

"I thought you liked the fish more," Mother said. "I had the chef make it the way you like."

"I do. But I always leave the best for last. That way, the last thing I taste in every meal is delicious."

"Hmn." Mother's antennae bent in humour. "Wait until you do your tour of service. Military cooks have a unique skill for making everything taste bad. Luckily, they work you so hard you're too hungry to care."

Having grown up with a chef who tailored every meal to the individual preferences of each family member, Ahk couldn't imagine that. Even quick snacks were works of art.

Remembering Bon's gorgeous carving and the sudden discovery of his talent, Ahk twitched in surprise. "Is cooking our chef's talent?" she asked with some dread. She'd heard of wealthy families hiding useful Corrupt from the Redemption so they might profit from their talents.

"No dear," Mother said. "She learned from many years of practice. Kyu Sah Noh has been with the family for a long time. Were she Corrupt, and cooking her talent, she'd have starved to death years ago."

Having seen Kyu Sah Noh, Ahk knew the chef wasn't in danger of starvation.

Shoving another leaf into her mouth, Ahk changed the subject, asking, "Are military skerry a lot faster?"

"Yes, they fly much higher, where the air is thin and the winds fast. The crew wear heavily quilted vests, thicker than this one." She tapped her thorax with a craft claw. "Sometimes, during emergency manoeuvres, they go so high you'll freeze and die, even with the heaviest vest. The crew gather around the ovens in the shelters until it's time to dive again. It's difficult to control skerry at that altitude. Sometimes they go too high and disappear, never to be seen again." Mother's antennae gauged Ahk's reaction, checking to see this wasn't too upsetting a topic. "Sometimes they reappear weeks later, the crew frozen solid. Once, a dead skerry crashed in the Nysh desert. Its crew wore uniforms no one recognized. They weren't from Yil either. No one knew whether they came from some distant island we'd never had contact with, or if they came from here but spent lifetimes drifting frozen in the clouds before the skerry died."

Ahk shuddered. There was something terrifying about a cold death. In the plays and stories, it was always described as a slowing of life, blood thickening, organs turning to gel before ceasing to work. The limbs died first, becoming heavy lumps. An ashkaro would lie helpless and immobile as the cold crept deeper, awake and conscious until it reached their guts. She imagined a skerry populated by perfectly preserved dead.

When she finished her meal, chirping happily as she ate the last delicious steamed fish, Mother brought her to a reading room with a lit fire and bookcase including some of Ahk's favourites. After making sure

THE STORM BENEATH THE WORLD

Ahk was settled and comfortable, Mother left to do whatever it was she did all the time. Never still, never bored, even high over the queendom and presumably out of contact with her employees and partners, her mother was a bundle of energy.

Selecting a book and curling into a reading hammock, Ahk wondered if being heir to the family business wasn't such a great thing after all. Mother never had time to paint or draw or pursue hobbies. It seemed that every moment of her life was given to the running of the family's interests.

For the next three days they flew above the Nysh Queendom. They were so high Ahk felt like she might reach up and touch the clouds, parting them to reveal Alatash. Mother said it was an illusion of distance and size, and that no skerry had ever gone so high. The gods, she said, were forever beyond the reach of the ashkaro.

Late in the third day, the windward horizon changed. The unbroken forest they'd flown over most of the day ended suddenly, an abrupt and hard line beyond which lay manicured estates, sprawling homes, and vacation resorts. After the homes, there was…nothing.

The world ended.

Beyond the edge of the island, a roiling storm reached forever, blurring to nothing in the distance. Lightning twisted through snakes of writhing cloud. Bubbles of flame rose from the dark depths to *pop*, spraying tiny sparks.

Pointing them out to her mother, who stood beside her at the rail, Ahk said, "Fire bubbles."

"Bubbles." Mom laughed. "Each of those *bubbles* is a thousand times bigger than *A Slow and Gentle Descent into Dark*. Many are larger than the entire queendom."

Ahk couldn't make the scale comprehensible. Existence was a river of unending wind upon which sailed colossal creatures so large thousands of ashkaro lived upon their backs like gnats and so ancient the gnats had evolved from unintelligent hive insects to city-dwelling masters of their environment. Above the islands, clouds stretched forever in every direction. Below, the hellish storm of Kratosh, so far away and so impossibly massive that what appeared to be tiny bubbles dwarfed the queendom.

Fly too high, and we freeze. Drop too low and we burn.

As if all this weren't already too much, one of her teachers, an ancient bright, said that if you travelled far enough north, you'd reach the stormwall. She said this storm separated the river of days from another wind river, and that sometimes alien creatures came through the storm on strange vessels. She also told the class that there was another similar storm to the south and that the air there became unbreathable. She said ashkaro venturing too close to the southern stormwall asphyxiated. Much of it was stunning blasphemy, but even the Redemption turned a blind eye when aging warrior females started babbling about their experiences.

We live in a tunnel, rushing toward…

Toward what?

Did the river of days go on forever? Some thought the gods were waiting at the end, but how could that be true if they were in Alatash?

Ignoring Ahk's confusion, her mother kept talking. "Much like the air above is too thin and too cold, the air below is too thick and too hot. If you dove deep enough, your innards would boil long before you reached the storm."

"Don't the Sisters of the Storm in the Yil Queendom throw blasphemers to the storm? If you're dead before you reach it—"

"They believe the souls live on, that Katlipok claims them."

"Oh."

Breathless, Ahk stared at Kratosh, the storm beneath the world, domain of the fallen god. She could well imagine an eternity of torment in such a place. Savage heat so brutal it baked souls dry. Drier than the leeward desert. Terrifying as the thought of freezing to death was, the idea of burning forever was scarier.

A shadow swept across the skerry's deck. Mom ducked, reaching instinctively for her weapons. Looking up, she stilled, all six eyes and both antennae searching the sky.

"Kratosh!" her mother swore.

Ahk looked up. Another skerry, smaller and darker than the one they rode, hung between *A Slow and Gentle Descent into Dark* and the light of Alatash. Writhing tentacles reached down, searching. One found the flagpole and coiled around it, tearing the family crest.

"Who is that?" Ahk asked.

Drawing her stab sticks, Mother said, "Go inside. Lock the doors. Don't come out until I get you."

"Who is it?" Ahk repeated, fear shaking her voice.

"Go! Now!"

Ahk ran as more grasping tentacles made contact and began pulling the two airborne creatures together. Weapons drawn, crewmembers hurried everywhere. Many carried stab sticks or spears. A few bore longbows and quivers of arrows.

Seeing a lower caste bright donning a vest of wood armour, Ahk confronted her. "What's happening?" she demanded.

The bright dipped a hurried bow. "Pirates. They don't usually attack skerry this big. They're either desperate, stupid, or insane." She glanced past Ahk. "Or they've come for something specific. Not to worry, we'll make short work of them." Dipping another curt bow, she added, "You should stay out of sight until it's over," and left without waiting to be dismissed.

Ahk headed inside, stopping a few strides down the hall.

If pirates aren't a threat, why am I hiding?

For that matter, where did one hide on a skerry?

Most doors had locks, but that was more to let others know you didn't want to be disturbed than to keep anyone out. As Mother said, everything was constructed of the lightest wood. There was no wall a determined ashkaro couldn't kick their way through.

Stay calm. Think.

Pirates would search both the crew and family quarters as that's where all the wealth and spoils would be. They'd probably raid the pantries for food, too. Should she leave the gondola altogether, hide on the skerry itself? The thought was terrifying. What if the wind blew her off? A fall from this height would shatter her carapace.

Skittering back to the door, Ahk pushed it open to peer outside. As she looked, a barbed arrow lanced down from above to puncture the exoskeleton of the female she'd just talked to. The ashkaro fell, writhing in agony, until another arrow pinned her head to the deck.

Looking up, Ahk saw ashkaro sliding down ropes, two arms

loosing arrows while the other two controlled their descent. Landing on the deck of *A Slow and Gentle Descent into Dark*, they attacked the crew, fighting to clear an area. The pirates fought like a well-trained military force, arrows falling from above with deadly accuracy. The moment they cleared an area of deck, Mother's security forces retreating to regroup, another slid down the ropes. This one, a small, scarred dull female missing a steering leg from the femorotibial joint and one craft claw, landed awkwardly, stumbling. Her carapace, warped and contorted, looked like it had been melted and then hardened again. The other pirates retreated, antennae bent away from the newcomer as if both scared and disgusted. Ahk stared in horror; such abominations were killed at birth so their souls might be reborn in another body closer to the perfection the gods demanded.

Limping a few steps, the dull said, "Fear. You fear me."

A score of strides away, Ahk's muscles locked rigid. The female shook with waves of obscene pleasure and spread her misshapen arms wide as if welcoming a lover.

"Fear me!" the cripple screamed, moaning in ecstasy. "My enemies fear me. Cower!"

For a heartbeat, no one moved. Crew and pirates alike stood rooted. One by one, the pirates shook off their fear. Dazed and still darting nervous looks at the dull, they went from crew member to crew member, killing. Locked in a rictus of terror, their victims didn't react.

A scuffed bright pirate bearing a spear approached her mother.

No, no, no. Ahk couldn't move.

Crouching behind Mother, the pirate pushed the spear against the back of her neck, working the tip into the overlapping plates of her carapace.

Please no. Please, please, please, no.

With a satisfied nod, the bright shoved a claw-length of wood into Mother's brain, twisting and wiggling the haft before dragging the weapon free. Her mother collapsed, tremors running through her body.

Unable to move, unable to make a sound, Ahk's screams echoed through her mind.

Another bright descended on a rope to stand beside the limping dull. Instead of dominating the lower caste, she stayed a respectful step back.

"Where is she?" demanded the dull. "Where do you see her?"

The bright hesitated, antennae searching in every direction. "I...I no longer see her."

Turning her attention on the cowering bright, the dull growled, "You told me she was here. Did she jump off?"

Twitching in fear, the bright said, "I don't know."

"Send the harpoons down. I want this thing falling into the storm when we're finished. Search everything!"

THE STORM BENEATH THE WORLD

JOH

For hundreds of generations the queens' political clout has eroded. Some see this as social reformation, males and dulls achieving rights unheard of in the lifetime of the previous generation. Others claim it's the result of the political manoeuvring of the inner council, those elected by the highest families to protect their interests. The Redemption, no doubt with its own agenda, preach such changes are the will of the gods and that we move ever closer to that final day.

Whatever the reason, the reality is that not having a singular ruler weakens us.

When questioned on her intentions regarding the coming meeting of our islands. Queen Yil Een Ahn Kyn Ah Phy-Rah fed her inner council to the storm. The Mad Queen is now the sole ruler of the island. While I question her methods, she has successfully both militarized and mobilized an entire island while we still argue about increasing the budget of both the Queen's Claw and Queen's Wing. There are families suggesting they should be allowed to continue trading with the Yil Queendom even though we'll be at war within the next year!

Sometimes, I think that leaving the hive was a terrible mistake.

—Fourth Officer Vynu Shuu, Queen's Claw

Joh helped Rel manoeuvre the unresponsive dull female into the wagon, an awkward process in the dark. Noticing her broken wrist when she groaned in pain, the priest took a moment to wrap the joint, immobilizing it so it might heal properly.

"What's your name?" the priest asked, voice gentle.

THE STORM BENEATH THE WORLD

Her antennae swayed loose, eyes focussing on nothing. "Wex," she said. "Wex Jel."

"Do you have any other wounds?" Rel asked.

She didn't answer.

With a shrug of his upper wings, Rel returned to the front bench. Joh followed. The priest snapped the reins and the skirrak set off.

"What's her talent?" Joh asked, keeping his voice quiet.

Rel stared off into the dark. "No idea."

The massive eight-limbed beasts hauled the wagon through the desert without complaint, their lumbering progress never slowing. Wood wheels clattered over hardpacked earth, crushing tufts of sharp, thick-leafed grass beneath them. Sometimes a skirrak tore a plant from the ground and devoured it, hanging clod of gritty dirt and all, without breaking stride.

Joh turned to look at the newcomer sleeping in the back of the wagon. They'd found her sprawled awkwardly in the dirt, all eight limbs splayed as if prostrating herself before the gods in prayer. Such displays of vulnerability were usually saved for private worship. There'd been a dead female ashkaro nearby, a dim shape in the night.

I think the corpse was a bright.

It was impossible to be sure in the dark, but there was something about the sleek carapace suggesting a higher caste.

Rel had noticed the body and said nothing.

He didn't even ask if Wex killed her.

Though with no one else in sight, it seemed likely she was the murderer. This was every kind of wrong. Murder was one of the few crimes punishable by death. While the priests said everyone was equal in the eyes of the law, there was a special hell for any dull daring to raise claws against their betters. Yet instead of carting Wex to the nearest town to face judgement, Rel helped her into the wagon and continued toward the school.

Whatever awaits us there must be more important than justice.

Shadows grew long as Alatash sank toward the windward horizon behind them.

Joh shuffled on the seat beside Rel. "Are we almost there yet?"

"No."

"I'm thirsty." He hadn't had water in two days.

Rel turned a secondary eye in Joh's direction.

"That wasn't a suggestion," Joh added. "Just a statement of fact."

Rel passed Joh a water skin.

"We left the road to find Wex," said Joh.

One of Rel's antennae nodded agreement.

"You didn't know she was there when you picked me up though. Otherwise, we would have taken a more direct route."

"I check at scheduled intervals to see if there are new Corrupt nearby."

Did discovering her talent get that bright killed?

Deciding not to ask, Joh said, "You can only sense the Corrupt after they've discovered their talent?"

"Of course," answered Rel, flicking the reins even though the skirrak hadn't changed pace. "Every ashkaro has a talent. We only become Corrupt when we discover it, when we feel that first rush of pleasure that comes with using it."

Remembering the first time he accidentally suggested Dad let him play outside a little longer, and the incredible wave of contentedness as his father returned indoors, Joh said nothing.

Rel said, "It's a spot of luck we happened to be so close."

"Oh," said Joh, suddenly understanding. "Sensing Corrupt is your talent. You get that feeling every time you use it. You must be blissed out of your mind right now!"

Rel shot him a dark look, antennae bent toward Joh as if studying prey. "Like any talent, the more I use it the less I'm able to resist the lure. I have learned the control required to use it sparingly."

"The Redemption says that once you discover your talent you're doomed. All Corrupt fall to the lure. Are you, a priest, telling me the church is lying?"

The priest's antennae relaxed. "Each use pushes me one step closer to falling to the lure. I'm as doomed as any." A main eye turned in Joh's direction. "I spend myself in service to the queen."

He hasn't been banished because the queen finds him useful.

All his life Joh had been told the Corrupt were sent to the desert or a Corrupt island if they were dangerous. This priest travelled freely, using his talent, with the queen's blessing.

There was an interesting lesson there: *Make sure you're useful.*

"What happens when the lure becomes too much?" Joh asked. "What happens when you can no longer resist and spend your days sensing the Corrupt around you because it feels too good to stop?"

Rel didn't answer, which Joh guessed was an answer.

If the queen found Joh's talent useful, he wouldn't be banished. That said, like Rel, he'd be asked to use that talent in her service. When he inevitably fell prey to the lure, Queen Nysh would cast him aside.

"Are you well paid?" he asked the priest.

"Servants of the queen never starve."

That sounded like a no.

No matter what he'd told Rel about his talent being harmless, he knew otherwise.

When the queen decides I'm more dangerous than useful she'll banish me.

He'd heard stories of lawless chaos, starvation, and death. Not part of the queendom, Corrupt islands had no government, no ruler. Those with powerful talents briefly rose to rule for a time before falling to the lure. As a small dull, he'd rather not learn the truth.

They rode on in silence, Joh contemplating what a future serving the queen as a Corrupt might look like and what use she'd find for his talent.

Suggesting things, obviously.

But as queen, couldn't she tell everyone what to do? Why suggest when you could command?

The only ashkaro she couldn't compel were those living on the Corrupt islands she banished them to.

And those living in other queendoms, he corrected.

They travelled through the night, the skirrak never slowing or tiring. Rel answered Joh's questions with grunts and dismissive waves of an antenna. Giving up, Joh watched the desert, secondary eyes checking the sky for danger. Unwilling to test the priest's patience, he decided not to ask why they weren't stopping. Instead, he turned on the bench and peered back into the darkness of the enclosed wagon. The dull female lay shrouded in shadow. Though not much bigger than Joh, she was everything he wasn't. Her carapace was streamlined and deadly, the barbed spikes of her raptorial arms unusually bright.

A complex mix of emotions chased his thoughts in circles. Writ deep in the blood of every male was a desire to find a dangerous female, someone fast and brutal, capable of both hunting and defending the home.

That's not the way things are anymore.

This dull priest was proof! He travelled alone, without a female to watch over him or give him orders. He was trusted to do what must be an important job. Farms having long replaced hunting parties, no one starved now. Even the most helpless dull male could find a meal if he was willing to work.

And yet, everything about Wex sang songs of worship in Joh.

You aren't worthy. You'll never be worthy.

Was that true, though? He was travelling toward a school where he would be taught how to use his talent, how to control it. That must elevate him somewhat.

I could suggest she find me attractive.

He felt filthy with the thought.

Never.

Sometimes he slipped up and accidentally made suggestions. On the rare occasions he did it intentionally, he was trying to help. Telling someone how they should feel was a terrible invasion.

Suggesting she like him wouldn't achieve anything. They'd likely be split up once they reached the school. He'd probably never see her again and if he did, she wouldn't recognize him anyway. She'd barely noticed him as Rel helped her into the wagon.

"It's rude to stare," said Wex, a barely visible shape in the shadows of the wagon.

Joh flinched, embarrassed, and turned in his seat, facing forward. "Sorry."

"Where are we?" she asked. "Who are you, and how did I get here?"

Joh glanced at Rel, looking for guidance.

"If climbing into the back of the wagon to explain things means you aren't bombarding me with questions," grumbled the priest, "then for the love and light of Alatash, please do that."

THE STORM BENEATH THE WORLD

"I keep asking questions," said Joh, "because you haven't told me anything."

"Then tell her whatever you *do* know."

Hesitating, Joh wondered what exactly that was.

"Please," said Wex. "Just talk to me."

Swallowing his fear, Joh clambered into the back.

"Hello," he said, antennae polite and unthreatening. "My name is Joh."

"Wex Jel," she answered, apparently having forgotten that she'd already told them her name. "Are we going to Brickworks #7? Am I to be tried for my crime?" She stared off into the dark and whispered, "I killed Cayr Rie Chi Lo."

She killed a four-name bright?

Joh glanced at Rel sitting in the front. The priest didn't appear to have heard the confession.

Wex was doomed.

There was no hiding from the Queen's Claw. Deepest desert, church-run school or no, they'd bring her before the court. The deceased bright's family would demand justice. No matter how much the church preached that the goal of civilization was the redemption of the ashkaro, some sins were unforgiveable.

Was there something he could do to save her?

WEX JEL

Nysh City, the political and religious heart of the Nysh Queendom, is home to near half a million ashkaro. By comparison, over three quarters of a million call Yil City home. What's more, the Mad Queen has introduced legislation commanding every citizen, female and male, bright and dull, to serve in the military. Queen Yil has militarized an entire island.

—Bash Sero Yui Kahl, Senior Chancellor, the Queen's Council

The little dull male fell silent. He glanced at his craft claws, cleaning them with fastidious little nibbles. The older dull priest driving the wagon—she couldn't remember his name—ignored them. Flicking the reins, he mumbled to the trudging skirrak who in turn ignored him.

Wex checked her own craft claws, found them caked blue with dried blood.

I killed Cayr Rie Chi Lo.

The dull looked up with a twitch of fear.

Joh. Such a nothing dull name. A single grunted syllable for a single grunt creature.

That was her mom, forever proud of that second name separating them from the filthy rabble.

She realized he hadn't answered her question. "Where are you taking me?"

"A school called Amphazar," said Joh. "Somewhere in the desert."

"The Queen's Claw will come for me," Wex said. "I killed a bright."

Joh looked from Wex's bloody claws to her face. One main eye checking to see if Rel was listening, he said, "It would probably be for the best if you never mentioned that again." His antennae gave a small flutter of pleasure.

He's right.

The Queen's Justice would find her no matter what.

"Rel can sense those with talent," Joh continued. "I'm guessing you discovered your talent during that fight."

Wex said nothing and he bobbed his head as if agreeing. "We're going to a special school where we'll be taught to use and control our talents."

"*Our* talents?"

"I'm Corrupt too," he said, oddly unbothered by the admission. "Though I think your talent will be of more interest to them than mine."

"Why?"

"They're teaching Corrupt so we can serve the queen."

Considering what he'd seen and the terrible crime she admitted to, Joh seemed surprisingly unafraid.

"I suspect," he continued, "whatever it is we're being trained for will outweigh any past crimes."

"He's right," said the old priest. "As long as you're at the school, you'll have no trouble with the law."

Wex thought that over.

"Are you saying that if she leaves the school, you'll give her over to the Queen's Claw? Not leaving her much of a choice are you."

"Be very careful how you word your next sentence," said the priest.

Joh's mouth snapped shut.

The priest is scared. He's afraid to let Joh speak freely.

Did he worry Joh would spill some secret? That seemed unlikely as the younger male had already grumbled about how the priest hadn't told him anything useful.

Joh knows why we're being taken to the school.

And he said her talent would be of interest there.

Though she didn't understand the details, her talent appeared to be murder.

They want us to kill for the queen.

She wanted to feel that euphoric rush again and hated herself for it.

Even without her talent, tearing this little dull male apart would be nothing. His talent must be something scary then. Probably not physical, either. While most talents were for something simple like painting or cooking or making tools, she'd heard of rare talents where a Corrupt could cause her victims to stop breathing until they died.

Joh turned to the priest. "Rel, are we there yet?"

The priest groaned. "Get some sleep. Both of you. We'll arrive in the morning."

"Unless you sense another Corrupt," said Joh.

"Go. To. Sleep."

With a shrug and an amused glance at Wex, Joh curled up in the back of the wagon, wings tight, all four arms wrapped around his upper thorax. He was careful to give her plenty of space.

Wex lay down too. Exhausted as she was, she didn't expect to sleep. Over and over, she saw the world slow, Cayr's finely crafted stab sticks moving in a predictable arc, the gaping hole in her defences screaming *Here! Right here!* at Wex. But it wasn't a fault in Cayr's skill that Wex saw. The bright was a better fighter than she would ever be.

It was a weakness.

She bent an antenna toward Joh.

What's yours?

He had many, some obvious. He was small and unskilled in combat. If threatened by a superior foe, he'd likely curl up in submission. None of that was her own talent speaking, she felt no pleasure at the observations. Was her talent only finding gaps in an opponent's defences?

Except it wasn't until she took advantage of Cayr's weakness that she felt the full crushing weight of the lure. She didn't want to think about that.

Someone's real weakness changes.

Just as in a fight, a weakness might only exist for a fraction of a moment and then disappear. Joh's weakness would change depending on the situation and who he faced.

Pretend it's me he's facing, what's his weakness?

THE STORM BENEATH THE WORLD

It was a silly game. She could kill him even knowing nothing about him. But if he was here in this wagon, being taken to a school to be trained to kill for the queen, he was somehow dangerous.

One of his antennae moved, bent a little in her direction, a secondary eye focussed on her in the dark. Not great at seeing detail, particularly at night, that eye watched for movement. Was he worried she might attack him? No, his antennae showed no hint of fear, and she didn't think him capable of such subterfuge. She remembered the way he studied her earlier when he thought she was sleeping.

He likes me.

It wasn't her talent speaking, simply a realization. She wasn't sure how she felt about it. A one-name dull from the desert was a step down from even the boring two-name bright her mother had been trying to arrange Wex's marriage with. Kratosh, a runt dull like Joh was a step down from everything, and that was without even considering that he was a Corrupt.

You are too.

For all the church preached the new equality of brights and dulls, males and females, the Corruption was the true equalizer. Yesterday, Wex had been a two-name dull with a career laid out before her and marriage prospects. Today, she was worth no more than this dull male.

"Did you kill someone too?" she asked.

Joh shook his head. "It'd probably be better if you didn't ask about my talent." A tremor ran through his antennae.

"I won't then," said Wex, suddenly disinterested.

Up front, Rel bent an antenna back in their direction. "I warned you, Joh."

Joh shot him an annoyed look. "Sorry. Suggestion," he said to Wex. "When I suggest things to people, they usually listen."

She'd never heard of that talent before and decided it must be incredibly rare.

"Sounds useful," Wex said. "Why didn't you want to tell me?"

"I was worried you'd be afraid of me."

Afraid?

Then she saw it. He called it suggestion, but it was more. He could tell people what to do and they'd obey. That, she decided, was scary.

"Could you tell someone to kill themselves?" Wex asked.

"I would never do that."

"But *could* you?"

Rel leaned back, making no attempt to hide that he was listening.

"I don't know," admitted Joh. "The further a suggestion is from a person's nature, the less likely they are to do it."

"That's now," said Rel, "wait until he's had some practice and grown in power. Wait until he's addicted, unable to stop himself from mumbling suggestions to everyone. Even if he's the nicest ashkaro in all the queendom, he'll be dangerous."

Wex saw no surprise in Joh's posture. He'd already thought this through.

They'll kill or banish him before he reaches that point.

And yet here he was, calm despite being small and helpless. Wex's talent for finding an opponent's weakness and stabbing them suddenly seemed paltry. There'd be a period, the duration of which depended on his self-control, where he'd be both powerful and in full control of his faculties. It could be days, but it might be years. Were he not dealt with in time, he might challenge the queen herself, throw the island into anarchy. By the time Rel understood the true danger, it would be too late.

Someone needs to watch him.

Someone he wouldn't see as a threat. Someone he trusted.

Someone he likes.

Wex's main eyes, so adept at tracking movement and seeing detail during the day were near useless at night. Her secondary eyes saw a blurred monochrome world beyond a few strides, always alert for predators. Her antennae moved constantly, tasting the world, feeling the movement of air.

The skirrak trudged on, heads swaying in rhythmic time to their eight-legged stride. They looked like they'd fallen asleep walking and were too dumb to stop.

The three sat in silence as the wagon rumbled over the uneven ground. The jostling rocked Wex, pulling her toward sleep. It was too much. Discovering she was Corrupt. Murdering Cayr. Being hauled off to some strange school to serve the queen. Exhaustion made her thoughts heavy and sluggish.

She mumbled, "We're not following a road."

"Like I said," said Joh. "Rel senses Corrupt. I'm guessing the school is almost entirely populated by the cursed."

Wex winced. She should have thought of that.

"You should sleep," Joh whispered. "You've been through a terrible trauma. It wasn't your fault. You'll feel better in the morning."

Catching the scent of preserved grubs, Wex's antennae woke her. Her belly grumbled complaint, her throat coated in dust reminding her she'd neither ate nor drank in over a day. The leeward horizon glowed gold promising the return of Alatash.

Yesterday was a blur of exhaustion. She killed Cayr, but maybe it wasn't entirely her fault. The bright challenged her; the fight hadn't been Wex's idea.

I tried to leave!

Cayr pressured her into the fight, teasing her.

Prostrate in the desert sand, praying to the gods for forgiveness, she'd thought her life over. She bemoaned the loss of things she hadn't wanted. She hadn't really wanted to marry that overly servile male, only agreeing to it to make Mom happy. Now, she had the opportunity to serve the queen. There could be no higher calling, no greater honour. There wasn't a female alive—dull or bright—who didn't dream of the chance to fight for her queen.

"Feeling better?" Joh asked.

Wex nodded an antenna, pushing herself into a sitting position. He looked different. There was an indefinable *something* about him she hated to admit she rather liked. For one, he was smarter than she'd expected. He was also oddly unafraid of the Defiled priest.

He's a brave little thing, she thought fondly.

She regretted how quickly she'd dismissed him as not worth knowing. He was easily the most interesting one-name dull she'd ever met. Sure, he was a little on the small side, but runt was such a cruel word.

The skirrak continued their relentless plod, once again pulling up and devouring great clods of earth and leathery leaves as they walked.

THE STORM BENEATH THE WORLD

Rel sat as he had, thorax hunched, wings hanging limp down his back.

Joh pointed with an antenna. "Look."

Backlit by Alatash, the leeward horizon looked strangely flat. Details grew with the coming day. Ahead, a clay brick fortress rose from the desert. Crumbling brick walls surrounded the inner structures. Repairs had been done, though not recently. Once this might have been a mighty fortification, but now it would be easy for invaders to wander up the gently sloped sand piled against the windward wall. Whatever gates had once enclosed the main entrance were gone, no hint of them remaining. Seeing the walls, the skirrak increased their pace, Rel sat straighter, his wings fluttering to dislodge the sand gathered there.

Half an hour later she understood how badly she'd misjudged the scale. Growing up in Brickworks #7, she'd thought the factory the largest imaginable structure. A full story taller than even the biggest bright home, it had been dwarfed by the chimneys belching filth into the sky day and night. The outer wall of the school would have towered over even the tallest smokestack.

The skirrak headed for the fortress.

As they drew closer, she realized the entrance was a section of collapsed wall. Part of it had been sloppily rebuilt to give the hint of structure, but most of that had fallen in. No ashkaro stood guard. Seeing no motion or activity to suggest the place was occupied, never mind an operating school, Wex leaned back to stare up at the crenelated wall. From up there, archers could rain arrows down on invaders. If there were anyone up there.

"Why have a fortress in the middle of the desert?" Wex asked.

"The only constant in life is change," said Rel. "Even on the leeward-most edge of the island, if you dig in the sand, you'll find the bones of fish. You'll find trees buried so long the wood has become stone. Once, long before there were ashkaro, the island was smaller and covered from horizon to horizon with lush forests. Things lived and died, and more things lived atop their remains. As the island grew in area, it grew in girth too, millions of years of death heaped upon death. In time, the island became so large the wind's moisture no longer reached the leeward side, having dumped all its rain on the far side."

"I don't—"

THE STORM BENEATH THE WORLD

Rel waved Joh to silence with a raptorial claw. "Many hundreds of millennia ago, there were thousands of queens on this island, thousands of hives battling for domination. With countless centuries of unending war, that number was whittled down to four queens. Though not yet the desert it is today, the windward side was already dying. This fortress was built by one of those queens, though we don't know her name. It has been rebuilt and abandoned so many times you'll find an awful confusion of architectural styles within."

"Why put the school out here?" Wex asked. "It must cost a fortune to bring in food and water."

"It does," agreed Rel. "We train Corrupt at this school, teaching them not only how to resist the lure, but also how to use their talents. Some are extremely dangerous. I've had students capable of calling storms, and summoning lightning. Others can control feral creatures, binding tramea or nests of rafak to their will. Try as we might, we are not always successful. Talent and willpower are two very different things." He bent an antenna in Joh's direction. "You never know who someone is until they've been tested." He sat quiet and contemplative for a while. Then, "I think we lost something when we abandoned the hive. Gone are the days when we turned all we are to serving our queen. Selfish individuality has replaced working for the greater good and we are diminished for it."

"On the other claw," Joh said, "I think such a sacrifice means more when made by choice."

Much as Wex craved the chance to serve her queen, the thought of mindlessly sacrificing herself held no appeal. Something in the priest's attitude niggled. He seemed like a kindly old man, though surprisingly educated for a dull. Yet he discussed losing students—and she had to assume they'd died—with a complete lack of emotion.

Whatever we're to be trained for is dangerous and requires dangerous Corrupt.

As a two-name and daughter of a shift manager, Wex was more educated than most dulls. She'd read enough to know that once, long ago, male drones were placed at the front of an army. Though sluggish and clumsy, their size slowed an enemy, buying the faster, smarter females time to plan and act.

We're drones to him.

THE STORM BENEATH THE WORLD

That wasn't quite right.

Despite knowing he too would be banished, Rel served Queen Nysh with all he was. He would sacrifice himself and every child in that school to achieve whatever the queen required.

We're sacrifices.

Rel probably saw it as redemption.

Was this a path to earning forgiveness for her sins?

"Are there bright students here?" Joh asked, interrupting her thoughts.

"No," said Rel. "There's a second school deep in the windward forests. It's called Kaylamnel."

Wex grunted a laugh. "The school for brights is in a lush forest and named after a beautiful flower, whereas the school for dulls is named for a worm that hides under the sand for decades until it rains."

Rel shrugged his upper wings, a dry flutter. "You'll be fed. There are wells. You might not soak in deep baths, but your carapace won't turn white and crack. The other options for an ashkaro with a talent for killing, are much worse."

"For a teacher," mumbled Joh, "you're not very good with children."

Eyes and antennae again facing forward, Rel said, "Your childhood ended the moment you discovered your talent."

THE STORM BENEATH THE WORLD

SHAN WYN VAL NUL NYSH

As a Sister of the Storm, the young Yil Een Ahn Kyn Ah claimed to have received a vision from Katlipok. The god told her Queen Shah Qwyn Hul Zsan Din had strayed from the true path, seeking selfish self-aggrandizement instead of serving her subjects. Sister Yil assassinated Queen Shah at the next cabinet meeting, spiking her limbs to the table and then splitting the back of her carapace wide to expose her sins.

The Mad Queen Yil now preaches that Katlipok commanded her to unite all the islands in the river of days under a single queen. All whom resist, she says, must be sent to the storm.

After so many generations of advancement, it's incomprehensible to see an entire island retreat toward the days of hive.

—*A History of the Mad Queen*, by Chuo Sdai Rhaj Een

Shan stood in the shadow of the Grand Temple of Redemption, staring up at the monolith of clay bricks, each one painted a different colour from its neighbours. Once a shimmering rainbow when the temple was first constructed some twelve hundred years and three or four queens ago, now they were a slur of flaking greys barely hinting at their original beauty. Centuries of industry stained everything in Nysh City. No matter how hard the acolytes assigned to scrubbing the exterior worked, nothing was clean for long.

Only the Redemption was allowed to use such painted bricks. Everyone else made do with various shades of yellow, red, and brown, depending on where the clay was harvested and the skill of those working the kilns. After hundreds of years, however, it was difficult to tell them apart. The brothels offering their fake bright glitter-glued males and the temples of the Redemption looked much the same.

A gust of wind shoved spinning funnels of gritty dust from an alley. It danced in tight pirouettes between Shan, the Defiled priest, and the remaining Redeemer, and then fled down another laneway. Apparently lost in their own thoughts, Myosh and the Redeemer ignored it. Shan wanted to follow the dust.

The blue-black Redeemer returned. "Defiled, your tramea are on the way."

"Would this not be easier from the aviary on the temple roof?" Myosh Pok Tel asked. "This alley is a little tight."

The Redeemer with the scarred, shimmering green carapace gave a careless shrug of her upper wings. "I don't care who backs your disgusting sect, you'll be dead before I allow you to set claw inside this temple."

Showing no more than a flash of annoyance in her antennae, Myosh asked Shan, "Have you ever flown a tramea?"

"You do know the feral ones *eat* ashkaro, right?"

"I'll take that as a no." The priest turned in a circle, studying the alley. "Lift-off will be tricky."

"Maybe we could hire a carriage?"

"On the bright side," said the Defiled, "if you fall off and die, my life suddenly becomes a great deal easier."

Myosh was right, this was a narrow alley. Winding lanes disappeared in every direction. Bending an antenna, Shan checked on Knek, the apparently speechless thug Myosh dragged everywhere as her personal executioner. The dull appeared to have forgotten about Shan and stood squinting at something filthy wedged in his right craft claw. Myosh stared at the sky, shading her main eyes with a raptorial claw.

Run. The Redeemers won't leave their post. Lose the priest and her big idiot in the alleys.

A few sparks to distract and maybe blind them for a moment and—

"If he makes a run for it," said Myosh still searching the sky, "would one of you be so kind as to put a spear in him?"

THE STORM BENEATH THE WORLD

The scarred green Redeemer studied Shan. "Too pretty to kill."

"Pretty or not," said the blue-black, "if he's with this Defiled, he's a Corrupt. I'll kill him with pleasure."

"Really?" asked the green, waving a raptorial arm at Shan. "Not even a hint of regret for wrecking something so perfectly crafted?"

"I wasn't going to run!"

Myosh cut Shan's protest off with a wave of her claw. "Don't bother. You're not smart enough to be a good liar and I'd know even if you were." One of her antennae straightened, intent. "Here they come."

A soft buzz grew to a bone-shaking roar as two tramea plummeted from the sky. Shan cowered, ducking behind Knek to hide from the predators. Happily, even the big dull retreated in fear. Myosh and the Redeemers didn't so much as flinch.

Ridden by two of the Queen's Wing, the flying corps of the military, the descending tramea kicked up clouds of dust and debris, the two sets of wings screaming different notes.

Peering from behind Knek, Shan marvelled at the monstrous carnivores. He'd seen thousands from a distance but never one this close. There were always messengers darting about the city sky delivering mail or reports for family business. Squads of the Queen's Wing flew regular patrols, and he often bet at the weekly races where daring female brights rode semi-feral tramea in gruelling slalom courses or jousting tourneys. This was the first time he stood close enough to appreciate the size and horrendous stench of the vile creatures. At a safe remove they were beautiful, the light of Alatash shimmering on carapaces, flitting through hoops, darting through the air like hurled spears. Up close, he was keenly aware they were apex predators. In the leeward desert these things hunted and killed ashkaro, dragged them into the sky and hauled them back to the nest to be drained by their young. He'd seen grim paintings of tramea hives, the husked and sun-bleached shells of ashkaro littering the ground.

Their long, segmented tails swayed with mesmerizing grace, curved barbs glistening. Knowing one of those stingers could punch clean through him left the fact they also happened to be deadly venomous kind of moot. He couldn't look away.

"They—" His voice cracked. "They stink like death."

"Feral tramea drape themselves in rotting intestines to hide their scent from prey," said Myosh. "They smell much worse than this. The trained ones…" her wings shivered in a shrug. "The second you turn your back they're rubbing faeces and anything dead or rotting they can find into their joints. Can't stop them."

"You get used to it," said a yellow bright as she dismounted.

She had a long spear clutched in one raptorial claw and wore a bow slung across her back with a quiver of war arrows. The insignia on her vest marked her as a squad leader, the two hooked tramea stingers hanging sheathed on her lower thorax proclaiming her a combat veteran. Shan's mother had one too, though she no longer wore it. She said Queen's Wing were only allowed to claim such trophies if they killed their opponent in single combat and collected the stinger themselves. Until this moment, he'd never appreciated what that meant.

"Liar," said the other pilot, slipping from the saddle, an intricate contraption of fibrous straps, wood, and what looked like bone harvested from those disgusting squishy vertebrate things that burrowed in the swampier forests. "It's more like you lose the ability to smell anything at all."

Both pilots noticed Shan, nodding appreciatively as their main eyes lingered on the brilliant red and gold of his carapace. For all his bulk Knek managed a pretty good job of becoming invisible in the way ugly dulls do.

"Don't suppose you need an escort?" said the yellow bright, one antenna bending teasingly toward Shan.

"No," said Myosh. "We're bound for Kaylamnel."

The pilot grunted disappointment, passing the Defiled the reins. "Make sure *Violence is Always the Answer* comes back unharmed, or I'll hang your head in my trophy room, and I don't care what your filthy talent is."

"If she doesn't return unharmed," said Myosh, "it's because I'm already dead. In which case you're welcome to whatever body parts best suit the room."

The other pilot offered her reins to Shan. "This is *Kill Them All and Let Katlipok Sort Them Out*."

"That's a mouthful," said Shan, accepting the reins. Reminding himself he was the queen's nephew, he straightened. "And bordering on blasphemy." He wouldn't allow these saddle jockeys to intimidate him.

"She'll answer to *Kill Them All*," said the pilot, unconcerned. "Though if you shorten it past that, she'll start butchering things. And she smells fear, so gird your ovaries or you're in for a rough flight."

Shan ignored the jab, squaring his shoulders and reaching for the haughtiest expression of wings and antennae. "I'll be quite fine, thank you."

The pilot snorted a laugh. "Need help getting into the saddle?"

He studied the chaotic contraption. "Are there straps to keep me seated?"

"Fear of falling to your death should do that."

"And *Kill Them All* smells fear," muttered Shan. "Fantastic."

Myosh swung effortlessly into her saddle, instantly at home. She sat, wings twitching in impatient annoyance, as the pilot helped Shan onto his own tramea, an effort apparently requiring all too much overly friendly and lingering contact. Once he was finally situated to the pilot's liking, the two stepped back, waving Knek, who still stood hunched like he hoped he might disappear into his own exoskeleton, out of the way.

"Take him inside and have him report to whoever seems appropriate," said Myosh, waving a claw at the dull. "He isn't Corrupt, just slow and stupid."

Knek said nothing, but an antenna twitched in hurt.

"We'll put him to work mucking the tramea aviary," said the yellow pilot. "You wouldn't believe how much frass these things create each day."

Myosh turned her attention on Shan. "We have a three-hour flight ahead of us. If you're going to fall off, try and do it right at the beginning so as not to waste too much of my time."

Composing his wings, neatening his vest, and doing his best to look haughty, Shan said, "I shall endeavour to plummet to my death as soon as we've gained sufficient altitude."

"Is that humour or attitude?" the blue-black Redeemer asked the pilots. "I like a funny male, but who has time for snark?"

If there was more, Shan didn't hear it. Myosh snapped the reins, and her tramea's wings became a buzzing blur and then a windstorm roar. His mount did the same, and he felt the vibration rumbling through his innards.

Three hours of this, and my guts will be grub-mash.

He screamed in horror when *Kill Them All and Let Katlipok Sort Them Out* heaved itself into the air, wings kicking up a blinding cloud of sharp dust. The only saving grace, he decided, all eight limbs clinging to the horrendous killing beast he rode, was that if he couldn't hear his screams, probably no one else could either.

Somewhere near the end of the first hour Shan's fear faded enough he could almost appreciate the beauty of being so high in the air a fall would shatter his carapace to mud. Myosh's mount led the way, *Kill Them All*, following without apparent need for commands. Though marginally quieter now that they were aloft, the staccato beat of wings remained deafening. He briefly considered trying to turn the creature and fleeing—certainly the Defiled priest wouldn't hear him leave—but he had no idea how to fly a tramea and even less idea how to get one to land. Even if he somehow managed, the damned thing would probably kill and eat him while he tried to disentangle himself from the saddle.

Another hour passed, the cold creeping into Shan's carapace and making him sleepy. He regretted not asking for a blanket. Much as they would have mocked him, he wasn't sure he'd survive another hour of this.

Don't want to disappoint Myosh by dying right at the end of the journey.

Looking forward, he saw the priest wrapped in a thick blanket.

Where had she got that from? He was sure she hadn't been carrying it. Too uncomfortable to be afraid of upsetting his mount, Shan searched the saddle, squealing once when he leaned too far. He discovered saddlebags hanging on either side. Digging through the first, he found a loaf of some ground and compacted meat baked to a brick-like consistency. Breaking off a corner and jamming it into his mouth, he learned it tasted worse than what he imagined an actual clay brick would taste like. In the other saddlebag he found a blanket and collection of incomprehensible tools—most likely for tramea care and cleaning—several viciously sharp bone knives, a powerful staff sling, and a pouch of hard pebbles.

THE STORM BENEATH THE WORLD

The thought of using the sling to kill the priest died faster than his earlier idea of fleeing. Even if he managed to hit her, which seemed unlikely as he had only the vaguest idea how to use such a weapon, by now his mother would have struck his name from the ledger. If he went home, Mother would give him back to the Redemption.

Where can I go?

He had no wealth of his own beyond the few scrips in his purse, enough for a nice dinner but not much more.

Shan stared, unseeing, into the distance. He'd lost more than money. His entire future had been stolen. He no longer had family.

So alone.

Ahead, the clouds darkened, promising rain.

The priest's tramea banked and lost altitude and his own followed. Thoughts of dinner were replaced by a desire to remain seated.

They fell toward unbroken jungle, trees blanketing the land as far as Shan's main eyes could see. Perceptive to movement, his secondary eyes kept a wary watch on the sky. When *Kill Them All* finally evened out, streaking no more than a body-length above the foliage, he realized he'd lost the blanket. The snarled morass of plant life below finally broke. At the centre of the clearing sat an ancient structure of moss-covered bricks. It looked more like an abandoned temple from the days of the hive wars than a place of higher education.

Myosh is part of some hive sect. They're going to sacrifice me to Katlipok.

There were other buildings too, but Shan was too busy imagining himself cornered by feral females seeking to indoctrinate him into their hive. Hadn't he seen that in a play?

The area had been cleared of trees and grass, cracked clay bricks pressed into the dirt to create a massive public octagon big enough for scores of ashkaro to gather. Another octagon had more recently been painted into the centre of the clearing, delineating the official landing area. Myosh aimed her tramea for it, sweeping down to land with consummate ease. By the time Shan's tramea touched ground, a process he missed as he hid behind his raptorial claws, the priest had already dismounted. His own attempt at a graceful dismount ended with him sprawled on the timeworn bricks, his numb legs no longer willing to support his weight.

THE STORM BENEATH THE WORLD

"Get up," Myosh ordered. "I must introduce you to Headmistress Chynn Wyl Gyr Daw. And if you ever use anything less than her full name, she'll have your carapace split wide and your guts scooped out with a wooden spoon."

Picking himself up and dusting off his thorax, Shan said, "I'm already quite scared enough without you trying to add to it with your fanciful—"

"It was meant as a warning," said Myosh. "If you don't believe me, call her Chynn." She sniffed, glancing toward the ancient structures. "Make life easier for everyone."

AHK TAY KYM

> *We ride the eternal river of days toward the moment of our redemption. Bordered to the north and south by the howling stormwalls, those limits set by the gods of Alatash themselves, the river of days has no beginning and no end. It is all reality, and it is all time. Claims of strange monsters and contrivances coming through the stormwalls are purest blasphemy.*
>
> —The Redemption

The fear holding Ahk in place fell away like breaking the surface in a murky pool. Though still terrified, she once again thought clearly. Still standing with the door cracked so she could see the deck, a pirate dashed past her without so much as a glance in Ahk's direction. The malformed dull and subservient bright stood in hunched conversation too quiet for her to hear. Beyond them, her mother lay still and dead, the last tremor having faded to nothing. The pirate skerry floated above and off to one side, tentacles still gripping the flagpole and structures on *A Slow and Gentle Descent into Dark.*

Four more pirates, lumbering dull males, descended to the deck carrying long harpoons with wedge-shaped heads. Marching to the dull, they stood ready, awaiting orders.

A Slow and Gentle Descent had been allowed to drift and a gulf of emptiness lay between the skerry and Nysh Island. Ahk's stomach twisted as she realized that for the first time in her life nothing separated her from the storm beneath the world.

"Either we find her," the twisted dull barked at the pirates, "or we're killing this skerry and reporting our failure to Queen Yil."

THE STORM BENEATH THE WORLD

The pirates spread out, searching.

"You saw her before we left Yil," said the foul dull. "You promised she was important, swore it was critical that we either had her in our possession, or made sure she was dead."

"I never said I saw her death," whined the bright, voice defensive. "She will be broken to nothing, horribly disfigured. I've seen that much."

The dull ignored the protest. "Broken to nothing isn't the same as dead. How have you lost her now that we are so close?"

The bright fluttered her wings in helpless apology.

The deformed dull turned in an awkward limping circle, studying the corpse-littered deck. "We haven't already killed her?"

"I don't think so."

Completing her circle, the dull again faced the submissive bright. "If your talent wasn't so useful, I'd feed you to the storm."

The bright cowered, wings folded tight, antennae bent back and lying flat.

"Forget the child for now," the dull instructed. "Give me a reason not to throw *you* overboard. How long do we have?"

The bright ducked her head and became still. Shivers of pleasure fluttered her wings and antennae. "We were seen. A squad of tramea have been dispatched. We don't have much time."

"Can we escape?"

The bright let out a soft moan of bliss. "If we climb high, we live to see Alatash set. Beyond that…" She shrugged her wings.

"By all the Dead Gods of Alatash!" the dull cursed. Gesturing at the four lumbering dulls with harpoons, she said, "Damage this skerry's membranes in as many places as you can. You!" She pointed out a loitering bright. "Burn everything. If the girl is still on board, Katlipok can have her soul. Everyone else, back to *An End to a Means*."

As the pirates scrambled up the ropes, the four with the harpoons searched for chinks in *A Slow and Gentle Descent's* carapace. Finding gaps where plates overlapped, they shoved the wedge-shaped head in, levering it back and forth. Working in pairs, they drove the harpoon deep until the wound sprayed a geyser of air and blue blood. When they'd stabbed the beast in a dozen places, the dull ordered them back to the pirate skerry.

THE STORM BENEATH THE WORLD

The bright told to set fires moved from gondola to gondola with a torch. Each time she left a structure, smoke billowed from every window. Realizing the bright was heading toward her, Ahk retreated from the door, searching for somewhere to hide. The hall was empty. Back in her room, she might duck into the armoire, but the pirate would throw it open to light the clothes within.

Fear and indecision froze her. She should run. Mother would stand and fight.

The hall darkened as if Alatash had suddenly dimmed.

Elation roared through Ahk, smothering thought as the door swung open, and the pirate entered.

Slowing to a stop, the torch wielding bright hesitated, antennae quizzical. Her attention slid past Ahk without hesitation. With a confused flutter of wings, the pirate stalked past her, bearing the crackling torch into the crew quarters.

One thought forced its way through the rapturous haze: *She didn't see me.*

That was impossible. Though dim, the hall was hardly so dark someone could miss an ashkaro youth pressed against one wall.

A moment later smoke filled the hall and again the bright passed Ahk, returning to the deck. This being the last gondola, she'd abandoned her torch.

Creeping to the door in confusion, Ahk watched the bright nimbly scamper up the last rope leaving only the crippled dull behind on *A Slow and Gentle Descent*. Antennae twitching with ill-concealed rage, the malformed dull again searched the deck, studying the corpses and smoking gondolas. Her gaze slid past Ahk's hiding spot without slowing.

With a bark of anger, the dull gripped the rope with both raptorial claws and yelled at the pirates above to haul her up. The burning skerry apparently forgotten, she looked toward the island, searching the sky.

Ahk looked too, praying for some sign of rescue. With a sudden spasm, she realized the island had risen. She now saw the colossal tentacles hanging beneath it. Her teachers said they hung all the way down to the storm and that the islands used them to draw sustenance and possibly for steering, though she couldn't imagine that.

One of the wounds left by the harpoon-wielding dulls sputtered, spraying a blue mist.

Nysh Island isn't rising, A Slow and Gentle Descent *is falling.*

Even knowing it was true, she couldn't feel it. The skerry was too big, too permanent. The loose excess of rope coiled on the deck uncurled and rose into the air.

"I'm falling." Saying it aloud made it more real. "I'm going to sink into the storm with this dying skerry."

Katlipok, the banished Queen of the Storm, awaited her.

Ahk didn't move.

Run and grab the rope.

The pirates would capture her, but at least her soul wouldn't go to Kratosh.

They didn't see me.

It was, she knew, impossible. Or rather there could be but one reason the pirate had missed her.

That wave of pleasure as she hid. How many times had Pol Mek Nan preached about the addictive nature of discovering one's talent? The lure. The Corruption. With little to compare it to, she'd imagined it felt something like Mother telling her she'd done well at her studies. That wasn't it at all. Hiding felt so good she was tempted to remain here, invisible, until she burned in Kratosh.

I'm Corrupt.

Cold rage replaced icy terror.

She was Ahk Tay Kym, heir to the family. She was the daughter of warriors. For a thousand generations, back to the days of hive, her family served queen after queen.

All that was gone now, as dead as Mother. The Corrupt inherited nothing.

But that didn't change who she was.

I am a predator, a hunter. A warrior.

She was a daughter, and she would have her vengeance.

Rage seethed through Ahk.

Those pirates served the Mad Queen Yil. Spies. Assassins. Whatever their reason for being here, they invaded the queendom.

I serve my mother. I serve my queen.

There was no higher calling, even for a Corrupt. The Redemption said all ashkaro—even those who fell to the lure—could be redeemed. This was it, her one chance.

She would be the spear of bloody retribution.

Ahk left the gondola, dashing onto the deck.

You can't see me.

Pulsing tremors of euphoria left her lightheaded. Leaping to grab the rope, she hung swinging below the crippled dull, waves of blinding joy filling her carapace until she thought she'd bust. The crippled abomination looked down, antennae showing her surprise. Searching the oddly swinging rope beneath her, she looked up to shout at the pirates on the skerry above to stop messing around. They pulled faster, tying off the rope once she was aboard.

Ahk swayed in the wind, an arm's length beneath the deck. Far below, the storm roiled with seething anger. Tongues of flame licked at the sky, stuttering lightning leaping like bridges of arcing light.

The Redemption said the servants of Yil were assassins, foul murderers worshipping torture and suffering. They said the entire queendom had gone insane and that Yil's priests threw innocent ashkaro off the edge, feeding them to the storm in ritual sacrifice.

They want punishment, I'll give it to them.

About to haul herself onto the deck and kill whoever was closest, Ahk hesitated. The cripple said the bright's talent was seeing glimpses of the future, and the bright said the crew would live to see Alatash set that evening. Did that mean Ahk would die without killing a single enemy? How could she fail so completely?

She also said she didn't know what happens after.

The bright knew they lived at least until Alatash set. Ahk decided to wait until dark and then creep from room to room, murdering her enemies as they slept.

Gripping the rope with both raptorial claws, she locked them closed. Even if she fell asleep, they wouldn't release their grip.

Losing altitude, *A Slow and Gentle Descent into Dark* fell away behind them as the pirate skerry fled toward the island. Instead of heading straight back, they cut a long curving arc toward the northern edge. No doubt they hoped to avoid the Queen's Wing sent to intercept them.

Ahk's rage simmered as she hung over the boiling storm clouds of

THE STORM BENEATH THE WORLD

Kratosh. Eyes unfocussed, she imagined what she had to do, picturing the scene over and over. She found herself oddly comfortable with the thought of killing. She should have felt guilt or doubt, but these were invaders, servants of the Mad Queen. She would never have sought to do them harm, but they came here. They murdered her mother and the crew and killed the glorious *A Slow and Gentle Descent* who'd loyally served for hundreds of years.

Perhaps we aren't evolved as far past the days of hive as the priests like to claim.

Alatash sank below the horizon and for the first time Ahk saw the storm beneath the world at night. As hellish as it looked during the day, only now could she appreciate the horror below. It was easy to believe a god lurked there, devouring the souls of the irredeemable. Kratosh stretched beyond the reach of her eyes in every direction.

Forever hell.

However long the river of days was, Katlipok was there at the beginning, and she'd be there at the end.

Though Nysh Island was inconceivably massive, the lights of distant cities like tiny sparks, it was a gnat floating above the endless nightmarish inferno. Everything Ahk ever knew, every generation of her ancestors stretching back to the beginning of time, had lived on that island. If it fell, the queendom would burn like a dry leaf tossed into a roaring bonfire.

This morning she was the heir to the Kym family holdings. She was important, destined to take her place at her mother's side and someday rule the family.

Now, hanging over the fallen god's hell, she was insignificant.

Tired, Ahk slept.

She woke when the deck of the pirate skerry fell quiet. Ahk waited longer, until no one moved. They'd post a guard to watch the sky but would never expect someone to already be aboard. Pulling herself up, she summoned that nothing feeling, pleasure singing through her limbs. Beneath it lay an exhaustion reaching deep into the meat of her.

I am nothing. No one sees me.

Finding a spear leaning against the rail, Ahk first killed those patrolling the deck. It was easy. They saw nothing. She crept behind each one, took careful aim with the spear, and spiked their brain as they'd done to Mother. When all was silent and still, blue blood shimmering black in the dark, she entered the crew gondola and went from room to room, murdering the invaders in their sleep.

She left the abomination to last. Though this foul creature hadn't personally killed Mother, somehow, impossibly, she was in charge. No doubt due to her talent for instilling fear, such an overturning of the natural order was obscene. No self-respecting bright would ever bow before a dull, and certainly not such a broken and helpless one.

Ahk stood over the sleeping dull. It would be so easy. That cowering bright who saw the future could have killed her any time she wanted, and yet had obeyed the hideous monster. Everything about the Mad Queen's servants was wrong. Like their blasphemous religion, they were anathema to the natural order.

As a child, Ahk had pestered Mother about her time in the military, asking how murder could be a sin and yet killing during war was a noble path to fame and glory.

It all made sense now.

Killing is wrong except when it isn't.

Lifting the bloody spear clutched in two raptorial claws for added strength, Ahk stilled.

I want her to know it's me.

Adjusting her aim, she slammed it through the dull's upper thorax and the loose webbing of the hammock, pinning her to the floor beneath.

The malformed dull grunted in surprise, eyes suddenly focussing.

"Go on," said Ahk. "Tell me I'm afraid of you."

Spasms ran through the impaled ashkaro. "She said you'd be broken to nothing, horribly disfigured."

"She was wrong."

The dull coughed a bloody laugh. "Shorn and alone, she told me. Shorn and alone." Gore leaked out the back of her carapace, painted the impaling spear blue. "She's never wrong."

"You deserve this. All of you."

The dull's throat clicked as she tried to swallow. "Do we?" She sounded weak and fading fast. "Queen Yil is Corrupt and yet does not suffer the lure. Chosen of Katlipok, she is our salvation."

Everyone called Yil the Mad Queen. It made sense now.

"You are as insane as your queen."

Ahk left the doomed dull to bleed out, the pitiful creature's whispered prayers—shorn and alone, shorn and alone—falling away behind her. Though the word had several meanings, in ancient times hive ashkaro would clip their enemy's antennae, deafen, and blind them. The pitiful victim was left trapped and alone, an unfeeling soul locked in a carapace.

Ahk returned to the deck, stared dazed at the floating creature that had been home her entire life. Beyond the Nysh Queendom Alatash lit the leeward sky, silhouetting the island. Even at this range it was impossible to see it all. Years of schooling and she couldn't make any of it real. It was impossible to believe everything she'd known, from the many families to the schools and shops, her mother's estates, and the queen herself, rode perched on the back of a massive skerry.

Moving to the railing, she gazed at the sprawling forests. Leaning out, she looked down, following the curve of the island until distance smeared it to nothing. Mother said she flew a skerry below the island once on a military exploration mission. Though they stayed well clear of the colossal tentacles hanging from the island's belly, she said they reached down into the storm. Then, Mother had said the most blasphemous thing Ahk ever heard: She said she didn't know if there were gods above the clouds in some shining city, but seeing those monstrous tentacles, looking up and seeing the entire world, she could easily believe the island itself was a god. 'Maybe they're all gods,' Mother had whispered to herself, as if she'd forgotten Ahk's presence. 'Maybe the gods didn't abandon us. Maybe we abandoned them.'

Only now did Ahk begin to understand.

With a start she realized the island had grown larger. The skerry, probably unhappy at being out over the storm, was taking her home.

Then what?

She was Corrupt. Even if Mother was still alive, Ahk would be banished, stripped of family and future.

They'll send me to the desert.

Ahk studied the blood-slicked deck, corpses sprawled where they fell. She was dangerous, and that meant banishment to a Corrupt island.

She looked down at the hellish firestorm of Kratosh. That would be a better death than falling to the lure and dying amid the filth and poverty of the Corrupt. She saw no sign of *A Slow and Gentle Descent into Dark*. Had it already fallen into the storm, taking mother and the crew with it, or was it too far away to see, an infinitesimal dot against the forever expanse of hellfire?

If it hadn't already, Mother's corpse would eventually reach the storm.

Katlipok will claim her soul.

Or at least she'd try. Fearless, Mother would fight anyone.

Can she still be reborn?

Had that foul dull robbed her mother of any chance for redemption?

Maybe I'll let the skerry drift forever.

If the ashkaro who crewed it came from Yil, the beast wasn't native to this island. Bereft of direction, it might decide to return home.

Already tired, a wave of exhaustion crumpled Ahk to the deck.

I don't care. I'll go where it goes.

Too tired to think, hollowed by the trauma witnessed, gutted by the terrible things she'd done, Ahk tucked all four legs beneath her.

Maybe everyone was wrong.

Maybe we're already in hell.

JOH

One moment the sky was clear, the clouds above calm. Without warning a heavy fog fell and no one could see more than the length of a raptorial arm. A peculiar fog, it devoured sound, plummeting the entire aviary into silence. Then, the wind whipped up fast, tearing skerry from their moorings and scattering the uncaged tramea. An hour later, when the storm died and the fog lifted, the caged Corrupt were gone. The skerry they'd been imprisoned in was one of the few still at its mooring. The Queen's Claw posted as guards however were dead. Eight veteran warriors murdered, apparently without landing a single blow of their own. Most perplexing was the lack of wounds on the dead. It was as if they all just lay down and died.

—Second Officer Wuy Jwu Shein Xik, Queen's Claw

Rel guided the wagon through the gaping hole in the outer defences and into the crumbling fortress.

Pointing out a long two-story brick structure that looked both newer than the rest of the fortress and still antediluvian, he said, "Student barracks; that's where you'll sleep." One antenna gesturing at what looked like an abandoned temple, he added, "Over there is the main school where lectures will be held. Reading and writing if you can't already. History and politics. The old castle," he nodded toward the fortified remains, "is where the teachers stay. You aren't allowed in there. Ever." A raptorial claw waved at a large clearing littered with wooden combat dummies and an obstacle course. "Physical and combat training."

"You'll teach me how to fight?" Joh asked.

"Don't be ridiculous."

A lumbering giant of a male with a patchwork carapace of light and dark brown hammered at one of the dummies with what looked like most of a tree, splintering it to pieces.

Rel shook his head in annoyance, muttering, "Bin has the self-control of a mating tramea. I told him to hold back."

Joh asked, "Where do people practice their talents?"

"Depends on the talent," Rel answered. "Students considered dangerous are taken out beyond the wall, where they're unlikely to hurt anyone. Those with talents like Wex's practice in the field here. Your own talent, while dangerous, isn't a physical threat. Most of your time will be spent in class. First, we'll work on getting you caught up on your basic education. We'll also work on your self-control. Though we all fall to the lure, that can be somewhat postponed."

"Just long enough for us to be useful," said Joh.

Guiding the wagon toward the barracks, Rel watched Joh with one main eye. "Is that such a terrible thing?"

Sitting at his side, Wex studied Joh as if intently curious about his answer. It was more than a little unnerving.

"Not the worst thing," Joh answered. *I guess.*

"You aren't prisoners," added Rel.

"We're totally free," said Wex. "I can choose to be handed to the authorities and brain-spiked, and Joh here can opt for banishment to a Corrupt island anytime he wants. Fantastic choices."

"Bad options," said Rel, "are better than no options at all."

Wex looked unconvinced.

With a tug on the reins, the priest turned the skirrak toward a palatial home located at the centre of the compound. "Raht Shram Yrn Nyst is the headmistress."

"Bright nobility in the middle of the desert?" Joh asked. "What's her talent?"

"Aside from terrifying students and staff, I don't think she has one. Queen Nysh herself assigned Mistress Raht to this posting. I am neither brave nor stupid enough to ask why."

Rel guided the wagon to a halt in front of the house. "Climb out and dust yourselves off while I see if the headmistress wants to lay eyes on the new arrivals."

Wex and Joh bounced out of the wagon with a flutter of wings to soften their landing. Rel clambered down more slowly, wincing, and groaning and stretching all four wings to shake them. Once everything was settled back into place, he looked over his two charges, tutting, and brushing off bits of the road. When he decided they were as presentable as they'd ever be, he climbed the steps to the front door. Knocking once, he retreated to stand at Joh's side.

"If you make even the slightest suggestion to Mistress Raht, I'll kill you where you stand."

A mix of male and female dulls gathered inside the doorway of the student barracks to watch from the shadows.

"Are all the teachers here Corrupt?" Joh asked.

"Quiet," snapped Rel.

The door swung open, and an elderly ashkaro stepped into the light of Alatash. Joh had seen brights before, but for the most part, that just meant they had more colour in their carapace. Mistress Raht was what he imagined gods looked like. Shimmering and shining, her exoskeleton polished to a mirror-like gleam, she reflected the clouds overhead. Yet this was no pampered noble. Her limbs showed thickenings where they'd been broken during fights, her thorax pocked with circular wounds suggesting she'd been stabbed a great many times.

"Rel," she said, voice like the crunch of stomped insect shells. "You were supposed to be back weeks ago."

The priest bowed. "I found the four Corrupt I'd sensed. One, a dull female working the clay mines, was more dangerous than I knew. Being able to sense them doesn't mean I know their talents."

"No excuses."

"My apologies." He bowed lower, antennae brushing dirt. "I left them in the wagon when I went looking for water. Most of the local wells were dry. When I returned, she'd…" He blew out a shaking breath. "They were *ruined*."

Ruined? Not dead? Joh listened in surprise. The priest had made no mention of collecting other children.

"What was her talent?" Mistress Nyst asked.

"If I had to guess, surgery, or something of a medical nature. She managed to render them helpless, and then got to work. They were broken, carapaces splayed." He shuddered. "But they were all still alive. She'd clearly lost herself to the lure. I killed her and put the others out of their misery."

"A shame," said Headmistress Raht. Cold eyes studied Joh and Wex. "And these two?"

Rel nodded an antenna at Wex, who stood at attention, all four claws clasped before her thorax in polite humility. "This is Wex Jel. She has a talent for killing. Not sure of the details yet, but she murdered a combat-trained bright with a sharpened twig."

"Could be useful," Mistress Raht allowed.

"And the small one is Joh. His talent appears to be suggestion. His limits haven't been tested. For the most part, he seems disinterested in abusing his curse."

The old bright examined Joh. "We'll change that." She returned her attention to the priest. "If he makes any attempt at *suggesting* things to the teachers, spike his brain immediately."

Joh blurted, "What about my fellow students?"

Rel hissed in appalled shock at the impropriety.

"He'll need someone to practice on," Mistress Raht answered, stepping back inside, and closing the door.

Rel sagged with relief once she was out of sight. "Come."

He set off toward the barracks and the youths huddled in the doorway ducked from sight.

Wex and Joh hurried after him.

Leaning close, Wex whispered, "Are you insane?"

"When you are small and dull and male," said Joh, "everyone's expectations are extremely low. I find it's best to exceed those expectations. In the wrong direction."

Wex's antennae flicked in consternation. "My mother said to always make a good first impression. Those who stand out get the best postings."

"I don't want a posting. I don't want to be noticed." Joh dashed a look back toward the house. "Particularly not by that terrifying old bright."

Wex grunted something between a laugh and agreement.

THE STORM BENEATH THE WORLD

Reaching the barracks, Rel led Joh and Wex inside. Lined with weapon racks hanging on every wall, the main hall stank of moulting and discarded carapaces. Long tables sat at the far end. Dust hung in the air, sand covering the floor. At the back, a set of shallow steps led to the second floor.

"Your rooms are upstairs," Rel said.

"Private or shared?" Wex asked.

"Private."

Joh, who'd never owned anything, never had his own space, said nothing.

The promise of regular meals. A well with clean water. His own room. He felt Wex move at his side. *Someone to talk to who might not hit me.* These were luxuries beyond imagination.

Outside, the wind moaned through the open doorway. The ceiling showed many patch jobs of varying degrees of success. In some spots it looked like someone had slathered mud over the damaged bricks.

Four dull students loitered at one of the tables, pretending to study texts or clean weapons.

Noticing how they gathered in a clump at the same table, Joh thought, *We may no longer be a hive, but we crave proximity.*

It was, he decided, an interesting conundrum. His natural inclination was to remain apart. Stay small. Stay hidden. Avoid attention at all costs. But if he did that, they'd label him as strange, an outsider. Few words were more loaded with danger. Even those from other towns were treated better than any ashkaro who lived there and yet set themselves apart.

We belong or we don't.

Rel pointed out one of the females, a grey dull with darker ashen streaks. "Des, this is Wex and Joh. Get them situated, make introductions." He nodded an antenna at Wex. "And no fighting this one until I've had a chance to test her. I don't want to have to bury more corpses this week than I already have."

He left without another look, his words drawing all attention to Wex.

Joh stepped behind her, making himself smaller.

Des approached, studying the new arrivals. "So, Wex. I see some colour there. A two-name?"

The others followed, the power dynamic immediately clear.

"I'm Wex J—"

"One name or five, it doesn't matter now. Rel thinks you're dangerous, eh? What's your talent?"

"I don't want to talk about it."

"We'll find out soon enough. We'll be trained as a team."

"A team?" asked Joh, peeking out from behind Wex.

"Not everyone makes the team," said Des. "Most fall to the lure and are shipped out."

A female with a mottled carapace of matte green streaked in brown said, "They say the dropouts are sent to a Corrupt island, but why would they bother? We're two days from the edge. Much easier to throw them to the storm."

"Zyr," said Des, "don't interrupt."

"Sorry, Des. Just—" She shut up when Des turned a single main eye on her.

"Others die during training," Des continued, casting an appraising eye over the diminutive Joh. "The small and weak. The dumb and unlucky."

"We mostly get the dumb," said Zyr.

"Once Rel is sure he understands your talent," continued Des, "he'll tell us anyway. No secrets here, sister."

Wex's antennae folded back in shame. "I killed someone."

Antennae everywhere perked at that.

"Killed?" Zyr asked. "With your mind?"

"With a stick."

Des snorted amusement. "Not so dangerous then. Can't kill what you can't hit."

Wex shrugged her upper wings. "I never wanted to hurt anyone."

"And the runt cowering behind you is Joh?" Des asked, circling to get a better look.

"He's not a runt," said Wex, moving to stay between Joh and Des. "He's just small."

Zyr bent a quizzical antenna toward Joh. "Isn't that what runt means?"

"Is he dangerous?" Des asked "He doesn't look dangerous. No way he survives. Probably die the first time we spar."

"Touch him," growled Wex, "and I will show you my talent."

Joh concentrated on keeping his antenna relaxed and free of expression as guilt flashed through him. He'd done a terrible thing and, though it might have felt good in the moment, he knew it was wrong. Scared that she'd abandon him at the school, leaving him alone again, he'd whispered suggestions to a sleeping Wex that she should be his friend.

I'll find some way to make it up to her.

She was his first and only friend.

Whatever it took, he would be worthy of her friendship.

WEX JEL

Reports of wealthy families maintaining pens of Corrupt—these so-called Hidden—so they may profit from their talents are purest fantasy. No bright would stoop so low.
—Councilmember Adag Loir Yehin Lo, on the night of her arrest

Wex waited, all six eyes searching Des for weaknesses. She saw moments of distraction as the other ashkaro tried to decide what to do about the threat.

She doesn't think I will attack her.

She realized she'd misread the interaction. Des wasn't Cayr Rie Chi Lo. She wasn't looking for a chance to embarrass the stupid dull. This was the bluffing and posing of two females figuring out their place in the hive. One would back down, the other would be seen by those gathered as the dominant female. After that, there'd be no tension, everyone comfortable with their place. This rarely happened back in Brickworks #7. The brights who ran the factory were of such a higher rank no one would think to challenge them. Even their children strutted the streets like visiting queens. There'd been more friction among the dulls who lived there. As a two-name and the daughter of a shift manager, Wex had rarely been challenged.

Even with Des focussed on the social aspects of the moment, Wex saw no glaring weakness and felt none of the mad rush of pleasure she experienced killing Cayr.

I don't have stab sticks.

Was that it? Did she need a weapon before she could use her

talent?

Des bristled, wings fluttering like she might attack. It was all a show.

"We're supposed to be a team, right?" said Joh from behind Wex.

Des' wings relaxed a little, lost some of their combative expression. "I'm team leader."

"Yes, of course," agreed Joh. "But a team leader's job is to make sure everyone works together."

Antennae twitching with uncertainty, trying to decide if this was an insult or trap, Des nodded agreement. "I make sure we're a good team."

"No doubt," said Joh, stepping tentatively out from behind Wex. "The whole point of working together is to achieve some goal, right? And that goal is the priority. In our case, we're being trained to serve Queen Nysh."

As there were no brights around to get angry about the shortening of the queen's name, everyone ignored it.

"Serving the queen is the only part that matters, right?" said Joh.

Ah, the question that's not a question. Wex's mom used to do that to her all the time. *He's setting her up.*

As disagreeing to such a statement was near unthinkable, Des had no choice but to agree. "Of course."

"And so, the leader of the group is whoever will keep the group united in such a way to best serve the queen."

The gathered ashkaro nodded.

"And that's me," insisted Des.

"Of course," said Joh. "Of course. And if that changes, as the current group leader and someone loyal to the queen, you would, of course, want to step aside for the new leader."

Des froze, finally seeing the trap. If she disagreed with Joh, she was admitting to being a bad leader and disloyal to the queen. "But I'm the best."

"Of course," Joh said again. "As great a leader as you are, Des, I think we can all agree that until everyone knows each other better, it's too early to make any final decisions."

Again, the ashkaro nodded, even Des, though she seemed less

happy about it.

Did he just turn us into an actual team and then suggest that someone might be better suited to leadership than Des?

And all in such a way that Des agreed and would be unable to argue when it eventually happened. She couldn't tell if he used his talent or simply been surprisingly clever for a male.

The question: Who did Joh think should lead the group?

She realized she knew. He was her friend and sought to support her in any way he could. He wanted Wex to lead the group. But why? She didn't think it was the typical male need to be with an important female. They were friends, but not *that* kind of friends.

Whatever the little male's faults and deficiencies, he would never abuse the trust of a friend. He might slip up a bit here and there, accidentally suggest things to smooth over awkward moments, but he meant well.

The big male they'd seen thrashing the combat dummies with a tree entered the barracks, ducking to fit through the doorway. Up close, he was easily the largest ashkaro Wex had ever seen. The patchwork brown carapace had the unfortunate effect of looking diseased, the lighter sections looking like an exoskeleton fungus common among the poor. His head, a blunt wedge, left no doubt as to his intellect.

Unaware of the room's tension, he waved at the group. "Who the new ones?" Waggling flirting antennae at Wex, he struck a pose to best show off his size and strength.

Wex ignored him.

"They're new students," said Des.

"Got that," said the big male, "from the fact I'd never seen them before and they're in the student barracks."

"This is Wex and Joh," said Des. "Wex and Joh, meet Bin. He lost a battle of wits with a combat dummy and yet still thinks he's clever." She held up a craft claw to stall response. "And no, Bin, we don't know their talents."

"While we're at it," said Joh, moving to put Wex between himself and Bin, "a round of introductions might not be a terrible idea. And maybe if we all say a word about our talent, we'll better understand each other and our place here."

THE STORM BENEATH THE WORLD

Des nodded in agreement. "I was about to suggest that. So, as you know, I'm Des, the team leader. My talent is speed." She puffed up a bit, wings fluttering. "No one is faster." She gestured at the male with the black carapace. "That's Kam. His talent is making medicine. That's Zyr with the matte green and brown. I've never seen her miss with a bow. Bin, the big clay-for-brains, has a talent for smelling bad."

"It's strength," corrected Bin.

"Or a strong smell." Des bent an antenna toward a male so nondescript Wex hadn't noticed him. "And that's Kris Kork. He's a mimic."

"Mimic?" asked Joh. "What can he mimic?"

"Mimic?" said Kris, sounding exactly like Joh. "What can he mimic?" Colours swirled through his mud carapace and a heartbeat later, the most gloriously beautiful bright Wex had ever seen stood among the lowly dulls.

"Don't *do* that," snapped Des. "You know what will happen if one of the teachers catches you using your talents outside training."

Kris's wings gave a small shrug, and he looked like himself again. "He asked."

"So that's the team," said Des, turning back on Wex. "Now introduce yourselves."

"I'm Wex Jel, my mom was—"

"No one cares," said Des. "Get to the important stuff. What's your talent?"

"I'm not entirely sure. I've only used it once."

"When you killed," said Zyr. "You felt it then, the pleasure?" She shuddered. "Imagine only being able to get that rush when you murder someone."

For the first time, Des looked uncertain. "Your talent is literally murder?"

"I don't know," admitted Wex. She wanted to flee the accusing stares, the terrible judgment. "I've only been in one fight, and I was using a stab stick I made."

"They're training us to fight and kill," said Zyr, moving closer, "but I've never been allowed to loose my bow at a living target."

"I've never hit anything but dummies," agreed Bin.

THE STORM BENEATH THE WORLD

"That's not true," said Kris, "you hit me once."

Bin laughed. "That's what I said."

In a heartbeat, the students surrounded Wex, main eyes focussed on her, antennae straight and attentive.

They aren't disgusted!

"Remind me not to spar with Wex," joked Kam.

"We need to get her some proper stab sticks from the armoury," said Zyr. "I want to see what she can do against Des's speed. No one can touch Des."

Antennae crooked, Des looked caught between pride and fear.

"I don't want to hurt anyone," Wex said. "I don't want to kill anyone. What I did…" She couldn't express how terrible it had been and how incredibly good it felt.

"No one accept the enemy," said Bin. "Murder isn't murder if you murder a Sister of the Storm."

"By Kratosh," swore Des, "you are dumb as watery mud."

Bin seemed unbothered by the words, reminding Wex that these students had been together a while. As was always the case, they'd formed a bond based on their shared experiences. They were dulls and outcasts, Corrupt banished from any chance at belonging.

They need this. She glanced at each one, only now seeing how they stood as a united group. *I need this.*

"This," said Wex, stepping aside, "is Joh."

They glanced at the diminutive ashkaro. A weak male was clearly less interesting than a female with a talent for killing. Murder might be wrong, but ashkaro were predators; their blood ran with ten thousand generations of killing.

"We've been in dire need of someone with skill in claw-to-claw combat," said Zyr.

"Hey!" Bin looked hurt.

Des poked the big male. "You're strong enough, but you're too slow to kill anything but trees and other males."

Bin grunted, apparently mollified.

"This is Joh," Wex repeated. "He has a talent."

Something in her voice caught their attention.

"And?" said Des.

"It's suggestion."

Zyr bent an antenna to scratch at her shoulder. "Suggestion? What use is that?"

"Try suggesting that I'm hungry," said Bin.

"I think you might be hungry," said Joh, voice small.

"I am! By Kratosh he's powerful!"

"Idiot," scolded Des. "You're always hungry."

"That's true," agreed Bin. "I was already hungry."

"You should probably go get a snack," said Joh, a shiver running through one antenna.

"Brilliant!" Bin slapped the smaller ashkaro on the back, sending him staggering. "I can see how this talent will be no end of use!"

Zyr looked from Bin to Joh. "How so?"

"Well now I have someone to blame everything on. Just got to say that Joh told me to do it and I can get away with anything. Anyway." He glanced at the door. "I'm going to the mess hall to scrounge up a snack."

Though no one commented when he wandered from the room, Wex felt a cold fear at the glow of pleasure she saw in Joh.

He sent Bin away and no one even noticed!

She tried to remember everything Joh had said since their meeting. Most of the first night was a blur of shock and horror.

He wouldn't do that to me, would he?

No. Joh was her friend.

THE STORM BENEATH THE WORLD

SHAN WYN VAL NUL NYSH

If we were meant to let the dulls live on the windward side of the island, then why do their carapaces so perfectly match the dry dust of the leeward desert? This is simple logic!

—Shih Nher Wui Fal, bright socialite

With a distant, gentle rumble of thunder, the gods blessed Shan with rain. Soft and warm, it pattered his carapace like kisses. Spreading his wings to rinse them of the clinging dust of Nysh City and the long flight, he basked in the cleaning downpour.

Maybe things aren't so bad.

By Kratosh it felt good to be clean again!

Glancing over his shoulder he saw ash sluicing from his carapace.

Ash? Where did that come from?

Nyk Arl Zon. He roasted her alive with his new-found talent, baked her to soot and cinders leaving a scorched and empty exoskeleton.

Horrified and entranced, he watched the last of the bright life he took rinse away. Murky water followed the grooves of his carapace, leaving him gleaming and spotless, rainbow slicked with golden fire. Truly, the gods blessed him with beauty. It was, he decided, a two-pronged gift, much like the forks he used to scoop molluscs from their shells at dinner. Nice as it was to so often be the centre of attention, none of those staring females saw past his stunning perfection. They never took him seriously.

Stepping away from the ashen mud, Shan took in the so-called school. While clearly of ancient origins, every building blanketed in thick moss, the structures were well-maintained. The central temple, an eight-sided pyramid, showed half a dozen different colours where bricks had been replaced over the centuries. Several buildings that looked like palatial homes fallen on hard times lined the perimeter. Most looked older than the family estate, which dated back three queens or more. A sprawling single-story building, walls lined with open windows, served as a schoolhouse. Young ashkaro brights wandered from a score of converted mansions with manicured grounds. Many clutched books and scrolls, hurrying toward the schoolhouse.

"Student housing?" Shan asked, gesturing with a craft claw.

Myosh grunted an affirmative, ignoring him as she folded her blanket, tucking it back inside the saddlebags. If she appreciated the cleansing rain, she showed no sign.

Shan decided not to mention losing his blanket. Hopefully, by the time anyone noticed, he'd be long gone.

"Looks crude," he grumbled. "How many housed in each building? Is it cramped? Private rooms, or shared dorms? Are the meals—"

Myosh silenced him with a look. "Follow."

She set off toward a mansion separated from the others. Trimmed hedges lined the walkway, the surrounding grass clipped neat and straight with manic care. Though falling well short of the family estates in and around Nysh City, the place would suffice for a reasonably appointed vacation property. At least, if it weren't plopped in the middle of a school for filthy Corrupt.

"Is that where I'm staying?"

"Don't be daft. That's Headmistress Chynn Wyl Gyr Daw's residence. Stay behind me and be quiet. If you speak without the headmistress' permission, I'll have your wings torn off."

"Rude."

His mandibles snapped shut, wings and antennae stilling when Myosh shot him a hard glare with a single main eye.

Approaching the massive home, Shan realized every window was shuttered with heavy wooden slats.

Myosh snapped, "Stay!" without checking to see if he obeyed and marched up to the doors.

So rude!

THE STORM BENEATH THE WORLD

Knocking once, she folded both sets of claws over her upper thorax and retreated several steps, head and shoulders bent in subservience.

The door swung open immediately, an elderly female standing hunched in the entranceway. Once, long ago, her carapace might have been bright and shiny. Bent and scarred with countless ill-healed war wounds, the four-name bright could pass for a dull. One raptorial arm and one craft arm ended at the first joint, blunt and useless appendages hypnotically drawing Shan's attention. The remaining two claws held canes of shellacked wood. She used them to shuffle awkwardly forward for a better look at her visitors.

By Kratosh, she looks older than the temple!

And how long had she stood there waiting for someone to knock?

"Myosh," she said, voice desiccated like the pinned wings of the sandflies displayed in his collection at home.

"Headmistress Chynn Wyl Gyr Daw," said Myosh, bowing low. "I have brought you something interesting, I think."

Wanting to argue he wasn't some*thing*, interesting or otherwise, Shan decided to keep his mouth closed when the headmistress slid a milky main eye in his direction.

"Talent?" the headmistress asked.

With the headmistress keeping one eye on him and the other on Myosh, Shan wasn't sure whom the question was directed at. Fearing the Defiled tearing his wings off, he remained silent.

"Fire," answered Myosh. "He blasted a rather important bright to nothing. She was gone, only a steaming carapace."

Both filmy eyes turned to Shan. "Interesting indeed. There have been…developments. The Sisters of the Storm have infiltrated some of the leeward cities. Enemy skerry have been spotted lurking in the clouds beyond the island, watching. There are reports of attacks on vacation resorts on the windward edge."

"The Mad Queen grows reckless," said Myosh.

"Mad as she might be, Queen Yil is far from stupid."

Myosh dipped a shallow bow as if accepting what might have been a mild rebuke. "I'd like to quarantine Shan here for two weeks to be sure he has the strength of character to resist burning the other students."

"One week," said the headmistress. "We might be months from war instead of years. All programs are being accelerated."

"Respectfully, Headmistress Chynn Wyl Gyr Daw, he's too dangerous to—"

"That's why he's here," said Chynn, talking over the Defiled. "One week. Watch and test him as you see fit. After, if he's still alive, begin training." The headmistress sniffed. "We don't have time to coddle a trophy male. Make a warrior out of him."

"Out of *him*?" Myosh snorted a laugh, quickly dipping another apologetic bow. "My apologies, Headmistress Chynn Wyl Gyr Daw. He's from the Nysh line. A nephew or something. He's never done anything more difficult than enjoy a dessert."

Shan bristled, wings fluttering in ill-concealed rage, but resisted the temptation to defend himself. He'd show them soon enough.

Grunting what might have been a laugh, the headmistress turned in tiny shuffling steps. Leaning heavily on her canes, she retreated indoors, muttering to herself.

"Follow," said Myosh, setting off toward the pyramid.

Tired of being snapped at like a dull servant, Shan jogged to catch up, walking alongside the priest. "She seems nice."

"Ah, the cowardly insults of the wealthy."

"Fine," said Shan. "Your headmistress seems like a crippled and senile war veteran who's been stabbed in the head too many times. Her understanding of etiquette—the basest modicum of polite society—is as lacking as her ability to take even minimal care of her carapace."

One antenna bent a little in Shan's direction, hinting at the mildest appreciation. As if being rude made him more likeable instead of less.

Peasants.

"When you've fought as many battles as Chynn," Myosh said, "when you've sacrificed half as much for our queen, you can be as rude as you want. She has more than earned it."

"What happened to never using anything less than her full name?"

"Don't be smart. It doesn't suit you."

Reaching the ancient temple, Myosh led him inside. Scrubbed clean of moss, the interior walls were better maintained than the exterior. A young bright female sat at a small desk flipping through a stack of papers with nimble craft claws. Her raptorial claws held more paper and a sharpened stick of chalk made from a blend of some starchy green plant matter and water. Enough light made it this far that she needed neither lantern nor torch. Reading the papers clutched in her upper claws, she made notes with the lower ones without looking.

Spotting the priest, the female rose to stand behind the desk. "Mistress Myosh." One eye studied Shan from the tip of his antennae to his lower tarsal claws. "A new student?"

"Maybe," answered Myosh. "If he survives the week, he'll join you in school. Now, Kask, if you would be so kind as to fetch me a torch?"

"Of course. One moment." The student dashed into the dark beyond her desk.

Kask returned with a lit torch. Passing it to the priest, she said, "Going into the wine cellar?"

"I wish. Deeper."

"The old dungeon?"

"Indeed."

Sensing the cold tone, Kask averted her antennae. "I'm on watch until the evening meal, Mistress Myosh. If you require any assistance, I'll be happy to help."

Myosh tilted her head in contemplation. "There is something you could do. I require a large quantity of dry leaves and kindling. Dry enough to ignite at the slightest spark."

"There's plenty in the woodshed," said Kask. "How much should I fetch?"

"Enough to cover the floor of an isolation cell."

"Of course." With a last appreciative glance at Shan, Kask exited the temple.

Myosh stood with crossed arms, her demeanour uninviting to small talk.

The student returned a moment later, pushing a wooden wheelbarrow piled high with kindling.

"I want you to lay it out on the floor of the cell," instructed Myosh. "A nice even layer. No stone exposed." Gesturing at the hall, she said, "Lead the way."

Lifting the torch, Myosh followed Kask deeper into the temple.

THE STORM BENEATH THE WORLD

Shan trailed along behind, moving slowly to avoid tripping on anything hidden in the gloom. Dancing flames drew his eyes, painted gyrating shadows on the brick walls. He'd lounged in front of enough cozy fireplaces to know the entrancing nature of fire, but never had he noticed its incredible beauty. Flickering claws of flame, the embrace of warmth. It was hunger and it was power, a force of destruction and change, and yet also used to build. In the desert, brickworks kilns fired bricks, baking them so they might build homes. Weapon makers used fire to harden spears of bone and wood. The hottest ovens produced glass for use in windows and spyglasses.

Though he'd never seen it himself, being unwilling to leave Nysh City, Mother said the storm beneath the world was an ever-raging fire.

Kratosh, realm of Katlipok. It was said those loyal to the Mad Queen Yil worshipped the fallen god. *They'd appreciate my talent there.*

He'd been born on the wrong island. His beautiful carapace glowing like golden fire, he'd probably be considered holy, someone to be exalted.

He studied Myosh from behind.

One little spark.

With the torch held before her and Shan trailing behind, the priest would never notice.

The thought alone sent teasing shivers of pleasure through him.

No!

He had to bide his time, prove he was strong enough to resist the lure. One week was nothing. Once freed, they'd realize his power and usefulness. If the deranged old headmistress was correct, and war with the Yil Queendom inevitable, they'd need him. After all, he was a descendant of Queen Nysh!

It won't be long before I lead a squad of my own!

He pictured himself as the first male to lead a squad of dangerous Queen Claw. While the Queen's Wing got all the glory, and was where all the highest ranked brights served, the thought of flying left him nauseous.

If the gods wanted us to leave the ground, they'd have given us bigger wings.

They passed doors and rooms in the dark and Shan, lost in thought, ignored them. They turned into a long hallway that wound its way deeper into the earth, the temperature dropping as they descended ever lower.

Shan imagined battling enemy soldiers, hunting them through the forests and burning them to ash, all in the name of his queen.

I'll be a hero.

No, he'd be *the* hero, saviour of the Nysh Queendom.

The more he practiced, the better he'd become. Eventually, he'd be so powerful he wouldn't need a squad. They'd send him hunting the enemy on his own. Just like the romantic plays, the old Lone Rafak archetype.

The Redemption said falling to the lure was an axiom: once addicted, the Corrupt grew in power until they died, either through starvation and self-neglect, or slain by the Redemption's Keepers.

That's ridiculous. Not in a million years would Shan neglect his carapace! It was unimaginable!

Kask stopped her wheelbarrow before a wood door with a single small window at face height. Myosh waited patiently as the student lifted the thick beam barring it closed and swung the door open. Shan moved closer for a better look.

"Dump it inside and spread it around," said the priest.

Kask did as instructed, and then exited the featureless brick cell. Arachn webs choked every corner and hung dangling from the ceiling like sad streamers at a dull party.

Do dulls have parties?

He couldn't imagine what they might celebrate.

Branches and crunchy dry leaves littered the floor, a filthy carpet no doubt riddled with pests.

"You have *got* to be kidding," Shan said. "I can't stay in there for a week. What will I do? How will I pass the time? Will meals be delivered? Where's the sleeping hammock? How will I clean my claws? There's not even a buffing towel!"

"You'll manage," said Myosh, "or you won't. There's enough flammable material in there if you attempt even the smallest spark, you'll burn alive."

Antennae suddenly perking with interest, Kask examined Shan with renewed appreciation.

"Oh," said Shan.

"You'll be fed each day. Assuming we don't forget."

"Fantastic. Can I get a look at the dinner menu?"

"You will be checked upon at random times. If we find you've cleared a spot so you can make sparks, we'll spike your brain."

"Lovely. I think I'd like to begin with molluscs as my first course. For seconds, a palate cleanser would be nice. Refreshing mentha leaves, perhaps?"

"In," commanded Myosh, ignoring his attempts at humour. Or perhaps not recognizing them; it was so hard to tell with priests. They were a humourless lot. Probably came from their lives of subservient denial.

Shan entered, the twigs and leaves crumbling beneath his claws. There was, he now saw, a narrow slot in the door through which meals could be passed.

"That's not nearly wide enough to fit an entire roast through," he said.

Myosh swung the door closed, plunging his cell into darkness, little of the torch light reaching the small window. He heard Kask drop the bar into place.

"Um," said Shan.

"Yes?" demanded the priest.

"How do I…you know?"

"I'll be back in eight days," said Myosh, ignoring his question. "I expect to be sweeping your ashes into a bucket. On the off chance you resist the lure, at that point you'll be welcomed to Kaylamnel."

"And here I thought I was getting the reception any visiting nobility might receive. Any chance you could leave a bucket in here?"

"Come," he heard Myosh's voice, muffled through the heavy wooden door. "Let's get lunch. I'm famished."

What little torchlight made it through the cracks and window dwindled to nothing.

Standing in the dark, Shan reached out a craft claw to touch the door. It wouldn't burn easily, but there was more than enough kindling here to start a roaring blaze.

If you don't cook, you'll choke to death on the smoke.

THE STORM BENEATH THE WORLD

It was, he decided, a rather cunning prison to be slung together so quickly and with so little thought.

The lack of a bucket was an unfortunate oversight.

Or was it?

"I really was born in the wrong queendom," Shan mumbled as he tried to make himself comfortable.

THE STORM BENEATH THE WORLD

AHK TAY KYM

We think of the storm beneath the world as Kratosh, the hellish domain of the fallen god. Having studied the raging fires through the latest in telescopic technology, I tell you the storm is more complex than we believe. I saw dark shapes, strange and yet teasingly familiar, rise out of the storm. Creatures live down there. I suggest to you it is not the hell of banished souls, not home to the Queen of the Storm, but rather a distinct ecosystem as different from the islands as the desert is from the windward jungles.

Furthermore, I have travelled north to the stormwall. I did not see the result of gods. I did not see a constructed *barrier. Rather, I saw the result of two powerful and conflicting wind systems. When combined with legends of alien creatures and contrivances passing through the stormwall, I can only believe that there is a second river of days, travelling in the opposite direction, on the far side. I propose we launch a research skerry with the intent of attempting to pass through the stormwall.*

—Chur Kin, Dull Philosopher – shortly before being banished for blasphemy

Ahk woke staring at the vicious point of a fire-hardened spear. Focussing past that, she saw a pale blue bright dressed in the uniform of the Queen's Wing standing over her.

"Move," said the soldier, "and I'll kill you."

Armed soldiers searched the Yil skerry, checking bodies and throwing the gathered weapons into a pile. A Wing Commander, carapace a silvery gold glowing in the rising light of Alatash, stood waiting with raptorial arms crossed over her thorax. Several tramea perched on the upper deck, eyeing each other with vicious loathing as they waited for their riders to return. A score more, ridden by ashkaro armed with longbows, flew escort.

A soldier exited the crew gondola and approached the officer, snapping a sharp salute. "More dead inside, Wing Commander." She gestured at Ahk with an antenna. "That's the only survivor."

The officer focussed on Ahk, dismissing the soldier with a flick of a craft claw. Raptorial arms still crossed, she approached. "Pirate?" she said, "Or Yil spy?"

"Neither," answered Ahk. "I am Ahk Tay Kym, heir and first-born daughter of Szin Say Kym."

"I know Szin," said the officer. "Can you prove that?"

Could she? The skerry she left home on was long gone, probably fallen into the storm by now.

"No," said Ahk. "Not easily."

The officer gave a dismissive twitch of one antenna as if the request for proof had been mere formality.

"A little too convenient," said the soldier still standing with a spear pointed at Ahk. "I bet the real Ahk is dead."

Ignoring the soldier, the Wing Commander studied Ahk. "I see some of your mother in you. How is it you survived where the rest of the crew did not?"

"I survived because I killed them."

Golden carapace aglow with the light of Alatash, the Wing Commander waved the soldiers aside. "Explain."

Starting with her departure from the family estate, Ahk told the story of how she came to be here. She spoke of the crippled dull leading the Yil crew and of how she could paralyze with a word. She told them of the subservient bright who saw flashes of the future. Eyes unfocused and unseeing, Ahk recounted the death of her mother and the crew, of sneaking aboard the Yil vessel and killing to avenge her mother.

"How?" demanded the officer. "How did a child kill an entire crew, most of whom were soldiers?"

Was there any point in lying? Eventually, someone would learn the truth. Even now Ahk felt the lure, the teasing temptation to use her talent again, to disappear. If she was doomed, why drag it out?

"I am Corrupt." For a heartbeat, she gave into the lure and felt an incredible rush of pleasure.

The armed soldier recoiled, spear rising in threat.

"No!" barked the officer as Ahk reappeared before their startled eyes. "Don't touch her."

"Throw her to the storm," growled the soldier. "Out here, no one would know."

"It'd be a mercy," agreed the officer. "But I have orders." She straightened, her fear and startlement falling away. "Prepare my tramea with a second saddle. Pack food, water, and blankets for two. I leave immediately." Raptorial arms still crossed, she gestured a craft claw at Ahk. "She's riding with me."

The soldier dipped a quick nod of antennae and dashed away to carry out her orders.

No longer threatened with impalement, Ahk stood.

Seeing the question in the set of Ahk's antennae, the Wing Commander said, "There is a school for your kind."

For a moment Ahk was confused. Her kind? Corrupt? Brights from good families? Murderers?

"Corrupt with useful talents," added the golden officer. "Out of respect for your mother, I give you the choice: I will take you to Kaylamnel where you might serve your queen before the Corruption takes you. Or you can step overboard and fall to the storm. The former might feel like a reprieve, but the latter is a mercy."

Unsure what the correct answer would be, Ahk contemplated her mother's death.

Yil's assassins robbed her of all chance at redemption.

Killing these few wasn't enough, didn't come close to soothing her rage.

"What will I learn at this school?"

"To fight the Mad Queen."

"I shall serve my queen until my last day."

"I would expect no less from the daughter of Szin Say Kym."

The soldier with the spear returned to announce the Wing Commander's tramea was ready. Though the officer showed no concern, the soldier watched Ahk with revolted distrust.

Approaching the beast, the officer stepped close, caressing its antennae with her own. It made a contented rumbling sound, one predatory eye, black like molten night, tracking Ahk. Never had Ahk been this close to a tramea, and she marvelled at its deadly beauty. She admired the sleek carapace, overlapping bands of an orange that was almost red, and glistening black. The long tail, ending in a viciously barbed stinger, swung and twitched as if itching to stab something.

The beast stank like the abattoir district in Nysh City.

"This is *Spearheading the Dawn*," said the officer, checking the straps on both saddles and nodding with satisfaction. "Stay well clear of the front half unless you feel you possess too many limbs. And stay clear of the back half unless you wish to be numb and paralyzed for the journey to come." Flipping open a saddlebag, she rooted through the contents, resettling a few things so they were packed more snugly, before tying it closed. "I am Wing Commander Koh Lin Tav Aah Rez." A secondary eye darted a look at Ahk. "You can call me Koh for the duration of the trip."

Ahk bowed low in thanks. "I am honoured, Wing Commander. You may call me Ahk."

Koh checked the weapons—four spears, a longbow and two quivers of arrows—strapped to the tramea. Finding everything to her liking, she turned to the waiting Queen's Wing. "Get Ahk seated."

The soldiers helped Ahk up into the saddle, making sure she was well situated before backing carefully from the tramea. Koh hopped into her own saddle with a wing-assisted jump, settling quickly into place. She looked entirely at ease riding the monstrous predator.

"Wing Commander," said the nearest soldier. "Will you take a few of the Wing with you?" She made a point of focussing on Ahk. "Just in case?"

Koh took up the reins. "No. Escort this skerry back to the tower." She looked toward Nysh Island. "I shouldn't be more than three days."

"Of course, Commander."

At some unseen signal from its rider, *Spearheading the Dawn* lumbered to the rail. Graceful and deadly as they were in the air, tramea were not well-suited to land. Crouching, its wings blurred into a tornado of motion. The soldiers scattered as the beast hopped over the railing. For a terrifying moment it felt like they'd fall all the way to the storm, the wind a deafening roar. Then, the wings caught traction turning the plummet into a steep, controlled dive. Finally banking and heading toward the island, *Spearheading* gained height.

"I will never tire of that!" Koh called from in front of Ahk. The wind snatched her voice, shredding the words.

Ahk understood. Though pale in comparison to the pleasure of using one's talent, the joy of flight filled her. Long had she dreamed of following in her mother's steps, serving her tour of military duty in the Queen's Wing.

That will never happen.

She wanted to laugh and scream with the pain of loss. A day ago, she'd been worried about what would happen to Bon, the dull fieldclaw who used his talent to make a carving of her. When Mother crushed the figurine, it had felt like she'd erased him from existence. Only now did Ahk understand how little she'd understood.

Would Bon be offered a place at Kaylamnel?

She doubted it. Where Bon made gorgeous carvings, she murdered a dozen spies. When art and beauty were held against death and violence, the worth of both became clear.

Pretty was nice. Killing was useful.

Sitting behind Koh, the wind whipping through her antennae, Ahk realized she felt no guilt. Yil's people killed her mother. They sent the ancient and beautiful creature that was *A Slow and Gentle Descent into Dark* to the storm.

No, it wasn't guilt she felt at all.

It was rage.

Rage, and a desire to strike back at those who hurt her.

Ahk wanted vengeance.

CHAPTER - JOH

For the Redemption is the claw and the wing of the gods. But if you do wrong, be afraid, for queens do not bear the spear for no reason. They too are servants of the gods, agents of wrath to bring punishment on the wrongdoer.

—The Redemption

Weeks passed in a blur of repetition. Mornings were a breakfast Joh felt guilty about eating every day. After that, it was hours of learning how to read and write and sitting through long classes on the history and economics of the Yil Queendom. When he pointed out that he now knew more about the enemy than he did his home, the teachers seemed pleased with themselves.

After lunch and more guilt, Rel lectured him about the importance of self-control in resisting the lure. Sometimes the priest led him in exercises designed to teach one such self-control. As far as Joh could tell, this meant enduring long periods of discomfort with no reward. Sometimes he was told to hold a particularly awkward pose for as long as possible. If he managed to hold the pose a bit longer each day, Rel labelled it a success. Seeing the pattern, Joh made sure to fail long before he needed to and then stretch each lesson by small increments.

When he asked the priest when they'd test the limits of his talent—careful not to show how desperately he craved that euphoric rush—Rel said it would only happen after he understood his own limits. It was an awkward trap as he'd already intentionally lied about those limits to set low expectations. Not that anyone expected much from a dull male.

Dinners were team-building events with Rel forcing each student to discuss their day and the lessons learned. The discomfort of speaking aloud in front of the others distracted Joh from the guilt he would have otherwise felt. After dinner Rel led the students in prayers for redemption.

Even though the school was deep in the desert, there was no end of water. If he was thirsty, he drank and felt guilty, remembering the two whites. If his carapace felt dry or showed signs of unhealth, he was splashed with water and more guilt. It was important, they told him, that his carapace remain healthy. When he asked if a dull with an unhealthy carapace would draw attention in the Yil Queendom, they sent him for more classes on self-control.

Each evening he fled to his room, always the first to leave the gossiping students. His hasty retreats were noted but no one said anything, instead glancing at Wex to judge her reaction.

Finally alone, he crawled into his hammock to think. From the moment he discovered his talent, he'd been careful not to use it on his father.

I left him his freedom and it got him killed.

He could have suggested his father stop poisoning himself. He could have recommended his father stop eating fenrik leaf and be more polite to the two-names who ran the local farms where he occasionally found work. All of those things would have been good for his father.

If taking his freedom would have been evil, was letting him slowly kill himself good?

If there was a balance, Joh couldn't find it.

Joh woke confused and disoriented. Everything felt wrong. The ceiling was impossibly far above him, occluded in shadow.

"Dad?"

His own voice jolted him fully awake.

He was alone in his room, a space four times the size of the shack he'd shared with his father. Rain never leaked through the roof, and the wind never howled through cracks in the walls.

He rose, disentangling himself from the sleeping hammock, and descended to the main floor. Wex and the other students stood gathered around a table upon which more food had been laid out. They chatted quietly, antennae bent toward whoever was talking as a show of attention, support, and respect. Wex noticed him and dipped a nod in his direction, waving him over.

Waving back but making no move to join the group, Joh studied the gathered youths. Where most ashkaro moulted seven or eight times—nine, if they were particularly large—before reaching adulthood, none of the students looked old enough to have seen their fourth.

Why are all the students so young?

With the guidance of the Redemption most ashkaro went their entire lives without discovering their talent. Those poor few who did discover it usually did so as adults.

That explains why there are so few students.

It didn't, however, explain why there wasn't a single adult student. What did the young offer that a full-grown ashkaro might not?

Obedience, a desperate need to be accepted, and an ingrained respect for their elders.

No matter how far we get from the hive, it will always be a part of us.

Belonging was everything. Even though everyone was free, they belonged to an island and that island belonged to a queen. She might no longer be the absolute ruler, a veritable god overseeing the lives of her drones, but if the queen decided on a course of action, it happened. Joh had never met anyone who'd so much as seen Queen Nysh yet everyone agreed she was the greatest queen. Yil, on the other claw, was the Mad Queen. No one had met her either. After questioning the other students—and more subtly the teachers—he realized he didn't know anyone who'd met an ashkaro from another island. The distances were too great.

We assume our queen is the best and repeat lies about other queens.

Or maybe they weren't lies. How could he know?

Who had travelled the incredible distance between the two queendoms, met Yil and spent enough time with her to decide she was insane, and then returned to Nysh to tell everyone?

Did the ashkaro in the Yil Queendom refer to the Mad Queen Nysh, or did they have some other derogatory name?

He wanted to laugh, to shake himself free of these blasphemous thoughts.

THE STORM BENEATH THE WORLD

Blasphemous?

Nysh wasn't a god. She might live three hundred years, where his life expectancy was closer to thirty-five, but she was still blood and carapace.

How can I think like this?

He barely remembered his mother and his father had rarely been around, often disappearing for days. He never had a hive, never belonged.

Wex gave him a concerned look, and still he hesitated to join the group.

Shel San Qun, the town priest, preached the dangers of solitude to the ashkaro mind. 'Though no longer hive,' she said, 'we are creatures of proximity. We need to rub wings, hear the hum and buzz of life to sleep. Alone, we go mad. Alone, we seek comfort in selfishness. Alone, we forget the truth: we are one. From dull to bright, we are bound in purpose. To exist without purpose is to not exist at all.'

For how many years had Joh existed without purpose? He'd never considered himself the worse for it, but perhaps he was unable to see the flaws in himself.

On the surface, it made sense that the school should be out here where the students couldn't hurt anyone, but there was more to it than that. Out here, the children were separated from everything they'd known. There were teachers, but no parents. There were enough empty rooms to know the parents could have lived here too.

They take Corrupt children because we are easier to shape, more compliant. We will strive to earn our place in this strange little hive they've created for us because it's in our blood to do so.

Out here, there was nothing else to belong to.

They will shape us into a violent little hive to do their bidding.

Would any of the students think to question? He doubted it. Watching them talk and argue, he felt very much alone for the first time. He'd never had anyone to talk to, to share his fears and doubts with. How much better would life be if he had someone like himself, someone who questioned the way things were, who needed answers beyond 'because that's the way it is'?

Wex, sleek and deadly, watched him with one eye while still

conversing with the others. His friend fit where he could not. She would fight for her queen without questioning because that was what she was supposed to do. He could change that, perhaps, but dared not. He'd already done too much in suggesting she be his friend. He had to do better, to earn her friendship.

I won't fight for our queen, but I will fight for my friend.

Des, Zyr, and Wex were being groomed as the group's killers. Kris, the mimic, would presumably be their spy. Kam's medical skill would keep them all alive.

And I'll get them through any closed door.

This would be a military unit of Corrupt. Unlike the Queen's Wing and Claw, they'd have no rights, get nothing in return beyond eventual banishment, and that only if they survived.

What he couldn't decide was how he felt about that. What did it matter if the Mad Queen planned on conquering the Nysh queendom?

What will change for me if we have a different queen?

He felt another flash of guilt at the thought.

He'd heard that on Yil all Corrupt were thrown to the storm no matter how trivial their talent. But then, like Queen Yil being insane and their entire island being barbaric and warlike, he had no way of knowing if any of it was true. Everyone assumed he'd blindly believe whatever he was told. He doubted being a Corrupt dull under Yil's rule would differ much from previous life.

Rel entered the barracks. Spotting Joh standing alone, he waved him over. "Come! It's time for your next lesson." As always, he turned and left without waiting to see if he was obeyed.

Joh watched him go. With nothing to be gained from antagonizing the priest, he decided to follow.

Outside, Alatash had crested the leeward horizon, lit the clay bricks of the ancient school orange and red. Small vertebrate lizards and squishy rodents scampered about the rough scrub, hiding in tufts of brown grass. A rafak snake, no more than the length of a craft arm, dove from above, snatching up a fleeing lizard and swallowing it whole. At that size they were ignored, useful in keeping the pest population down.

Joh shuddered. Dad often mocked his small size, saying that someday a rafak would carry him away.

Rel marched out into the centre of the field and stopped, turning to face Joh. He ignored the flitting snake.

Hurrying to join the priest, Joh ducked his antennae in quick apology for dawdling.

"The faculty here is small," Rel began. "We all serve in multiple rolls. I am not only tasked with finding new recruits, but I also teach history—to those we think will have need of such education—and control."

This was a little different. Usually, he launched into lectures about how suffering hardship not only built character—whatever that was—but also left one more able to resist temptation.

Two questions sprung to mind, and Joh chose what he thought might be the least dangerous. "Who decides who needs to learn history?"

"I do." When Joh didn't ask another question, the priest continued. "We have no control over who the students will be, what their talents are, or when they will join us. Yet we must create cohesive units from whatever we have to work with."

"We are to be a team." He'd figured that much out on the first day, but it was still nice to have it confirmed.

"Since we have so little control, we must change tactics with each unit depending on personalities and talents."

I wonder what he thinks of my personality. Joh nodded to show he was listening.

"While the other students you met started before you and Wex, none have been here longer than a few months. They are your team."

Is he chastising me for staying apart from them?

"As such," the priest continued, "we must decide how to best shape you as a team so your talents complement each other." One eye moved to follow the rafak as it darted after something it had seen in the dry grass. "Every team needs a leader."

Joh's antennae perked up, suddenly interested. "You want to know if I might be a suitable team leader?" It made some sense. As a small, unimposing male, none of the females would see him as a threat.

"No," said Rel. "You are the last ashkaro I would nominate as team leader."

Antennae carefully expressionless, Joh accepted Rel's decision. It was always better to be seen as complacent and subservient. "Des already sees herself as the leader," he said instead. "Though she's a little confrontational," he added, feeling a small shiver of pleasure. The priest thought Joh's talent was making blatant suggestions—and those were the most effective at achieving immediate results—but he'd found such subtle things as tone of voice, body language, and pointed observations often worked just as well. If Rel couldn't see that Wex would make a better leader than Des, he was an idiot.

"Young females tend to be confrontational," said the priest. "Des will mature out of that behaviour."

"We're going to live long enough to do any real maturing?" Joh asked, pointedly.

One of Rel's wings twitched. "The other students already know her."

"True," Joh agreed. "And no doubt you know her much better than I." He glanced back toward the barracks. "Truth be told, I don't know Wex that well. But she did say her mom was a shift manager at a brickworks. That means she received a better education than most of us, and grew up walking a line between the brights running the place and the dulls working it."

"Like that bright she murdered?" asked Rel.

Joh fluttered his wings in an embarrassed laugh. "Point taken."

I should sneak into the teacher housing and plant suggestions as they sleep.

Even though Wex would make a much better team leader than Des, he wouldn't; it would be a terrible abuse of his talent. It would also be incredibly dangerous. If he slipped up and one of the teachers figured it out, they'd either kill or banish him.

Joh considered his fellow students. Kris's talent for mimicry was interesting.

I'll have a talk with him later. It would be handy if he's studied and can mimic all the teachers and students.

"Soon," said Rel, "we're going to begin teaching you to control your body language. A spy who is so easily read is not much of a spy at all."

He's testing me.

To keep the teacher from examining the previous conversation too closely, Joh changed the subject. "Do you think I need to learn history? I've always been curious. There's an oral tradition dating back many queens, but much of it is so fanciful it must be myth. Or maybe—what's the word for when there's more to a story than meets the antennae?"

"Allegory, or perhaps parable. Though, really, what story doesn't contain layers and themes beyond the obvious?"

"Right. There are tales of the sky darkening with tramea as enemies from another island attacked. I heard that once, long ago, an island unlike all others flew past us in the wrong direction and that everything living on it was twisted by some foul disease. How can any of that be true?"

"If the river of days runs an infinite distance in either direction," answered Rel, "what *isn't* possible?"

"That's the non-answer adults always give when they don't know the answer."

"Because that was the typical non-question children ask when trying to distract adults."

WEX JEL

For the body does not consist of one member but of many. If the craft claw should say, "Because I am not a raptorial claw, I do not belong to the body," that would not make it any less a part of the body. And if the antennae should say, "Because I am not an eye, I do not belong to the body," that would not make it any less a part of the body. If the whole body were an eye, where would be the sense of hearing? If the whole body were a craft claw, where would be the strength?

We are each a part, but nothing alone.

—The Redemption

Wex, Des, Kam, Zyr, Bin, and Kris Kork gathered around the breakfast of leaves and grubs laid out for them. No one thought to wake Joh, and she felt a stab of guilt when he wandered down from the second floor looking blearily confused. She understood. She too often woke startled to discover she wasn't in her room back in Brickworks #7.

Many nights she lay awake wondering if anyone thought to tell her parents. Mom would be worried. She tried asking Rel once, but he made excuses about the queen's secrets and told her not to worry.

And what exactly did she want Mom to hear? That her daughter was Corrupt and had murdered a bright? It would be better if they thought she wandered out into the desert and was eaten by a feral tramea.

Joh noticed the students and she waved greeting. Nodding back, he made no attempt to join them.

He's nice, she decided, *if a little odd.*

She wished he'd join them. Setting himself apart like that would bother the others.

THE STORM BENEATH THE WORLD

A moment later Rel entered the barracks. Ignoring the knot of students, he gestured at Joh to follow. The little dull looked annoyed for a moment when the teacher's back was turned, but dutifully obeyed. It was a small rebellion, though one she never would have considered.

There was something off about him.

He's smarter than I expected.

He was too watchful and too comfortable being alone. Back on that first morning after they arrived, Wex had woken, heard the students talking in the main room, and scampered down to join them. Joh descended soon after, took one look at the gathering, and wandered outside on his own.

"Today is combat training," announced Des, drawing Wex's attention back to the group.

"It is?" Wex asked, plucking a dried slug from the table and popping it into her mandibles. She'd lost track of time, and rarely paid attention to the schedule.

"Three Day is always combat. Just like Four Day is always politics and Yil etiquette."

"Eight Day is best," said Zyr. "We get to hunt." Her wings shivered with excitement.

"Big surprise there," said Des. "She blisses out every time she looses an arrow."

It felt strange to casually discuss their talents. Someday Zyr would crave that euphoric rush so bad she'd put arrows in anything and everything, her fellow students included.

"And I like to eat," added Zyr, one antenna bent in wicked humour. "These dry husks are better than what I had at home but if I bring down a wild skirrak we feast for days!"

Never having eaten anything larger than a particularly plump grub Mom once brought home from some social function at the brickworks, Wex couldn't imagine so much meat.

Picking up a grub, Bin popped it into his mouth, swallowing it whole. "Hurry up and kill something already. I'm starved!"

Is that Joh's suggestion still at work?

She couldn't remember how he'd worded it. It was probably nothing. Bin was always hungry and, according to the others, always had been.

A tangle of emotions—excitement, fear, and guilt—that had nothing to do with food wrestled for dominance. Combat training! She imagined holding real weapons like those Cayr Rie Chi Lo possessed. Her claws itched to feel the smooth wood, polished to perfection.

"Oh ho!" crowed Des. "Wex here is a little too thrilled by combat training. Well, forget finding anyone's weaknesses. Fel Shyn teaches combat and she's untouchable."

"Untouchable?" Wex asked. "Is she skilled, or is it a talent?"

Zyr cackled. "She's a veteran of the Queen's Claw. I heard she saw action on a feral island that got too close to Nysh. The ashkaro living there must have been trapped for a long time. They'd reverted to hive. A savage queen with mindless drones and warriors. I even heard there were ruins, like they'd once had a civilization of sorts and then everything fell apart."

"Don't listen to her," said Kam, the dull male with a black carapace, sidling closer. "Zyr has a fantastic imagination and a tendency to make things up."

Zyr bristled. "I heard it from Nuin, before she left."

"And where did Nuin hear it?" Kam asked.

"Nuin?" asked Wex, interrupting. "A teacher?"

"No," said Des. "A student. She was in the group before this one. Her talent was linguistics."

"Where'd they go?"

The gathered students glanced at each other, checking the doors to see if there were any teachers in antennae range.

"Once they feel like we can work as an effective unit," said Des, "we're sent away. They won't *officially* tell us where." Seeing Wex about to ask another question, she added, "I heard most end up serving on Yil as spies or seconded to a diplomat."

"Spies?" Wex asked.

"And assassins," added Zyr.

"Counter insurgents," said Kam.

"War," said the hulking Bin, rising to his full height.

Kris Kork, who'd remained quiet until now, stepped forward. His carapace shimmered and shifted and in a score of heartbeats Rel stood among the students. Only the slight difference in size betrayed the mimicry.

"Infiltration of the upper hierarchies of Queen Yil's inner circle," Kris said, voice identical to the teacher's, "will be crucial to our efforts. Having loyal assets placed among the highest ranks of the Sisters of the Storm could mean the difference between victory and defeat." With a shudder of pleasure that started at the tip of his antennae and ran the length of his body, his carapace returned to its usual muddy green.

"My guess," said Des, "is that we're going to help Kris get a spot on the Mad Queen's council. Obviously, we'll have to kill whoever he replaces." She didn't sound upset at the idea of murdering someone she'd never met. "We'll also have to make sure Kris has time to study them, down to food preferences and what Rel calls *behavioural tics*. Then we'll use his influence and our own talents to sow chaos and undermine the power structure from within."

"And when we start succumbing to the lure?" Wex asked.

Zyr answered, voice sober. "I'll find a concealed place on a rooftop and assassinate as many ranking Yil brights as I can."

Wex wasn't sure if killing random ashkaro from a rooftop still qualified as assassinations, even if they were from another island.

"Maybe the Mad Queen herself," added Kris. "If we can get close enough."

Bin tapped quietly on the table, getting their attention, and bent an antenna toward the door. A dull female with a carapace showing hints of yellow stood waiting. She held two long spears in an odd cross-grip, the butt of each held in a raptorial claw, the top clutched by the opposing craft claw. Wex immediately saw that with such a grip, she'd be capable of a formidable defence while still being able to stab her opponent.

More than anything, she wanted to test that defence.

"That's Fel Shyn," whispered Des.

"If you've finished stuffing your faces," barked the teacher, stabbing a spear in the direction of the gathered students, "it's time to train." The other spear poked in Bin's direction. "You, big thug—"

"My name is Bin, Mistress Fel Shyn."

"Did I ask your name, you dull lump of rafak droppings? No. Do you know why?"

"Because I'm so pretty you couldn't possibly forget?" asked Bin, antennae showing humour.

"No. Now fetch two stab sticks from the armoury." She turned, spinning on her lower claws as if in a military parade, and marched out.

"Woo!" crowed Des. "I think we're going to see just how good our new student is!"

Bin dashed out the rear door, presumably off to the armoury, while the rest led Wex to the field. Fel stood waiting, both spears spinning lazy yet mesmerizing circles as they passed among her four claws with consummate ease.

"You were wounded when you first joined us," she directed at Wex. "Is it healed?"

"It is." Wex held up the damaged arm so the teacher could examine where the carapace had thickened around the break.

"Good," snapped Fel without looking.

Bin came lumbering up with a pair of scuffed but solid-looking stab sticks. Fel bent an antenna in Wex's direction, and the big male passed Wex the weapons.

A whirlwind of conflicted feelings chased through Wex.

The memory of the moment she saw the gap in Cayr Rie Chi Lo's defences. The sublime bliss of using her talent only to realize she'd murdered someone. The neat hole in Cayr's exoskeleton. Blood.

She wanted to hurl the weapons away.

She needed to once again feel that mad rush of euphoria.

The sticks felt good. Infinitely better than the crude pair she'd crafted herself, but inferior to Cayr's glorious set. These were real weapons, well-used and built for combat, not display. Wex accepted the stab sticks, testing the weight and struggling not to show her excitement.

Elsewhere on the field, Rel and Joh were bent in conversation. Neither seemed to have noticed the knot of students.

"Rel tells me you killed a bright," Fel Shyn said. "Not an adult, but a youth with some combat training."

Wex nodded, antennae sagging in shame.

"He said your talent is with stab sticks."

"I'm not sure that's correct," Wex admitted. "I'm not particularly skilled with them."

"As you have only just discovered your talent, you wouldn't be. How did you kill her?"

Wex struggled to find the words describing what happened. "I saw... I couldn't hit Cayr," she started again. "She was better than I. She kept hitting me and I couldn't stop her. Every time I tried to hit her, she blocked me with ease. But then I saw a hole in the pattern she wove. I knew if I put the stab stick exactly *there*, I'd hit her." She wanted to say more, to explain that all this was Cayr's fault, and that she hadn't wanted to fight, but sensed the teacher would see it as weakness.

"We will fight," decided Fel Shyn.

"I'm not sure that's a good idea," Wex forced herself to say, though she desperately wanted to feel that incredible pleasure again. "I might hurt you."

"You won't," said Fel Shyn. "Everyone, stand back."

The students retreated, making a clearing for Wex and Fel Shyn. Spears again in that cross-armed grip, the teacher circled Wex, forcing her to turn to keep her in sight. Knowing she was no match for Fel, Wex raised her sticks, waiting for the teacher's attack. When she saw the gap, as she felt strangely sure she would, she'd try to pull the blow, touching the teacher instead of stabbing her. Surely, that would be enough of a demonstration.

"You're not attacking," said Fel Shyn, still circling.

"I don't know how to fight."

Fel attacked, one spear sweeping aside Wex's defences, the other spinning and then stabbing her in the thorax with the blunt end. Wex backed away, and the teacher, not letting up, followed. Unlike Cayr, Fel made no attempt to disarm her opponent. Instead, she rained blows upon Wex, never hard enough to crack or permanently damage her carapace, but enough to keep her stumbling in retreat. A swung spear cracked into the left shoulder of her raptorial arm while the other darted forward to punch into the shoulder of the craft arm on the other side.

This was nothing like fighting Cayr in the desert. The young bright had been more skilled than Wex, but Fel was a warrior, a veteran. She fought with calm and deadly intent, emotionless and in control. Struggling to defend herself, Wex retreated before the onslaught. Fel and the gathered students followed, the fight ranging beyond its original confines. Blow after blow landed leaving scuffs in Wex's carapace.

"No fight," said Fel, landing another vicious chopping blow, "was ever won by retreating."

Wex wanted to argue, but the other spear swept her front legs from under her, and she went down in a tangle of limbs, rolling away to gain space.

Fel followed, allowing her to rise before attacking again. "If you don't hit me, I will beat you helpless." A thrust spear butt impacted the elbow joint of Wex's left raptorial arm, numbing it. "I can damage your limbs and joints such that you will likely make a full recovery."

She's right. I can't win going backwards.

She'd been too busy trying not to get hit to look for an opening.

If she's going to hit me anyway—and Wex saw no way to stop the teacher—*I might as well get a few shots of my own in.*

Digging the claws of her powerful jumping legs into the soil, Wex held her ground. Giving up on defending herself, she attacked. Fel knocked aside her first attempts with ease, her antennae hinting at some appreciative pleasure. That momentary respite was all Wex needed. She launched herself at her opponent with no thought of injury. She swung and stabbed with mad abandon, Fel's attacks still landing. Wex knew she'd feel them later.

An opening!

Gone even as the thought formed.

The palest taste of pleasure, teasing at the bliss to come.

Pressed by Wex's unskilled barrage, Fel changed tactics. Though she refused to retreat, she also ceased attacking.

Still unable to land a blow, Wex experimented. She grabbed at Fel's craft arms, or intentionally left herself exposed to draw an attack. Fel ignored every feint, blocked every attack, stepped over Wex's leg-sweeping attempts as if they'd been choreographed, and acted as if she hadn't noticed the openings left. No matter how unpredictable Wex tried to be, no matter how insane her attack, Fel reacted as if she knew exactly what Wex planned.

Another opening again filled the instant Wex recognized it. Warmth built in her abdomen begging for release. It felt nice, though still fell well short of the incredible bliss she felt when she killed Cayr.

She's too fast!

Each time Fel contemptuously flicked aside another attack, her antennae quivered.

She's happy, but not because I'm attacking.

Wex lunged forward with both sticks simultaneously, throwing her weight behind the weapons and Fel sidestepped the attempt, moving even as Wex decided what to do.

She's not happy she's winning or that I'm doing well.

The knot of students broke apart to make room as Wex rolled through them in an uncontrolled tumble, and reformed around the fighters once Fel closed the distance.

She's happy because she's using her talent.

Sticks spinning, stabbing, and swinging, trying to distract her opponent, Wex attacked. Yet another opening in her opponent's defences gone even as Wex tried to take advantage. Fel was leagues more skilled in combat, but that wasn't what Wex saw. Each time Wex decided her next move, Fel already knew what she was going to do.

Mind reading?

It seemed a waste to use such an incredible talent for beating up students.

Deciding to test the theory, Wex thought, *I'm going to swing at your head!*

Fel either ignored the thought or hadn't heard it.

I didn't actually intend *to attack.* Could the teacher read that, or had she heard Wex's earlier thought about testing if she could read thoughts?

"Can you hear my thoughts?" Wex blurted.

"Don't be ridiculous."

Wex attacked again and was once again blocked at every attempt.

"But you *are* thinking too much," said Fel, whacking Wex on the shoulder as punctuation. "You have a talent, not skill." *Crack!* The other shoulder stung. "Stop thinking. *Feel.*"

Remembering how it felt when she killed Cayr, the incredible calm, the way all worry and fear fell to nothing, the slowing of time until dust hung still in the air, Wex let go.

She attacked. Though still shy of the first time she used her talent, euphoria filled her.

There, an opening. Hit it.

Blocked, barely.

Another. Strike!

Parried.

Fell retreated a single step.

By all the gods above and Katlipok in Kratosh below this felt glorious!

Wex followed.

There. There. There. Holes everywhere.

She struck.

Blocked again.

Someone said something.

What did words matter when the gods split your carapace and poured love into your darkest recesses?

Opening. Attack.

Blocked, but even that defence made more openings.

"Stop!"

Talking during a fight is dumb, some calm and distant part of Wex thought. *It makes more gaps.*

She attacked those openings.

In full retreat, spears weaving a blurred web of defence, antennae and wings showing the joy of a female in mid copulation, Fel parried the attacks.

She's enjoying this as much as I am!

It hadn't, then, been Fel who ordered her to stop.

A weight crushed Wex to the ground, bending a craft arm beneath her so she screamed and lost a stab stick. The other stick was torn from her grasp, and she roared in feral rage as the pleasure fell to nothing. Gutted emptiness, the horrible dark left when one was robbed of the light of the gods, remained in its place. That, and the sick knowledge she'd do anything to fill that wound.

A powerful raptorial arm slipped around her torso, claws blocking the breathing holes along her abdomen.

She didn't care. The light of the gods was gone, stolen. She'd been so close!

Carapace dented and cracked, Fel stepped into view. Rather than show anger at being hit, her antennae pulsed in waves of post-coital contentment.

    The world faded to black.

THE STORM BENEATH THE WORLD

SHAN WYN VAL NUL NYSH

The small vertebrates digging in the mud beneath our claws are interesting creatures. Their brains are entirely unlike those of ashkaro. Instead of having four distinct hemispheres, they have only two which are intimately connected. My suspicion is that where we can manipulate all eight limbs at once, looking in two different directions while our secondary eyes watch the sky and antennae test the air around us, these pathetic creatures are limited to one—or at most two—thoughts at any one time.

—Wuy Nsan Jil Nan, A Treatise on Vertebrate Biology

Locked in a dark cell, far from the light of the gods, time ceased to have meaning.

At least that's what the poets and storytellers said was supposed to happen. Quite frankly, Shan was beginning to think not one of them had spent time in a dark cell. Time didn't become meaningless. Quite the opposite. Time became everything!

All I have is time and every second of it is excruciatingly boring.

Nuhir Sih Quan Nhai, the so-called Grandmother of Modern Philosophy, was said to have spent months alone doing nothing but thinking.

She must have had the intellect of a mollusc.

Being trapped alone with his thoughts was Shan's new definition of hell. At least in Kratosh, you'd be distracted by your burning soul. And while time might not be meaningless, with no sight of Alatash passing overhead, it was impossible to judge its passage.

His stomach rumbled in hunger. How long had he been down

here? Days? They hadn't fed him once. His water bowl had been empty forever!

They've forgotten me.

He was going to die down here. Someday, a thousand years from now, a student would be sent down to sweep the basement of this ancient temple. She'd discover his husked carapace wound in spiderwebs and crawling with carrion beetles.

Shan imagined the young ashkaro cleaning around the corpse, maybe even sweeping the dust and debris into the gutted exoskeleton.

A rattling sound echoed through the dusty clay brick halls.

Should he call, remind them he was here?

Showing weakness in front of females was always a mistake. They acted as if suffering was somehow character-building, as if all existence were a contest and whoever had the worst life won. Instead of being evidence of past mistakes, battle scars and war wounds were badges of pride. As if the ashkaro who got through life without breaking a single limb wasn't provably smarter than the ones who threw themselves into danger at every opportunity. Mother was sixty years old and still bragged about the wounds she received first during training and later when flying patrol around a Corrupt island. Back before she died, his grandmother used to wave the stump of her severed claw in his face and tell him in excruciating detail how she lost it fighting a full-grown rafak.

Females never grow up.

They acted like rambunctious juveniles from the moment they were born until the day they died or were eaten by something. Really, the more you thought about it, the funnier it was. With a life expectancy of forty years, most males died of old age. With a life expectancy of twice that, few females reached sixty-five, many dying in wars or entirely avoidable accidents during flashy shows of bravery.

And they say we're the dumb ones.

Deciding he'd rather starve to death than show weakness, Shan sagged with relief when he heard someone approaching his cell. Rather than give them the satisfaction of knowing he'd suffered—and maybe it was a little character building, he did now feel like he'd matured—he contemplated his options. Choosing his most courtly pose, the one that said, 'I'm less than entirely impressed with the quality of the service here,' he waited.

What little he saw through the small window set in the door grew brighter. Whoever carried the torch stopped out of sight and fumbled about lodging it in a holder. Shan listened, shifting his stance to better express his displeasure, as the heavy bar was lifted and set aside. When the cell door swung open, he cringed from the flood of light, eyes unaccustomed to the brightness after so long in the dark and ruined his pose.

A bright female, all jagged angles, viciously barbed raptorial claws, and cold black eyes, stood holding a plate heaped with food balanced in one craft claw. Her carapace, shot through with colours from red to a deep leaf green, flickered in the torch light. A selection of weapons hung about her exoskeleton.

Shan's breath caught. Reckless and juvenile as females might be, there was something endlessly enticing about the truly dangerous ones. Mom often made fun of him for liking 'bad girls.'

The guard, still holding his food and making no attempt to enter, took her time studying Shan. "Kask wasn't kidding. You're easily the prettiest thing I've seen in years. Not that there's much competition here. I'd say you're a six out of eight."

"A six?" he demanded, appalled.

"Maybe a seven if you got cleaned up and were displayed in better light."

"I am Shan Wyn Val Nul Nysh," he said. Perhaps if she understood his lineage, he'd get the respect he deserved. "And I do believe—"

"I'm Izi Doq Qen Jin Vur. And it's a pleasure to meet you, Shan." She lifted the torch to get a better look. "A real pleasure, indeed." She glanced at the leaves and kindling littering the floor of his cell. Was that the briefest tremor of fear in her antennae? "I see you've behaved yourself. So far. We have a pool running on how long you last, so if you wouldn't mind holding off until the third day before immolating yourself, I'd see that as a kindness."

"A kindness?" Shan sputtered.

Izi shrugged her upper wings. "Of course, me betting in a pool like this is kind of unfair, what with my talent being luck."

THE STORM BENEATH THE WORLD

Shan forgot the complaint he'd planned. "That's not a real talent."

"I am so lucky," she said, leaning to one side to better appreciate the colours of his abdomen, "that if I decided to use my talent you would definitely kill yourself on the third day."

"I would never!"

Izi ignored his protestation. "It's not a huge amount of scrip, but no one likes to lose. Honestly, it's more about standing. And of course, knowing my talent, everyone is going to be surprised if you *don't* die on the third day. Folks will wonder if something happened when I delivered your food. No doubt they'll assume you flashed a little underbelly and seduced me."

Shan crossed all four arms protectively over his thorax and retreated from the light.

Izi took a single step into the cell. "A pretty thing like you, in a place like this? So many lonely females. It wouldn't hurt to have a friend here," she leered, antennae reaching suggestively toward him. "I could be a friend."

Shan backed into a corner, fear building in his abdomen. The temptation to burn promised bliss. The wood and kindling on the floor assured a hellish death.

"Do you know what happened to the last female who tried to hurt me?" His voice only shook a little.

"No, no, no. I don't want to hurt you. Quite the opposite." Again, her antennae teased. "Maybe it'll hurt a little bit, but you'll like it."

"I burned her to nothing."

Izi's antennae snapped straight, her advance ceasing. "Are you threatening me?"

"No. But I will defend my honour to the last."

"Your *honour*?" Izi snorted, placing the plate on the ground. "You males are so sensitive. I was just having a little fun. You need to learn how to relax." Exiting the cell with a sensuous and deadly leisure, she closed the door. Giving him a last look through the window she said, "If you do ever want a little extra something with your dinner—maybe a honey sweet—I'm sure we can come to an arrangement."

Shan heard the wood bar drop back into place, the scrape of claws on stone as Izi collected the torch.

Desperate to stall her departure, he called, "How often am I to be fed? I've been here forever."

"Forever?" Izi snorted again, a genuine laugh this time. "You're to get three meals a day. Each time we'll check to see if you've burned anything." She made an unhappy buzzing noise, her antennae twitching against each other. "Look, Myosh ordered me to push you a little to see if you'd break. That's all I was doing. And you've only been here three hours."

"Izi?" Shan said. *Please don't leave. Not yet.*

"Yes?"

His mind raced, searching for something to say, some reason for her to stay. "Is your talent really luck?"

"It is. Don't worry though. I would never use it to hurt you." Eight heartbeats of silence. "Unless you anger me."

Was she teasing him? He couldn't tell. In a way, it didn't matter. Maybe the priests were right, and someday he'd starve or immolate himself making bigger and bigger fires, but Izi would likely die in a dank alley rolling eights on a dice over and over.

We're all doomed.

"Shan?" Izi said. "I was just kidding. I know I came off a little forward there, but I haven't seen a male worth having in two years." She sniffed, and he heard her drag a raptorial claw along the grain of the wood. "I'm sorry if I scared you. I was just following orders."

Not wanting her angry with him or tempted to turn her luck—if that was a real talent—against him, he said, "I understand." Then, he added, "I'm going to last the whole week."

"No one believes that. There's not a single bet on day eight. Anyway, I haven't placed a bet. That seemed cruel. The thing with talents that most folks don't understand is that sometimes we use them without meaning to."

That sparked an idea.

"You should bet that I make it. I promise you'll win, even without your luck."

And if you do accidentally use your luck, all the better for me!

"Not like I can punish you if I lose."

"Yeah," said Shan. "There's that."

"You're all right," said Izi, moving away down the hall. "For a male."

"Wait!"

"Yes?" She sounded annoyed now and he wished he'd thought of this earlier.

"I need… I need a bucket."

"I'll see what I can do."

Then, she was gone.

Shan sat in the dark. By all the gods in Alatash above, he'd give anything for a moment of light.

One spark, just to see that there's nothing crawling in my food.

No. Myosh was doing this on purpose. The priest was evil, setting everything against him. The darkness was nothing more than another attempt to push him to use his talent so she could be rid of him.

Shan shuffled forward, feeling for the plate. Finding it, he sank down into the dry debris, legs folding beneath him. The food was cold.

A few small sparks and I could warm it a bit.

Another attempt to trick him, no doubt.

Lifting the plate to his mandibles, Shan hesitated. Just because they were treating him like an animal didn't mean he had to behave like one. As best he could with the lack of tableware, Shan ate a civilized meal. The grubs, perhaps acceptable if one were a dull servant or lacked a refined palate, had clearly been sitting out for some time. Their normally pliant flesh had the consistency of drying tree sap. If any attempt had been made at spicing the meal, he detected none of it. Finishing, he returned the plate to the door and retreated to the corner he now thought of as his.

The whole damned cell is mine.

Still, this corner felt safest.

Eight days and he'd be free.

And then what?

He'd never been privy to Mother's business, though he knew she had military contracts and maintained her rank in the Queen's Wing. You couldn't live in the same home and not overhear a few things. And maybe he eavesdropped a few times, curious what the females were up to during their closed-door meetings. Hushed voices. Maps and scrolls hastily swept aside if someone entered the room unannounced. Previously, his interest had been purely a nosey curiosity born of the fact he wasn't supposed to be interested.

'War is female work,' Mother would say every time he asked questions.

Shan would point out the new male squads in the Queen's Claw and her antennae would move in amused condescension. 'They're grunts, the first to fall. At best, a distraction while the real warriors work elsewhere.'

The queendoms of Nysh and Yil were drawing closer together. He'd been hearing that for years. At first, most of Mother's meetings had been about trade, acquiring a fleet of long distance skerry and crews to pilot them. There had also been discussions regarding exotic foods and materials she might import, and questions as to what Nysh had that Yil lacked. Later, when it became obvious the islands were heading directly towards one another, likely to mate, the talk turned to war. For a while, trade continued—just because they were enemies didn't mean you couldn't make a profit. Then, a year ago, he overheard one of Mother's employees report that two skerry, loaded with goods, had been sent to the storm by the Mad Queen's soldiers.

Trade was done and it was time to make a profit off the coming war.

In discovering his talent, Shan lost any chance in playing a part in that. As a male, his role would have been minor, but at least there'd be social events to attend, and some secondary business matters might be left to him. Once he proved himself—and he had no doubt he would have—Mother would have given him an upper management position. The other females might not like it, but he was the queen's nephew, and his mother owned the company. From there, a favourable marriage and a life of leisure. It wasn't his fault he was born gorgeous, but he gained nothing by not taking every advantage the gods saw fit to bless him with.

Shan shook his head, caught between anger and wonder at the vicious perversity of life.

The life he was supposed to have was gone. Were he anyone else, that would have been the end of him.

Shan's antennae shivered with excitement. He was Shan Wyn Val

THE STORM BENEATH THE WORLD

Nul Nysh, nephew to Queen Nysh Na Kan Oh Rok An-Rah. War was coming, and his talent was fire. The first time he discovered his talent, he burned an ashkaro to nothing. Given time and practice he could do so much more. Burning a lone opponent would be nothing. Though the female officers would likely be unable to overcome their ancient preconceptions of a male's abilities and promote him to officer, he'd still play a critical part in the struggle to come.

In typical female understatement, Myosh had described him as "interesting" to Headmistress Chynn Wyl Gyr Daw. Try as she might, she'd been unable to hide how impressed she was by his power. A power that could only grow.

Until it consumes you.

He shook off the unhelpful thought.

Making a nest like a feral tramea, Shan folded his legs beneath him and slept.

He dreamed of fire, of the expression on Nyk's antennae as she realized she'd made a terrible mistake in cornering him. Maybe he wasn't naturally brave, but he could be. He dreamed of the way she came apart like dry leaves thrown into a blaze, crumbling and fragmenting. He saw her carapace curl and darken, charred by the incredible heat. Shan dreamed of fields of carapaces, empty and blackened, the queen's enemies burnt to ash. He dreamed he was a god, that he challenged Katlipok for domination of Kratosh. The new ruler of the storm—why wasn't there a masculine term for queen?—he was the first male god.

Shan woke to the smell of smoke. He searched the confines of his lightless cell for the glow of embers and found nothing. Retreating to his corner, he prayed to the gods of Alatash that the scent would dissipate before his next meal arrived.

AHK TAY KYM

> *I appeal to you, sisters, by the mercies of all the gods of Alatash, to present your bodies as a living sacrifice, flawless and whole, and thus acceptable to the gods. This is the truest spiritual worship. Be conformed to this world, but also be transformed by the renewal of your mind as an individual. For by the grace given to everyone among you, none must think of herself more highly than she ought to think, but to think with sober judgment, each according to the measure they have earned. For as in a hive, we have many members, and the members do not all have the same purpose, so we, though many, are one body in Redemption, and individually members one of another.*
>
> —The Redemption

Wing Commander Koh delivered Ahk to Kaylamnel, a school hidden in wildest jungles and far from any city. The Wing Commander stayed only long enough to explain to the terrifying headmistress how they found Ahk. She went into great detail as to the number of dead, and the manner of their deaths. She mentioned that Ahk claimed to have killed them herself while evading detection, and flew out the moment the headmistress dismissed her.

Headmistress Chynn, carapace showing countless war wounds, one raptorial arm looking like it had been viciously twisted off at the elbow, studied Ahk. Her secondary eyes watched a group of young ashkaro sparring with blunted spears.

"I knew your mother. Her loss is a grievous wound to the queendom."

Ahk bowed thanks, unable to speak for fear she'd break down.

'Emotion is a strength,' her mother often said. 'An inability to control when you express it, however, is not.'

An antenna bent in Ahk's direction as Chynn adjusted the canes she relied on to remain upright. "You told Koh you killed near twenty Yil spies." The ragged stump of a raptorial arm waved as if to suggest this was a claim Ahk had best defend with rigour.

To the headmistress, a Wing Commander and five-name bright was just 'Koh.' That scared Ahk more than the elderly ashkaro's cold regard.

Ahk told the headmistress everything, leaving out no detail, no matter how unflattering.

"And they couldn't see you?" Headmistress Chynn asked.

"Several looked right at me and didn't react."

"Interesting." Chynn scratched at a mandible with a craft claw. "I wonder if you're truly invisible, a chameleon, or somehow convincing them they don't see you."

A tremor of pleasure ran through Ahk's antennae at the thought she might be asked to display her talent.

Chynn grunted, noting Ahk's reaction. "You'll need to learn better control." The splintered stump arm gestured at a nearby clump of buildings. "You'll find Myosh Pok Tel there. Repeat your story to her. Leave out no detail. After, she'll introduce you to the other students and see you settled."

The headmistress shuffled back into her home without another word.

After hearing Ahk's story and asking several questions, Myosh, a middle-aged female bright wearing the garb of a Defiled, studied her. "Izi's group, I think. Come."

The priest led her across the school grounds toward a row of sprawling estate homes. Tangled in vines and creepers, the bricks were cracked and ancient. The roofs showed repairs which themselves looked old. Several similar buildings lined the school's cleared perimeter, thick jungle no more than a score of strides beyond the manicured lawns. It was a strange place for such a community. Though cleared and obviously cared for, every structure looked like it had sat long abandoned and only recently been put back into service. In the centre of the grounds sat a massive octagonal pyramid. It looked impossibly old, the bricks larger than any she'd seen and of a strange colour.

"Was this a vacation resort?" Ahk asked.

"Long before Nysh Na Kan Oh Rok An-Rah, a queen decided there would be a city here, centred around the pyramid, which was already ancient. She died, slain by one of her daughters, and the project was abandoned."

"I've never seen bricks that big or that colour."

"We believe they were imported from another island." Myosh gestured at one of the crumbling estate homes. "Your cadre will share this house. There are other cadres in different homes. You will not interact unless explicitly ordered to do so."

Ahk fluttered a wing in mute acceptance. As a three-name bright, Myosh was of similar standing. Not knowing the priest's family, she wasn't sure if she should be deferential. There weren't many three-name families with higher standing than Ahk's. Due to her business acumen, her mother moved in circles beyond the station she was born to. On the other claw, being a priest of the Redemption, even as one of the Defiled, gave Myosh status beyond mere names. Feeling off-balance, torn from the life she'd known, Ahk played it safe.

"Cadre?" she asked, antennae bent in polite query.

Approaching the main entrance, Myosh threw the door open without knocking and entered. Ahk followed.

"There are several cadres studying here. For the most part, they're defined by your time of arrival. Sometimes, if we see two talents likely to clash, or the possibility one student's talent might complement that of someone in another group, we'll shuffle members."

Ahk took in the home's interior. Everything was decrepit, the furniture and finishings long outdated. They stood in a lobby that would have once been a spacious main foyer for greeting guests but was now crowded with equipment and weapons. There were splintered vests of wood armour. A complete set of tramea barding, shellacked clay plates woven into wood and fraying fabric, hung gathering dust on the wall. She wasn't sure if it was meant as art or awaiting repair. A stack of broken spears leaned in one corner while unstrung shortbows lay heaped in another. Beneath the barding sat a clay urn filled with napped stone arrowheads. Where there should have been soft woven rugs only bare brick showed, scuffed, and faded from centuries of use.

"Each cadre has their own house," continued the priest. "You will not set claw in any other cadre house unless ordered to do so. The kitchen and dining room are at the back on the ground floor. The staff will prepare your meals, and no, they don't take requests." Myosh waved a craft arm at the far end of the foyer where a curved staircase wound its way up to a second floor. "Your personal rooms are upstairs. There are half a dozen empty chambers, so you have your pick."

"How many students in my cadre?" Ahk asked, feeling like it was expected she show some curiosity despite her numb emptiness. Her thoughts constantly slid to her mother's death, and she hadn't slept properly in days.

"Including you, there are currently six."

"Currently? More are expected?"

Myosh's wings fluttered discomfort. "No." She sighed. "I suppose you'll hear it from the others soon enough, and better you get the truth rather than some fanciful story. There were more. One student, a bright with a talent for etiquette and social situations, disappeared one night."

"Disappeared? Where did she go?"

"The other two," said Myosh, ignoring the question, "died during a training accident. One of them had a talent for controlling trees and plants. He lost control."

How can losing control of a plant end in the death of two ashkaro?

Unable to imagine how such a talent could be useful or dangerous, Ahk kept the question to herself.

Myosh leaned back to shout "Izi!" up the stairs. "Come meet the new student."

An instant later, a bright female with a carapace banded in green and red bounded over the banister, ignoring both decorum and the stairs. She dropped into the lobby with a flutter of wings to slow her descent. Immaculately maintained weapons hung from several belts. A quick glance showed stab sticks, bone knives, a shortbow slung across her back, and a quiver of blunted practice arrows.

"This," said the priest with annoyed patience, "is Izi Doq Qen Jin

Vur, the cadre leader. For now."

Izi ignored the priest, making no attempt to hide her scrutiny of the new arrival. "What's your talent?"

Myosh shook her head in mock disgust but said nothing, waiting.

Though Ahk had seen a few five-name brights at Mother's business meetings, she'd never been introduced to one. Standing before a member of one of the highest families in the queendom, Ahk shivered with awe. She bowed low. "Izi Doq Qen Jin Vur—"

"No need for that," said Izi. "Who we were, our family names, mean nothing here." She glanced at the priest. "We're a team."

Which didn't change the fact that what must be the only five-name bright within a week's walk was clearly being groomed for leadership.

Unsure what the correct etiquette was in such a situation, Ahk mumbled, "Um, I suppose my talent is hiding."

"Hiding, eh? That could be useful, I suppose."

"Ahk Tay Kym is being modest," said the priest. "She killed a dozen Yil spies. By herself." The priest retreated toward the door. "Introduce her to the rest of the cadre and get her situated." Both antennae bent in Izi's direction. "As you said, family names mean nothing here. Prove you are worthy to lead."

Both students dipped quick bows as the priest left.

Once the door closed, Izi visibly relaxed, her wings losing their tension. "I wasn't kidding about our names not meaning anything. But not because we're a team."

Ahk understood. "It's because we're Corrupt."

Izi looked glum. "One month ago, I was accepted into the Queen's College to be fast-tracked for an admiralship. My mother's old posting was to be mine upon graduation. Eight wings of combat tramea as my very first command." She grunted a pained laugh. "Now all I command is four Corrupt youths and even that might get taken away if I don't dance to Myosh's every whim." Her attention returned to Ahk, and with it some humour. "Call me Izi. Everyone goes by their first name. My talent is luck, and yes, it's a real talent. I'll show you later when there's no chance of a teacher popping in to surprise us. Come on upstairs and I'll introduce you to the others."

Ahk followed Izi up the winding staircase, the steps creaking and groaning beneath her claws. At home there'd been carpet runners to protect the wood floors, but here they'd been torn out long ago. Countless claw marks scored the ancient wood.

Izi gestured at a closed door at the top of the stairs. "My room." Passing that, she approached the second door on the far side of the hall and rapped with a craft claw.

"What?" answered a female voice from within.

"New student," said Izi. "I'm supposed to introduce her."

The door swung open and a female bright, carapace streaked with soft shades of purple, stepped into the hall.

"This is Iyik Nal Hyr," said Izi. "Her talent is her antennae. She can sense the faintest scent and listen to whispered conversations in nearby rooms. Useful for spying on teachers." Izi waved a craft claw at Ahk. "Iyik, this is Ahk Tay Kym. Ahk's talent is stealth or being invisible, or maybe killing Yil spies."

"My talent isn't killing," Ahk corrected with polite deference.

"Myosh said she took out an entire skerry of the Mad Queen's warriors."

Unsure if it would be polite to correct the five-name again so soon, Ahk said, "It's possible they weren't *all* warriors."

Izi ignored the protest but also seemed unbothered by the correction.

Iyik left her room and joined them in the hall as Izi banged on the next door. A bright female with a glistening green carapace answered, studying Ahk.

"This is Bash Scv Zxan Liss," said Izi. "Bash's talent is balance. Ahk's talent is stealth."

Bash grunted a greeting and followed them into the hall.

"Next," said Izi, pounding on another door, "is Shil Sen Huh." The door swung open to reveal a male with a lustrous gleaming black carapace. "His talent is seduction, so be careful around him." Izi flicked an antenna in Ahk's direction. "Shil, meet Ahk. Her talent is killing males who try and seduce her."

Shil's wings fluttered in humour. "Nice to meet you." He was attractive enough, but Ahk felt nothing for him beyond an appreciation of a pretty exoskeleton.

THE STORM BENEATH THE WORLD

Turning away, Izi headed toward the next door. "Come, I've saved the best for last."

Everyone followed, Iyik snorting in amusement. "Best is highly subjective."

"Prettiest?" ask Izi.

"I'll give you that," agreed Iyik. "If you like them vacuous and self-absorbed."

"Who doesn't love a trophy male?" Stopping before the door, Izi banged on the wood. "Stop buffing your carapace and come meet the new student."

Ahk heard a male grumble something unintelligible.

"He says he is neither vacuous nor self-absorbed," whispered Iyik. "And he's angry that the ways of the modern city—equality for males and all that nonsense—haven't reached this 'rafak nest of thrill-seeking vipers.'"

"Thrill-seeking vipers?" asked Izi, pretending shock. "Does he mean us?"

When the door opened Ahk found herself facing the most stunningly gorgeous male she'd ever seen. His carapace, a magical swirling rainbow of lustrous reds and golds, each colour sharply defined, looked like it had been buffed by a team of beauticians just seconds ago. Everything about him was flawless. His pose, the slight swaying of his abdomen to catch and reflect the light pouring in through the open window. He knew he was glorious and, haughtily annoyed expression aside, gloried in the attention.

"Was I right," said Izi, "or was I right?"

She was right. Shil paled in comparison.

"Ahk, meet Shan Wyn Val Nul Nysh."

The male's name penetrated the distraction of his beauty. Another five name! And more than that, he was a Nysh, a direct descendant of the queen. Awed as she was at meeting Izi, this male was royalty. She wanted to bow, to apologize for the rudeness of the other females, but they showed none of her reverence.

"Anyway," continued Izi, ignoring Shan's angry pose, "Shan's talent is fire. He burned someone to ash."

"Less than ash," said Iyik. "I heard there was only an empty carapace when he was done."

Shan retreated into his room, flustered and upset. "It was a mistake. She attacked me."

"He is, I suppose, the most dangerous student here," continued Izi with an ironic bent to her antennae. "The gods are capricious and malicious. Imagine, giving all that power to a trophy."

"I'm not a trophy."

Izi waved him to silence. "Come," she said, turning her attention on Ahk. "I'll show you to your room."

Shan watched them leave, all six eyes and both antennae following Ahk, while Iyik returned to her own room. It was an uncomfortable level of attention, more than a five-name male should ever give a mere three-name.

Picking a door apparently at random, Izi shoved it open and entered. Ahk followed.

"They're all the same," Izi said, gesturing at the room. "Sleeping hammock. Drawers for all the clothes you don't have because you've been struck from the family ledger in shame. A desk for studies and shelves for all the books and scrolls you're not allowed to remove from the library." She nodded at the ceiling. "Each suite comes with a fine selection of arachn, weblings, and other assorted things that crawl on you while you sleep and nest in the creases of your carapace." Izi dashed a quick look at Ahk. "I'd tell you to take a moment to unpack, but you don't have anything, and we have a training exercise scheduled, so…" She shrugged her wings. "Today we have spear throwing practice. If you've never thrown one before, don't worry about it. None of us have hit anything yet."

Izi led them all back to the ground floor where everyone took their turn selecting one of the less damaged spears from the pile heaped in the corner.

"Maybe if they gave us some decent weapons," grumbled Iyik, "we might look less like helpless children."

It wasn't until they were back outside that Ahk realized how musty the house smelled. Her antennae felt like they'd accumulated weeks of grime in just a few minutes.

Seeing her pause to clean herself, Izi said, "You get used to it."

"No, you don't," said Shan, trailing behind. In the light of Alatash he was even more beautiful, a work of art the gods could be proud of.

Across the field another cadre worked on unarmed combat training. Wrestling under the watchful main eyes of a veteran of the Queen's Claw, they practiced joint locks, sweeps and throws involving intricate use of multiple limbs, and submission holds. Ahk guessed the oldest student, a bright female with a scuffed carapace in dire need of a bath and a scrubbing with a hard-bristle brush, was maybe three years older than herself.

Izi droned on about obstacle courses and whoever ran the fastest time winning a reprieve from the filthier duties, but Ahk ignored her, entranced by the skill shown in the other cadre. She was to have begun combat training under a private tutor that summer. The memory of what she would never again have stung hard and deep.

Again, she saw the spear shoved through the back of Mother's neck, wiggled around to destroy the brain.

I'll kill them. Every Yil spy and assassin.

The Mad Queen herself, should Ahk somehow get close enough.

The scuffed female was paired with a large bright male. They circled each other, probing and testing. The female, much faster, teased her opponent, making jokes about rubbing his pretty mandibles in the mud.

Noting Ahk's attention, Shan stopped to stand beside her. "Beautiful, isn't it."

"Hm?"

"Fighting. Well, maybe not the fighting, but the skill." He sighed wistfully. "I could watch females fight all day."

"Are we going to learn that too?"

"You bet," said Izi, joining them. "Shan cheats though."

"I do not!"

"He just looks so good you feel guilty about messing him up and then he runs away."

Shan darted one main eye in Ahk's direction. "That only happened the first day. No one warned me!"

The scuffed female lunged teasingly at her opponent and the male, stunningly, caught one of her raptorial arms. Even as she reacted, pulling away and lashing at his face with her craft claws, he ducked, sweeping her front steering legs out from under her. She crashed forward into the mud and in a practiced move he spun to land on her back as he kicked out her jump legs with his own.

Izi guffawed, a crass bellowed laugh that echoed across the field. "Stev isn't going to like that."

Crack!

The bright male exploded, carapace splitting in an instant. Blue gore and guts rained down upon the rest of the cadre gathered around the wrestlers.

"What happened," managed Ahk in stunned disbelief. She couldn't have seen that, must have misunderstood.

The Queen's Claw overseeing the training launched herself at the scuffed female and burst like an over-ripe fruit. The brutal *snap* of her exoskeleton rupturing staggered Ahk.

The begrimed female, spattered in blue, antennae pulsing in waves of euphoric elation, picked herself up from the mud. She faced the rest of her cadre, craft arms stretching wide.

"The lure," said Shan.

"Kratosh!" Izi grabbed Shil, dragging him away. "We have to run!"

Crack!

Crack!

Crack!

Three more students detonated in rapid succession. No longer recognizable as ashkaro, their carapaces looked like splintered branches twisted into nightmare shapes. Here, a recognizable main eye hung from a ropey strand of tissue. There, part of a craft claw lay tangled in intestines.

The last student, a lumbering male, turned and fled.

Crack!

He looked like Katlipok herself had risen from the storm and ripped him inside out, scooping his guts and slinging them into the air.

"I could burn her," said Shan.

He didn't move.

Slicked in mud and blood, the female searched for more victims. Students and teachers fled screaming in every direction.

Someone will get a long bow.

Spotting Ahk and Shan standing together the bloody female sang a clean note of joy. She sprinted at them, a deranged dash driven by insatiable need.

"I could," mumbled Shan. "I could. But." He lifted one leg as if about to flee, and froze, trembling.

Ahk's fear fell to nothing, drowned in a wave of ecstasy. The charging female barely reacted, antennae shifting in a moment of confusion before her attention locked on Shan. Ahk dashed forward, angling to intercept.

"Oh," said Shan standing frozen behind her. "She left me?"

Wrapped in a thick blanket of her own joy, Ahk gave no thought to what she planned or what would happen if the Corrupt female saw her. Ramming the butt of the spear into the soft earth, Ahk lowered the sharp end. Somewhere behind her, Shan squealed in horror.

The charging female crashed into Ahk, impaling herself on the wedged spear, her inertia punching it through her carapace, driving it deep into her thorax.

By the time Ahk managed to lever the corpse off and stand, students and teachers had gathered. Some congratulated her on her quick thinking and skill while others eyed her with distrust.

Bliss fading, she stood over the student she killed. *That's our shared fate: we fall to the lure and die, or fall to the lure and are killed.* She didn't know how to feel. If not stopped, Stev would have continued using her talent, bursting students and teachers. But killing her felt nothing like slaughtering the Yil spies on the skerry. That had been vengeance, justice. This…

What was this?

"You didn't abandon me." Shan stared at her, both main eyes and antennae following her every move.

How could she tell him that, lost to her own talent, she hadn't given him a single thought?

"You saved me," he said. "You saved my life."

Myosh hustled into the gathering mob, scattering students and teachers alike with harsh words. "You," she snapped at Izi, who'd returned looking sheepish. "Get your team back into your cadre house.

No one leaves until ordered to do so!"

Izi led her team home.

Strangely exhausted and unwilling to answer the barrage of questions, Ahk retired to her room. Crawling into the sleeping hammock she dreamed of her mother's death and how good it felt to pass unseen through the world.

JOH

We can talk about 'equality for all' in the eyes of the law, but the reality is that not all are equal. The dim-witted dull male in the far desert will never be the equal of a five-name bright female descended from queens. The concept is purest delusion, and society treating the measurably inferior as equal to the greatest among us, madness.

We call them 'gods-given rights,' but the reality is our queen gave us these rights. What one queen gives, another can take away. It is the way and always has been. This flash society of cities and titles, males strutting the streets as if they bear real responsibility, is a momentary aberration. Like a malformed abomination, all Queen Nysh has wrought shall be thrown to the storm.

Queen Yil Een Ahn Kyn Ah Phy-Tah, the One True Queen, is coming.

—Transcript from the *Trial of Pfar Ain Syl Pah Maiy*

Joh sat alone in his room. Never had he spent so much time in a brick structure. Half an hour in the local church with his father was very different from sleeping in a brick-walled room night after night. Every sound echoed, harsh on his sensitive antennae. In here, the world smelled wrong, ancient and dusty. Dry as their shack in the desert was, he'd gone to sleep each night listening to the flora and fauna beyond the thin reed walls, catching their scents. Each night the desert shaped his dreams, part of him ever wakeful, secondary eyes alert for danger, antennae testing the air for predators.

While it was nice to be safe from such dangers, the room was too still, too quiet. It felt like he slept in a mausoleum. Separated from the world, he missed the danger. How could the brights in their brick homes live like this day in and day out?

Rising, he paced from one wall to the other, tasting the stale air, listening to the sound of his claws on the brick floor.

Carpets. Rugs. Tapestries.

Such odd words. He'd never seen any, but suddenly they made sense. Something to soak up some of the reflections, maybe hold the scents of the outdoors. Funny, the more the brights separated themselves from the world, the more they faked the very thing they sought to escape.

Joh stopped pacing, faced the door. Across the hall, Wex had been confined to her room.

I should talk to her.

What comfort could he offer a two-name female who almost killed someone?

He sighed, remembering the brutal fight. Two females, sleek and terrible, in pitched battle. Weapons blurred, each attack and response so fast he couldn't follow it, only figuring out what might have happened after the fact. It was probably the sexiest thing he had ever seen in his short life.

Probably? There was no 'probably' about it.

Dad often bemoaned the tight violence of females, but there was no denying the appeal. No one could ever be as dangerous as Wex, and so no one could ever be as provocative. Last night, instead of dreaming of tramea stalking the sky, he dreamt of her. It was the first time he'd ever noticed a female in that way. Previously, they were something to be wary of, to avoid if possible.

What am I doing?

Even ignoring the difference in standing and the fact he was a runt of a one-name male, they had no future together. Corrupt, all the students were doomed. Their end was inevitable.

You could suggest that she loves you.

Joh hissed, antennae lying flat in deepest shame. "If you do that, I swear by all the gods in Alatash I will spike your brain."

It was bad enough he suggested they be friends. Were he not so scared of the school's purpose, the teachers, and other students, he'd undo what he'd done.

I need someone on my side.

It felt like a justification rather than a reason.

It is. You only decided that after *doing it.*

Taking a step toward the door, he hesitated.

Classes were cancelled, the teachers meeting in Headmistress Raht Shram Yrn Nyst's home to discuss Wex's fate. Despite how close she'd come to dying, Fel Shyn seemed the least concerned. Having watched the fight, seen the blissed-out expression on Fel's antennae, Joh suspected he understood: the combat teacher finally met someone who could push her. While the teachers deliberated, Wex had been ordered to remain in her room. No doubt they feared she might succumb to the lure and kill her fellow students.

She wouldn't.

Or he didn't think she would. He'd never more than scraped the barest edge of his own talent. While it felt good to suggest things to people—particularly when he knew it would help them—he was sure he could resist the lure. Truth be told, it was hard to credit the Redemption's claim that all Corrupt fell to the lure. Back home, weeks passed where he never gave it a thought. Now, it was like the teachers pushed the students to make their talents central to their lives. It made sense, he supposed.

The more we use our talent, the stronger we'll be.

Why then were they upset by Wex's fight with Fel?

She must be further along than me, closer to falling to the lure.

Which meant they were trying to decide if Wex's talent outweighed the potential loss of another student.

A sharp knock on the door startled Joh. That was another problem with these rooms: the doors blocked his senses. He felt trapped in here.

"Yes?" he asked.

"We're going for lunch," said Des. "You coming?"

"Yes." He hesitated. "I'll be along in a moment. I want to see if Wex is hungry. I can bring her something."

"We're not supposed to talk to her," said Des, repeating Myosh's command.

Someone groomed to lead ought to be better at thinking for themselves.

"Are you going to tell on me?" Joh asked.

"Of course not."

"I'd do the same for you," he lied.

Though Des might not be as terrifyingly enticing as Wex, she was still capable of killing, and it never hurt for people to think you were friends.

Des scraped at the far side of the door with a claw. "Don't get caught."

She left, clawsteps fading to nothing.

Joh went to the window, pushed one shutter open enough to peer through the crack, and waited to see the students follow Des to the dining hall. Pulling it closed, he slipped into the hall, crossed to Wex's door, and knocked politely.

"Joh?" she asked.

Startled, he said, "How did you know?"

"Who else could it be?"

That was an odd question. Did she think he was the only one thoughtful enough to check on her, or that he was the only one dumb enough to ignore the teacher's command?

Unsure, he said, "Everyone has gone to the mess hall."

"I know. I was listening to your conversation."

Either she was a lot more perceptive than he, or her antennae had been pressed against the door.

If she knew why he was here, should he just ask what she wanted to eat and be done? Would trying for more be weird or unwelcome?

Suddenly uncertain, he mumbled, "Uh…can I come in?"

The door swung open and Wex stood there looking dishevelled, her wings twitching and unsettled. One antenna bent toward him while the other seemed lost in thought. She ushered Joh into the room. Entering, he pushed the door closed behind him.

"I'm not hungry," she said.

His excuse for being there snuffed, he searched for something to say. "It wasn't your fault." *That was dumb.*

Wex gave him a flat look.

"Fel is responsible," he added. "It was her idea. And you didn't hurt her." He remembered the scrapes and dents in her carapace.

"Much."

"I could have killed her."

"You would have stopped first."

"No," Wex said. "I wouldn't have."

"Anyway. Fel's talent being what it is, I'm not sure you could have won."

Wex looked at Joh with doubt. "You don't get it. I was improving the whole time. She was too, but I was improving faster."

"Eventually, if the fight went long enough, you would have evened out."

"Why?" Wex asked. "Why can't one talent be more powerful than another?"

He didn't have an answer.

"It doesn't matter," she added. "Fel is older and would have slowed first. I saw it happening. The holes got bigger, and I got closer each time. She didn't try to stop the fight either. Even though she knew I'd kill her. It felt too good."

"It's what they want," said Joh. "It's why you're here. We're Corrupt and doomed—"

"You're terrible at cheering people up."

"But we have an opportunity to serve few others will ever get." Though, in truth, he remained unsure how he felt about dying in service to a distant queen.

"You're saying I shouldn't feel bad that my talent amounts to killing people?"

"If you kill me, you should definitely be overcome with guilt."

The flat regard remained, but something subtle changed in the bent of her antennae. A hint of humour. Maybe something more that he didn't understand.

Uncomfortable, he changed the subject. "Des didn't want me to talk to you."

"She's doing as she was told."

"Exactly. But is obedience a good trait in a leader?"

Wex's antennae perked up. "There are military ranks for a reason. Everyone is supposed to follow the orders of those above them."

"We're not in the military. Not really. I think we're going to be spies. Or maybe assassins."

She nodded agreement. "They'll send us to Yil. We'll be far from any ranked officer, forced to think for ourselves."

"The others follow Des because she's the loudest, but that's a dumb way to choose a leader. You're the smartest in the class. Des throws herself at problems but you *think*."

Both antennae bent toward Joh, testing the air. "I'm not sure I'm the smartest."

"Then who?"

She cocked her head to one side, one antenna bent in mocking query.

"Oh," he said. "No." Was this because he suggested they be friends? He thought he understood. Wex had to believe there was something special about him that made her friendship make sense. "I don't think so. Anyway, I could be the smartest ashkaro in all the queendom and no one would follow me."

"Times are changing," Wex pointed out.

"Not fast enough to matter. We don't have that long. We either die in service to our queen or starve in some filthy alley."

"What if you used your talent to suggest I never use my talent again?" asked Wex. "You could save my life."

Would that work? He'd never attempted something so drastic. He didn't want to. If she refused to use her talent, they'd eject her from the school. He'd lose her forever.

You promised you would earn her friendship. "Do you want me to try?"

Wex leaned toward him as if she might brush her antennae against his. "No."

His heart broke. *Is she refusing because she won't abandon a friend?*

He was about to admit his terrible crime, when someone outside raised their voice, shouting as if speaking to a crowd.

"Maybe the teachers have decided," said Wex, heading to the window, "and are announcing my fate."

Swallowing his admission, Joh followed, standing at her side as she pushed the shutters open.

Below, at the edge of the field where the students trained, a small skerry had lowered itself enough to tangle the trees with its tentacles.

THE STORM BENEATH THE WORLD

Slathered in black paint and looking tattered and unhealthy, it would all but disappear in the night. Ropes hung from the single gondola mounted on its back. Ashkaro stood at the railing with longbows while others had descended to the field. Several surrounded a gloriously colourful bright female who bellowed into a wood speaking trumpet. Spears and shortbows held ready, they guarded her.

Students exited the dining hall and stood in a tight group centred around Des, looking uncertain.

"We're being attacked?" Joh said, disbelieving.

If whites had mobbed the place searching for food and water, he would have understood. While insane, it would have fit into his worldview. But brights flying in on a ratty skerry? Why would anyone attack a school of dulls out in the desert?

"Your gods didn't abandon you," the bright female beneath the strange skerry shouted, voice amplified by the speaking trumpet. "They're dead! Only Katlipok, remains, Queen of the Storm!"

"Blasphemy!" hissed Wex.

Joh knew he should agree but said nothing. The bright's words were strangely convincing.

"Katlipok blessed Queen Yil Een Ahn Kyn Ah Phy-Rah," the bright continued. "No longer must ashkaro fall to the lure. Katlipok meant our talents to be a gift. We were meant to stand beside our creators. The jealous gods in Alatash cursed her gift. She is rage and she is vengeance! Katlipok slaughtered them for their sins of pride! Their glowing corpses will light our world forever! Your weak queen worships dead gods, your Redemption is a lie." She gestured at the students. "You, the children Corrupt, loathed by your own people, see better than any. Join us and be whole. You need not die, starving or murdered, banished to some horrid island."

Blasphemy or no, she made sense. For thousands of years queens rose and fell on the islands, and not once had the gods visited or shown any sign they cared. Either they were dead, or they'd abandoned their creation, but it hardly mattered. In the end, the result was the same. All the gods left their creations was the light of Alatash sweeping across the sky.

Joh imagined a dead city, littered with the glowing corpses of bright gods, worshipped by ashkaro ignorant of the truth.

"There is one god!" screamed the bright. "And she is death! She is the storm!" Students shuffled closer to listen. "What sick queen trains children to be spies and assassins?"

"She's right," said Wex.

"But," said Joh, struggling against a blood-deep need to agree with Wex, "the Mad Queen."

The preaching bright's voice filled his head, left little room for thought. Just moments ago, he'd denigrated Des for her mindless obedience, and here he was, blindly accepting the words of the enemy.

Are we the villains?

No! It couldn't be! Everyone said Queen Nysh was good and beautiful and that she ruled with fair claws.

If she's so fair, why are most dulls forced to live in the leeward desert while the brights live in the windward forests?

Out in the field the bright's voice rose, thick with emotion. Antennae pulsating with waves of intense love, she spoke truth and needed all who heard to understand. No one could lie so perfectly.

Joh focussed on her antennae.

She's using her talent.

He tried to think, to distance himself from her words, and failed. Maybe she said what he wanted to hear or gave voice to things he only dared dream. How could he know?

I can't.

What could he do? Runt. Male. Dull. All the words everyone used over and over and over. He was nothing, could do nothing. Mesmerized by the speech, Wex stood at his side so close they almost touched.

I'm nothing, but she's something.

"Wex," Joh said.

Still watching the speaking bright, she bent one distracted antenna in his direction.

"Wex," he repeated. "I don't know if we should believe her."

With obvious effort she pulled herself from the voice and faced him.

"You need to question everything," he added.

For a long moment she stood rooted, eyes locked on his, antennae reaching toward him like they might caress. He wanted that more than anything.

Wings fluttering in confusion, Wex turned to again gaze down at the field. The students and many of the teachers had gathered around the speaking bright, hanging on her every word.

"Children," called the bright, "come, join with your sisters! Your true sisters, the Sisters of the Storm! Serve the One True Queen, the only path to redemption!"

Someone lowered a rope ladder from the skerry and the students obediently shuffled toward it.

"Queen Yil Een Ahn Kyn Ah Phy-Rah, servant to Katlipok will save us all! Only when she has united *all* the islands under one true queen can we know freedom from this curse! The Queen of the Storm has spoken, and we must obey!"

"What she says makes sense," said Joh. "Right?"

"Oh," Wex said. "I have to kill her. I have to kill her now."

Grabbing her stab sticks, she dashed from the room.

Confused, Joh followed.

WEX JEL

We found the dying skerry less than a day from the northern stormwall. With one exception, the crew were dead. Some had starved. Many looked to have taken their own lives. All were elderly. The sole survivor, Zjeen Chay Nash Kio Phin, claimed she left the Yil Queendom forty years prior on an exploratory mission. Zjeen said they took a squad of skerry through the stormwall and that they discovered another reality on the far side. They found a race of carnivorous reptilian gliders who built cities on massive coral trees that reached up out of the storm below. There were, she told us, no islands at all.

They were taken prisoner and saw other ashkaro imprisoned there, though couldn't converse with most due to differences in language. If true, this would suggest ashkaro have arrived there from many different and widespread islands. She said they managed to stage a grand escape during which most of the ashkaro were slaughtered. Fanciful and insane as her story was, we did find a number of devices of unknown purpose on the skerry.

After our Redemption priest declared it all blasphemy, we threw Zjeen and all artefacts overboard.

—Queen's Wing Report [REDACTED]

You need to question everything.

And she did.

With a single careless suggestion, the veil had been ripped from the world.

Wex's heart slammed against her carapace. Maybe she hadn't

THE STORM BENEATH THE WORLD

believed everything she heard, but there were ashkaro you were *supposed* to believe. High ranking bright females, with knowledge backed by an education Wex could only dream of. Such ashkaro spoke the word. If a five-name bright female told you something was true, you believed it. That was community, ashkaro working claw in claw toward a single goal. That was how society was supposed to work.

Wasn't it?

It's hive.

Memories inundated Wex. The things Mom said that she'd blindly believed. Every sermon. The Redemption itself! Nothing was sacred. Nothing was above the need to scrape it apart, to examine every aspect until it was understood.

Suddenly, everything she'd ever learned was in question.

That's not true.

With the slightest thought, much of it was either clearly false or at least not entirely true.

You need to question everything.

Even as she rushed down the stairs, some distracted part of her quailed at the implications. It was a command, not a suggestion.

We've misunderstood Joh's talent.

Calling them suggestions undermined the truth, belittled his terrible power.

He commands.

Worse than that was the idea she'd spend the rest of her existence doubting everything. There was a comfort in faith, in knowing what your betters said was true.

She recalled an old axiom her mom once told her: Beauty is in the eyes and antennae of she who witnesses it. Truth was like that. Maybe there was some underlying reality where a truth existed, but no part of ashkaro society worked on that level. Everything was perception, reaction, and emotion.

Truth is a myth.

You need to question everything.

She wanted to scream at Joh, to rage against this terrible injustice. Those words changed everything. In that instant the bright speaking out in the field became a voice of poison.

Wex didn't have time to ponder whether the Yil bright spoke truth—whatever *truth* was. All that mattered was that she was manipulating those loyal to Queen Nysh.

Why does that matter?

If the queen entered the room and addressed Wex directly, Wex would still have to question whatever she said. That was wrong. So wrong. The queen's word was law.

It matters because they're my friends.

Were they? Some, maybe. Joh—despite how terrifying his talent was—definitely.

It matters because they're on my side.

Hive against hive. Us against them. Hatred of other.

It was sad and it was terrible, but at least it was true.

She wanted to pick the thought apart, question every detail, but didn't have time.

He told me to question everything because he can't use his talent on himself.

Jumping the last steps, she landed hard, already moving through the lobby, smashing through the front doors. The sticks felt good in her claws. Balanced. Ready. Joh followed somewhere behind her.

Wex sprinted for the field. The archers who'd descended to the ground didn't seem to notice her, but those on the skerry did. An arrow punched deep into the earth to her right, and she changed directions, ducking and dodging. A second arrow careened off her carapace leaving a long groove. More arrows fell from above, indiscriminate now as the archers loosed in panic. Someone screamed, a high-pitched note like steam escaping a clay pot. Focussed on the preaching bright, Wex saw all the best places to stab her. The bright noticed her, and the number of gaps shrank as she drew her own stab sticks from sheathes hidden behind her thorax.

Passing Des, Wex yelled, "We have to kill her!"

A single archer stood between Wex and the enemy. A dull male, he held a long bow with arrow nocked and pulled to full draw in paired craft and raptorial claws, and a ready spear in the other set. The arrowhead, stone knapped to a deadly edge, seemed to fill her vision. Dropping low as she ran, jump legs spreading wide and bending at the femorotibial joints, she saw the archer's aim dip to follow her.

A slow dumb male.

Preconception proven untrue by recent experience, that questioning segment of mind offered up.

Wex jumped, a powerful wing-assisted leap, and the arrow passed beneath her.

He was well-trained, better than Wex. He fought by instinct, no thought slowing his actions. But she was female, born to hunt, born to protect hive and queen. A few hundred generations of civilization were nothing. Killing was in her blood, writ deep in the chitin of her exoskeleton.

One main eye tracked his craft claws, the other watching the raptorial arms. Secondary eyes alert for other dangers, she saw the holes in his defences. It was a puzzle, like the intricately cut ones the brights from Brickworks #7 gave to their children. Except the correct placement of the pieces shifted as her opponent saw her attack, made his adjustments to meet her. Wex moved a claw, saw him react, saw how it changed the gaps.

I can move him where I want.

With practice, she would dance enemies like puppets, create the openings she needed instead of watching and waiting.

The dull's spear swept up in an impaling thrust. Simultaneously, a craft arm reached for the quiver to grab another arrow—likely to be used as a stabbing weapon—and a free raptorial arm swept in a scything arc.

Wex used her wings to alter the path of her descent. Even before she landed, she was switching the stab sticks to her faster craft claw to leave her raptorial arms free. Sweeping aside the arrow, she shattered his craft arm with a stab stick, at the same time deflecting his spear with her raptorial claws. With the second stab stick she penetrated his skull with a quick thrust. Jubilation lit her soul. This was what the gods wanted of her. This was why she existed. There was no questioning the euphoria. The weapon came free blue with blood, and she spun past the confused male, already moving toward the bright as his punctured brain struggled to understand what happened. He made a noise, a soft and interrogative *huh*, as she plucked the spear from his weakening grip.

Find the weakness. Kill. Give the gods a chance to show their appreciation.

Something struck Wex's abdomen as she charged the bright female. She felt an instant of sharp pain washed away by predatory focus. Stopping to nurse wounds was death. The hunt was all that mattered. Kill the threat, figure out if you'll survive later.

Wex closed the distance, four rear claws churning dirt in a burst of speed. Where she saw the male's skill, his intentions and reactions, in the female she saw only fear. This was no warrior. She faced a pampered noble, a lesser daughter who never did time in the military. Where violence lay just beneath the carapace in Wex, this noble came from a long line of courtiers. The savagery wasn't gone, just buried deeper, hidden beneath layers of civilization.

In Wex, killing lurked within easy reach.

The bright needed time to find it, to peel back the façade of culture.

Time she didn't have.

There. There's the weakness.

Wex killed her, one stab stick slamming deep into her skull, the other puncturing the bright's heart while the spear slid effortlessly through the raptorial arm joint to impale the guts.

Blessed bliss washed the last questions away.

Kill and kill and kill, said the gods. We made you to kill.

More pain. Impacts staggered Wex as she moved past the twitching corpse. The spear was lodged in the bright's carapace, trapped in the joint, and she left it behind. Stab sticks raining gore, she was ready to kill again.

Des passed Wex in a blur, impossibly fast.

More pain. Something punctured Wex's thorax, grating on her innards. She ignored it, following Des.

By the time Wex reached the bottom of the rope ladder, Des was already on the skerry, killing with mad abandon. She was a ghost, flickering moments of solidity as she slowed long enough to batter her opponent, breaking joints and leaving crippled victims, before she again blurred. Des fought without finesse, relying on her speed advantage. Even seeing the gaps in her friend's defences, Wex didn't ever want to face her as an opponent.

I'd never stab her before she killed me.

THE STORM BENEATH THE WORLD

The difference, Wex saw, was in where Des felt the lure. With each burst of action, her antennae quivered with pleasure. She gloried in the movement, not the violence, not the killing. If anything, slowing to defeat an enemy pulled her from the lure. For Wex, it was all about the moment she beat her opponent's defences, found the hole, and killed them.

Weapons clutched in her craft claws, Wex clambered up the rope with her clumsier raptorial claws. She gained the deck and discovered Des had already cleared an area. A bright male, six of his eight limbs bent at shattered joints, groaned in agony.

He's helpless.

Something in her itched with hunger. He was all gaps. She stabbed him through the skull as she moved past, her antennae straightening with a small pleasure. It was too easy to enjoy; she needed a challenge to access that incredible rush.

Another struggling ashkaro, trying to drag herself away with a broken craft arm.

Wex killed her too, following the path of Des' destruction.

Another and another, each kill bringing enough gratification to push away the pain. Or at least make it less important. The Yil ashkaro were a pathetic, ratty bunch, now that she saw them up close. They looked half-starved, many showing poorly healed wounds.

Are they all Corrupt?

Glancing over the railing, she saw the students and teachers, having shaken off the influence of the preaching Yil bright, fighting the last few grounded archers.

I should have stayed down there. I could have killed more.

The uneven fight would be over in moments. Already, several students were on their way up the rope ladder.

Drawn by the need for another taste of that beautiful bliss, Wex followed Des, killing the other student's leavings.

Why doesn't she kill them herself?

Leaving wounded enemies was sloppy.

Wex stabbed another through the heart.

Des's personality matched her talent. Always fast, she never stopped to consider her actions. She spoke the instant a thought arrived, acted on every impulse.

Maybe Joh is right, and I should lead.

Wex found a shimmering bright trying to pull herself upright and stomped on her back, pinning her to the deck.

"Please," whispered the gorgeous bright. "We had no choice. She speaks and we—"

Wex cracked her in the back of the head with a stick. Maybe the bright spoke truth, or maybe she lied. Where Wex would have once struggled with questioning such an imposing ashkaro, never mind killing one, she now had no choice but to question everything. It was possible the preaching bright held the crew in thrall and, given the opportunity, they'd leave peacefully, but it didn't matter. They were *other*, servants of another queen. The moment they set claw in Nysh's queendom they had to die.

Wex raised the stick, seeing the softest spot in the carapace of the bright's neck. She hesitated. *Why does it matter that they came from elsewhere?*

Why did that make them enemies? As long as the two islands remained safely separated, there had been trade. Mom talked about how some of the bricks from Brickworks #7 eventually made their way to the edge of the island and were transported by skerry to the distant queendom. She hadn't known why. Likely, she told her daughter with some pride, they were of a better quality than the Yil brickworks could achieve. Wex had also overheard the children of the brights who ran the factory bragging about the sweet and strange fruit imported from Yil. Such delicacies were beyond the budget of a manager like her mom. As the islands drew closer, trade increased, taking advantage of the diminishing travel time, until suddenly the islands were too close and trade all but stopped. Though what 'too close' meant and who decided what qualified as a comfortable distance, Wex had no idea.

Everyone saying the islands were enemies, that war was the only answer, didn't make it true.

Or does it?

Wex's head hurt, and she killed the bright to diminish the pain.

This was terrible. She'd been so much happier when she questioned nothing.

No, you only questioned less.

THE STORM BENEATH THE WORLD

There had been order and reason to her life. She'd *known* where she stood. The constant examination was bad, but the fact there were so rarely answers was enough to drive her insane. She would ask Joh to undo what he'd done. Surely, a simple suggestion to stop questioning would save her from the hell of knowing she would never truly *know* anything.

Pulling the stab stick free of the dead bright's skull, she flicked the clinging brain matter away.

Do I want that?

She'd been happier, but what was happiness worth when founded in ignorance at best and lies at worst?

Really? I must question if I want to be happy?

Yes.

Behind Wex, the other students gained the deck, swarming the skerry.

Someone touched her shoulder, said something that sounded concerned.

Wex turned to find Kam, black carapace gouged with superficial wounds, staring at her, antennae perked in fearful worry.

"What?" she demanded.

"You're hurt," he said.

"I'm fine."

Are you though? Stop!

Kam's antennae said that was not the case and he gestured at her thorax and abdomen. Four arrows jutted from her carapace.

"That's why it hurts," she said, oddly relieved to finally find something with an answer.

Kam opened a pouch of medical supplies, ground plants with coagulating properties, and various sized wood plugs to block wounds closed until they had time to heal. "Hold still. I'll pull them free."

When he yanked the first one out, she considered killing him to numb the pain.

No. He's a friend.

Was he?

She growled in anger and Kam cowered. Where normally such a display from a male might bring some small pleasure, now it left her uncomfortable.

How does that subservience make him *feel?*

Was it real, or feigned?

She dragged her thoughts from the male, ignoring him as he worked. *I want to be happy.* It was true, as far as it went. But happiness wasn't everything; she already knew that. *What matters more, being happy or understanding things?*

Startled, Wex realized she cared more about understanding the world than being happy. If that was the case, she'd have to be very careful what she said to Joh. Her friend could undo what he'd done in a heartbeat.

Is he my friend?

Yes, he was. Where she didn't know if Kam was, with Joh she was certain.

But why *is he my friend?*

That she could not answer.

SHAN WYN VAL NUL NYSH

For eight thousand lifetimes of ashkaro did the Queen of the Storm wait for One True Queen to be born, the one queen who would unite all islands under a single rule and bring about the final ascension. In Queen Yil Een Ahn Kyn Ah Phy-Rah did Katlipok find that queen.

Chosen of the Storm. First Daughter of the Last God.
She is the Word and the Way.
She is the Spear and the Claw.
The blasphemers will not come quietly to the truth. It is our calling to bring them and, should they refuse, banish them to the storm.

—The Sisters of the Storm

For weeks after Stev lost herself to the lure, the school was on military lockdown, the students confined to their cadre houses. An armed squad of Queen's Claw escorted them to every class, ready to kill anyone who looked like they were enjoying themselves too much. Iyik said she overheard one of the teachers mentioning that they had a Corrupt with a talent for spying who could see into the student rooms any time she wanted.

'If they catch us using our talent without orders to do so,' Iyik had told her fellow students, 'they have orders to spike us.'

And so, night after night Shan lay awake imagining sparks dancing in the air. When he did sleep, nightmares of burning Nyk Arl Zon in the school hall plagued his dreams. Over and over, he heard her horrible screams even as he craved that euphoric rush. Each morning he woke to the stink of smoke.

And then there was Ahk.

Sure, he'd noticed her right away. Gleaming raptorial claws. Bright barbs, curved for killing. She moved like water over rounded stones, smooth and liquid. All grace. Though only a three-name, she looked brighter. At first, it had been simple physical attraction, the appeal of a dangerous female.

And then she saved him. Afterwards, he couldn't stop thinking about her.

I owe her my life.

Prior to discovering his talent, he could have given her his names. That would have been ample payment for any heroism. Corrupt, he'd lost that. But now he could offer something better: Shan would fight at her side.

First, however, he'd have to find his bravery. When Stev rushed him, he'd folded to the ground and cowered. It'd be embarrassing if it wasn't the only reasonable course of action when a murderous female charged a male. Except he wasn't *just* a male anymore. He was a corrupt male with a talent for fire.

Everything had changed. He'd grown up with reasonable expectations—sprawling family estates and a good marriage—and all that was gone, shattered the instant he discovered his talent. He had known who he was supposed to be, what everyone expected of him, and none of it included bravery or danger. He didn't however know who he was now. This new life was difficult to accept. None of the arranged marriages his mother talked about would ever happen. He'd never have a family, never raise children. He was a dead end, meaningless in the grand scheme.

I might as well be a dull.

What a terrible thought! How did they do it, muddling through their obscure and unimportant lives?

By all the gods in Alatash, I am not a dull. I will not live a dull life!

Those very gods had already given him the answer. Terrible as Kaylamnel seemed at first, this was exactly what he needed. The teachers grumbled and complained that such power had been granted a male, but he'd show them all. He'd find his bravery and learn to control his talent.

THE STORM BENEATH THE WORLD

Though he still felt ill when he thought back at what he did to Nyk in the school hallway, he would master his revulsion.

Burning the queen's enemies will feel different.

They were evil and he'd be doing the queen's bidding. Terrible as it might be, he would know he was righteous.

I'll show them a male can fight.

Another month passed listening to Myosh drone on about control, suffering through what the priest called 'character building' exercises. Mostly they seemed to be about surviving discomfort and facing adversity in one form or another. Sometimes it involved missing meals or the class sitting motionless and silent. Whoever stayed still and silent the longest got everyone else's dessert. The females, inevitably twitchy, always lost and it came down to a competition between Shan and Shil Den Huh, a bright with a lustrous black carapace and all the wit of skirrak droppings. Accustomed to reading romances in the family library for hours on end—and blessed with a good memory—Shan spent the time daydreaming those stories. He always won. Knowing the value of appearing generous, he shared his desserts. Mostly with Ahk.

Though still forbidden to patronize with the other cadres, the restrictions eased. The students were allowed more free time and the escorting Queen's Claw loitered farther and farther behind. By the end of the next month no one followed the students at all, and Iyik reported hearing that the spying Corrupt had been sent away. Tensions faded and the routine fell back to whatever had previously passed as normal for a school filled with dangerous children.

When in the classroom, they learned everything there was to know about the Yil Queendom in excruciating detail. They studied street maps until he dreamed in octagonal blocks, teasingly familiar and yet unlike what he knew of Nysh City. They practiced speaking with a Yil accent, every word harsh and angular, and ate weird food imported from Yil for every meal. The new spices left Shan belching late into the night, forced to savour the foreign flavours once again.

Now that most restrictions had lifted, the teachers again explored the talents of the children under their care. Shan was given permission to make small sparks, the teachers ready to flee the instant he lost control. Sometimes they asked for specific colours, and for the most part, he was able to give them what they requested. Once they decided he wasn't going to burn the school down, they asked for larger fires, heaping kindling, and later piled logs. Though they still demanded utmost control, ready to smash him to unconsciousness if he twitched wrong, he lived for these moments of purest bliss. With every fire, no matter how much they asked for, he knew he could do so much more.

On other days, Myosh chose crueller torments for her students. She'd supply them with blunt sticks and order them to spar. Where Shan thought sparring was supposed to involve two ashkaro tapping their sticks together in a choreographed dance, the females seemed to think it meant beating him senseless. To make the exercise punishing for everyone, no one was allowed to use their talents. If Myosh suspected that someone cheated, they were banished to spend a full day in isolation. No one wanted that, instead allowing themselves to be occasionally hit rather than chance the priest's suspicion. While it meant Shan managed to land a few blows he probably otherwise never could have, he also ended each day feeling like he'd never walk again.

Ahk never complained, never seemed tempted to use her talent. She held her own against the others, finishing most fights with the fewest new dents in her carapace. Izi, who'd ruled the little hive for months, accepted Ahk's martial superiority with a good humour so thin as to be transparent. Ahk was either unaware she was upstaging the other female, or uncaring. To Shan, both possibilities were equally alluring.

'Suffering is strength,' Myosh often told the class as they lay sprawled and wheezing in the grass. 'If you can't stand a little pain'—at that point she'd invariably glare in Shan's direction—'how can you possibly resist the lure?'

It was eight kinds of stupid. Like being knocked about by a bunch of females made him any less likely to burn. If anything, after a particularly brutal day, resisting the urge to turn Izi to an empty and steaming carapace was more difficult. She didn't need luck to be a better fighter than Shan.

For months Shan watched Ahk, waiting for the chance to properly introduce himself. She socialized little and talked less, spending much of her free time staring at walls like she wanted to tear them down. She was polite to teachers and students, deferential to those who outranked her, and answered every question in curt tones, as if distracted.

When Izi shared with Shan the details of Ahk's terrible experience, he understood. Such trauma would change anyone. When Izi went into even greater detail, regaling Shan with how Ahk snuck on board a Yil skerry and murdered the entire crew, he had some altogether less wholesome feelings for the new student. Many nights he lay awake thinking about her, hating himself for falling for another dangerous female.

It rained most mornings, the teachers and students gathering in the open field to rinse the dirt from their exoskeletons. Sheened in water, glistening like a fiery rainbow, Shan caught every eye. After, he pretended to ignore the females' cajoling and focus on his lessons. Each night, the hunger to make sparks clawed at him, a constant itch he dared not scratch. When he finally slept, he dreamed of Nyk's screams as he burned her to nothing.

Each day Myosh read news reports, flown in from Nysh City, pushing the class to look for patterns and argue the deeper meaning hidden behind possible enemy actions. Military skerry went missing, all crew presumed lost. Squads of the Queen's Wing, mounted on war-tramea, spotted shapes lurking in the clouds. When they went to investigate, they found nothing. There was often news of the sudden and mysterious death of high-ranked bright females.

'Assassinations, or bad luck?' Myosh would ask.

When Izi asked if Nysh was doing the same in the Yil Queendom, the priest neglected to answer. Where everyone else seemed to assume that meant yes, to Shan she looked embarrassed that their own war efforts were less successful.

"Outside!" Myosh bellowed from the ground floor. "Everyone outside now!"

Another pleasant daydream of the terrible things Ahk might do to Shan faded. Rising from his reading hammock, he followed the other students as they trooped out the front door to find the Defiled priest awaiting them.

Shan stretched in the warming light of Alatash. The air pleasantly damp, insects flitted from flower to flower, pursued by harmlessly small rafak snakes.

"Is war inevitable?" he blurted. He'd been thinking about it a lot. At this rate, he'd fall to the lure before he had a chance to do anything that might impress Ahk. "And if it is, why are we still trading with the enemy?"

Whatever she'd called them out for momentarily forgotten, Myosh gave a weary sigh of tested patience. "It's not that simple. The Queen's Council—"

"Could Queen Nysh not overrule them?" Izi interrupted.

"Of course," agreed Myosh. "But you must remember the council is made up of all the highest-ranked and wealthiest ashkaro in the queendom. Many hold interests in companies relying on trade with Yil. While they understand that at some point that trade will cease, they want to profit until the last possible moment."

"That's insane," said Shan. "That means their counterparts on Yil are also profiting. The queen should put an end to all trade!"

The priest fluttered her wings in a shrug. "Queen Nysh is not like the old queens. She rules, but we are no longer a mindless hive. There are a dozen five-name females from royal bloodlines on the council who would dearly love to be the next queen." Seeing Shan about to ask another question, she waved him to silence with a craft claw. "All that is a distraction. Interesting, and worth pondering, but not why you're here."

The class stilled.

"Ah," said Myosh. "Now I have your attention. You'll have to forgive me, but I'm going to give you a little background first."

"I'll consider myself lucky," whispered Izi, "if she gets to the point before I die of old age."

"Or boredom," added Iyik.

Myosh ignored them. "How do the Sisters of the Storm treat the Corrupt in the Yil Queendom?"

"They throw them to the storm," said Shan, happy to know the answer.

"Correct," said Myosh. "Or at least, that's what we thought. It now looks like our spies were fed bad information."

THE STORM BENEATH THE WORLD

"Or," said Ahk, voice soft, "our spies weren't ours at all."

The priest stared at Ahk, both main eyes and antennae examining the student. "Perhaps. A few years ago, we learned that the Corrupt of Yil were not fed to the storm as we previously believed. Or at least, not all of them. Instead, they have been hiding them in secret schools and training them to work as teams."

"That sounds weirdly familiar," Shan muttered.

"Yes," agreed Myosh. "Except they've been doing it for decades. Maybe longer."

"So," said Shil, startling everyone, "while we've been banishing our talented to the desert or shipping them off to islands to die, Queen Yil treats hers like ashkaro."

Shan stared at the black carapaced male. Shil almost never spoke and was so quiet Shan often forgot he was there.

"We don't know how well they're treated," said Myosh. "They might be tortured daily."

"So just like here," Bash grumbled.

"Do we have reason to think their schools are worse than ours?" asked Shil, waving a craft claw at the lush surroundings and ancient structures. "This isn't as nice as what most of us are accustomed to," he said, "but I'd rather be here than in the desert."

"Or starving to death on a Corrupt island," added Bash. Her mandibles snapped shut when Myosh directed an antenna in her direction.

With a rare thoughtful look, Izi said, "It's better in Yil than in Nysh?" She darted a guilty glance at the priest. "At least for Corrupt."

Shan hated the thought, loathed the fact it had been spoken aloud. He expected better from a fellow five-name. Speaking ill of the queen—even obliquely—wasn't done! Suggesting Queen Nysh might have made a mistake was barely shy of blasphemy. At least in polite society.

He realized Myosh had been talking and stopped to stare expectantly at him.

"Uh…" he said. "What?"

"If you spent less time staring at your reflection in your own carapace," the priest said, "I might not have to repeat myself. I asked if you'd figured out what you're being trained for." She clearly didn't expect him to answer.

Shan pointed at Ahk. "Stealth and killing." He turned an antenna toward Izi. "Lucky enough to bend the odds in any situation." She mumbled something about not being lucky enough to bed him and he ignored her. Shan slid one main eye toward Bash. "Impossible balance. I've seen her walk on ledges no ashkaro could ever manage. Iyik's perceptions make her a perfect spy. She can listen to a conversation across a crowded hall and often does." Gesturing at Shil, he said, "I can't remember what his talent is. He never speaks."

Shil's antennae turned away in awkward embarrassment. "Seduction."

"Why do we need a male with seduction when *I'm* here?" asked Shan, shifting a little to best catch the sun.

Izi snorted a laugh. "He has a point."

"Shil was here first," said Myosh. "And pretty as you might be, seduction is *not* your talent."

Shan accepted that without comment. Anyway, she was wrong. He could bed any of the females here. Except Ahk, whom he couldn't work up the courage to talk to.

"And my talent is fire. You've kept me reined in tight, but you know how powerful I am."

"And so?" asked Myosh.

"Well, we aren't being trained for diplomatic missions," answered Shan. "You're teaching us Yil customs so we can fit in. We've all learned to passably fake a Yil accent, except for Bash, who is awful at it. We know their culture. We know their foods and their geography. We know their cities and the layout of the main streets."

"We're going to be tourists," quipped Izi.

"Look at us," said Shan, "the brightest of the brights. Well-bred and educated. All of us from the best families. We're going to infiltrate Yil society."

"And?" asked Myosh.

"And we're going to be assassins."

Killers. Shan kept his antennae expressionless as he remembered Nyk's empty carapace boiled clean. *Murderers.*

The children at Kaylamnel were being trained to be the villains in the story the ashkaro of Yil told themselves. Shil's talent, his place in the cadre, now made sense. Shan's gorgeous carapace and Shil's talent for seduction would give them access to the highest ranks of society.

We'll be the trophy males they joke about.

A shiver of anger ran through Shan. No matter how impressed the females were with his fire, he would never be anything more than another pretty male.

AHK TAY KYM

The Redemption says that Alatash, a city home to all the gods, rises from the leeward side of the island and sets on the windward side. If the river of days is infinitely long as they also claim, how did it get from windward back to leeward? Where did it go?

—Awar Dun Nih Yhir, Philosopher

Ahk hung suspended in her hammock, listening to the chirp of morning insects beyond the window. The deeper *buzz* of a rafak snake flying past in search of breakfast shivered her antennae. Soon the students would be called to the morning meal and the illusion of peace would end, replaced by lectures on the Yil Queendom and ever-stranger training programs. It felt like the teachers made it up as they went. Not once had she seen a detailed lesson plan. Kaylamnel was unlike any school she'd known. While the ancient buildings and converted homesteads gave the feel of age, there were signs the teachers and students were recent intruders. Corners clogged with dust compacted with age. Unused rooms where the air hung still and silent.

Sometimes the teachers asked Ahk to demonstrate her talent. They'd order her to disappear and then sneak up on one of them. If she managed to touch her target without being seen or sensed, she won. Careful to hide the incredible rush of joy she felt each time, she'd vanish before their eyes. For her, nothing changed. The teachers were as they had been, and yet somehow unable to look directly at her. Eyes slid off her like she'd been slicked with melted fat. Or like she was a hole in reality.

Ahk always won.

THE STORM BENEATH THE WORLD

Sometimes, they'd order her to disappear and then reappear a moment later, testing her control. Vanishing felt good. Returning to the world of judging antennae did not. She always did as instructed, but each time the desire to remain unseen grew.

Someday, she'd disappear forever.

She feared and longed for that moment. To an ashkaro, nothing was worse than being alone. Yet her talent would make her last days the most joyous time of her life. She'd die happy, locked in bliss.

Swinging in her hammock a few claw-lengths above the ground, she felt separated from everything. It was as if in coming to this strange school she'd been severed from the river of time. The island she'd known was gone, passing by just beyond reach. Her mother's murder had been a different life. She was a ghost here, forgotten.

Weeks slipped by with worrisome ease.

After visiting Grandmother Kym, the elderly matron of the family, Ahk's mother once said, 'Time devours all.'

At seventy-eight, Grandmother Kym had little to do with running the family businesses. Ahk's grandfather had passed at the ripe old age of thirty-nine some thirty years prior, and Grandmother, a self-proclaimed romantic, never remarried. Which wasn't to say that there weren't always shiny younger males about her lush estate on the windward edge of the island. 'Entertaining dalliances,' Grandmother Kym called them. 'Pretty distractions.'

Mother used to talk about her own mother in hushed tones filled with awe. Grandmother Kym was a warrior, a force not to be reckoned with but to be feared. One of the first three-name brights to build a true empire, she travelled in circles beyond the station she'd been born to. She'd met the queen, battled savage hive ashkaro on feral islands, ridden tramea out over the storm in pursuit of pirates. Ahk's mother also once told her that grandmother claimed to have seen the northern stormwall. Mother admitted, very quietly indeed, that Grandmother Kym was prone to bombast and hyperbole. Particularly when it came to exploits so far in the past no one could contradict her.

A year and a half later, Grandmother Kym was dead.
Time devours all.
She came here, fresh from her mother's murder, brimming with

rage. She'd been ready to hunt every Yil spy, stalk and kill the Mad Queen herself. The anger wasn't gone, but the months blunted it.

How long will they keep us here?

Would she still carry the hate needed to kill in another eight months?

A polite knock sounded at her bedroom door. It was too early for breakfast or classes.

"Yes?" she said, annoyed.

"It's Shan."

Ahk stifled a groan. The pretty male, self-obsessed, always posing and buffing his already gleaming carapace, constantly stole looks at her during class. Tempting as it was to send him away, he was a five-name and distant nephew of the queen. Even though Myosh said that none of the old social etiquettes mattered now, that they were all Corrupt and thus severed from family ties, it was impossible to shake generations of programming.

Disengaging herself from the webbing of her hammock, Ahk said, "Enter."

The door swung open, and Shan Wyn Val Nul Nysh slipped into her room, all four legs doing a dainty dance. Antennae bent in subservient apology, he faced her. Though lustrous and gorgeous, he somehow managed to look ruffled, wings not quite sitting right, one antenna twitching and awkward. He stared, mandibles moving, and said nothing.

Ahk dipped a polite bow as required. "How can I help you, Shan Wyn Val Nul Nysh?" she asked, careful to use his full names.

"Shan," he said. "Please just call me Shan."

She waited, both main eyes and antennae bent in his direction. Having learned from the best, she knew how to make those of higher rank feel rude and unwelcome.

"Um, I, uh…" He sank suddenly to the ground, legs folding beneath him, abject and submissive, as if awaiting punishment. "How do you do it?" he mumbled.

"It?"

"I only killed one, and it plagues me. Nightmares. Every night. I can't sleep. I keep seeing—" He shuddered. "They say you killed sixteen."

"More," she said. "I think." Ahk grunted a laugh. "Wasn't counting."

"Does it bother you?"

She thought about it for a moment. "No." *And now please go away.*

"Is it because of what they did? Because they killed—" Shan cut off, stared at the floor between them.

Ahk's head hurt, her insides felt squeezed tight. "I heard the bright you killed threatened you. Weren't you defending yourself?"

"Yes, but…" Shan gave an uncertain flutter of his upper wings. "Mother always said, 'Females will be females.' She said that any male who looked like me should expect a certain kind of attention."

Grandmother Kym said much the same, the casual dismissal of a juvenile female's tendency to brash and violent behaviour. Ahk's mother, of a different generation and slightly more comfortable with the changing social norms, would look tolerantly pained, though she never bothered trying to correct Grandmother.

Conflicted, Ahk wasn't sure what to say. The male was stunningly gorgeous and knew it. He primped and preened, constantly posing to best catch the light and show off his shimmering carapace. Anyone who intentionally drew attention to themselves, as he did, deserved some of what followed. Things had changed a lot in the last eighty years, but such cultural shifts took time. Males enjoyed more freedoms, held jobs the previous generation wouldn't have dreamed of, but they were still males. Equal in the eyes of the law hardly meant real equality. No matter how well-educated a bright male might be, they weren't as smart and had none of the natural leadership or aggression of the females.

"You were defending yourself," Ahk said, deciding to stay on safe ground. "With no chance in a physical confrontation, you had no choice but to use your talent."

Shan looked doubtful. "The Redemption says killing is wrong, yet I never saw a courtroom. All was forgiven in an instant because of how I killed Nyk." He scraped at the floor with a steering claw, not leaving a mark. "It seems unfair that I should get away with it."

Unfair?

"We're at war," said Ahk. "Fair doesn't matter. Fair doesn't win battles, and that's all that matters."

"Is it? And even if it is, should it be?"

"Ask the Mad Queen if she's worried about fair."

One of Shan's antennae bent in acceptance. "Killing those Yil spies really doesn't bother you?"

"They killed my mother."

"And so that relieves you of guilt?"

"Slap a tramea," she said, repeating her mother's words, "get stung."

Shan rose, bowed deeper than was required. "Sorry for bothering you." He seemed disappointed.

"I think," said Ahk, already regretting the decision to say more, "you haven't asked the question you came here to ask."

"We're being trained as assassins," said Shan. "They will ask me to burn our enemies as I burned Nyk. The Redemption says nothing survives the flames. Burn a body, burn the soul. It's how we used to punish murderers before we abandoned the hive and became civilized."

"Civilized." Ahk snorted. "Sometimes I wonder if that was a mistake."

Part of her longed for the mindless simplicity of warring for one's queen untroubled by doubts or questions of morality. *How can morality play a part in war?* It was ridiculous.

"Spoken like a typical female," said Shan, opening the door to leave.

"Whined about like a typical spoiled male," Ahk countered. "We are Corrupt. None of what we were matters. Not your names, not my family's businesses. The queen speaks, we obey. If she orders us to kill, we kill and thank her for giving us meaning."

"What if meaning doesn't come from a queen?" asked Shan.

He left without waiting for an answer, closing the door behind him in such a way she felt his chastising disappointment.

I will never understand males.

After breakfast Myosh called Ahk's cadre to the field.

The students gathered around their teacher. Iyik, as always, watched everything, main and secondary eyes constantly roving, antennae always in motion. Izi, who somehow yet again ended up with the largest and plumpest slug at breakfast, absently clawed at the dirt with a foreleg, still hungry and searching for grubs. Bash stood relaxed with that weirdly perfect poise she possessed. She looked ready to spring in any direction and attack. Shil and Shan stood separate from the females, a half-stride back from the main group. Lustrous black carapace hot in the morning sun, Shil watched everyone with a focussed intelligence unnerving to witness in a male. Shan, on the other claw, worked at buffing out a non-existent smudge while managing to check his face in the reflection of his own exoskeleton. Scuffed and dull, Myosh's carapace looked like she hadn't cleaned in days.

"Tell me, Izi," said the teacher, "did you use your talent at breakfast?"

"No," said Izi.

"Lies," said Myosh with a shudder of pleasure. "We're going to do something different today."

"We do something 'different' every day," grumbled Izi. "I don't know what normal means anymore."

"Today," continued Myosh, ignoring the student, "you are going on a team-building excursion."

"Excursion?" asked Shan. "We'll leave the school grounds?"

A flutter of excitement passed through the female students. No one had set claw beyond the walled compound since Stev fell to the lure.

"You're going camping," Myosh answered. "Just the six of you."

"Pardon," said Shan. "Camping? As in sleeping in the *dirt*?"

"As in sleeping in the dirt," agreed Myosh.

"Will someone bring us meals?" Shan asked.

"No." An antenna bent in his direction when he looked ready to ask another question. "You will kill your own dinner, or you will starve."

"We're going to starve," said Shan.

"You will work as a team to make your kill. The details will be left to you, depending on the circumstances. There is an important caveat."

"Let me guess," grumbled Bash, "we're not allowed to use our talents."

"Wrong," said Myosh. "You must each use your talent to contribute to the kill."

Izi snorted a laugh. "That's fantastic. Shil is going to have sexy times with a wild skirrak."

Myosh ignored her. "I will ask each of you when you return how your talent contributed. I will know if you're lying."

She's looking forward to it, Ahk realized. It hit her then how much Myosh changed in the months since Ahk's arrival. The Defiled priest had never been vain, never cared much for the appearance of her carapace. Now, however, she looked like one of those dulls who begged on the streets of Nysh City. Both antennae bending toward whoever spoke, desperate to catch the scent of even half-truths, her craft claws shook. She'd shrunk, caving in on herself.

She's succumbing to the lure.

Ahk wanted to laugh and mock, to call the teacher out for the absurdity of lessons on control when Myosh herself had failed. More than that though, she wanted to take the teacher from this place that pushed her to use her talent.

Leave the school. You'll live longer.

She wouldn't though. Out in the forests there were no lies to hear, and she craved that. Here she had purpose. She served the queen.

Remembering Shan's suggestion that there should be something more, Ahk felt an uncomfortable tremor of her own.

That'll be me some day.

She'd disappear from the world. No one would witness her slow death.

Having never seen the ravages of the lure, Ahk didn't know how long Myosh had. Would she last several more years, crumbling to nothing as she searched every word and sentence for lies?

"You may not return for three days," continued Myosh. "If at that point you are unsuccessful, you will be deemed unfit to serve the queen. If anyone tries to run away," she glanced at Shan, "you will be hunted and killed. Go." She gestured at the open gate with a craft claw. "Now."

Izi taking the lead, they left the school grounds. She slowed before pointing toward the southern forest and then heading for the trees.

"Why this way?" asked Bash, hurrying to match Izi's pace.

Izi shrugged her wings. "I find it's best not to worry too much about such things. Based on how good it felt to pick this direction, you can assume this is the lucky one." Seeing the distasteful bent of Bash's antennae, she added, "What? Myosh said we were to use our talents. You want to wander lost the whole time, or walk straight to where we're going to find easy prey?"

"I guess," answered Bash. "Still feels like cheating."

"We're *supposed* to cheat! You think they're going to send us to Yil so we can rely on our *skills*?" She gestured at Shil. "What regular skills do you have?"

"My mother planned on marrying me into some family who owned a tramea aviary on the windward edge of the island," he answered. "I can read and write and have a decent grasp of history. My hobby was poetry."

"Poetry is always useful when assassinating foreign dignitaries," said Izi. She nodded at Ahk. "We already know she's a killer, so we can leave her out. Iyik, talent aside, what skills do you bring to your new career as spy?"

"I have hundreds of hours in the saddle," said Iyik. "I was being trained to join the Queen's Wing. I can joust, am skilled with the long and short bow, and can fight with spears and stab sticks."

"I stand corrected," said Izi. "We're a team of hardened killers."

"I've never actually fought or killed anything," Iyik admitted. "It was all sparring and target practice."

"I'm sure it's exactly the same," joked Izi. "And you, Shan?"

"We're going to sleep in the dirt?" Bash said, managing a passable mimicry of Shan.

The others laughed.

"I think you underestimate how dangerous we could be as a team," said Ahk, feeling the need to come to Shan's defence, and distract the others from ganging up on the pretty male. "The real question is whether we have a leader good enough to make us a team."

Izi's wings shuffled in smug composure. "I'm too lucky to be saddled with a team I can't master."

"I hope, for our sakes, you're right," said Ahk, and she meant it.

The others agreed.

The group entered the jungle expecting to walk into effortless prey and found nothing but little rafak that fled before they got close. The first few minutes were easy going, the trees well separated, the light of Alatash shining through the foliage.

"I thought you were going to use your luck," complained Shan. "I don't want to spend the night out here."

Bash said, "Everything of any size lives deeper in the forest."

As if to make her point, a small gruesome thing with all its bones hidden away beneath meat and matted fur scrambled through the undergrowth. The students retreated with sounds of disgust.

"I read," said Shil, "that on Yil those things are considered a delicacy." He shuddered with revulsion.

"They could use them as a test," said Bash. "Put a plate of raw vertebrate in front of you," she mimed doing so with a flourish, as if at a fancy restaurant in Nysh City, "and then if you refuse to eat, they know you're a spy."

"I'd rather be brain-spiked," said Shan, "than eat one of those. Anyway, I'd choke on the fur."

"They peel it off," said Shil.

Everyone stared at him like he'd said the most insane thing imaginable until Shan blurted, "Where are the tents and cooking equipment? Where are the refreshment stations? Where are the family retainers to carry it all? This isn't camping. This is living like a filthy dull!"

"Not all dulls are filthy," Ahk said, thinking of Bon, her dull friend from home. A pang of guilt, muted and distant, folded her wings tighter. "And they're not all stupid."

Shan waved a dismissive craft claw at Ahk. "I know it's fashionable to pretend dulls and brights are equal, but it's just us here. You can drop the act."

Izi bobbed her head in agreement. "We had hundreds of dulls working our farms, and they were all dirty and stupid."

"Farming," said Ahk, "is dirty work." She locked main eyes with Izi. "Are you smart enough to know the difference between intelligence and education?"

"Yes," Izi answered, voice hard, antennae straightening in defensive anger. "Smart ashkaro get an education."

"Not all ashkaro have the same opportunities," Ahk pointed out.

Izi stood her ground. "Sure they do. Anyone who passes the

entrance exam can go to university."

"Not only are the schools expensive, but you need years of *education* to pass that exam," Ahk said. "Which is funny, because I know quite a few university graduates who are idiots."

"Those who call me stupid," growled Izi, "tend to be unlucky."

Shan spoke into the tense silence. "I graduated from the best school in Nysh City."

Izi turned a main eye in Shan's direction and snorted a laugh. "Did I just lose an argument because of you?"

Did he do that on purpose?

If he had, the pretty male was smarter than she thought. Was the stupidity an act, habit learned from bending to social expectations, or camouflage?

Shan fluttered his upper wings in a shrug. "I want to get this finished so we can get back to the school and cooked meals and comfortable beds."

Tensions dissolved, Izi looked away, studying the trees. "Fine." Antennae quivering with pleasure, she turned in a circle, stopping when she faced into the denser jungle. "This way. Iyik, let us know when you sense something. That'll be two talents used. All we'll need then is for Shil to seduce our prey while Ahk sneaks up on it, Bash does a perfectly balanced dance on its back, and Shan burns it to a pile of ash. We'll probably have to convince Myosh the ashes used to be alive."

Everyone followed Izi, pushing through the tangled vines and branches, arguing about how they could each use their talent to contribute. Ahk slowed to trail behind. Even though they ignored her, prattling among themselves, and joking that Myosh wouldn't be happy with whatever helpless creature Izi led them to, she felt the weight of eyes. Something watched them. Wild tramea were rare this far windward, preferring the drier air and easier prey to the leeward end of the island. Danger lurked in any forest. It could be a mature rafak snake flying hidden in the foliage above, or even other ashkaro. Though none ever strayed onto her family estate, she'd heard stories of roving bands of Corrupt. Usually, they weren't so much dangerous as annoying, travelling the island trying to sell their talent for a meal. Sometimes they were vagrants and thieves, bending their gods-given skill to crime and murder.

THE STORM BENEATH THE WORLD

Sharp nettles scraped carapaces and Shan grumbled. Dank mud clung to claws, and he complained about the smell. The foliage above choked out the light of the gods and the students wandered through a murky half-light. Shan moaned about when they would pause for the first meal break.

Iyik held up a closed claw, signalling a halt. Head lifted, she tested the air, antennae searching.

"See," said Izi. "I told you I'd lead you to something quick."

Iyik's upper wings fluttered in annoyance. "I smell rafak. More than one, I think."

"A nest?" Shan asked.

Grown Rafak were solitary creatures, not given to hunting in groups.

Crushing the hunger down deep, Ahk hissed at the others. "Something is wrong." She wanted to vanish, to hide.

Izi studied the thick forest with main eyes and antennae. "I neither see nor smell anything."

"We're being watched." No, that wasn't quite right. "We're being hunted."

Izi's antennae gave a small quiver of bliss. "I'm too lucky to get hurt, and I sense nothing. We have to trust our talents."

Two long, barbed arrows punched into Izi's carapace, lodging deep in her thorax. All four legs buckling, she crumpled.

THE STORM BENEATH THE WORLD

JOH

Reports of the decreasing distance between the Nysh and Yil queendoms have proven correct. Current estimates suggest that, unless they change direction and pass each other by, the islands will meet within the year.

—Senior Officer Bhen Szie Kul Ahj, Queen's Wing

By the time Joh made it onto the training field, it was all over. Students and teachers wandered the grounds, looking lost and confused. Some, better able to pull themselves together, saw to the wounded. Several lay motionless, limbs splayed in the dirt. In some cases, the arrows jutting from their exoskeletons made it clear what happened. Others leaked blue from cracked carapaces, skulls and limbs broken. A few looked unhurt yet were clearly dead, motionless in a way alien to living ashkaro. Littered among the fallen were Yil spies and warriors. Beneath the haggard skerry floating over the field lay the shattered ruin of more corpses. For a heartbeat, he couldn't understand what could have done such damage. Then, looking up at the skerry above and seeing Wex at the rail looking down, he understood. Ashkaro wings might assist a jump, or slow a short fall, but beyond a certain height the fragile wings tore and broke. Too heavy for flight, limbs slim and built for speed, ashkaro landed poorly.

Judging from the torn carapaces and splintered shells, these hadn't stood a chance.

Did they jump or were they thrown?

Above, Wex turned from the rail and limped out of sight. Kam followed, posture bent and subservient as he fussed over her wounds and was ignored.

What do we do now?

Something was gone. Missing. Stolen.

Purpose?

Somehow, the Yil spy and her talent for oratory—he didn't know what else to call it—had taken that. While the Mad Queen's followers killed many, that Corrupt's speech did the real damage.

A Corrupt with corrupting words.

The floating skerry, hanging tentacles gripping trees at the edge of the forest and latching onto nearby structures, began to lose height. Joh watched its graceful descent. Wex must have been guiding it down. She alone still moved with purpose.

If she has purpose, so do I.

"Joh."

Eyes and antennae focussed on the skerry above, Joh flinched in surprise. Rel stood beside him, a craft arm hanging loose. Carapace dented and gouged, the old dull priest looked like he'd been through a battle.

He's tougher than he looks.

"Your talent is sniffing out the Corrupt," Joh said. It came out sounding like an accusation. Maybe it was.

Rel, staring up at the skerry, said nothing.

"You check regularly. You can't help but use your talent."

Nodding, Rel said, "Once a day." He glanced at Joh, antennae bending away in shame. "On the days when I'm strong enough to resist doing it more."

The confession felt like a betrayal. The old priest's talk of resisting the lure was worthless garbage.

Joh set aside his anger. It was a pale and weak thing anyway, worth nothing. "What is the range of your talent?" The mystery was a better distraction than raging at a teacher.

"I can sense the Corrupt who are a day or more distant."

"Then you should have sensed them coming," said Joh. "Why didn't you?"

Rel shrugged, helpless. "Maybe they had a Corrupt capable of blocking my talent. I've heard of that."

Joh thought through the implications. "That would mean they not only knew where the school was, but also the talents of at least some of the teachers."

Still gazing at the skerry, antennae listless, Rel said, "The school is a secret."

"Not a very good one. You rode around in your wagon collecting Corrupt children. You weren't particularly secretive. In the months we've been here, I've seen regular deliveries of supplies. It was different ashkaro every time, low caste brights, and the occasional dull. They know where the school is and have some idea what happens here. How many of your superiors know about the school?"

A twitch in Rel's antennae said it was a lot.

"So," said Joh, "it's not a secret. Likewise, the enemy will soon know they failed."

Enemy. The word used so often to describe Yil suddenly felt wrong. Were they really the enemy, or had there been some truth to the orator's poisonous words? If turning the students of Amphazar against Queen Nysh had been the goal, Joh wasn't sure they'd failed.

"We might be in danger," he added.

Though whether that peril lay in more spies and assassins, or from the students and teachers, he wasn't sure. How would Queen Nysh react if she heard her school of dull Corrupt might have been turned by the enemy? Knowing how powerful some of the students were, she might decide to rid herself of a possible threat. He doubted Nysh would bother banishing them to the desert or some distant island.

Rel pulled his attention from the skerry. "Where is Fel Shyn? She'll know what to do."

Joh studied the field until he spotted Fel's sun-faded yellow carapace, arrows jutting from it in all directions. Her skill in combat must have drawn their attention. For all her ability to predict an opponent's moves, she couldn't know what everyone everywhere planned and had been vulnerable to arrows from above.

"She's dead."

"Oh." Rel looked toward the headmistress' house, hesitating. "Then we'll have to see Headmistress Raht Shram Vrn Nyst."

While Joh agreed, he felt a pang of anger at handing the

responsibility for deciding his fate to a bright, no matter how terrifying she might be.

"Come with me." Rel set out.

Joh hurried to catch up with the larger male.

They found the door to Headmistress Raht's home splintered and laying on the front step.

Rel slowed, glancing back over his shoulder toward the distant field. "Do you have a weapon?"

"I wouldn't know what to do with one if I did."

"Kratosh!" swore the priest. "Stay behind me."

"Should we get Wex?" Joh asked.

"No time. Raht might be in danger."

"Then we'll *definitely* be in danger."

Grabbing a handy chunk of broken door, Rel crouched, shuffling forward.

Joh followed more slowly. *Should I suggest we wait?*

The priest was distracted, might not notice. On the other hand, eventually, someone would have to enter the house. And if they found the headmistress dead, Rel would remember Joh telling him to wait.

"Maybe," Joh began.

One main eye turned in his direction.

"Maybe I should find a weapon too," Joh finished. Selecting a spike of wood, he added, "Ready."

Rel grunted something that may have been doubt and entered Raht's home.

Inside, they found a scene of violence and ruin. Smashed furniture littered the floor. A dead bright Joh had never seen before lay in one corner with a broken broom handle crammed halfway through her skull. In the second room, a long hall with a massive table capable of seating eight, they discovered another corpse. Headmistress Raht lay upon the table, vacant eyes staring at the ceiling, antennae limp, joints smashed, legs bent at terrible angles. Judging from the amount of blue blood pooled around her, she must have bled to death. Her wings had been torn off, fire-hardened wood spikes driven through each splayed limb, pinning her. Someone had carefully sawed her thorax open, exposing her insides. Wet and glistening green. Gleaming tubes of yellow. A rainbow of organs, inert and cold.

Even her insides are bright.

Pulling his attention from the body, Joh forced himself to look elsewhere. Everything, the floor and walls, the beams above, was splashed blue. Bloody claw prints cut winding paths.

"They didn't just kill her," said Rel. "They tortured her."

Only half listening, Joh traced the footprints, turning to see where they left the room, heading back into the house.

"Why?" asked the priest, voice cracking. "Why would someone do this?"

Joh followed the bloody trail into the main foyer. He said, "They questioned her," over his shoulder.

"Why? They already found the school," said Rel, joining him.

"Is there something only Raht might know?"

He saw it then. It was so obvious he hated himself for not seeing it sooner. Amphazar was a school of Corrupt dulls hidden in the leeward desert. But no matter what everyone might pretend, the Corruption struck everyone equally. There were as many Corrupt brights as dulls. He had the dim memory of Rel mentioning it just after they found Wex but couldn't remember details.

"Did Mistress Raht know where the bright school is?" Joh asked.

Rel cursed. "Yes. It's in the forests south of Nysh City. I accidentally found it when searching for students." He turned one main eye on the dead bright. "Raht was as tough an ashkaro as I ever met. I bet she didn't tell them."

"She didn't," said a female bright standing at the main entrance.

At least Joh thought she was a bright. She was so splashed in blood it was difficult to be sure. Beneath the gore, he saw strange vestments, unlike anything the Redemption wore. An embroidered badge of intricate detail depicted the roiling storm beneath the world.

She's a Sister of the Storm.

The Mad Queen Yil's elite wing, the Sisters were creatures of myth and nightmare. In the Redemption temple back home, he'd heard stories of how they broke sinners and Corrupt alike, dragging them to the edge of the world to be thrown to Kratosh. They were Yil's sharp claw of the law, assassins lurking in the shadows.

Holding two vicious stab sticks, the female blocked the door. "But you," she said to Rel, "will tell me what I need to know." In one raptorial claw she clutched a length of rope trailing out of sight around the corner.

She was outside when we came in. She could have escaped but came back.

She must desperately need the location of the other school.

Her wings fluttered in anticipation, and he recognized that desire.

"Your talent is torture," said Joh.

"Pain," she said. "My talent is pain." She slid into the room, graceful and deadly, a trained warrior. "There's a difference."

"Perhaps," said Joh, "you should hurt yourself."

She slowed, antennae quivering with need.

"I think," he added, "that you should keep hurting yourself until I tell you to stop."

Eyes and antennae following Joh, she gave the rope a tug. A stunted and bent male, carapace hideously misshapen, craft and raptorial claws bound closed, shuffled into view. His eyes wandered in different directions, unable to focus on any one thing. Antennae drooping in listless languor, he seemed unaware of his surroundings.

She ignored my suggestion!

Frozen in fear, Joh watched as the sad thing scraped at an arm with a bound claw as if trying to pry himself open.

The bright stepped into the headmistress' home with a menacing glide. The pathetic male followed like a trained pet.

"My little Beq here is all but lost to the Corruption," she said, "unable to stop using his talent." One secondary eye turned in Beq's direction. "I have to feed and bathe him so he doesn't stink too much, but he clings to life."

"He blocks talents," Joh said. "That's how you got here without Rel sensing you."

It was also how she ignored his suggestion.

Staying between Joh and the door, she moved closer. Rel and Joh retreated, backing into the room where Raht lay dissected on the table.

The blood-spattered female's antennae shivered in anticipation. "Beq doesn't have much range," she said. "If I need to hurt someone," her mandibles snapped and clacked like she meant to eat them, "I send him to the next room."

THE STORM BENEATH THE WORLD

Joh's thoughts raced. Wex was still up in the skerry. Everyone else wandered the field in dazed confusion. No one would come to their rescue. This bloody Yil bright would kill them both. She'd take her time, as she had with Headmistress Raht. She'd carve them. Saw their carapaces open, poke and prod. If pain was her talent, she would inflict horrendous agonies upon them. Later, Wex would find him, spiked to a chair, organs spilling about his legs.

We must do this on our own.

He knew exactly how it would happen: she'd incapacitate them, render Joh incapable of speech, and then send her pet from the room.

Two unarmed and untrained males against a Sister of the Storm. They didn't stand a chance.

Unless we kill Beq.

"We have one chance," Joh whispered to Rel.

"I know," the priest answered. "Be quick."

Rel screamed and launched himself at the Sister. For an instant, Joh hesitated, having thought that he would distract the bright while the older Rel dealt with Beq. This, he realized, made more sense; the moment the Corrupt male was incapacitated, Joh could use his talent to stop the female. If he attacked her himself, she might kill him before he had a chance to be useful.

The Sister, however, did not hesitate. Releasing the rope, she caught Rel in her raptorial claws, holding him helpless. She reared back, balancing on her rearmost legs, and struck with her forelegs. The damage was terrible. Long gashes appeared in the priest's carapace, dark blue blood gushing. And still, she held him, using her craft claws to grip his raptorial arms and pull them wide, leaving him exposed and helpless.

Don't watch you idiot!

Never having been in a fight, Joh had no idea how to hurt someone. Killing was unimaginable. Should he run for help? No. Rel wouldn't last that long.

Forelegs braced against the priest's thorax, the claws of her powerful jump legs digging deep into the wood floor for purchase, the Sister pulled one of Rel's craft arms off. He screamed as it came free, a retched squeal of agony. She didn't need her talent to cause terrible pain. Rel clawed at her with his remaining craft arm, weak and ineffectual.

THE STORM BENEATH THE WORLD

Move!

Joh forced his attention from the horror. He needed a weapon. Anything.

Raht, spiked to the table! Grabbing the nearest wood spike, he tried to pull it free. His claws slipped on the blood-wet wood. Behind him, Rel wailed again, a pitiful sob of terror.

The spike hadn't so much as budged. Giving up, Joh snatched the nearest chair, a thing of carved beauty and fibrous webbing, and turned back in time to see the Sister club Rel with his own arm while simultaneously driving two stab sticks deep into his thorax. Held helpless, Rel sagged in her grip.

Not dead, Joh prayed as he scrambled, claws skidding on the blood-slicked floor, to get past the Sister. With typical female alertness, one main eye and an antenna followed him. She moved, blindingly fast, and Rel's arm hit Joh in the face, blood splashing his mandibles. He staggered, stunned by the impact.

Rel, weakening quickly, tangled his limbs around the female. He made no attempt to defend himself, grappling desperately to trap her legs. Over and over, she drove stab sticks into his body, snapping the joints of his arms backward, and trying to peel him off.

Joh ducked past the two and hurled himself at the dull male, knocking him to the ground. Clutching the chair in four claws he raised it over his head. The dull stared vacantly past him, made no attempt to defend himself.

He's helpless.

This was wrong. The Redemption said it was a sin to strike the weak, that it was the holy calling of the strong to protect those incapable of protecting themselves. Everything he'd ever been taught screamed at him to stop this violence. Behind him, Rel fell. It sounded like a bag of damp slugs thrown to the ground.

In that heartbeat instant Joh knew right and wrong were, at best, myths, at worst terrible lies. The Redemption called murder a sin while teaching females to kill. They preached peace and obedience to the dulls while training assassins in hidden schools.

Control.

It was all control.

THE STORM BENEATH THE WORLD

"If you kill Beq," said the Sister from behind Joh, "I will be freed to show you pain unimaginable."

Ashkaro Female and Male

WEX JEL

But if you obey her voice and do all that she says, then she will be an enemy to your enemies and an adversary to your adversaries.

—Sisters of the Storm

With the Yil Skerry brought low enough it could be safely moored, and Des staying behind to search for clues as to their mission, Wex retreated down the rope ladder and back to the training field. She left behind a scene caught somewhere between peace, and nightmare. Corpses littered the deck, each with a neat hole somewhere critical. Only a few bled, having died almost instantly. The school grounds were worse. Teachers and students lay dead, punctured by viciously barbed arrows rained down from above. Fel Shyn must have drawn a great deal of attention, avoiding the arrows until enough Yil archers focussed on her that she couldn't predict them all. Though three thick-shafted arrows pinned her to the ground, the grass around her looked like a prickly shrubbery with all the near-misses.

Sudden fear thrummed through Wex. She stopped, surveying the field of dead and wounded.

Oh gods, no. Where is he?

She couldn't see Joh anywhere.

Did he follow me, or stay back in the student barracks?

She wasn't sure. Driven by the realization of what she must do, she'd acted without thought. Slow and weak, Joh would never survive such violence. Picking her way through the dead, heading back toward the barracks, she spotted familiar carapaces. Zyr's matte greenish brown showed from beneath the bulk of a larger female. Both were dead, the archer's skull smashed with a heavy club. Kris Kork, the mimic, sat hunched and silent, his exoskeleton a slurred storm-cloud of emotion, sometimes the blue-black of old blood, sometimes showing flickers of fiery rage. He looked unhurt.

Wex felt a pang of sadness and regret. Gentle creatures, males weren't built for such horrors. Much as she understood the queen's reasons, trying to train them as assassins was a mistake. War should be left to the warriors, those born with conflict writ deep in their blood.

How did he survive?

His talent, of course. Kris would have constantly shifted his appearance depending on who was near, friend or foe. No doubt that shame was part of what now bent him.

Turning away, leaving the broken male to his grief, Wex saw big Bin's muscular body. If anything, he was proof she was right. Massive and strong as he was, a single female had killed him. Bin had been systematically dismantled with great skill, joints shattered, soft spots punctured. The ashkaro who killed him lay dead at his side, stabbed from behind, likely by another female.

Wex reached the edge of the field. She hadn't seen either Joh or Rel. She prayed the two had hidden somewhere safe. There were no bodies here, the hard dirt paths the teachers and students followed each day looking as they always did. Wex stopped, antennae craning in every direction as she searched for sign of her friend. About to call out that it was safe, she saw the shattered remains of Headmistress Raht Shram Yrn Nyst's door lying crooked on the front step.

Stab sticks clutched in craft claws, Wex sprinted to the headmistress' home. One main eye watched the windows of the second floor, alert for archers. The other studied the doorway. Her antennae tested the air for unfamiliar scents, any sign an unknown ashkaro hid behind the next corner.

Fresh blood.

A lot of fresh blood.

Up the steps to the entrance, legs tensed and ready to leap in any direction if someone waited within. Beyond the gaping entrance, darkness. The stench of blood was stronger here, sharp and biting.

Wex slid into the headmistress's home, weapons ready for

violence.

And stopped.

So much blood. Horrendous carnage beyond anything she'd seen on the field.

A crooked and runty male she didn't recognize lay on the floor, the lower half of his face crushed in. Mandibles a blue ruin, he stared sightlessly at the ceiling, antennae limp. A broken chair lay beside him, one leg dripping gore.

Movement!

Wex flinched, crouching to make a smaller target, and froze.

A female crouched on the ground, legs bent beneath her. Painted in blood, her carapace was cracked and open, internal organs writhing and pulsing within, slippery purple, yellow and green snakes gurgling and slurping. Someone had methodically broken both her raptorial arms and claws at every joint. They hung useless. Her secondary eyes were gone, clawed out. Leaning back as she was, both main eyes focussed on her own splayed innards. With one craft claw she sawed at choice organs, careful not to cause enough damage she'd bleed out quickly. The other craft claw snipped her remaining antenna off, the tiniest bit each time.

Snip.

A shiver of orgasmic pleasure and unimaginable agony.

Snip.

A soft sigh of bliss undercut by a whimper of pain.

Snip.

Joh stood before the female, watching her hurt herself.

He's alive! She wanted to scream her thanks to the gods.

Her little Joh was alive! She'd been so worried she'd shied from contemplating what would happen if she found him otherwise.

Snip.

Though bleeding from a few minor wounds, he seemed unhurt.

Snip.

"Joh?"

He didn't react.

Snip.

Stepping closer, Wex saw into Headmistress Raht's dining room. The elderly bright lay splayed on the massive table. Like the female still torturing herself, she'd been sawed open, carapace splayed wide. Unlike the Yil female, she was very dead. Rel lay crumpled on the floor before the table. His craft arms had been pulled off and tossed aside. Two stab sticks stuck from deep in his carapace.

Snip.

"Joh?" Wex repeated.

One eye moved to focus on Wex. The other remained locked on the grizzly scene.

"What happened?" Wex asked, voice gentle.

"I suggested she hurt herself. Since that was her talent—and maybe what she wanted—she did."

Snip.

Wex glanced at the female. "A Yil assassin?"

Joh nodded. "They came to find out where the other school is."

She remembered Rel mentioning something about a school in the windward forest. That could wait. Too many questions wrestled for dominance. Was Joh's talent so powerful he could suggest to someone that they kill themselves? He might be the most terrifying weapon in Queen Nysh's arsenal. Send him to Yil, let him walk the streets suggesting the locals rebel against their queen. He could turn armies. Convincing as she was, the bright orator out on the field was nothing compared to little Joh.

"They know," he said. "They know everything."

"They?"

"The Mad Queen. The Sisters of the Storm." He laughed, a sick and cracked sound, and made a weak gesture in Rel's direction with a craft claw. "They not only knew exactly where our school was, but also his talent. That bright speaking in the field was right: we've already lost."

"They don't know everything. They didn't know about you. They didn't know about me. We haven't already lost because we're still alive."

Snip.

Wex gestured at the Sister torturing herself. "We *won*. If anything, they made a mistake in coming here."

Something changed in the set of Joh's wings. He bent an antenna toward the male with the crushed face. "His talent was blocking other's talents. I've never heard of that. It must be incredibly rare."

"They spent him and lost," Wex agreed.

"That orator was dangerous."

"She's dead. Her talent was nothing compared to yours."

All attention on Wex, Main and secondary eyes. Both antennae reaching toward her like he offered himself. "We were lucky this time, but you're right. We can win."

A couple of months ago she wouldn't have looked twice at this undersized dull. Now, there was something about him she couldn't understand. He haunted her dreams. After killing the invaders, his safety had been her first thought and her only concern. Seeing Fel and Bin dead hadn't touched her. Even Rel's corpse—and she'd liked the old priest—failed to bother her. Finding Joh alive had filled her with indescribable joy. Had the gods of Alatash come down from their glowing city to proclaim her the saviour of all ashkaro, she wouldn't have been happier.

"Together," she said.

Joh shook with contained emotion. "Together."

Snip.

Wex stepped past her friend and spiked the female's brain. Tremors ran through the sundered body as the soul fled.

Turning back to Joh, she said, "They might return. They may have even sent more than one cadre in case the first failed."

"Because we're dulls and can't amount to anything," Joh said, "they're more interested in the other school. Rel mentioned it was in the forests south of Nysh City."

Forests and jungles. Towering trees soaring into the sky. Lush foliage and gloriously damp air. Wex had seen illustrations in old and faded books, but never anything taller than a johak tree. With its eight streets and clumped homes—brights on the windward side of the factory, the dulls downwind—Brickworks #7 had seemed like a seething metropolis compared to the neighbouring towns. Nysh City, home to near a quarter of a million ashkaro, was unimaginable. Mom used to tell her stories about how some of the bricks they made ended up in the queen's palace. The memory stung. More than anything she wanted to go home, go back to the simplicity of life as a shift manager's daughter.

I'd give anything to hear Mom's voice again.

"We have to go there," Joh continued. "We have to warn them."

They couldn't stay here in Amphazar, that much she knew. The other school, on the windward side, would be populated by brights. The teachers would be four and five-name citizens, many with military experience.

They'll know what to do.

While the dulls of Amphazar might not be welcomed there, at least they were of the same queendom. In the end, nothing else mattered.

"Do you know where the school is?" Wex asked.

Joh winced. "I know the vicinity." He held up a craft claw, stalling her. "But we can find it. I have a plan."

Fondness for the little male flooded her. Shocked as he was by what he witnessed, he was already recovering. *He's tougher than he looks.* Which was good. He'd need to be very tough indeed to survive what was to come. And she very much wanted him to live.

Joh looked toward the front entrance. "How is Kris Kork?"

"Alive."

"Good. He's going to pretend to be Headmistress Raht."

Wex saw it immediately. A four-name bright holding military rank, any question she asked would be answered immediately. With the headmistress and Rel both dead, there would be no one to stop them. Any teacher who tried to get in their way could be persuaded by Joh that this was the best course of action.

"Do you think Kris can manage that?"

Joh gave an embarrassed flutter of wings. "I have no doubt he can."

Wex laughed. "He's been practicing?"

Again, that shrug of wings, this time a little guilty. "I asked him to. Seemed prudent."

"Who else?"

"What do you mean?"

"Who else can Kris mimic?"

"Everyone. Though he's better at some than others. Honestly, his Raht isn't great because he couldn't spend enough time with her to master the finer details of her body language. On the other claw, no one spent much time with her. I doubt we'll run into anyone who knows her well enough to catch the deception."

"You had him copy me?"

"Of course. I asked him to watch me too, in case something happened, and I died. I'm not important, but you never know." An antenna twitched in morbid humour. "He was really good at being me. It was kind of upsetting. As if all I am is rote responses to stimuli."

Joh wasn't bad at mimicry himself. He sounded a lot like the teachers. "Why?" Wex asked. "What were you planning?"

"Planning?" he asked, startled. "I'm trying to plan for everything. They're training us to be spies and assassins, but they're not particularly good at it."

He's right.

Few of the teachers were real teachers, and she was certain none of them were experienced assassins or spies. It seemed obvious in hindsight, but how had Joh reached that conclusion first?

He's smart for a male.

She considered the statement, questioning her assumptions. If he figured something out before a female, then maybe he wasn't smart 'for a male.' *He's smart.* That statement felt more accurate and made her feel good. No doubt, his intelligence played a big part in why they were friends.

Maybe smarter than me.

Or perhaps smarter than she had been before he suggested she question everything. Did that make sense? Was asking questions all that separated the intelligent from the stupid?

She realized that Joh must have put this together, deciding to use Kris to get them out of the school, in the time between fighting the Yil bright and Wex's arrival. When she first entered, he hadn't been staring in horrified shock at the scene of bloody violence, he'd been planning.

"Do you think the teachers at the bright school will be better?" she asked.

"They can't be worse." He hesitated. Then, "I suggested the assassin," he bent an antenna toward the dead ashkaro who'd been clipping her own antennae, "answer a few questions while she hurt herself. I had to know more about the Mad Queen. I needed to know if she was everything that orator claimed. She told me that Queen Yil's talent is commanding islands. She said Yil visited the neighbouring islands and gave them orders. The smaller ones move faster than the big. They were sent ahead and now circle Nysh. Some are above us, hidden in the clouds. Others are far enough away we can't see them. She put soldiers on them too."

Even a small island could support thousands of ashkaro.

With no choice but to question every possibility, Wex clawed at the problem. "The Yil queendom is leeward of us. Queen Nysh will move most of her troops to that side of the islands once they're close enough. Then, Yil's soldiers will attack from the far side."

Panic tightened Wex's chest. No one had said anything about Queen Yil having already conquered other islands. If it was only a couple of small farm islands, perhaps it wouldn't be a big deal. If she'd already conquered an island the size of Nysh, she might have killed their queen. The survivors would have sworn loyalty and made Yil their queen on the spot. How could you fight something like that?

There was only one answer: "We have to kill Queen Yil."

In the days of hive, the outcome of a queen's death depended on the circumstances. A queen taken by illness or age, or who fell to a challenger within her hive, would be quickly replaced. But when a queen died during war with another hive, the survivors scattered. Many would join the victorious hive. Others wandered lost until they stumbled across another hive or starved. Much as things had changed, basic ashkaro nature had not.

If Mad Queen Yil died with the two islands separated by months of travel, she'd be replaced by one of the high-caste bright females in her own court. The islands would hopefully return to their natural behaviour, likely once again drifting apart. But if Yil fell with Queen Nysh nearby, her subjects would beg to join the victorious queen.

By all the gods of Alatash! It would be safest to kill the Mad Queen while the two islands were still far apart. On the other claw, if they waited until they were closer, Queen Nysh would end up ruling both.

That can wait, Wex decided. The decision was too important for a dull and, with Raht dead, there was no one left with any real authority.

"Tell me what we should do," she said, stunned to be asking a one-name male for direction.

"We need to save the island. I think that means finding the bright school."

The answer was too fast, too simple. But it was his answer.

"We already have a skerry we can use," she said.

Joh inched tentatively closer, an antenna reaching out to caress hers, the softest, most daring touch. "Perfect."

A new thrill shivered Wex's wings. She was going to do what few leeward-born dulls could dream of. She'd see the windward forests. Maybe they'd even visit Nysh City! Joh would be with her all the way. She'd protect him, and he'd do what he could to support her.

At the least, they'd report what Joh learned. If the bright school was also training Corrupts, maybe she and Joh would complete their training there. If there was more she could do to serve the queen, she wanted the chance. Joh would follow her, of course, and it would be dangerous, but saving the queendom was more important than any one life.

Is that true?

She thought it over and realized she couldn't find an easy answer. In the end, time robbed everything of meaning. Queens came and went. She knew enough history to understand Nysh wasn't the first and wouldn't be the last. Many generations ago there'd been thousands of hives on this island alone. Even civilizations rose and fell, the oldest buildings in this run-down school were testaments to impermanence. In the end, everything and everyone died. If that was true, how could it matter if one queen triumphed over another? In a few hundred years, both would be gone anyway.

If nothing I do matters, why do anything?

Because doing nothing wasn't in her blood.

She could take Joh and a few others and flee the island and the war to come. They had a skerry, could go anywhere. Maybe they'd find another queendom or a small island where there was no leeward desert.

If nothing matters, why not fly to Yil?

If half of what she'd heard was true, they'd be accepted there and not considered outcasts as they were here, at home.

Wex laughed. "Asking questions isn't the same as knowing answers."

Joh gave her an odd and confused look, one antenna bending.

THE STORM BENEATH THE WORLD

I was wrong!

Time didn't rob everything of meaning. There was still now, and now meant something. It had to. She'd been thinking on too large a scale. Time only robbed the big things—queens and civilizations—of significance. Now was always about the small things. The next meal. Friends and family.

Joh.

Queen Nysh didn't matter because she was too big. She was a nebulous idea with no impact on the moment. But Joh was right now. He mattered.

Joh was the only thing that mattered in a pointless existence.

THE STORM BENEATH THE WORLD

SHAN WYN VAL NUL NYSH

For the most part all islands travel leeward, driven by the winds. Having tracked several smaller islands, I can definitively say they have some control over their north/south position. They are also capable of reducing speed if they choose.

Generally, smaller islands travel faster than larger islands, presumably because the winds move them more easily. They're also more capable of altering their north/south position and steering. Looking at the historical records, it's clear that smaller islands often overtake the larger, slower islands. If the smaller island is populated—and most are—there often ensues a brief period of trade. More rarely we see short and brutal wars as one attempts to conquer or pillage the other. Several of the farm islands currently trailing along behind Nysh were once entirely separate micro-queendoms.

Occasionally these cays are populated by unfortunate castaways from islands far back along the river of days. There are ancient reports of ashkaro with radically different cultures and languages.

—Gmar Klor Ihns, Court Cartographer to Queen Nysh

Sprawled in an ungainly heap of limbs, tangled in the mad riot of vines, Izi bent an antenna to touch an arrow jutting from her thorax. A shudder of pain ran through her. "That was…" Her mandibles clacked, wings fluttering weakly. "That was unlucky."

Shan stared, frozen in place. With no idea where the arrow came from, he didn't know which way to run.

Someone yelled, "Get down!"

THE STORM BENEATH THE WORLD

Shan spun in time to see the others scatter, diving behind trees and into bushes. Ahk was gone like she'd never been there.

"Where should I—"

Something knocked him down, smashing him into the muck, and then Ahk was on top of him, face pressed close to his. Her eyes glossy, antennae shivering in the throes of bliss. It was a look he'd hoped to someday put there himself. On the one claw, his heart soared at the realization she felt this depth of emotion for him. On the other, her timing was abysmal. Mom always warned him that females only had one thing on their mind when it came to males like him, but he'd never really believed it.

Pinning him down, Ahk leaned into the embrace until their antennae entwined.

"Maybe this isn't the right time for—"

"Shut up," she hissed. "I'm hiding us both."

Oh. His heart fell. The quiver in her antennae wasn't for him at all. She was using her talent. *She can hide me, too?* His desire not to be pierced by arrows outweighed his curiosity and he kept silent.

Crouched low, clutching two spears in a cross-handed grip, Iyik slipped from the foliage. She turned a main eye on Shan, staring directly at him. Though he doubted she saw him and Ahk in this undignified position, her talent being perception, she no doubt knew where they were.

"We have to run," she whispered.

Bash, hiding behind a tree, shook her head. "Can't leave Izi."

Iyik retreated a few skittering steps, looking like she was about to flee. "This is bad."

Three mature rafak flew from the knotted chaos of hanging creepers with a sinuous grace that left Shan's stomach turning. Less disgusting than the furry rodents, they were still vertebrates, their verdant reptilian scales gleaming. The snakes spread out, wings needing space in the crush of thick forest. They looked like the Queen's Wing flying their tramea in a wedge shape over the yearly parades celebrating Nysh's coronation. Though not quite large enough to carry off a full grown ashkaro, these were adult specimen; their sting would cause paralysis lasting hours. Maybe even kill.

THE STORM BENEATH THE WORLD

"They don't hunt in groups," Shan blurted, echoing his earlier thought. Which, in hindsight, was stupid because they were flying in a perfect formation.

Still on top of him and all too distracting, shivers of orgasmic pleasure ran through Ahk's body as she hid them.

Does her talent hide sound?

The flying snakes focussed on Bash and Iyik. Shil, hidden in the bushes, screamed once and went silent. Izi lay still, leaking blood. Shan prayed she played dead and worried she wasn't playing.

The rafak broke formation, one darting directly over Shan and Ahk. They spread out, circling around behind where Bash and Iyik hid. The largest of the three lunged toward Bash, jaw wide, its folding fangs dropping into place. Rearing back its upper body, the barbed tail darted underneath, stabbing. Fleeing, Bash leapt away. The instant she was clear of the tree, a thick-shafted arrow punched through her skull. She folded, collapsing in a loose heap of limbs.

They're using the rafak to flush us from cover!

Ahk's antenna stroked his and he struggled to ignore her. He had to think! The other two snakes went after Iyik. In a moment she'd have to choose between facing two grown and deadly rafak—and likely being paralyzed and helpless—or leaving cover and risking death.

Two arrows had hit Izi at the same time, but only one struck Bash. There was a second archer somewhere. Probably manoeuvring for a better angle on Iyik.

Ahk's antennae tangled with his and forcefully dragged his head closer to hers. At any other time, it would have been incredibly erotic. Now, it was a distraction he didn't need. He had to do something, but not something stupid. Not something likely to get him killed.

"Use your talent," Ahk whispered, face pressed against his. "Burn the snakes."

Burn.

Finally.

A chance to show what he was capable of. A chance to impress this terrifyingly deadly female. A chance to show everyone they were wrong about him.

And he hesitated.

"Before they kill Iyik!" Ahk growled.

But he didn't know where the archers were, and the moment he loosed the fire, they'd know exactly where he was. No way Ahk's talent could hide that. Saving his fellow student would expose him to attack!

"Wait," he whispered to Ahk. "Wait!"

The rafak which had gone after Bash, beating wings rippling in the dappled light from above, spun to face Shan. A squishy forked slither of wet muscle slipped from its mouth, testing the air. Long ago, in another life, his private tutor had told him vertebrates could shove bits of their foul innards outside of their bodies.

Tongues. She said they were called tongues.

The flying snake twisted and coiled through the air, barbed tail hanging beneath it. Stopping no more than two strides distant, it swung, swaying and hypnotic, with each beat of its wings.

Shan and Ahk froze, neither breathing.

Burn it!

He couldn't. Not with the snakes within striking distance and at least two archers lurking nearby.

Iyik screamed as the two rafak attacked, tail barbs stabbing lightning fast. Shan didn't see if she'd been hit. She stumbled from cover, robbed of her perfect grace. A dull female with two longbows rose from the bushes behind Iyik and took careful aim.

One of Ahk's claws found Shan's craft arm and squeezed hard. Eyes glazed with joy, antennae tangled around his own, she turned both main eyes on the archer, pleading.

Not yet! He might save Iyik for a moment, but there were three rafak and possibly another assassin hidden in the trees. Much as he wanted to explain, he dared not move.

Iyik collapsed, spasms twitching her antennae, and then stilled.

The archer, one arrow trained on the fallen student, moved to keep a clear line of sight.

More scared than when Nyk cornered him, fire built in Shan's gut. Burn the rafak. Burn the archer.

THE STORM BENEATH THE WORLD

Rafak

THE STORM BENEATH THE WORLD

He imagined long, wispy wings going up in smoke, the sinuous coiling bodies plummeting to the ground. He'd stand then, wreathed in flame, and burn the exposed archer. He'd sweep fire through the trees in case another hid there. He wanted to feel that unfettered joy once again.

Ignite the world! Incinerate it all!

Ahk is on top of me.

He needed to burn wild and free, and yet if he failed to maintain rigid control, she'd die like Nyk. Haunted by nightmares, he couldn't let that happen. He'd hated Nyk. He couldn't imagine the guilt of killing someone he liked.

"That was easy," said a bright female stepping from behind a tree barely three strides from where Shan and Ahk lay. Her golden carapace, shot through with pale yellow swirls, had been smeared dull and muted with mud. An assortment of weapons, stab sticks, spears, and a shortbow, hung slung across her abdomen, all within easy reach. She moved like a warrior. Waving an antenna at the rafak, she said, "Hashu, back those stinking things away."

A dull male rose from where he hid and bowed to the bright. His antennae sagged in rapture, and the flying snakes retreated from the clearing.

"This one," said the archer, "is still alive."

Shan realized she wasn't a dull at all. Like the first, her exoskeleton bore a thick layer of drying muck.

Having spent his entire life trying to be clean and presentable, this was an appalling breach of decorum. They were disguising themselves, hiding like Ahk did, but without talent. Understanding the why made it no easier to accept. Such things weren't done. Brights pretending to be dulls and dulls pretending to be brights was against the laws of nature.

Armed with spears, two more dulls—real ones this time—stepped from the underbrush. One moved to stand over Iyik, the mud-spattered bright relaxing her bows. Their already matte carapaces needed less disguising, yet both wore a shellacking of mud. Spreading out, they remained watchful and alert, as if expecting trouble to come charging from the forest at any moment.

There were more of them than Shan had thought. Even Ahk

stopped her squirming attempts at communicating. Surrounded, they lay still, hardly daring to breathe.

If I'd lashed out with fire, we'd be dead.

The golden bright pointed at Iyik. "That one matches the description for Iyik. The green one there is probably Bash, which means the colourful one with all the reds and greens should be Izi." She grunted a laugh. "Not so lucky after all."

"I killed Shil in the bushes," said the other dull, hoisting a bloody spear.

They know us all!

The golden bright studied the downed students, antennae sweeping about, searching. "We're missing one. Where is Shan?"

"He's a male," said the other bright. "Either stayed back at the school to preen or fled into the trees at the first sign of trouble."

Shan bristled, only to be calmed by a caress from Ahk's antennae.

The gold bright scowled. "Just as well. I wasn't too excited about facing a jumped-up male with a talent for fire. Too unpredictable. You never know if they're going to fold and cry, run away screaming, or panic and attack everything."

They didn't mention Ahk.

It made sense. These assassins must have left Yil before she arrived at the school.

The dull standing over Iyik drove a spear through the helpless student's eye and into her brain. It was so sudden, so casually violent, a gasp of horror escaped Shan.

The gold bright's antennae perked up. Her attention slid past Shan and Ahk. "I thought I heard something." When no one else reacted or confirmed, her wings gave a flutter of annoyance.

"This one is hurt," said the male dull crouched over Izi. "Doubt she'll survive the night."

The bright spoke over her shoulder, not bothering to turn. "Kill her." Like the act was nothing. Barely worthy of notice.

Seeing Bash murdered was bad. A four-name female deserved better. A fighting chance, at the very least. He couldn't watch Izi Doq Qen Jin Vur, a five-name bright, go the same way. The fact she was Corrupt and banished to this grubby little school changed nothing. It didn't matter that she mocked Shan at every chance, or that she thought he was a vacuous trophy male. Izi was royalty.

Coward!

He hadn't resisted the lure when Myosh tossed him in a cell, he'd simply been more afraid of the repercussions. Instead of acting to save Bash or Iyik or Shil, he chose to stay hidden and safe.

You always look for reasons to do nothing.

But there were always good reasons to do nothing! Even now, if he and Ahk stayed hidden, these assassins would leave.

They'll kill Izi first.

No amount of luck could save her.

But we'd survive!

Doing nothing was the smart decision. Doing nothing meant they'd live to report back to the school. Surely that was important too.

Ahk pulled him close, claws digging into his carapace. "Burn them."

His main eyes locked on hers, antennae entangled. He couldn't move, couldn't speak. Fear froze him.

I can't.

For so many reasons.

He might accidentally kill Izi. He might burn Ahk. He was surrounded. Someone would attack from behind, drive a spear through his skull. If he and Ahk died here, there'd be no one to report what happened.

"Burn them," Ahk whispered, "or die."

AHK TAY KYM

The Redemption says the stormwalls define the northern and southern limits of reality, but that doesn't change the fact that objects are constantly being ejected from those stormwalls. Most often it's dead vegetation, little of which is recognizable. Occasionally it's the storm-twisted corpses of monsters or crafted objects of unimaginable purpose. Once every few years we see something alive. Such foul creatures usually die soon after, falling into the storm beneath the world. Though I haven't seen it myself, there are ancient reports of ashkaro coming through the stormwalls on dying skerry.

Enough exits the stormwalls that cargo-cult islands have sprung up along the edges. Having toured such islands with a cadre of the Queen's Wing for protection, I found those living there to be insane loaners and outcasts from one queendom or another. Some were willing to trade what they found for the supplies needed to survive out on the ragged edge. Others had regressed to cannibalistic hives who worshipped deranged queens, their islands lined with the spiked heads of trespassers.

—Gmar Klor Ihns, Former Court Cartographer to Queen Nysh

Seeing Shan would not act unless forced, Ahk released him, rolling into the bushes.

Startled by his sudden appearance, the Yil ashkaro stared at him in shock until the golden bright said, "I think we found Shan." She studied the cowering male. "Seems a shame to ruin something so pretty."

"You don't have to," stuttered Shan. "I won't—"

"Kill him."

THE STORM BENEATH THE WORLD

Having heard the rumours of how Myosh found him, how he'd burned a bright female in self-defence, she thought he only needed a push.

She'd made a terrible mistake.

Shan lay, helpless and unmoving, hiding behind his arms.

They'll butcher him.

He was weak. No warrior blood ran within that stunning carapace. Gathering her legs underneath her, Ahk made ready to pounce. Maybe she could take one hostage.

A dull stepped close to Shan, raising an already bloody spear.

Mud bubbled, damp leaves furling and turning brown. The dull standing over Shan boiled, steam screaming from every joint. The spear crumbled to ash, the knapped stone head glowing red as it fell. The gold bright said something, retreated a step, and was gone. An empty carapace, cracked and smoking, stood for a heartbeat as if held aloft by a ghost, and toppled. Snake wings turned black and curled to nothing. The rafak landed awkwardly, writhing in the steaming mud.

Shan swept the trees with fire. Scorching heat blew out from him in every direction, uncontrolled roiling chaos. A thrown spear never made it, ashes scattering in the tornado winds spiralling around the gorgeous male.

Ahk gasped for breath, found nothing. Her insides burned, the wet foliage of the rainforest suddenly becoming dried kindling. Her wings were in agony as she tried to hide from the firestorm. The world was smoke and death, it clung to her. Agony stabbed through her head as if someone tore out her antennac and was gone. No air to breathe, she couldn't scream.

Shan rose to his feet, roaring like an enraged god.

Lord of the Storm.

Such an insane and blasphemous thought. Creation was a strictly female act, there could be no male gods.

Ahk curled tighter, hiding her main eyes from the fire.

The agony fell away, left her stunned and relieved. Alone in the sudden silence, she sensed nothing. For all the roaring firestorm, no air moved against her antennae, and she smelled nothing of the charred and smoking carapaces now littering the forest floor.

THE STORM BENEATH THE WORLD

Am I dying?

The Redemption said fire burned everything, carapace and souls alike, leaving nothing.

A perfect nihility beyond black. Not cold, but devoid of pain. She floated, untouched by the suffering of life, as if the gods of Alatash had severed her from the world of the living. Shan's hellstorm, Kratosh brought to the island of Nysh, must still rage, but she was alone.

I am the darkness.

That wasn't right. Not yet.

Nothing, she wrapped herself in the perfect black, hid from the world. She hadn't known she could hide others; she'd done it without thought.

I can hide everyone.

Ahk imagined the gods looking down and seeing only the storm. She'd hide the ashkaro and the islands.

We'd be free of their disapproval.

The ashkaro would finally be their own masters. If the first step in their social evolution was leaving the hive, surely leaving the gods must be the second. Afterall, what had they done for their creations? The gods gave them talents and then cursed them for using those skills.

Maybe I won't have a choice.

She'd fall to the lure as all must, using her talent, growing in power. Unable to help herself, she'd hide others just to feel that rush of pleasure. To the world, they'd disappear.

An island of ghosts. Lost. Wandering alone.

Only the results of their actions would be seen.

She'd heard of haunted islands, abandoned cities and empty streets. The citizens mysteriously gone. Were they there, hidden by some Corrupt's talent run amok?

And what of Shan?

His talent was more terrifying that hers. Lord of the Storm. How powerful would he be at the end? Would he burn the island itself? Would it spiral, aflame and dying, into Kratosh?

The dark called to Ahk, inviting her to hide.

JOH

Modern males often complain that they are overlooked for higher positions in politics and business because of ancient preconceptions dating back to the days of hive. This is purest garbage. My decision not to hire males has nothing to do with their flighty and overly emotional nature.

Simply put, a male will work for a few short years before leaving to raise a family or retiring at thirty due to old age. A female, on the other claw, will remain a loyal employee for sixty years or more.

It's a simple question of Return on Investments.

—Nik Bor Rel Lli, Matriarch of the Lli Family Businesses

'Tell me what we should do,' Wex had said, surprising Joh.

'We need to save the island,' he'd answered. 'I think that means finding the bright school.'

It was ridiculous! And worse, he only suggested it because he thought that was what she wanted to hear! What he really wanted to do was flee and hide, wait for the war to end, and return to his quiet life. Wex would never accept that. Females needed to *act*.

You're going to get yourself killed trying to deserve her friendship.

"We need Kris Kork," Joh said. "He's going to pretend to be Raht. He'll order everyone to get the skerry ready for us and then tell them he's decided to escort us to the other school."

"It's called Kaylamnel," said Wex. "Rel told me that once. The school for brights is named after a pretty flower."

"Typical," Joh muttered.

Wex's upper wings fluttered agreement. "What about the other students? Should we bring them with us?"

"I don't think so. The Sisters of the Storm knew where the school was, and they knew at least something about the teachers. There might be a spy among us."

"I hadn't thought of that," said Wex. "You could suggest to everyone that they tell us if they're a spy."

And I hadn't thought of that.

"I could, but it'll push me closer to the end. I think it's more important that you, me, and Kris make it to the other school. Nothing matters more than saving the island."

He was surprised when Wex didn't question that they mattered more than the others. Had he accidentally suggested that she always agree with him at some point in the past? He couldn't remember doing so, but sometimes things slipped out and he didn't know he'd influenced someone until that shiver ran through him. It seemed like lately he was making an awful lot of small suggestions. Most of the time it wasn't intentional—hey, you should try the grubs, they're fresh—and then some student would be shovelling food into their face while Joh stumbled away, distracted by waves of bliss.

What was a suggestion but an attempt to manipulate someone into doing what he wanted? Except was it really an attempt if they had no choice but to do as suggested?

Rel calling my talent suggestion *was a mistake.*

He'd known people tended to do as he wanted for some time. He used to think it was because he had good ideas. When he figured out that wasn't the case, he became more careful.

There are other words for what I do.

Command?

No, even a command could be ignored. Joh's talent robbed ashkaro of choice.

What do you call someone who enslaves others?

He hated the answer.

"What do *you* think we should do?" Joh asked.

How long could he go on asking questions and hoping others figured out the right answer?

Wex glanced toward the front entrance. "I saw Kris out on the field. I don't think he was hurt. I'll go get him. You stay here. If someone comes…" Her antennae bent, uncertain. "Keep them out. Tell them Raht doesn't want to be disturbed."

It was a good plan.

"Be fast."

Wex left at a sprint. Joh rocked back on his rear legs, torn between the glow of joy and shame at what he'd accidentally done. It didn't matter that he'd only meant it as a request that she not dawdle. It had been an innocent mistake.

Looking at the shattered remains of the door laying on the front steps, he swore.

If someone shows up, I'll suggest they go away.

A cracked laugh slipped out.

What was the limit to his power? Was there anything he couldn't order someone to do?

What will you do if you learn you can command anyone to do anything?

There'd be nothing he couldn't have.

Friends? Everyone would love him.

Wealth? You should give me your family estate.

Power?

Joh shied from the thought. Dulls didn't have power, and dull males had even less. Such a talent belonging to someone like him went against the natural order. It was a cruel joke, the gods of Alatash laughing in mockery.

Or they gave me this talent because I'd need it to save the island.

Did saving the island justify robbing his fellow ashkaro of the freedom of choice? Except that wasn't why he was doing it. Nysh and her queendom meant nothing to him. All this was some pathetic attempt at earning redemption for suggesting Wex be his friend.

"I suggest you never use your talent again," Joh told himself.

He felt no pleasure.

"At the very least," he said, "never use it for evil."

Again, he felt nothing.

He looked at the ceiling, imagining the gods of Alatash looking down. "It would have been handy if I could make suggestions to myself."

Be happy. Do as you're told. Know your place. Free Wex from the compulsion of friendship. Live as the Redemption says you should. Be loyal to the queen.

I could tell myself not to feel guilty for the things I have done or the things I will do.

Joh faced the carnage. He was too small to move any of the bodies, and there was too much blood to clean up. The Sister of the Storm lay dead, blood pooled around her carapace. He killed the bright without having to touch her. The worst part was how good it felt to suggest she hurt herself. His talent didn't care what purpose it was turned to. Telling people to commit atrocities felt as good as suggesting they take better care of themselves.

The stunted male with the misshapen carapace, Joh *had* touched. Crushing his head in with one of Headmistress Raht's chairs hadn't felt good at all. That his victim hadn't seen his death coming didn't help. If anything, it made it worse. With the torturer he could tell himself it was self-defence. But the helpless male was different.

A soft knock on the doorframe startled Joh from his thoughts. Wex led Kris Kork into Raht's home. Kris froze, staring at the scattered corpses, carefully avoiding the blood. Seeing the dead Sister, he retreated in horror.

"They tortured the headmistress," Joh explained. "And killed Rel. They were trying to learn where the second school is."

"Second school?" Despite the shock, Kris's antennae perked in curiosity.

Wex explained their plan, such as it was: Kris would pretend to be Raht and commandeer the Yil skerry to fly them to the other school to warn of the danger. Fearing spies, they couldn't bring anyone else. After…well, someone at the bright school would know what to do next.

Pulling his attention from the Sister, Kris asked, "You know where the school is?"

"Kind of," Wex admitted. "We'll find it."

"Will you help?" Joh asked, resisting the temptation to tell the young male that he should.

Kris nodded and became Headmistress Raht, carapace a mirror-like gleam. "We need to move quickly. Raht has cleaning staff and all her meals are delivered to the dining room."

THE STORM BENEATH THE WORLD

Surprised, Joh nodded agreement. He'd suggested that the mimic should learn how to become Raht but hadn't realized how seriously Kris had taken the task.

"You," Raht snapped, poking an annoyed antenna in Joh's direction, "stop dawdling. There's work to be done!"

Even knowing it was Kris, Joh jumped to obey. If obedience to brights was so deeply written into his behaviour, perhaps his talent was less foul than he thought. Thinking back, he couldn't remember a bright ever showing the slightest hint they were aware of the responsibility that came with being able to order people about.

Out in the light of Alatash, Raht's exoskeleton reflected the clouds above, a constant shifting shimmer. She spoke with utter certainty, orders given with the confidence they'd be followed immediately. And they were. Within minutes, students and teachers hustled about the training field hauling food and water up to the waiting skerry. Wex and Joh remained silent, a respectful two steps behind the headmistress, and no one dared question them.

In record time the skerry was loaded, the corpses thrown overboard. The Yil dead were heaped into a pile, ready to be burned. It was an act of anger and hatred; the Redemption said souls consumed in fire were never reborn. Joh had no idea if the Yil believed that. It was said they cast criminals into the storm, but then he'd also been told they did the same with their Corrupt.

It doesn't matter what the Yil believe.

Burning them was strictly for the benefit of the survivors. It was punishment and revenge and justice.

How pathetic to cling to such sad displays. We should be embarrassed.

Joh saw only gritty determination on the antennae of his fellow students. Resisting the temptation to tell them to be better—to suggest that much of what they'd been told was somewhere between misunderstanding and manipulation—he bowed and trailed behind Raht.

When Kris arrived at the rope ladder leading up to the moored skerry, he faced the gathered crowd. "While I'm away, I want you to stay out of my home."

The antennae of several teachers bent in confusion and Wex

poked Kris from behind.

"Right," Raht said, voice again imperious. "I'm taking these two to Kaylamnel to report what happened here."

Splashed in gore, Des appeared out of the crowd. "Should I come, Headmistress? You might need my speed."

Was that a genuine question, or was she the spy they suspected lived among them? Would she kill them as they slept and take the skerry to report her success to her masters?

Joh leaned close to Kris and whispered, "No."

"No," said Raht. "You're in charge until I return."

Des's antennae straightened in surprise as did those of several teachers.

Without another word, the aging headmistress climbed the rope ladder. Glancing at each other, Joh and Wex followed.

Up on the deck, Raht said, "Which of you knows how to pilot one of these beasts?"

"It can't be that hard," said Wex, disappearing into the gondola.

Out of sight of those on the field, Kris dropped the disguise. "That last bit, putting Des in charge, was probably a mistake, but I couldn't resist."

"At the least it kept her from asking more questions," Joh said. He studied Kris. "When you were mimicking Raht you were using your talent, but I didn't see the pleasure in your antennae."

"All part of the disguise. But believe me, someday I will die pretending I'm anyone other than myself."

Something about the wording bothered Joh. Were ashkaro shaped by their talents, or was it the other way around? If the latter, what did that say about Wex? Was her ability to kill born of a fear of weakness or a need to protect herself?

And what of your ability to command others?

Small and weak, his talent made some sense in that light. What of Kris Kork's ability to disguise himself? Was he hiding from something?

The skerry shuddered as the hanging tentacles released the moorings.

"Ah!" said Kris. "That didn't take too long."

It was another hour before Wex got the tired creature moving.

THE STORM BENEATH THE WORLD

WEX JEL

> *Before the Mad Queen's ascension to power, the island worshipped the gods of Alatash in a religion not too far removed from the Redemption. After, in a fit of what can only be described as mass insanity, the entire island turned their back on the gods and worshipped Katlipok. Yil is now not only the queen and sole ruler of the island, but also the Voice and Claw of the Sisters of the Storm.*
>
> —*A History of the Mad Queen,* by Chuo Sdai Rhaj Een

With the skerry unmoored and finally propelling itself windward, albeit at an embarrassingly slow pace, Wex returned to the deck. Not nearly as far below as she'd hoped, the teachers and students gathered to watch the departure. Lifting a craft claw, she waved to Des, who returned the gesture before shouting orders at everyone to get back to work.

She always did want to be in charge.

Eventually they'd discover the corpses in Raht's home, one of which was the tortured headmistress. They might blame Des, at least until they figured out that Kris was missing and that he must have been mimicking Raht. Perhaps they'd decide Kris had fooled Wex and Joh, forcing them to travel with him. Or they might think Joh had coerced Kris and he was their hostage.

Staying back from the rail and out of sight of the training field, Joh said, "You figured out how to pilot the skerry pretty quick."

She shook her head. "Not really. There's levers and pulleys but none are labelled. I pushed and pulled things at random until it started moving."

"Let's call that a victory."

THE STORM BENEATH THE WORLD

Wex accepted that. "I suppose. It was pure luck the thing decided to head windward on its own. I'm not sure how to make it turn."

Standing beside Joh, Kris said, "We'll push and pull things until it turns." Edging closer to the rail, he asked, "Are we going as slowly as it looks?"

"I think so," admitted Wex. "At this rate it might be faster to drop the ladder once we're out of sight and walk."

The mimic looked doubtful. "I'd rather sit and move slowly than walk. Anyway, we'll still be moving while we sleep. That's got to count for something."

Joh fluttered his wings as if about to make a long jump. "Too bad ashkaro lost the power of flight. We'd make better time on our own."

"More proof the gods hate us," muttered Kris.

Confused, Wex asked, "What do you mean?"

"Oh," he said with a careless shift of wings, "Rel said that on Yil they believe the gods of Alatash stole our ability to fly when we turned our backs on them and followed Katlipok."

"*We* didn't turn our back on them," said Joh. "We hate the Queen of the Storm."

"Since when did religions make sense?" Kris asked. "Neither is particularly rigorous when it comes to consistency. The Redemption says the gods gave us our talents and then turned their backs on us when we used them. The Sisters say Katlipok gave us our talents so that we might take our place beside the gods and that they grew angry and poisoned the gift. We say Alatash is a brilliant city of order and beauty and that the storm is death and chaos. The Sisters claim Alatash is a place of unchanging stagnation and that the Storm is a place of rebirth."

Is there a difference between order and stagnation?

Unsure, Wex said nothing. While she'd never given it much thought before, now she had no choice. The Redemption preached of the endless cycle of birth and rebirth, forever moving closer to the day when the gods forgave the ashkaro, but they never said exactly *how* the souls were reborn. It just happened. Could both religions be correct? Could Katlipok ensure souls were reborn, as the Yil believed, while the gods of Alatash waited for their creations to achieve their redemption?

Or are both wrong?

THE STORM BENEATH THE WORLD

For thousands of generations of ashkaro the gods remained in their city, never interfering. Likewise, the Queen of the Storm never ventured from Kratosh. Blasphemous as the thought was, there was no evidence either religion was right. Wex quashed the urge to laugh. Such sacrilege was the one point where the two religions agreed; both would throw her to the storm for speaking the thoughts aloud.

Joh's shoulders slumped, his antennae drooping. "You paid more attention in Rel's classes than I did." He gazed at the receding school grounds. "I'll miss him."

Kris bent a quizzical and slightly embarrassed antenna in Joh's direction. "This is awkward, but I can't remember your talent."

Joh darted a glance at Wex and said, "It doesn't matter. I'm not terribly important."

Kris lost interest in the little male, wandering off in search of something to eat.

Wex watched him go, thoughts a chaotic whirl. No one ever talked about Joh or how scary his talent could be if turned to the wrong purposes. In fact, no one paid him much attention at all. The teachers rarely called on him to answer questions, and the students acted as if he wasn't worth talking to. Even the gossipiest ones never mentioned him, and Des, who loved nothing more than bossing everyone around, never barked orders at him.

He must have told everyone to leave him alone. Everyone except me.

She knew he was self-conscious about his size, and understandably so. Had he been much smaller, the local Redemption priest might have decided he was unfit to live. And if the other students had paid him any mind, they'd have picked on him. A runty one-name dull, he must have been subject to bullying much of his life. Suggesting people ignore him was probably an old habit.

Kris returned to the deck carrying a platter of dried leaves and grubs. Crossing to Wex he lifted the tray in offering. "Hungry?"

Selecting the fattest grub, she devoured it. "I don't recognize this breed."

Kris shrugged, unconcerned. "Food is food."

After Wex selected another slug and a couple of leaves, Kris popped a grub into his mouth before noticing Joh and offering him the platter. Joh shook his head.

Placing the tray on the deck, Kris faced Wex. "I have what might be a crazy question."

Wex cracked a laugh. "Crazy questions. Kind of my thing."

He gave her an odd look. "Make that two crazy questions: How are we going to find Kaylamnel, and what are we going to do once we're there?"

"Joh knows roughly where it is," said Wex. "It's somewhere south of Nysh City, hidden in the forests."

Kris said, "Any forest that can hide a school is going to be big."

"If we can't find it ourselves, we'll find a city and land. You'll pretend to be a bright and ask questions until we get an answer."

"Pretending to be someone else for that long will not be healthy."

Even though it was an understatement, he didn't seem terribly upset. Wex understood. Like all Corrupt, he knew the pleasure of the lure. No matter how much he feared the end, he craved that rush. He wasn't wrong though. She'd thought nothing of asking him to use his talent.

"Kaylamnel," said Joh.

Kris twitched in surprise as if he'd forgotten the other male was there.

"I hadn't remembered what the school was called until Wex mentioned it." He studied Kris. "But you already knew the name."

"I must have heard someone talking about it."

"Rel said it was a secret."

"You were with me when Rel first mentioned it," Wex said to Joh, thinking back to that wagon ride from the brickworks.

"If Rel told you both," said Kris, "it couldn't have been much of a secret."

Again, he wasn't wrong.

Joh looked to Wex for support. "The Yil assassins knew too much. What if Kris is the spy?"

Kris raised his craft claws. "Hey, you came to me. None of this was my idea."

"He's right," said Wex. "I think you're being paranoid."

Turning on Kris, Joh said, "Tell me if you are a Yil spy."

"I am a Yil spy," said Kris. Startled, his antennae snapped straight. "Hey. No, that's not—"

"Tell me how you were reporting to your superiors."

"I'd pretend to be Rel and send messages to Nysh City where we have an asset in the Messengers Wing. She passed the coded notes off to someone else who got them to our other assets in the city. After that I—" Kris's mandibles snapped shut.

"That's how they knew where Amphazar was," Joh said, antennae quivering with pleasure. He gestured at Kris. "And here we are, flying their spy to the bright school."

Kris retreated until Joh told him to stop. The mimic stood helpless.

"We can ask him anything and he'll tell us," Wex said. "We need to find out everything he knows and report it to the brights at Kaylamnel. They'll know what to do."

Will they?

She hated the question, because if the brights were half as smart as everyone thought, this spy wouldn't have infiltrated Amphazar so easily.

"Have you met Queen Yil?" Wex asked Kris.

Kris said nothing.

"Answer all our questions honestly, and to the best of your ability," commanded Joh.

"I have never met the Queen," Kris said.

Remembering something Joh said back in Raht's home, she asked, "The Sister of the Storm said Queen Yil can command islands. It that true?"

"Yes."

"How do you know?" Joh demanded. "Maybe it's the sort of garbage brights tell dulls to keep them afraid."

Kris shrugged. "Everyone knows. It's her talent."

Wex looked from Kris to Joh. "All that means is that *he* believes it. Something being common knowledge doesn't make it true."

"Do you actually *know*?" Joh demanded.

"The queen has taken skerry to other islands and commanded them. There are flotillas of smaller cays surrounding Yil."

"Explain."

THE STORM BENEATH THE WORLD

"We have more farming islands now than we did twenty years ago. We have killed the queens of dozens of feral islands and turned the drones and warriors into mindlessly obedient shock troops. Some of your Corrupt islands now travel with Yil. For years, our islands have been moving to surround Nysh."

"We know," Joh said. "The Sister of the Storm already told me that."

"When are they going to attack?" Wex asked.

Kris looked startled. "Attack? There will be no attack, no war."

"No war?" Wex asked. "But then…why surround the island?"

Kris puffed his wings with pride. "My mother is a Sister. She told me Queen Yil decided Nysh was too large to chance a war. She only wants the land."

"Only wants the land?" Wex struggled with the idea. "But *we're* here!"

"How will she remove the current inhabitants?" Joh asked.

"Queen Yil will order Nysh Island to dive. It will go low enough everyone dies, but not so low as to kill all the flora and destroy all the buildings. The pickets surrounding Nysh are there to make sure no one escapes."

Wex asked, "What happens after?"

"Once we've settled the island, forever joined it with our own, we'll have the resources to take the war forward without need for such mass exterminations. In time, we'll unite all the islands of the river of days under a single queen."

Wex and Joh stared at each other in appalled shock.

Joh's antennae drooped in despondent acceptance. "We can't fight that," he said. "We're just two dulls."

"We don't have to fight it," Wex said, desperately hoping she was right. "All we need to do is report what we learned. The brights at Kaylamnel will know what to do."

You don't believe that.

Kris snorted a mocking laugh. "No one will listen to you. We've been intercepting and changing reports within the Nysh intelligence network for years."

"We have *you*," said Wex. "You're our proof."

THE STORM BENEATH THE WORLD

Joh stared at his craft claws. "We can't bring him with us to Kaylamnel. Think about it. He can be anyone. Given the chance, he could be Queen Nysh. He's too dangerous."

"Too dangerous?"

"We have to kill him."

"Without me," said Kris, "no one will believe you."

Was that true? Wex's thoughts churned in the background, picking at the problem.

Joh studied the Mimic. "Just a moment ago you were saying no one would believe us." He looked to Wex. "You should kill him."

Stab sticks in her claws, she saw all the Mimic's weaknesses. It would be effortless.

"Stop!"

Weapons raised, Wex froze.

"I'm sorry." Joh's voice cracked. "I shouldn't have—I didn't mean it to be a suggestion. Tell me what we should do." Again, his antennae quivered with pleasure.

"We should kill him," she said, thinking, *Does he even realize he just gave me another command?* "You're right, he's too dangerous." She had the answer. "We don't need him. You can tell whatever brights we run into that they believe us. You can tell them to send reports to the queen."

"Kris," said Joh, voice soft. "Jump over the rail."

With no attempt at resistance, the mimic walked to the rail and leapt. Even as he fell, he changed, his abdomen becoming a long, spiked tail. Stunted wings grew large and caught the wind.

Joh and Wex watched the rafak fly away.

"I didn't know he could mimic more than just ashkaro," Wex said.

"I don't think the teachers did either." He sounded distracted, like watching Kris turn into a flying snake wasn't all that interesting. "They were remarkably inept."

"Are you all right?"

"I'm torn," he answered. "There are several lessons there, and I don't know which I should take to heart." His wings and antennae showed no hint of emotion, his voice strangely flat. "I ordered him to his death, and it felt good. When the lure takes me, I could walk through a crowd of innocents telling them to kill themselves and it would be bliss.

I don't want that power. I don't want to ever do something like that again."

When he didn't continue, Wex asked, "What's the other lesson?"

"Had I ordered him to jump to his death instead of just telling him to jump, he'd have fallen and died instead of flying away."

Wex understood the lesson: "You must learn to be more careful with your wording."

"Precisely."

Days passed, the Yil skerry continuing in the same general windward direction. With no idea where they were going, she saw no reason to correct it or try another course. Though she'd seen skerry floating so high in the sky they were little more than dots, this one remained stubbornly low despite her attempts to get it to gain altitude. The matte scrub of desert passed below, broken only by the odd patch of stunted johak trees huddled around an oasis.

Joh and Wex took their meals together, finishing the last of the grubs and rarely talking. They ate the fibrous leaves next, watching the level on the water barrel diminish.

While she understood the brights of Kaylamnel would make all the important decisions, she also knew she couldn't trust them. They'd want to write reports to the queen, make trips to Nysh City and arrange audiences. They'd want to plan, and none of those plans would involve Wex and Joh. Being Corrupt didn't change the fact they were dulls. Dulls never did anything important.

Queen Yil was closing with her prey. As soon as she was in range, she'd order Nysh Island into the storm.

We have to stop her.

Maybe Joh could do it. Maybe he could tell the mad queen to end the war. First, he'd have to get close enough to talk to her and that would never happen. Wex's talent for finding weakness wouldn't suffice.

We need more Corrupt.

She'd been wrong. They weren't going to Kaylamnel to report what they knew; they were going to conscript students who could help. Joh would have to *tell* them what had to happen. He might even have to order students onto the skerry.

Day by day, the desert changed. Small towns slipped by. Sometimes Wex and Joh discussed whether any were worth landing at to ask for directions. Most were smaller and dirtier than the brickworks where she grew up. The one time they saw a small city, the skerry ignored all attempts to turn it.

Browns and greys became pale green before giving way to lush colours Wex had never seen. The damp air smelled of life, the most beautiful scent ever. When Alatash rose the next day, they flew above endless forest. Trees tangled and coiled about each other as if wrestling for access to the sky. Rafak snakes flitted through the jungle, sometimes climbing to get a look at the decrepit skerry before disappearing back into the green.

That evening, as Alatash fell toward the windward horizon, the skerry began to lose altitude.

Joh joined Wex at the front rail, looking down at the trees. "I'd be worried about crashing if we weren't going so slow."

"We have no idea how tall those trees are," Wex said. "I haven't seen a break in the foliage in days. We could crash and then fall to our deaths."

"I tried suggesting the skerry go higher," joked Joh, "but it ignored me."

"It's a Yil skerry. Probably didn't understand your terrible accent."

SHAN WYN VAL NUL NYSH

Corrupt islands are typically ruled by a self-styled queen, a bright with no real lineage and only a dangerous talent to enforce her claim. Such 'queendoms' change rulers often as one queen falls to the lure or is slain by another with a more deadly talent. For the commoners, brights and dulls alike, life tends to be brief and brutal. Crime runs rampant.

That said, I think we're missing an opportunity here. If we could unite and militarize these banished Corrupts, they could present a formidable force in the war to come.

—Senior Officer Snur Elk Naj Myyr, The Queen's Claw

The echoing whistle of a rafak snake interrupted Shan's dream of dancing for Ahk.

Rafak? Here?

Where was he? Had they gone to the estate on the private farm island trailing along behind Nysh? There were rafak there because they hunted those disgusting furry little things and other pests. The fieldclaws were supposed to cull the flying snakes before they became dangerously large.

Did we go camping?

There'd been a fire, crackling and merry. And such pleasure! Had Ahk finally made her move? He'd been waiting, teasing, showing he was willing, and she'd still hesitated. It couldn't be that he wasn't pretty enough.

Again, he heard the *scree scree* of a rafak.

The babies don't make that sound.

THE STORM BENEATH THE WORLD

Damned fieldclaws. Mother always grumbled about how difficult it was to find good help, often joking that leaving the hive was the worst thing ashkaro ever did. 'Mindless' she liked to say when out of the public eye, 'is often better than utterly stupid.'

Shan woke sprawled in filth, ash clogging his breathing holes. For a panicked moment he retched, sputtering and wheezing, trying to clear them. Finally managing to blow them free enough he didn't feel like he was about to suffocate, he struggled to stand, all four legs wobbly beneath him. The stumps of burnt and splintered trees surrounded him. Many looked as if they'd exploded from the heat. His raging fire had created a clearing. Once an impassable snarl of jungle, the nearest tree was now eight strides distant.

Exhausted, he struggled to stay awake.

The forest loomed dark and threatening in the night, lurking shapes shifting with the wind. Each could be a tree, a stalking rafak, or a tramea hunting for a stupid ashkaro to feed to its young.

Checking to see if he was hurt, Shan loosed a horrified squeak. "I'm dirty!"

Caked in ash, charred wood, and baked mud, he looked like the lowest dull. Clawing at the crud contaminating his beautiful carapace, he scraped an area clean enough to see beneath. He sagged in relief. Disgusting as he was, and he shuddered to imagine one of his friends back home seeing him like this, it was just dirt. A long soak in the tub, and he'd be good as new.

Fire. Screaming. Enemies bursting as their innards boiled and expanded, splitting their carapaces like rotting fruit left in the sun to burst. Glorious raging flame. The mind-cleansing bliss of surrendering to chaos. Nothing could ever feel as good as losing himself to his talent. Control was the curse, not the lure. The gods wanted him to be happy and gave him the means. The damnable Redemption with their smug piety, telling the Corrupt that using their talent was wrong.

We aren't Corrupt, we're blessed!

How could priests who had never discovered their talent possibly understand? The Corruption was a gift. He struggled to imagine how different things would be if the Corrupt were embraced, trained to use their skills to the betterment of all, and cared for as they succumbed to the lure. What feats of technological innovation might the ashkaro reach? Imagine the works of art they'd create! All society would benefit.

If only we treated the Corrupt like they do in the Yil Queendom.

Shan understood where he was. He remembered the Yil assassins.

Checking the trees and seeing no rafak, he whispered, "Ahk?"

He shuffled in a dainty circle, antennae perked to catch the slightest movement in the air. Mounds of ash and detritus reached the first joint of his legs.

The nearest pile shifted as something buried within moved.

Fear swept away all thought of sleep. "Ahk?"

Had one of the assassins survived?

By all the gods of Alatash, what if he killed her? They'd never welcome him back to the school. Myosh would spike his brain.

He should run.

Where?

Leeward, to the desert? No one would look for him there because that was the last place on all the island he ever wanted to be. Maybe he could catch a ride on a skerry to a farm island, or even Yil. Was there still trade between the queendoms? He had no idea. He also had no money, having lost what little he'd possessed to Izi within days of being released from his cell.

You're pretty enough you'll never need money. Mother used to say that. He'd thought it meant he'd marry into another wealthy family and live the pampered life of a five-name bright male with direct lineage to the queen. Now, he was less sure. Would he trade himself for passage?

Never! I am Shan Wyn Val Nul Nysh!

Would he trade himself for passage if the only other options were death, or life on a Corrupt island?

Maybe.

Only if I can escape to Yil, where my kind is welcome.

The ash groaned and Ahk pushed herself upright. Grabbing him for support, she missed, toppling back to the ground in an ungainly heap of limbs.

"Are you—" Shan cut himself off as the dirt fell away from her carapace.

Where he was caked in filth, Ahk was charred pale and grey,

exoskeleton misshapen and bubbled from the heat. She shed flakes of burnt carapace with every movement. A thin yellow-blue liquid leaked from every joint. A good long soak would put Shan right again. Ahk was forever disfigured.

Standing, she clung to him, and he bent under her weight. Ahk was wrong. Terribly wrong. Her eyes met his and he wanted to push her away, to flee screaming from the horror. Revulsion wailed *abomination!* in his blood.

"Shan?" She leaned away, strangely expressionless.

"It's going to be all right," he lied, trying not to stare at the molten ruin of her carapace, struggling to hide his abhorrence.

"Shan!" she shouted even though he was right there, struggling to hold her up. "Shan!"

He saw it, stifled the urge to scream or run. Ahk's antennae were gone. Not damaged. Not snapped part way. Burnt to dust. Main eyes locked on his, exoskeleton twisted and malformed, she stared at him. Without her antennae, he could read nothing of her thoughts or emotions.

I did that to her.

Finally focussing past her disgustingly smooth head, he saw no wings behind her. Both sets were gone, slagged to melted nubs.

In a moment of glorious bliss, he crippled the only ashkaro he ever liked. Without her antennae, she lost much of the world. Never again would she sense the breeze, smell prey or the proximity of friends and family. She might touch an object with her claws, but they were dull things in comparison, incapable of sensing fine variations in texture and temperature. With wings and antennae gone, she'd lost most of her ability to communicate. She'd be both deaf and near mute, her mandibles speaking in blunt and emotionless sentences devoid of life and feeling.

"You're going to be fine," he said, wiping away at her charred exoskeleton like he might clean it. Black flakes crumbled to dust exposing the flame-bleached carapace beneath.

She's a dull now.

Worse, she'd look like a white, one of those poor dulls wandering the desert until their carapaces lost the last hints of beauty.

This is my fault.

THE STORM BENEATH THE WORLD

Ahk screamed "Shan!" at him again. "What happened?"

Unsure what to do, desperate for some way to make this easier, he gestured at where her antennae should be with his own.

She reached a claw up to feel.

And disappeared.

With ash everywhere, he should have been able to tell where she was, but he couldn't. She ceased to exist, a gaping wound in reality.

"Ahk," Shan said, "I know you're still here." What more could he say, I'm sorry? No words could convey his guilt.

"I'm here for you," he said. "I'm…an idiot."

Antennae gone, she could hear nothing.

All the shining gods above in Alatash, forgive me.

Though if he was to run away to Yil, perhaps he should be praying to Katlipok in Kratosh.

I can't leave her.

If he took her back to Kaylamnel, they'd kill him because he lost control of his talent, and for what he did to Ahk. Would she come to Yil with him? Even deaf and disfigured, she still was Corrupt, could be useful.

Ahk couldn't hear him, but she could still see. Shan held out a claw, nodding toward it with an antenna. "Take my claw," he said, unable to help himself. "I won't leave you."

He prayed she read the honest emotion expressed in the set of his wings and antennae.

Ahk flickered, curled in the ash, all eight limbs tucked tight around her abdomen, and was gone.

A stride away, another mound of ash shifted and made a low, grumbling groan. Shan froze in fear until Izi shoved a husked exoskeleton off her and peered blearily at him, main eyes coated grey. The arrows lodged in her thorax were gone, burned away or yanked out. Astoundingly, though filthy, she'd survived in better shape than Ahk.

"Shan?" she said. "What happened?"

I killed them. I ruined Ahk, left her a dull.

"They're gone," he said instead.

Ahk reappeared, shivering at Shan's feet.

"Oh," said Izi. Then, she slumped, limp.

Ahk, noting the direction of Shan's attention, turned to see who he'd been talking to. Spotting Izi, she rose on unsteady legs and stumbled to her side.

"She's hurt bad!" she shouted over her shoulder at Shan.

About to answer, he realized she'd turned away and wouldn't hear.

Shan joined Ahk and studied Izi. The arrow wounds were clogged with ash, which might be good or bad. He had no idea. At least she wasn't bleeding.

Noticing him at her side, Ahk shouted, "We have to get her home!"

Or should he and Ahk slip away now, while she was unconscious? If Izi was so lucky—and seeing her take two arrows left him doubting—someone would stumble across her, carry her back to the school. She'd be fine. That meant they could leave without guilt, right?

Shan touched the unconscious ashkaro's shoulder. "Izi?" He gave her a tentative shake. "Can you walk?"

Izi didn't react.

Great. She woke up just long enough to dislodge the ash so I could see her.

For a moment Shan wondered which was more powerful, Izi's talent, or his own bad luck.

"We should leave," he said.

Ahk brushed ash from Izi's carapace to get a better look at the wounds.

"We'll never be accepted here," Shan continued. "I'm a murdering Corrupt and you…" He choked down a surge of emotion, guilt crushing his heart. "And you're a white." There was nothing in all the world lower than that. Had she been born like this, her parents would have given her to the Redemption to be slain. "We should go to Yil and spend the rest of our lives there. Together."

"Help me carry her!" Ahk shouted.

She hadn't heard a word he said.

He made hushing gestures with his claws and tried to figure out how to tell her there might be a rafak somewhere nearby. Trying to mime a flying snake, he made a show of studying the trees and sky.

Ahk gave him a blank look and bellowed, "Have you lost your mind?"

Shan gave up. The snake had probably been scared off by all her shouting.

And if it does show up, I'll have a reason to burn.

He hated the muted thrill of anticipation that ran through him. Now that he didn't think he'd die in the next few heartbeats, fatigue made a creeping return.

Together, they struggled to lift Izi. Shan, never strong, suffered under the weight. Ahk, not much better off than Izi, collapsed to her femorotibial joints. Dumped to the ground, Izi screamed in pain but didn't wake.

Leaning over Izi, Ahk sobbed, "I can't."

Shan wasn't sure he could either. If he and Ahk couldn't carry Izi, there was no way he could carry both. Should he leave, return to the school for help? Tantamount to volunteering to have his brain spiked, he couldn't bring himself to suggest it. Not that Ahk would have heard him.

Getting her attention, he said, "We'll stay here until morning," hoping she'd somehow understand. With no antennae or wings to express emotion, he had no idea.

Maybe we'll get lucky, and Izi will die in the night.

Then there'd be no reason to return to the school. Once Ahk recovered a bit, she'd understand how bad things were. If she didn't kill Shan as punishment, maybe she'd come to Yil with him.

How am I supposed to explain all this to someone who can't hear?

Sitting beside Izi, Ahk bellowed, "How did they hit her?"

Shan fluttered his wings, admitting he had no idea. "Maybe one of the assassins was luckier than Izi."

She ignored his feeble attempt at an answer.

Shan and Ahk sat on either side of the unconscious student, watching helpless as shivers ran through her carapace. Insects flew and buzzed, circling to see if there was anything interesting, and then were drawn away by the remains of the assassins. Everything stank of charred exoskeleton and burnt meat.

Izi is dying.

How could that possibly be lucky? He snuck a glance at Ahk.

I'd rather be dead than live like that.

White, mutilated, deaf and cut off from the world. He'd read stories of what happened to ashkaro who lost the ability to interact with their peers. Social creatures, they caved in on themselves. Many stopped eating and hid from society. Most went mad from the isolation. Thinking back to his week in Myosh's cell, Shan shuddered. He couldn't imagine years like that. What was a life worth if it was spent separated, cut from all meaningful contact, forced to grunt simple shouted sentences devoid of emotion?

I'll protect her.

He had to. This was all his fault.

Shan touched Ahk's carapace, getting her attention. "We can't go back to the school."

She stared at him.

He pointed at his head, making a jabbing motion. "They'll spike my brain for losing control." He swallowed, needing to confess. "They'll kill me for what I did to you."

THE STORM BENEATH THE WORLD

AHK TAY KYM

There are small, fast-moving islands ruled by rogue queens. Prone to attacking other islands in savage raids, they tend to avoid the more prosperous windward coast, instead focussing on the leeward edge. These so-called 'pirate islands' are rarely large enough to support their population without such raiding and become desperate if victims are scarce. Rogue queens are more likely to chance making use of the Corrupt, making them extremely dangerous.
—Chal Uim Swen Dah, Court Historian

Choked in ash, Ahk was trapped in a still and silent existence. Smoke from burnt trees wafted past yet she sensed no breeze. The air rippled with heat, and she felt no warmth. No sound. No sensation of any kind. Her eyes worked, though all she saw was the pity, horror, and revulsion in Shan's antennae every time he looked at her.

Glancing down she saw the bubbled ripples in her melted exoskeleton. She looked like smeared mud, leeched of colour, and baked in the sun. Charred ruin, dead white exposed where it flaked away. No one survived such wounds.

I must be dying. Half fear, half prayer.

When she moved, a gritty grinding sensation filled her guts, sections of jagged and splintered carapace rubbing against each other. Exhaustion bent her; she wanted nothing more than to lie down in the filth and cease to be.

Shan said something, mandibles moving, antennae showing concern.

Ahk fluttered her wings in confusion, realized they too were gone.

THE STORM BENEATH THE WORLD

The majority of ashkaro communication was through a blend of pheromones and body language involving antennae, wings, and claws. Thoughts in an unfeeling cage, all she had left to communicate with were shallow words.

I'm dying, she thought again. She had to be dying. Nothing could survive this. *Please let me be dying.*

"Are you hurt?" she asked Shan, and he shied as if she scolded him.

His mandibles made meaningless movements and she read the denial in his antennae.

Unable to sense the movement of air, to taste the wind for friends and enemies, she was more alone than she'd ever been. She'd never again smell a friend, know that she was part of a hive. Tramea could be lurking behind her, and she'd never know. Twisting, she looked behind while her other main eye watched Shan. Her secondary eyes tried to see everything else. She kept trying to communicate with her wings and antennae, each time having to dumb her communications down to a few stupid words.

Realizing that every time she spoke his antennae bent away, she tried to stop shouting. It was difficult. Unable to feel any shift in the air, she had no idea how loud she was.

She needed to talk to stay calm, needed him to hear and understand. Ashkaro might have left the hive, but without some sense of belonging, she'd lose her mind. She desperately needed to know she wasn't alone.

Panic prowled at the edges, every shape and shift dragging an eye to it.

A secondary eye noticed a bright ember smouldering on one shoulder and she brushed it off. Another caught movement above and she tensed to flee or kill. Whatever it was blotted the sky.

Too big to be tramea.

Turning a main eye up, she saw long tentacles dragging through the trees.

Shan noticed it and said something she couldn't hear.

"It's a skerry," she said, again noticing the twitch of his antennae.

Too loud. She tried to apologize with her antennae and cursed.

THE STORM BENEATH THE WORLD

A skerry here, in the middle of the jungle? It had to belong to the assassins. They must have come to finish what they started. A secondary eye noticed Shan was still talking, and she ignored him.

Hide?

No. If she hid, she might survive.

Another secondary eye saw Izi laying curled in the ash.

Save her. Save Shan.

She'd kill whoever was on the skerry and then get the others back to the school.

Forcing herself to move despite her fatigue, Ahk grabbed a tentacle as it slid past. Shuffling to the nearest tree, she coiled it around the trunk. The skerry, acting on mindless impulse, grabbed hold, tightening the grip.

"Grab another tentacle," Ahk told Shan. "We've got to stop it!"

Though he cowered under her roared orders, he did as instructed, lunging after a dragging tentacle. Spotting another cutting a line through the ash, she grabbed it, looping it around a tree.

Belly barely clearing the foliage, the skerry shuddered to an ungainly stop.

Ahk grabbed Shan, ignoring the shiver of revulsion in his antennae. "I'll hide us." He shied again. Forcing herself to speak softer she added, "It's the assassins. We'll kill them when they descend to free the skerry."

She had no idea how they'd do that. Neither were armed, all weapons burnt to nothing or hidden in the ash.

So tired.

She dared not let Shan burn again. If he lost control, he'd kill the skerry and Izi would die out here.

One eye on Ahk, one on the skerry above, he said something.

Ahk dragged him close. The last time she did this, their antennae touched, became entwined. A moment blurred by terror, she'd felt something then, something new. Her mother often said there were two kinds of males: those you used to pass the time, and those you married. When Ahk first saw Shan's glorious carapace she'd known exactly which kind he was. But she'd been wrong. Afraid as he'd been, he overcame his fear. He'd wanted to run yet stayed.

She wanted that feeling again, the gentle caress of antennae, a touch so incredibly intimate it was usually only shared between life-mates.

Never again. Not with Shan. Not with anyone.

Corrupt, object of pity, carapace burnt ashen white, she'd be scorned by even the lowest dull.

A rope ladder dropped from the skerry, hung swaying.

"After they're dead," she told Shan, "we'll use the skerry to get Izi back to the school."

He babbled something she couldn't understand.

After that, I'll find a way to die.

Nothing could be worse than this solitary hell.

Clinging to Shan, sobbing for the loss of her antennae, Ahk turned her talent to hiding them.

She felt nothing, no pleasure.

The secondary eye watching the skerry above caught movement as an ashkaro looked over the edge of the gondola mounted on its back.

Again, Ahk tried to hide her and Shan and again she failed.

I've lost my talent.

Ahk wanted to laugh and to scream in horror. Somehow, the loss of her antennae took her talent too. She was no longer Corrupt. She could go home, return to her family, or whatever remained of it. That is, she could if she weren't irreparably damaged. With only sight and brute words shouted into an unresponsive world, she offered nothing the family would be interested in. She wasn't suited to minding even the simplest business. All who saw her would recoil in disgust.

She wanted to laugh. She'd cried when she learned she was cursed. The world had been so unfair. And now she would never again feel the soul-deep pleasure of using her talent. That loss was worse than all the rest of it combined.

"I can't hide us," she told Shan.

Looking up, he said something, heat building in him.

Ahk grabbed his face in her claws, forced him to make eye contact. "You can't burn them! We need the skerry to save Izi!"

One of Ahk's secondary eyes sent signals of mad panic as something scampered down the rope ladder to land behind her. Ahk spun and found herself facing a runt of a male dull, small and weak looking.

He must be Corrupt!

Otherwise, the assassins would never have sent him first.

The male's mandibles moved, his antennae showing calm. Ahk's raptorial claws lashed out, trapping all four of the male's arms and holding him helpless. He squirmed in panic, writhing to escape, and she twisted his left craft arm. Wings and antennae showing his agony, the male hung trapped. Both main eyes locked on hers he shouted something, begging or commanding, she couldn't tell. Rearing back on her jumping legs, Ahk braced against the male's thorax, preparing to rip his arms off.

Something hit her from behind, a glancing blow that left one of her raptorial arms numb. Cursing, she realized a second ashkaro had descended, unnoticed, from the skerry. Stab sticks blurred, striking the joints of her arms, somehow missing the trapped male. Needing to defend herself, Ahk tossed him aside. Whatever his talent, he was harmless.

She faced her new opponent, a female with a dark brown carapace streaked in shades of green. Though dull, she had the bearings of a warrior, sleek and deadly, stab sticks ready.

Instead of striking, the female moved to stand between Ahk and the runt male. Shan, as if suddenly awake, jumped to land in front of Ahk, blocking her view.

"Move!" she shouted.

Shan's antennae bent away in cowering apology, but he remained where he was, mandibles moving as he babbled at her.

"I can't hear you! MOVE!"

When she tried to shove him aside, he clung to her arms, tangling her, antennae begging for calm. This wasn't Shan. He would never hurl himself into the middle of a fight between two females. He might be dangerous but fell somewhat short of brave.

Ahk twisted him, bent his arms near breaking, and sent him stumbling away. With no unarmed combat training, he was completely unprepared, and fell sprawling in ash.

The female dull, still standing over her wounded companion,

crouched, legs bent and ready to fight. Her wing and antennae spoke fear and anger, though not in the way Ahk expected. The dull was scared the little male was hurt, angry he'd been attacked, and stood ready to kill any who approached.

Why isn't she attacking?

Shan scrambled upright, scattering ash and dust, about to hurl himself once again at Ahk. Seeing him, the wounded dull male waved a weak claw and said something. Shan stopped, antennae wobbling in confusion.

For several heartbeats, no one moved, all four ashkaro staring at each other, each tensed in case the other attacked.

They're young, like Shan and me.

The male said something, awkwardly picking himself from the ground, his left craft arm cradled against his thorax. Facing Shan, he spoke again.

Helpless and confused, Ahk watched the two males talk. Shan stood relaxed like he conversed with a trusted servant. The female, still between Ahk and the little male, remained poised for a fight but made no attempt to attack. Finally, the dull male touched his protector with his working craft claw. Antennae unhappy, displaying doubt and worry, she lowered her weapons.

Shan gestured at where Izi lay and then in the direction of the school. The two dulls darted uncertain glances at Ahk. She saw disgust and pity in the set of their wings.

Unable to hear any of what was said, incapable of detecting the subtle pheromonal information they shared, Ahk felt more separated from the world than ever. Her limbs shook as the fight leaked from her. Without her talent, carapace twisted and charred ashen white, she was nothing.

Leave me here to die.

She should beg the female for a mercy killing. It was rare for a bright to go to a dull for such a request, but Ahk had few options.

She couldn't, not until she knew Shan and Izi were safe.

Having apparently reached an agreement, Shan approached Ahk, though this time more carefully. He bent an antenna toward Izi. The other, he used to gesture at the swinging rope ladder.

THE STORM BENEATH THE WORLD

"They're going to help us get Izi back to the school?" Ahk asked, wincing when she saw all three react to her volume.

Shan's wings fluttered an affirmative.

Unsure if these were friends, or if Shan had fallen under the sway of a Yil assassin, Ahk saw no choice. Izi wouldn't last long out here.

Did this mean Izi had been saved in the nick of time?

Working in tandem, Ahk and the other female wrestled the unconscious Izi to the rope ladder. Tangling her limbs in the rungs, and then lashing her there with rope taken from the skerry above, they hauled her up to the gondola.

After, with much claw and antennae waving, it became clear the dulls had no idea how to pilot a skerry. Heading to the steerage, Ahk convinced the beast to release the trees it held. With much poking and prodding she got the tired and wounded skerry to gain enough altitude to rise above the foliage. With it finally in motion, she returned to the deck to stare down at the jungle below.

I should jump.

Unfortunately, they weren't high enough she could guarantee death.

Later. I'll find a way later.

JOH

The brighter the carapace, the duller the ashkaro.
—Anonymous

Reeling from the horror of seeing the mutilated female, head shorn of antennae, carapace cracked and diseased looking, flaking ash and weeping at the joints, Joh struggled to understand what had happened. At first, he'd thought her a white, but he'd seen real ones and she was not that. Seeing the burnt trees and cracked and charred exoskeletons, he realized she'd only recently suffered these awful wounds. He couldn't look away. The dead ashkaro in Headmistress Raht's home showed more expression, more personality than this…this…

Ghost. She's a ghost.

There was no other word. She was caught between death and rebirth. Her body looked like it had been ravaged by the fires of Kratosh. Her mind, trapped within, remained sharp. Joh saw it in the way her main and secondary eyes followed every movement, trying to watch everything. And by the way she kept looking over the railing to judge the distance. She wanted to jump to her death and yet hesitated.

Should I help?

One small suggestion and she'd be freed from her hellish existence to be reborn again. Were their positions switched, he hoped she'd do it for him.

She's the only one who can pilot the skerry.

Without her they might float right past the school, unable to turn or land. Giving her the death she craved might cost the other wounded bright female her life.

Later, when alone with Wex, he'd ask what he should do.

Joh prodded Shan Wyn Val Nul Nysh, the gorgeous male bright, with carefully worded questions, learning what happened. Students from Kaylamnel, they'd been set upon by assassins. Izi Doq Qen Jin Vur, the unconscious one, was supposed to be lucky, though she'd been taken out of the fight almost immediately. Ahk Tay Kym, apparently once a bright female, used her talent to hide herself and Shan, who burned the assassins. The male admitted to losing control of his talent. It was he who burned Ahk, and the guilt devoured him from within.

After making sure the unconscious Izi survived the rough trip up the rope ladder, Wex joined Shan and Joh. She nodded toward Ahk, who remained at the rail looking down into the jungle. "How did she survive?"

Shan's antennae bent in shame, but he didn't disagree. "I think she had to."

"Had to?" Joh asked, confused.

"Izi. I didn't see your skerry, that was Ahk. Without her, you'd have coasted by unnoticed. I could never have got Izi back to Kaylamnel; she'd have died out there." Doubt showed in the set of his wings, like maybe he hadn't planned on returning to the school at all. He wasn't terribly excited to be going there now.

"She's lost her talent," Shan told them. He laughed, a harsh bark of self-loathing. "It's my fault."

"She'll kill herself the first chance she gets," Joh said.

Shan nodded, one main eye turning to the rail as if he too considered jumping.

Joh said, "Don't jump. We need you."

He wasn't sure if it was true, but worried if Shan jumped, Ahk wouldn't be far behind, and they definitely needed her.

Shan's wings sagged. "I don't think I could anyway. I'm not that brave."

Was fleeing the repercussions of one's actions brave? With brights, who knew? Though one set of laws governed all society, there were differences in how they were applied. With brights, it often seemed that expectations and perceptions mattered more than the Queen's Law.

Ahk was an interesting case. Talking Shan down had been easy. A few subtle suggestions that they were all on the same side—and could be friendly, if not friends—and the pretty male accepted them as favoured servants. Joh had seen how his haughty demeanour annoyed Wex, though she said nothing. It must have been different for her, growing up the child of a relatively important dull female. As the eldest daughter of a two-name shift manager, she was accustomed to a certain level of respect. The few brights Joh had met had treated him like furniture or a poorly trained animal. Unlike Shan, Ahk ignored Joh's every attempt at suggestion.

She couldn't hear me!

With communication being a seamless blend of pheromones, antennae, wing language, and sound, he'd never given much thought to which aspects carried the power of suggestion. It was, he realized, a comment on how thoughtless the teachers at Amphazar had been. They'd talked about training and testing the limits of the students, but little real effort had been spent on understanding. Not that anyone would have expected him to run into an ashkaro like Ahk. Those suffering such debilitating wounds inevitably went mad from the isolation and took their own lives.

Joh glanced toward the malformed female. *This only just happened*, he reminded himself.

They needed Ahk to get them to the school, but after that, what purpose could she possibly serve? Whatever her status had been, she was a white now, less than Joh. Death would be a mercy.

He remembered the two whites who came to his home begging for water. Despite their desperate thirst, they'd been flawlessly polite, though both were larger than Joh. There'd been something honourable in the way the male refused to leave his fenrik addicted mate. No, honourable wasn't the right word. Respectable? Romantic?

Where are they now?

The female would have succumbed to her addiction months ago. He imagined the male sitting at her side, refusing to leave, as she died.

Ahk needs someone like that. She needs a reason to go on.

It would have been easier if she'd been able to hear him.

"Shan Wyn Val Nul Nysh," Joh said, bowing before the bright male. "Ahk Tay Kym needs you."

Both main eyes turned on Joh. "I know."

Was this the right thing to do? In a way, it fit the Redemption's parables: Shan was responsible for the damage to Ahk and therefore the result was his responsibility too.

"Ahk is your path to redemption," Joh said, "your path to forgiveness. You must give her a reason to live. You can never abandon her."

Never had Joh dared give such a blatant command to a bright. Wex stood to one side, watching with a single eye while pretending to study the dark jungle passing below. One antenna twitched a little, but she didn't otherwise react. While not tacit agreement, Joh decided that, at the least, it meant she wasn't upset with his choice. Though if she hadn't taken an instant dislike to Shan, he wasn't sure she would have felt the same.

Shan looked from Joh to Ahk. "I don't need some damned dull runt to tell me what to do."

He left in that way brights had when dealing with one-name dulls. It was as if Joh simply ceased to exist.

Wex moved to stand by Joh. "They're all going to be like that, you know. Back at Brickworks #7, the only time the bright children talked to us was when they wanted something." She waved an imperious antenna. "You, there, dull," she said, doing a passable impersonation of Shan's arrogant tone. "Fetch my rush ball from the mud!"

"I think we need Ahk," Joh said, an idea forming. There were too many scattered pieces to call it a cohesive thought, but they were fitting together suspiciously well.

Wex looked doubtful. "I understand why you told Shan to care for her, but what possible use could she be? If anything, she's a hindrance. She can't hear, can barely communicate. Whatever her talent was, it's gone."

"She can pilot a skerry," Joh pointed out.

"I'm pretty sure all bright females can pilot skerry, ride tramea, and fight."

"She's immune to my suggestions."

Wex thought about that for a moment. "She'd be immune to that Yil orator too." Her wings fluttered in a half shrug, admitting he had a point, but also letting him know she was far from convinced. "She's immune to manipulation. So what? What are the odds we run into that again?"

Yesterday, he would have said slim. Today, he was less sure. Somehow, Ahk mattered. A secondary eye noticed Izi shift and groan.

We almost missed them in the dark.

But because Ahk saw them, Izi was going to survive, and he and Wex were now on their way to Kaylamnel.

By all the gods of Alatash!

"Her talent is luck," he said, turning an eye in the direction of the unconscious bright.

"Didn't do her much good. She's badly wounded."

"But she's probably not going to die." His mind raced, trying to figure out the connections. "What is the one thing we must do?"

"Stop Queen Yil from sending our island into the storm."

"Right. Izi will recover, but not soon enough to join us. She's lucky enough that she's not going to Yil on a suicide mission."

"I feel like if she was really lucky," Wex said, "she'd have found a way out that didn't involve almost dying."

Joh couldn't argue against that. "Izi and her luck are going to stay here instead of going to Yil. But if no one stops the mad queen, the island is still doomed."

Startled by the implications, Wex's antennae straightened. "You're saying she's so lucky that we're going to save the island while she stays here all nice and safe?"

"Yes. Maybe. I don't know."

"How does that explain why we need a damaged white?"

"She's not a white. Not a true one."

Wex gave him a strange look. "No one is born that way."

She was right. Anyone who spent enough time in the dry air of the desert ended up a white.

"Look," he said. "You and I survived the attack on Amphazar. We took the enemy skerry and went in search of the school. It was us that found them. If I'm right, that's all the result of Izi's luck. And I think it means that everyone here—even Ahk—matters."

"If she's so lucky, then our success is all but guaranteed. We don't even need to try. We'll spin this skerry around, wander over to Yil and toss the mad queen into the storm." She gave him a flat look that said she believed none of it.

"First, I'm not sure anyone can be that lucky. Second, saving the island doesn't mean we survive."

"I'll sacrifice myself to save my family. I'll sacrifice myself for my queen."

"I know," said Joh. "But I'm not sure *I* will." *And if I decide not to let you, you won't either.*

Wex looked less surprised than he expected. "Either Izi is incredibly lucky and we're going to save the island—with or without you—or she's not, and you're wrong about all this."

Joh glanced from Wex to the helpless bright. "If I'm right, her luck trumps free will. As long as she's alive, we'll have no choice but to do whatever we must to ensure she survives."

"And?" She waited.

"And the only way to know we're free to choose is to kill her."

Wex stepped between Joh and Izi. "Why would that matter? Saving the island and Queen Nysh is everything."

Why couldn't she understand how terrifying it was to worry you'd been robbed of choice? He should tell her to kill the unconscious bright. Why even have this conversation when—

Joh froze. *This is what I do when I make suggestions.*

If he told Wex to kill Izi, she would. She'd have no choice.

"I see you thinking about telling me to kill her," Wex said.

She sounded casual, but her antennae were rigid with tension.

"I need to be better at hiding my thoughts," he half-joked.

She didn't react.

It would feel so good to tell Wex that it would be in their best interest if Izi died. It might be manipulation, but it was still truth.

You don't know that. Not for sure.

Joh shook his head. "I can't. I won't."

"We're going to save Izi," Wex said, antennae relaxing a little. "And then we're going to save Nysh. We're going to do it because it's the right thing to do. We're going to do it because then our dull lives will mean *something*."

Why couldn't she see that their 'dull lives' had meaning before any of this started?

I could walk away.

He could order her to land the skerry or deposit him in the nearest city. It might rob her temporarily of some small freedom, but she'd never truly be free if he was with her. If he cared about Wex as much as he thought he did, the best he could do for her was leave. If he was right about Izi's luck, Wex would go on and save the island, though she'd probably die doing so. He'd still be here, safe and alive.

She has a better chance of surviving if she has me.

What were his promises of earning her friendship worth if he fled at the first chance?

He wanted to laugh, to rage at the gods. Between Izi's luck and his increasingly intense feelings for Wex, he felt as if he had no free will at all.

Does she know?

That was a funny thought. If she used his feelings for her to manipulate him, he could hardly be angry. After all, he'd already suggested they be friends.

The gods, he decided were beyond cruel. He told Wex to be his friend and ended up falling in love with her. He was as trapped as she.

I'm going to die in some foreign queendom because I was afraid of being alone.

"I'm coming to Yil with you," he said. "But if we don't survive, I'm going to be really angry."

WEX JEL

Make a pilgrimage to the island's edge.
Look down into the hellstorm of kratosh.
Know its queen, Katlipok, stares back at you.
Feel her seething wrath at being banished from Alatash.
Understand she will drown everything you care about in fire.
She is death everlasting.

—The Redemption

Wex patrolled the skerry, searching the night sky for threats and watching over Izi, worried Joh might change his mind about killing her. Seemingly at peace with his decision, he went to the rear railing. His antennae moved and twitched as he studied the trees, no doubt worried about wild tramea coming after the wounded skerry.

The jungle below heaved and breathed, a mad riot of life perched atop the back of an unimaginable creature floating through an endless river of days. Most believed the islands were dumb beasts, unaware of the civilizations that had grown up riding them. But if Queen Yil could command them, didn't that mean they possessed some rudimentary intelligence? Ashkaro had been riding skerry and tramea for generations. She'd even heard that vicious rafak snakes could be trained.

What would an island think about?

During her brief schooling at Brickworks #7, she learned that the lifespan of islands was measured in hundreds of millions of years. When Wex asked how they knew that—when the oldest queen lived three hundred years and the most ancient texts dated back fifteen queens—the teacher talked about layers of dirt and dead plant matter accruing on the backs of islands. She told Wex that ashkaro had once been mindless insects flitting from flower to flower and that the gods gifted the first queens with intelligence. With generations of breeding, that intelligence slowly filtered down through the queens' offspring, first to her warrior daughters, and eventually all the way down to the lowest dull drone. The unspoken suggestion was that the gift was somewhat filtered as it passed to the lower castes.

On the one claw, it made sense. On the other, brights rarely seemed more intelligent than their dull counterparts. Having watched the four-name daughters of upper-management, Wex knew they could be as dumb as the stupidest dull. The only thing the brights had more of was knowledge. The dumbest bright child knew a thousand times more than the smartest dull. All brights received years of education, sometimes attending universities well into adulthood. As a two-name dull and daughter of a shift manager, Wex's two years of school was twice what most dulls got.

Exhausted, she drifted off, dreaming she was an island and that she carried the burden of lives upon her enormous back. She dreamed she loved them all and didn't mind that they worshipped imaginary gods in the sky instead of the one who bore them through the endless river.

Wex woke to discover Joh standing at the rear rail gawking at the foliage below. Alatash had crested the leeward horizon, returning the light of the gods to the ashkaro. She checked on Izi, finding her still unconscious, and then joined Joh. During the night the lush tangle of jungle had given way to a more civilized and equally green forest. The Yil skerry wobbled often but maintained enough altitude to clear the trees.

"See anything?" she asked.

"I thought I saw a rafak following us. It was difficult to see, kept fading into the foliage. Saw a couple of small tramea, too. There's so much living down there; I've never seen anything like it. Everything is so alive!" He turned his full attention on Wex. "I can never go back to the desert. Not after seeing this." He stretched all four arms wide. "I've never felt so good!"

Though hardly colourful, his mud-brown exoskeleton had darkened with the days of damp air. He wasn't large or strong or beautiful, but he possessed an indefinable quality.

He's growing braver.

Or perhaps he always had been, and she was getting to know him.

Suddenly embarrassed at her scrutiny, he folded his arms about his thorax and pretended to study the forest.

For all his faults, doubts, and fears, she loved him.

Wex's antennae straightened in surprise. Was that true, did she love him? He wasn't what Mom wanted for her. There'd been talk of marrying into a minor bright family, a huge advancement for a two-name dull.

Is he only worthy of me now that I'm bereft of any chance at a future?

Or had she changed? Joh wasn't at all what he seemed on the surface. Dull as his carapace was, he was surprisingly smart. His bravery constantly surprised her. Though small and weak, he defeated a Yil assassin and uncovered a spy. More than anything, his willingness to follow her to Yil, even though he didn't like her plan and was scared, spoke volumes for his character.

Shan returned to the deck. Having cleaned himself during the night and apparently put great effort into buffing his carapace, he was stunningly gorgeous in the light of Alatash. Though she felt desire stir in her abdomen, it was an appreciation for his beauty. He was a work of art the likes of which she'd never seen. Were there male gods, she imagined they'd look like Shan. While his fire made him dangerous, adding some allure he wouldn't otherwise possess, he lacked something.

Something? He's the prettiest male you've ever seen and a five-name bright.

Unattainable, Shan was everything a dull female could ever dream of. Yet he sparked no interest in her. Weird that she couldn't put a word to it, but there it was. Every time she looked at Shan, she saw a mysterious *lack*, as if he could never be what she wanted or needed.

Why, though?

She looked at Joh, saw his dull carapace and knew the quiet strength hidden within. He was loyal and wise and caring and would die at her side. Glancing at Shan she saw a pretty shell of a male.

Dad used to say that love was blind, that the heart wanted what the heart wanted and nothing else mattered. As he was an unrepentant romantic, Wex had ignored him.

She stifled a laugh. Sometimes wisdom came from the most unexpected places.

Shan found the best place to catch the light. Gesturing windward with an immaculate claw, he said, "We're here." His main eyes never left Wex, no part of him showing any sign he was remotely aware of Joh.

Why should he be?

Shan was so far above the highest ranked bright to ever visit the brickworks, she couldn't comprehend what his social standing must have once been. His family probably hired nothing lower than two-name dulls for the most menial tasks. In his world, one-name dulls weren't qualified to scrub toilets.

This was normal and right. This was the way of the world. Joh's ancestors were mindless drones. Yet he was so much more than that. What bothered her most was the inability to connect the Joh she knew with her expectations of a dull runt male. One had to be wrong. Either he was dim-witted, and she'd allowed her fondness for him to blind her, or what she thought of as the way of the world was incorrect.

You know that not all brights are intelligent, and not all dulls are dumb. What's the problem?

Ignoring Shan much as the bright ignored him, Joh moved to the front of the skerry. Uncomfortable with the questions, Wex joined him. As if of its own accord, one antenna bent to touch his. He slid sideways, moving closer.

"Someday," she whispered, "I want you to suggest to the world that it should make sense."

A shiver of humour ran through his wings. "Even the gods of Alatash couldn't do that."

She wanted to ask if he believed in those gods.

Below, the forest stopped abruptly, replaced by neat rows of crops. Dulls worked the fields, simple leather tool belts slung across their thoraxes. A bright lounged beneath a parasol, sipping a drink as another dull worked oils into her carapace. She ignored her charges. Beyond the working dulls lay a large, octagonal area where the ground had been covered in a tight pattern of interlocking bricks. Some still bore vestiges of paint, suggesting the area had once been a massive and intricate mosaic. Wex couldn't guess what it might have displayed. Most of the clay bricks had long ago been scuffed back to their base colours, muted reds and oranges. Thick moss and creeping vines covered the central structure, an eight-sided pyramid, though the entranceway had been kept clear. Sprawling mansions, many times bigger than Headmistress Raht's home, lined the central area. While everything looked impossibly old, it was all better maintained than anything she'd seen in Amphazar. Even the homes of the brights who ran Brickworks #7 were small and drab in comparison. Where the training field in the desert school had been hard-packed dirt, this one was lush grass surrounded by manicured hedges.

There were young brights everywhere, more than she'd ever seen in one place. They hurried about on unimaginable business, perfectly comfortable in their own carapace in a way no dull ever managed.

They know who they are, where they belong.

No matter where a dull went, there was always the chance some bright would come sauntering along and tell them to leave. Few owned anything beyond their scraps of clothing, most living in homes provided by the bright landowner whose farms or factories they worked. Wex's family, better off than any of the other dulls she knew, didn't own their house. The brickworks and all the surrounding property were owned by a bright too important to ever visit somewhere so filthy.

Eight guard towers surrounded the school's perimeter, a bright lounging in each. Wex recognized the uniforms of the Queen's Claw. Spotting the skerry limping in, barely clearing the trees, the guard sounded an alarm, striking a hollow wood tube with a hard stick. The *pok! pok! pok!* sound echoed through the clearing, and guards rushed from the barracks. In moments scores of longbows were aimed at them. Those with spears formed up around the landing area.

Shan waved from the rail. There was no mistaking the pretty male. Though still alert, weapons were lowered as those below stayed clear of the reaching tentacles. One of the brights waved a few dulls forward. Carrying huge trays of glistening grubs over their heads they hurried to feed the hungry beast, ducking away each time a tentacle reached clumsily toward them. Wex watched in horror as one of those writhing limbs suddenly lashed out, curling around a dull. The male screamed, dropping his tray, as his rear claws left the ground. The tentacle curled around the dull, effortlessly lifting him. In a heartbeat he disappeared beneath the skerry. The ashkaro below watched helpless, retreating.

The male's screams cut to hard silence as blue blood rained down on those who had not backed far enough away.

Leaning out over the rail Shan tutted. "He should have been more careful. Any fool could see this thing is starving." Seeing Wex's expression and misunderstanding, he said, "That's it. Won't be any more gore. They digest the entire exoskeleton." An antenna dipped in humour. "I bet crapping that out is going to hurt."

Stunned at the lack of remorse or horror, Wex said nothing. *That's all we are to them: skerry crap.*

Once the beast was low enough, the guards lashed it to several landing poles. A crew of well-dressed dulls moved forward—more carefully than those who fed the skerry—pushing a wheeled stairway. Everyone looked healthy. Even the dull carapaces were robust and lustrous. Back in the brickworks, she'd almost been able to pass for a bright, in the right light. Here, no one would mistake her for anything other than a dusty dull.

Waving Wex back, Shan retreated from the rail. "Better stay behind me until I've had a chance to introduce you. We're missing several students, and…" He glanced toward the steerage. Ahk had yet to return to the deck.

And you burned at least one.

Wex prayed the male didn't decide to try and blame it on the dulls they'd brought home.

Eight Queen's Claw armed with shortbows and stabbing sticks swarmed up the steps, spreading out as they hunted for enemies.

"This is Wex," Shan told the nearest female. "She's with me."

"And Joh," Wex said from behind Shan.

"Oh! Right! The little male is with me too." He sounded less pleased about that.

That was it. The soldier nodded to Shan and promptly ignored Joh and Wex.

Two soldiers lifted Izi and helped the student down the steps, carrying her off to a nearby building as if she were a wounded hero. When Ahk returned from the steerage, limping onto the deck, her carapace still shedding charred white flakes, the warriors backed away from her, antennae shying in horror at the sight.

Ahk gestured a claw at Shan and shouted, "Tell them!"

Shan winced at the bellowed command. "Right. Uh…Ahk was hurt." He darted a guilty glance in her direction. "Her antennae are gone. She can't hear or…or anything."

One of the soldiers guided Ahk off the skerry, though she refused to touch the mutilated student. The two waited at the bottom of the steps, Ahk staring blankly at nothing.

With the deck declared safe, a female bright, carapace a smear of soft pinks fading to green, climbed the steps. Everyone cleared a path for her, nodding respect.

"That's Myosh Pok Tel," whispered Shan. "Defiled priest. She's a teacher. Her talent is hearing lies."

Caught between the terror of being questioned by someone who would know if she lied, and the relief of knowing Shan couldn't lie to blame her for the deaths, Wex bowed her head and antennae, waiting.

THE STORM BENEATH THE WORLD

SHAN WYN VAL NUL NYSH

There are bright families who have made their fortunes off the Corrupt. Look at Ihl Lee Ahd Dhees, matriarch of the Dhees family. Thirty years ago, when she first took over the family business, they were struggling, most of their wealth lost to failed trade ventures with the Yil Queendom. Since then, they've dabbled in fashion, weapons manufacturing, culinary rarities, farming implements, carpentry, and a half dozen other fields. Each time they launch a company it does increasingly well for a few years, the product constantly improving until they are producing the best available, and then suddenly close the business. A few months later, they've reinvested their profits in a new venture and suddenly it becomes incredibly profitable.

We pretend most wealthy families don't have a Corrupt or two hidden away making trinkets for their amusements. But blasphemy on the scale of the Dhees family shifts economies and cannot go unpunished.

—Transcript from the trial of Keh Nil Lee Ahd Dhees

As was proper, Wex and the runty dull male retreated a step as Myosh Pok Tel arrived on deck. Heads bowed, they stood behind Shan, silent. It was a relief they didn't embarrass him; you never knew with dulls, and with these two being from the desert, he had no idea what to expect.

Myosh ignored them, studying Shan. "I send you to hunt one stupid animal, and you return missing half your cadre in a dying skerry I've never seen before. Explain." Her antennae quivered in pleasure as she listened for lies.

THE STORM BENEATH THE WORLD

Shan skirted the edge of the truth, not lying, but not mentioning every detail. He told the teacher how the students were attacked by assassins and rafak. He explained how they were caught unprepared and how Ahk hid them.

"Iyik, Bash, and Shil were all dead," Shan finished. "Izi was hurt. If I didn't do something, they were going to kill her."

Myosh glanced down to where Ahk stood, arms folded tight about her melted carapace like she sought to hide. The student's eyes twitched, trying to watch everything to make up for the loss of perceptions.

The teacher returned her attention to Shan. "You used your talent."

"To save Izi."

"Not entirely true." She grunted doubt. "You lost control."

He wanted to argue. It wasn't his fault! There were too many and they were everywhere. Had they been clumped in a small group he could have controlled the fire. Maybe if Ahk hadn't pressured him to act before he was ready, she wouldn't have been hurt.

"Say it," Myosh commanded.

"I lost control."

"What did I say would happen if you lost control and hurt a student?"

"You'd spike my brain. We'd all be dead if I hadn't done something," he added, struggling to keep his voice calm.

She grunted again, gesturing at Wex. "Who is this?"

"Student from the Corrupt school in the desert," Shan explained. "Her name is Wex Jel. If she hadn't arrived in the skerry, Izi would have died."

Myosh examined the dull female. "Are you really from the desert school?"

"Yes, Teacher Myosh Pok Tel. I am from Amphazar. As is Joh." She nodded at the runt male, who managed a passable bow and wisely remained silent.

"Tell me," demanded Myosh. "Leave out no detail."

Shan listened as the dull female explained how assassins attacked their school and tortured the headmistress. Wex had told him most of the story during the flight here, and he'd only paid attention to the interesting bits. Now, hearing it again—though in more detail, as she was careful not to lie—he found it even less interesting. As far as he could see, the assassins only attacked the desert school to find out where the real school was. The dulls panicked and fled in the skerry. Like the uneducated fools they were, they almost brought a Yil spy straight to Kaylamnel.

"What is your talent?" Myosh asked Wex.

"I'm not sure what to call it," Wex answered. "I see weaknesses, gaps in an opponent's defences. Given stab sticks, I can take advantage of them."

"Killing, then."

Wex's antennae shied in distaste, but she dared not correct the bright teacher.

Myosh noticed Joh. "What's this? A servant?"

"Another student from the desert school," Shan answered.

Myosh's wings flicked in dismissive disinterest. "I need to talk to Headmistress Chynn Wyl Gyr Daw." She waved the soldier near Ahk over. "I want these two," she bent an antenna at Wex and Joh, "put in separate rooms and guarded. No one sees them. Shan, you're with me."

His heart fell at the thought of having to repeat everything in front of the headmistress.

"Excuse me," Joh said, stepping from behind Shan.

Myosh turned a single annoyed eye in the dull's direction. "What?"

Joh hesitated, looking like he was torn between apologizing for the horrific breach of etiquette, and wanting to flee. Finally, he blurted, "Queen Yil can command—"

"Queen Yil Een Ahn Kyn Ah Phy-Rah," corrected Myosh.

The mad queen might be the enemy, but she was still a bright and a queen, and Joh was a dull male of the lowest order.

Shan retreated a step when the little dull's antennae bent in annoyance. Such a display was unimaginable on this side of the island.

"Queen Yil Een Ahn Kyn Ah Phy-Rah," Joh carefully enunciated each syllable, "can command islands and is going to order Nysh into the storm. We must stop her."

Myosh's antennae shivered. "You're not lying."

"No, I am not."

"You're also extremely rude and haven't been educated in even the simplest manners. The fact you're not lying only tells me you believe what you're saying."

"Technically," said Joh, "I suppose that's true."

"Dull males believe all manner of silly romantic garbage," announced Myosh, shooting an angry look at Shan as if all this was somehow his fault. "That hardly makes it true."

"I think," Joh said, "that you should believe what I am saying."

To Shan's surprise, Myosh turned to study the little male. After a moment's scrutiny, she nodded.

She believes him?

"Shan," take these two," Myosh waved a claw at Wex and Joh, "to the kitchens." A single eye turned toward Ahk. "Take her too," she whispered, antennae bending from the disfigured student in disgust. "Get her out of sight of the other students."

"We don't have much time," Joh said, as if addressing an equal. "You should bring all four of us straight to the headmistress so we can tell her what we know."

"Good idea," Myosh agreed.

Looking from the dull to the teacher, Shan said nothing. *Is she humouring the idiot?*

Waving at the soldier to bring Ahk, Myosh set off. The rest scampered after her, the dulls coming last. Shan followed, trying to figure out what had happened. Joh had made some insane claim and Myosh appeared to take him seriously. And now she led the mouthy and impolite dull to the headmistress, who was famous for her intolerance of stupidity and waste, and definitely intolerant of wasting her time with stupidity.

Myosh has lost her mind.

Or did she know something that made the dull's raving make sense?

Myosh approached Headmistress Chynn's home, a converted estate manner. The main door swung open the moment her claw touched the first step. Without a word, the guard there ushered them in, leading them into a long hall. Never having been in Chynn's home, Shan cast a judging eye on every fixture and piece of furniture. It was all nice, though terribly outdated. It felt like walking through the house of a family who'd fallen on hard times some generations previous. Old as it all was, he noted that everything was immaculate and polished to a hard shine.

In another hundred years, this stuff will be worth a fortune.

Today, however, it was all mildly embarrassing. At least to someone of Shan's standing.

They entered a sprawling office lined with bookcases and scroll shelves. Headmistress Chynn stood leaning on her canes at a table, pouring over maps pinned flat by intricately carved paper weights. Her carapace, polished to a mirror finish, gleamed in the candlelight. Shan had heard she was an unprecedented ninety-seven years old and that she'd served during a war against some island only she and Queen Nysh remembered. Chynn turned to face her uninvited guests, one eye still studying the maps.

She managed to look simultaneously frail and terrifying.

"Headmistress Chynn Wyl Gyr Daw," said Myosh, bowing with respect. She straightened, waiting to be told to speak.

Shan ducked his own courtly bow. The two dulls at the back of the party bowed low, almost prostrating themselves. Only Ahk failed the bare minimum of politeness. Shan winced when he noted her lack of courtesy. She barely seemed aware of where she was.

She's still in shock. She'll recover.

He'd find her the best doctors. Somewhere, there'd be someone with exactly the right talent to cure her.

"Myosh," said Headmistress Chynn, pointedly leaving off the rest of her subordinate's name. "Why have you brought *these*," she waved an antenna at the two dulls, "into my home?"

Noticing Joh, her antennae suddenly perked with interest. Both eyes locked on the runt dull, she approached him, shuffling on her canes. Everyone fled from her path.

"These are students from Amphazar," answered Myosh. "They come with an interesting story of—"

"Their names?" Chynn interrupted, antennae showing a flash of fear before recovering. Her eyes never left Joh.

Myosh pointed at Wex. "This is Wex Jel. The male is Joh."

THE STORM BENEATH THE WORLD

The queen aside, Chynn was the oldest ashkaro Shan had ever seen. If the years slowed her, he shuddered to think how fast she must have once been.

She hit Joh, snapping two claw-strikes into his throat, stunning him. Sweeping his front-most legs out with a cane, she cracked him on each side of the head with the spiked elbows of her raptorial arms as he stumbled forward. He collapsed like an emptied shell.

"If he moves," she said to the nearest guard, "kill him. If you let him speak, I'll put your head on the mantle."

The guard, who'd come escorting Ahk, stepped forward. She stood over the unconscious dull, spear raised and ready to kill.

"What the—" Shan snapped his mandibles closed, not wanting to draw the attention of the coldly murderous female.

Happily, Chynn ignored him.

Turning to Myosh, she said, "I was warned about this one by Headmistress Raht. He's Corrupt. His talent is suggestion, though Raht was uncertain as to his limits. They were having difficulty testing him. Teachers kept forgetting or getting distracted. Likely his doing; he didn't want them understanding his potential." One eye watched Joh while the other studied Myosh. "What did he tell you?"

Myosh answered without hesitation. "He said Queen Yil could command islands and that she was going to order Nysh into the storm, killing us all."

Chynn snorted disdainful doubt.

"He wasn't lying," Myosh added. "I would have sensed that."

"Unless he suggested that you believe him," Chynn said. "Most likely we'll have to kill him. It's the only way to be safe."

Suggestion?

Shan thought back to the skerry and his chat with the little dull. Hadn't Joh said something about Ahk being his responsibility because he was the one who hurt her?

I'd already decided I was going to care for her!

That was the kind of ashkaro Shan was. He had a big heart, his mother always said he was too caring.

"They saved us," Shan blurted. "Izi would have died. Rude as the runt is, I think we can trust them."

"He *told* you to trust him," Chynn snapped.

"He didn't though. He never once said I could or should trust him."

"He could have told you to forget he told you to trust him," Chynn stated. "The point is, we can't trust him or anyone he's had access to." She directed a look at Myosh. "With apologies."

The teacher shrugged it off. "I understand, Headmistress Chynn Wyl Gyr Daw, and it makes sense. I don't think I'm a threat, but I can't be sure. I should be watched until the truth has been ascertained."

"Until the truth has been ascertained?" demanded Wex. "Joh was right, we don't have time to wait for you brights to decide to act!"

Chynn ignored the outburst. "Myosh, you'll confine yourself to quarters."

Myosh bowed again. "Of course."

"If she says another word," Chynn said, flicking a contemptuous antenna at Wex, "silence her." Cold gaze sweeping the room, she added, "I need time to think." An antenna pointed out a waiting soldier. "I want messages and warnings sent to the queen. We need guidance. Have a tramea ready to fly within the hour."

The guard left at a run.

Chynn selected another waiting soldier. "I want news from Amphazar. See to it."

The Queen's Claw dashed from the room.

The headmistress examined the students. "Relieve them of weapons and lock them up," she said to the last two soldiers. "Separate cells." She pointed at Ahk, who stared at the floor as if none of this mattered. "The white too."

One of the soldiers collected their weapons, heaping them on the headmistress' table.

Dredging up every last bit of bravery, Shan said, "She's not a white. That's Ahk Tay Kym." He struggled to find a word that encompassed the damage she'd suffered and the loss of senses. "She was hurt when the Yil assassins attacked."

Chynn's antennae showed revulsion. "She's a white now." She clicked her claws and the soldiers hustled to obey. A battle-scarred bright female with a carapace of black shot with red, lifted the unconscious Joh.

THE STORM BENEATH THE WORLD

The other, a younger bright with a pastel blue exoskeleton, herded the obedient dulls and unresponsive Ahk toward the door."

"Him too," said Chynn, nodding at Shan. "We don't know if Joh made dangerous suggestions."

"Me?" Shan's voice cracked. "He didn't! I can't! Not again! I'm the queen's nephew!"

He lay on the floor, trying to make sense of the ceiling and to understand why his legs didn't work. Managing only a slurred mumble, he tried to argue, his thoughts mushy and sodden like someone drown them in a bog.

The soldier carrying Joh slung the little dull over a shoulder and grabbed one of Shan's jump legs with a powerful raptorial claw. She dragged him from the headmistress' chambers, his head bouncing off every imperfection in the floor.

Did she hit me?

He hadn't seen her move.

Somewhere between Chynn's home and the temple, Shan's limbs started to feel like they might work. He wanted to ask the soldier to let him go, to explain that this was all a mistake, but worried she wouldn't listen and might decide to hurt him again.

The soldiers took them to the dungeon under the temple. The one dragging Shan hauled him to a familiar cell, the floor littered with wood scraps and kindling. Each student was put into a separate cell, Joh tossed into one like a jumble of twigs. Seeing the soldier, who maintained a safe distance, point at the door, Ahk entered hers and promptly curled on the floor, pulling her limbs in tight.

Numb and silent, he allowed himself to be shoved into the cell. He couldn't pull his attention from Ahk, the way she caved in on herself, carapace still shedding ashen flakes.

That's my fault.

The kindling surrounding him screamed to be lit ablaze. By all the gods of Alatash he wanted nothing more than to lose himself to the bliss of his talent.

I can't. I'll hurt her.

"Throw the broken and ruined things to the storm." Ahk's voice echoed through the dungeon hall. "Disappear into nothing."

THE STORM BENEATH THE WORLD

My fault. I'll never burn again.
He knew he lied.

THE STORM BENEATH THE WORLD

AHK TAY KYM

After decades of studying the Corrupt I can say there is no rhyme or reason as to who gets what talent. There are brights skilled in carving pointless trinkets and dulls capable of calling lightning from the clouds above. There are females who can master stunning dances and males with a gods-given skill in the longbow. There are brights with a talent for weeding gardens and dulls who can create such exquisite works of art they can't possibly have the wit to appreciate them.

Either the gods work in mysterious ways, or they're utterly insane.

—Tah Ree Sah Fro Hok, Scientist

Throw the broken and ruined things to the storm.

Ahk pulled all eight limbs in, hugging herself tight. She'd felt betrayed when the gods cursed her with talent. Now, she wanted it back more than anything.

Disappear into nothing.

If she could sink into the floor and dissolve, never again see the looks of sick revulsion on the antennae of those around her, she would.

Throw the broken and ruined to the storm.

She was an abomination, useless to everyone. At least as a Corrupt she might serve the queen and have some purpose.

We think we've turned our backs on the hive but it's a lie. We will always be hive, always need others to survive, to give us meaning.

In the dark of the cell, huddled in a cage of her arms, she could almost believe she ceased to exist. Perfect silence. Nothing moved, no hint of air feathering her antennae. No scent of pheromones. More alone than Katlipok in the hellish storm of Kratosh.

Maybe the headmistress would take pity and end her miserable existence. Rot in a dark cell. Spike in the brain. Either was fine. What was time to the useless? What was life to the purposeless?

She remembered the headmistress' fear, the way she angled closer, shuffling on those canes, until she was close enough to strike. Why hit the little dull male? He was harmless. Even deformed and crippled Ahk could easily have killed him. But Chynn made a show of her feebleness, lulling the runt dull until she was within range.

Runt dull? Ahk laughed. *I don't know his name and probably never will.* What were the odds he knew how to write? Still, the question scraped at her thoughts. The dull reminded her of Bon, who'd discovered his talent for carving figurines and chose Ahk as his muse.

He'd choose someone else now.

When she'd realized Bon's fate, she'd felt overwhelming loss and pity. Now, he'd pity her. If he wasn't too disgusted. Whatever happened to him after she left was better than what happened to her. They likely shipped him off to some brickworks in the desert.

If only I'd discovered my talent a little sooner.

She'd give anything to be there with him.

Thinking back, she remembered the set of Bon's antennae. She'd seen something similar in the dull male on the skerry. *He seemed sad.* And not because of what happened to her, though she'd seen his pity. It was more like he had a difficult decision to make, and it weighed upon his slim carapace. That, and he was clearly smitten with the dull female he travelled with. Previously, she likely would have missed it, but robbed of her primary senses, she'd been unusually reliant on her eyes.

Is he Corrupt?

He must be. Headmistress Chynn hadn't just struck the little male, she'd put him down hard. And then a guard had stood ready to kill him. The elderly ashkaro was terrified of him.

His talent must be dangerous.

Shan had joined her in the steerage on the trip home, though he stayed well clear as if some disease caused her malformed carapace.

You caused it. It was almost funny. *The prettiest ashkaro I ever met turned me into the ugliest.* He'd babbled, mandibles and antennae moving and agitated, explaining or apologizing, forgetting she couldn't hear. She'd ignored him. What did it matter? What difference could he make?

He was talking because he didn't know what else to do.

Even though he kept his distance, he was there; that should matter.

She recalled the guilty set of his wings, the way his antennae shied in shame.

I should tell him not to blame himself.

She knew all too well the pull of the lure. Sometimes, when alone in her room where the teachers couldn't see, she'd hidden from nothing, just to taste that rush. Shan had hesitated and she'd thought it cowardice.

He knew his weakness.

Looking back, she saw a male dreading exactly what happened.

Shan would leave her before long. His guilt would fade. He'd go on with whatever life remained to a Corrupt bright. *He's too pretty, too shallow to ever be with something as awful as me.*

Her arms, curled tight over her head, ached with tension. Shifting, she stretched a raptorial arm to work out the ache.

Not dead after all.

Standing, she stretched her arms, feeling the useless nubs of her crisped wings move.

The guards and caged students—except the little dull male, who was still unconscious—gawked at her. Shan's antennae sagged in humiliation.

Why are they staring at me?

The nearest guard retreated a step.

"I've been thinking aloud, haven't I?"

The guard's antennae bent away in fear and distaste, but she nodded, retreating another step from the horrific monster.

Ahk considered her last thought: He's too pretty, too shallow to ever be with something as awful as me. It was true and yet still cruel.

Facing Shan she said, "That was unfair of me. You saved Izi, and that matters."

Shan shook his head in denial, mandibles moving.

I'll never abandon you. What happened is my fault. I can be more than what people think.

THE STORM BENEATH THE WORLD

Ahk stared at him, confused. Though she heard the words in her head, those weren't her thoughts.

Fantastic. On top of everything else, she was losing her mind.

You're mutilated and insane, does that mean you should give up?

She'd been so intent on what happened to her, she'd forgotten what the servants of Queen Yil did to her mother.

Perhaps vengeance might serve as both reason and purpose.

JOH

In the final throes of addiction, fenrick addicts can become as dangerous as the Corrupt. They will lie, steal, cheat, and kill for one more taste of the leaf. And yet we treat them with pity. There are social programs for addiction in the larger cities. Every Redemption priest has been trained in dealing with addicted ashkaro. I find it strange that we treat those addicts so much better than we treat the painter who has discovered her muse and will spend her last days creating ever more stunning works of art.

—Spin Har Dho, social commentator, Nysh City.

Joh woke, groggy and confused to find himself sprawled on damp stone. Leaning against the wall for support, he stood. The world felt tilted, threatening to hurl him back to the ground. Turning a circle, he found himself in a dank cell. The door was closed, no doubt barred on the far side. A small octagonal window, too high to see through easily, gave him a view of the dungeon beyond. Across the hall were more cells, doors closed.

Ahk, shorn of wings and antennae, looked deranged. The only times ashkaro bent their antennae flat back against their head was when they were cornered and terrified or suffering the deepest shame. It was the kind of expression that presaged violence. Wex peered through her cell window, main eyes meeting Joh's. If there were more cells on his side, he couldn't see them. Two bright females armed with spears and stab sticks stood huddled and whispering in the hall, darting nervous glances at Ahk.

It felt like something important happened moments before he

woke.

Still unsteady, he retreated into his cell. His antenna brushed against the clay bricks sensing faint imperfections. Dazed from being hit, he traced them, following faults and hairline cracks. A picture grew in his mind as the other antenna joined in, reaching out to caress stone.

This isn't random at all!

Someone had carved images into the wall. Invisible in the dark, the lines became a clear image when so traced. There were ashkaro, incredibly detailed and yet subtly wrong. Their wings were too large, antennae overly long and drooping. Bodies smaller and whisp thin, they looked like a strong breeze would take them away.

Was this artistic interpretation, or were these carvings so old they depicted ashkaro as they were during the days of hive?

Translated by his antennae, the picture grew in such detail he easily imagined the colours and scents. There was a jungle, air hotter and damper than that surrounding this school. Leaves bent and swayed in the breeze. Strange things darted through the foliage, sinuous and twisting like rafak, but scarier. Scores of ashkaro gathered around a wingless creature so disgusting revulsion threatened to crumple Joh to the floor. They worshipped it, offering newborns as gifts.

Was this what they thought the gods of Alatash looked like? That seemed wrong. The gods were always described as towering ashkaro with magnificent wings and carapaces of unsurpassable beauty. Even Katlipok, the fallen god, was depicted as a gorgeous, if terrifying, bright female. There was nothing in this squishy-looking creature to even suggest a sex.

The furless vertebrate, wrapped in gut-churning stretchy black instead of a proper carapace, turned to look at Joh. Its stone eyes bled smoke.

He backed from the wall. The image remained with him, locked in his imagination. These were the artistic ravings of a broken ashkaro.

This is a creation of talent!

It was too perfect, too powerful to be anything else. Long ago, some mad heretic Corrupt had been locked beneath this ancient temple.

Joh's sluggishly wandering thoughts snapped back to the present.

As soon as the headmistress saw him, she'd begun moving closer.

THE STORM BENEATH THE WORLD

Though he'd never met her, she looked as if she recognized him. Then, when she heard his name from Myosh, she'd lashed out with such speed he hadn't seen it coming. She'd very intentionally rendered him both helpless and unconscious.

Incapable of speaking.

The only way she would have known of his talent was if someone warned her. Headmistress Raht must have been reporting to Chynn. The headmistress at Kaylamnel no doubt knew the talents of all Amphazar's students, but she'd been most afraid of Joh's.

Raht warned her specifically about me.

Had all the teachers at the desert school been afraid of him? Most of his interactions had been with Rel. Had they been using the dull priest as a buffer between themselves and Joh? He imagined them watching Rel for changes, always wondering if Joh was manipulating the Defiled priest. What would they have done if the teacher seemed different one day, spike Joh's brain in a spasm of fear?

It seemed short-sighted. He could easily have found a way around it. For a school supposedly set up to teach Corrupt children, they were woefully unprepared for someone like Joh.

Except you had no idea.

He'd been blissfully ignorant of the teacher's thoughts and opinions about him. They must have had strategies in place should he prove dangerous. Archers ready to snuff his life at the first sign his intentions were malicious. Fellow students with stab sticks hanging innocently in scabbards.

Did they tell Wex to spy on me?

He didn't want to believe that, but how different would things have been had he not suggested they be friends when they first met in Rel's wagon?

No, they would have seen we were too close.

They couldn't trust her not to tell him.

Thinking back, he didn't remember anything suspicious. Considering how bad the teachers were at everything else, he doubted they were master spies when it came to him. More likely, they knew he was potentially dangerous and simply kept an eye on him. Then, when he showed up here in Kaylamnel, Chynn panicked, rendering him unconscious. Once they talked to him, they'd understand he was on their side. They'd release him and let him share what he knew.

Assuming that happened—and waking up in the cell of a psychotic heretic did little to ease his worries—what would Raht do next?

She won't believe me.

Had he not forced Kris to tell him the truth, he wouldn't believe Yil planned on murdering the entire population either. There were stories of ashkaro with talents that let them communicate with—or even command—wild creatures, but an island was altogether different. Wasn't it? The idea that not only could someone command an island to dive into the storm, killing everyone, but that they *would*, was too much.

Let's say Chynn believes me. Then what?

She'd send word to Nysh City. She might be an important bright, but the fact she was stuck out here running a school for the reviled of society said much about her social standing. Would anyone believe Chynn, and if they did, how long before someone acted on the knowledge? Having seen how long brights took to decide what to have for breakfast didn't fill him with confidence.

We can't wait for someone else to save the island.

If he was honest, it was only Wex he cared about. If he could convince her to abandon Nysh and go elsewhere, he'd be infinitely happier. He couldn't though, not without robbing her of her freedom to choose and he wouldn't do that.

Just like you wouldn't make the one suggestion that would have saved your father's life? Joh flinched at the thought. *Fine. I won't suggest we flee unless there's no other way to save her.*

For now, Wex cared about the island and that made it important. He'd do what he could to save their home and if, in the end, it looked hopeless, he'd make sure they fled together.

Joh bent an antenna to the wall, brushed the scene carved there, saw again the oddly shaped ashkaro gathered around the grotesque creature. Worship written into every pose, every antenna, there was no mistaking the power balance.

Religion and faith are writ as deep in our blood as hive. Much like the ashkaro's desperate need to belong, they were a form of slavery.

It was a strange thought, bordering on blasphemous.

THE STORM BENEATH THE WORLD

While never referred to as slaves, dulls everywhere knew what it was to have limited options. Where brights had access to the best schools, dulls were lucky if they got a single year of basic education. That brief schooling was invariably based around whatever the local brights decided the dull's job would be.

Making suggestions that must be obeyed is slavery too.

Having grown up without choices, he didn't want to be responsible for stealing those of others.

Even if he saved Wex from the doomed island, they had no future together. Though nothing could save him from falling to the lure, he could tell her to never again use her talent. He could save her, earn some shred of redemption.

Either slavery is wrong, or it isn't.

The reasons shouldn't matter. There was, after all, no difference between a reason and an excuse. It was all a matter of perspective. Saving her could be the reason for robbing her of choices or the excuse he used to get what he wanted.

Is it acceptable to rob Wex of some freedom if it saves her life?

It seemed like it should be and felt like it wasn't.

On the other claw, none of his concerns counted for much if they were locked in a dungeon when Nysh Island dove into the storm.

Joh returned to the cell door, stretching as tall as he could to get a better look. The guards were still focussed on Ahk, who mumbled to herself.

"Joh," Wex called across the hall, antennae reaching toward him in concern, "are you hurt?"

One of the guards shot Wex an annoyed look. "Silence!"

Joh shook his head.

Amazing. Even forewarned of his talent, Chynn couldn't believe a dull male could ever be a threat. The guards were within earshot. It would be easy to tell them to open the cells.

Slavery isn't wrong if it gets you out of a cell?

He wanted to explain everything to Wex, how the brights would ignore them or act too slowly to save the island. He wanted her to tell him what to do, what was acceptable and what was evil. It was too much responsibility. What in his life could possibly have prepared him for this?

"Joh?" Wex repeated. "What's wrong?"

"I said silence!" the guard snapped, thrusting her spear at Wex to drive her back from the window.

Ahk straightened, denuded head shocking as her attention locked on Wex. "Joh wants you to tell him it's all right to enslave the guards so he can save the island from the mad queen."

WEX JEL

The most dangerous Corrupt I ever saw was a storyteller. She travelled from city to city, weaving tales of heroes and freedom and equality for all. She told stories for meals or for a sip of water. She wove legends for blankets or the opportunity to sleep in a barn. No ashkaro left one of her story-telling sessions unmoved. Many left wracked with grief or anger, depending on the night's tale. Everyone left thoughtful, plagued by questions and doubts. As she grew in power, her stories becoming ever more intricate, ever more effective at capturing her audience's imagination, some began to follow her. Soon, she travelled with a mixed entourage of dulls and brights from all castes. Unlike the storyteller, few were Corrupt. They cared for her. They cleaned her and made her meals. They scavenged and scrounged for food or traded their wealth to support her. They kept her healthy long past the time when she should have fallen to the lure. She mumbled parables in her sleep, spun new myths as she ate, wove tales of rebellions and false gods as she walked. Sometimes her followers starved to death despite not being Corrupt. They could not bear to miss even an instant of her stories. More came, replenishing the numbers, her mob growing ever larger. They swept into prosperous villages and left ghost towns.

The queen sent assassins to deal with this nuisance and they too fell in love with her dangerous fictions. Desperate, the queen ordered her greatest warrior—her firstborn daughter—deafened and then sent her to assassinate the storyteller.

—Anonymous

Wex looked from Joh to Ahk and back to her friend. The two guards tensed, antennae straightening, weapons clutched tight in claws.

Shan, on the same side of the hall as Joh, said, "The runt can enslave people?" His attention slid to Ahk, his upper wings fluttering in agitation. "Did he tell me to care for Ahk?" Shan shook his head. "No. I'd already decided! I did!"

He didn't sound like he entirely believed himself.

"Enslave?" asked the pastel blue guard, turning to her superior.

"Kill him!" the battle-scarred soldier barked.

With no hesitation, the younger soldier hoisted a spear and approached the door to Joh's cell.

Joh stood at the window, made no attempt to retreat or protect himself, eyes never leaving Wex. He was so small, so physically unimpressive. His talent, however, was the scariest she'd ever seen.

Enslave? Having already spent countless hours questioning the extent and possible repercussions of his talent, she knew it to be true.

Ready for danger, scared and expecting attack, the soldier shuffled toward Joh. Refusing to retreat, he stayed at the window.

She'll kill him where he stands!

But they were brights, and she and Joh were dulls. The brights were in charge.

Why?

Because they're brights.

A circular argument with no end. Wex's thoughts spiralled, gaining speed as they clawed at the problem. Even as the pastel blue bright closed with Joh, she couldn't stop asking questions. She needed to understand.

The brights were descended from the hive queen's warrior caste. Everyone assumed they were smarter because they were shinier, faster, and deadlier. But the drones, those who later became the dulls, built everything. Early on, before the queens became sentient, they built massive hives on the backs of flying islands. When the gods lifted the queens from brutish animals to ashkaro, the drones built them bigger and bigger hives, ever more intricate works of art. The warriors went to war and the drones learned how to build defences. They built walls and traps. They built ramparts. The first crude weapons were crafted by the claws of dulls, as were the first bows and other machines of war. Brights had always been above such things and still were.

What is more difficult, building or killing?

The bright soldier reached Joh's cell, spear lifting, ready to kill.

Looking past the bright, Joh said, "Wex, tell me what to do."

"Enslave them," Wex answered without hesitation.

"You should release us," Joh told the soldier.

He sounded calm, unworried, and some part of Wex's mind picked at that. Had he been confident she'd give him permission, or did he not care if he died?

The raised spear hesitated.

"What are you doing?" snapped the battle-scarred red and black bright. "Kill him!"

"Put your spear down," Joh called to her. "You can relax. You're in no danger here."

The red and black's shoulders sagged as she lowered her weapon. Then, she snarled, dropping into a fighting crouch. "Ser Ahl Xun," she said to the other bright, "kill him. That's an order!"

Ser looked from Joh to her superior.

"Ser Ahl Xun," said Joh, "she's not being serious. You don't want to kill me." He looked past her at the other soldier. "Put your weapons on the floor," he ordered. "Stand motionless."

This time the soldier barely moved, catching herself before her weapons drooped. Sliding a pair of stab sticks from their sheath slung across her abdomen, she said, "I'll kill him myself."

"You don't want to kill me," Joh told her. "You and I should be friends."

We should be friends? Wex's heart squeezed tight. By all the gods, how many times had she struggled to justify her friendship with the runt dull?

No! He would never!

Why not?

Because he's my friend!

The black and red bright ignored Joh's suggestions, stalking the hall toward him, poised for violence. "I feel you pushing, *parasite*." She spat the last word. "You're wrong. I very much want to kill you." She shifted the spear, holding it across her body in one raptorial claw and one craft claw. She gripped the stab sticks in the remaining claws.

For the first time, Joh looked scared, attention darting between the two brights. "Ser Ahl Xun, protect me," he told the pale blue bright already at his door.

Ser turned to her commanding officer. Seeing the readied weapons, she drew her own stab sticks, matching the grip. Crouching, she stood ready.

Did he tell me to be his friend?

Wex saw what Joh could not. Due to the wording of his command, Ser would only defend him.

"That's not enough," she called through the window.

Joh darted a pleading look in her direction. Sheltered as his upbringing had been, he'd likely never seen violence. Certainly, he'd never hurt anyone. He didn't have it in him. Wex remembered the dull whose head Joh smashed in with a chair back in Headmistress Raht's home.

That's not why he's hesitating.

Once again, he waited for explicit permission. There was so much there she wanted to examine, but there was no time. The choice was simple: the life of this bright she'd never met, or that of her best friend, who may have manipulated her into that friendship.

Unable to let someone hurt Joh, Wex said, "Do it."

"Ser, kill her," he commanded.

Ser Ahl Xun skittered forward, keeping herself between Joh and the other soldier. The two females closed slowly at first. Ser used her stab sticks to bat aside the other's spear thrust, stabbing back with her own spear. Though Wex's talent let her see the weaknesses and opening in an opponent's defences, watching from a remove was completely different. These were two trained and experienced combat veterans at their physical peak. Where Ser had youth and speed on her side, the red and black, carapace scarred with past wars, had experience.

The red and black launched herself at her underling and the tentative testing turned into a mad flurry. Wex watched in awe as the hall echoed with the rapid staccato *clack* of wood on wood so fast it sounded like a single hummed note. She didn't see the death blow. There was the sound of splintering wood and then Ser lay spasming on the floor with a stab stick driven upward into her skull just behind her mandibles.

The red and black studied her victim with cold regard. Wex saw no hint of regret or remorse.

Dragging her stab stick free, the soldier faced Joh. "I'm going to break you for making me do that. Every joint and every limb." She stalked toward his cell. "I'm going to smash your mandibles so you can't speak. I'm going to tear out your antennae, so you look like that white abomination."

"You've forgotten something!" Ahk shouted from her cell, slowing the bright's approach.

"What did I forget?" the red and black bright asked, not taking her eyes off Joh.

"Shan," bellowed Ahk. "You forgot Shan."

The bright turned one eye so she could focus on Shan, who stood at the door of his cell, peering nervously out the window. "The pretty one?" she asked dismissively. "What about him?"

"I can't," said Shan, pleading. "Look what happened last time."

"It won't happen again," said Ahk. "I know you. You won't let it."

Shan shook his head. "I lost control. Down here, trapped in cells, I'd cook you all."

Decision made, the red and black again moved toward Joh's cell.

"He's not going to," Ahk shouted at Joh. "Not unless you *tell* him to."

Joh looked to Wex. Confused, she nodded permission.

"Shan," said Joh. "Burn her."

THE STORM BENEATH THE WORLD

SHAN WYN VAL NUL NYSH

You are the first step in our quest for Redemption.
Is your neighbour's business suddenly becoming unexpectedly successful? She might be Corrupt.
Has your sister hesitated to show her newborn? She might be hiding a malformed abomination.
Is your child spending too much time on her hobby? She may have discovered her talent.
Be alert.
Be watchful.
Report what you see.

—The Redemption

Burn her?
Shan looked down at the twigs and kindling littering his cell floor. Heat built in him, and he struggled to crush it back into place. If he used his talent in here, he'd be burned alive! Did they not know, or not care? Ahk must have gone mad, her sanity broken by the trauma suffered. She babbled nonsense, claiming people who hadn't said a word were talking.

"Shan!" Ahk yelled at him. "I'm not crazy." She made a broken cackling sound. "At least I don't think I am."

"Burn her," repeated the Kratosh-damned dull, as if Shan was his to command.

The nerve!

The fire built, clawing for release.

No!

The red and black bright shuffled closer to Joh's cell, alert for danger. For a moment one eye focussed on Shan. Seeing no threat there, it swung to the bellowing Ahk.

This was not at all like burning the Yil assassins in the forest. This was a member of the Queen's Claw, a loyal soldier! Shan might not like being locked down here, but they were on the same side. The terrifying Headmistress Chynn was in charge! Eventually, she'd see her mistake and release him. Anyway, if the runt dull really could enslave ashkaro, the soldier was doing the right thing.

Shan shuddered at the thought of a dim-witted dull with such power.

Imagine asking me—a five name bright!—to risk not only my own life, but the lives of everyone down here to save an ugly little dull!

"Shan," repeated Joh.

"I can't!" he screamed at the runt. "I made a promise!" The heaped kindling on the floor smoked, dried leaves curling as they darkened.

The bright soldier reached Joh's cell. The dull made no attempt to protect himself.

Eyes and antennae on Shan, the strange weight of their scrutiny crushing him, Joh said, "Burn her. Now."

Choice gone, Shan lost himself to the all-encompassing joy of his talent. Flames roared from him, an uncontrolled maelstrom of raging destruction. The wood and leaves, heaped in his cell all those months ago to test his control, ignited. He saw only white, the colour of purest bliss and foulest ruin. Someone screamed in agony, a single ecstatic note.

He hadn't wanted to.

He warned them.

After hurting Ahk he promised to never again use his talent. Less than a day later, here he was burning. Control was asking too much; those who teased him for being pampered were right. There was nothing in his life to give him the strength of character to resist the lure. It was impossible. This was the gods' curse.

You're weak. It's all your fault.

"Shan!" Ahk yelled from across the hall. "You're not weak. It's not your fault."

Her insistence on roaring out his every thought was annoying.

Guilt at hurting Ahk again crushed him. Every terrible thing everyone ever said about him was true. He was shallow and stupid and vain and cared only for himself. If he could burn himself to save Ahk, he would.

I'd give anything to save her.

"Then save me."

Shan snuffed the fire.

I didn't know I could do that.

"You did it," Ahk said. "I knew you could."

Smoke filled his cell, turned the hall beyond the little window into a blurred haze.

He couldn't tell her she was the only reason he was able to regain control. From the first moment they met, he knew there was something special about her, a connection. Even if only he felt it. Even if it was all in his imagination and she thought him a romantic idiot.

"It's all right," Ahk said, voice softening. "I'd rather a romantic idiot than a heartless killer."

The wood and leaves piled in his cell were gone. Only ash remained. He found his carapace unharmed, not a hint of char.

I didn't die.

Was he immune to all fire, or only the fire he made?

That seemed like the kind of thing the teachers should have tested.

And I'm still beautiful!

"Start small," suggested Ahk. "Don't walk into the next bonfire you see."

"Smart," he agreed.

Shan pushed a craft claw against the door to his cell and the wood crumbled apart like charcoal. Smoking embers scattered as they hit the floor. He squinted into the smoke. In the hall beyond, the other prisoners were returning to the windows in their own doors having fled to the back walls.

The red and black bright lay before Joh's cell, her carapace scorched. She twitched, whimpering in agony as a cloud of steam escaped a crack in her exoskeleton.

Shan stopped, staring in shocked horror. *She's still alive.*

Joh stretched as tall as he could to see out his window. "Unbar the doors."

THE STORM BENEATH THE WORLD

Shan moved without thought, lifting the smoking wood bars, and tossing them aside. He released Ahk last, and she stepped close as the door swung open, pulling him into an embrace. His antennae reached for hers, found nothing, and his heart broke anew.

I wish we could touch like we did when you were hiding us.

"Me too," she said.

Malformed and white, she'd lost her alluring grace. And yet, saving her had mattered more than the euphoria of the lure.

Maybe there's hope for me yet.

Perhaps he wasn't so shallow after all.

Ahk gave him an odd look, head tilted to one side, and said nothing.

Wex stood over the keening soldier. "What should we do?"

Releasing Shan, Ahk said, "Kill her. Her pain is deafening."

The wounded bright's exoskeleton hissed and popped, making crackling sounds as it cooled.

Not a bright anymore.

Hadn't she said something similar about Ahk? He wanted to laugh. Was this justice?

"No," Ahk said. To Wex she added, "Please, end her misery. She's in terrible pain."

Wex bent to collect one of the bright's stab sticks. It must have been shielded by the soldier's body as it looked undamaged. She stood over her, weapon gripped in both craft claws.

"I know," said Ahk. "It's not like killing someone in a fight."

"She's going to die anyway?" asked Wex.

The gnarled stumps where Ahk's wings had been wriggled in what was probably a shrug. "She'd rather die than live like this." Her head cocked to one side as she studied the soldier. "Like me."

Wex stabbed the bright through the head, spiking her brain. The burnt body stiffened, spasms running through the limbs, and relaxed.

Ahk stared, transfixed. "I feel her sliding away." Her mandibles moved as if searching for the right words. "I always thought death was sudden. You're alive," she clicked a craft claw, "and then you're gone. It's not like that at all. Some of her went the instant the wood punctured her brain, but some remains. She's fading, and yet clinging to life. So scared."

"Can you tell where she's going?" Shan asked. "Up to Alatash, or down to the storm?"

"No," answered Ahk. "It's more like she's…dissolving."

Joh fluttered his wings for attention. "We don't have much time. Even if no one saw the fire, the smoke will let them know something happened."

"Time?" Shan laughed. "To do what? They'll kill us for this."

"Queen Yil can command islands," Joh said as if it was the most normal thing in all the river of days. "She's going to order Nysh Island into the storm."

Hadn't he made a similar claim before? Shan hadn't been listening. The runt tended to babble. "You're insane."

"He's different." Ahk's wing stumps writhed again. "But then so is Wex and so are you. I don't know if you three are somehow special, or if everyone is if only you can hear their thoughts."

You can hear my every thought?

"I can." Ahk gestured at Joh. "He's afraid Wex will realize he—"

"We don't have time for this," Joh interrupted. "We have to save the island. *We* have to save the island."

"He's right," Ahk agreed. "His reasoning is sound."

"Or you're both insane," Shan said.

"Perhaps," agreed Ahk. "What's normal when we're so different from each other? Being Corrupt is the only thing that binds us."

That's not true.

"Isn't it?" she asked. "Would you have given a three-name bright—even one from a family like mine—a second thought? And you," she directed at Wex. "You're only friends with Joh because—"

"Ahk!" Antennae standing straight, Joh looked ready to flee back to his cell.

"There are worse crimes," she said, "than wanting a friend."

Wings tense, Joh ignored her. "We have to save the island. First, we must escape the school. The headmistress will never willingly let us go." He turned to Ahk. "Can you hear what she's thinking now? Are there any guards coming?"

"I hear only you three," Ahk said. "Maybe the stone of the temple is blocking me, or perhaps my range is limited. A blessing, I suspect. You three never shut up. It's an incessant bombardment of doubt and fear and," she glanced at Wex, "questions. I'd go mad if I had to hear more."

Shan's thoughts churned in confused turmoil. There was too much to take in. The stupid dull could tell others what to do and they had to obey. Well, except for this dead bright. Somehow, she'd resisted.

"Joh is many things," Ahk said, "but stupid isn't one of them."

Shan waved her to silence, trying to concentrate. The runt was right about one thing: they had to escape. Though supplies were delivered each week, and tramea came and went regularly, there were no skerry permanently stationed at the school.

"The skerry we arrived on is our only option," he said. "And it was in rough shape. I think it might be dying."

"It only needs to get us somewhere we can steal a healthier one," Joh said, darting nervous looks at Wex, who seemed distracted.

If Ahk could hear thoughts and said the runt was right, then maybe Queen Yil really could send Nysh Island into the storm. That was a problem for later though. Right now, all that mattered was escaping before Chynn spiked him for killing the soldier.

The hall fell silent except the *crackle pop* of the dead bright's carapace.

They're waiting for someone to tell them what to do. They need a leader.

He looked to Ahk. She nodded.

We'll stay with them until we're clear and then ditch them. I know people in Nysh City who will hide us. He wasn't sure if he was lying.

Ahk shook her head. "No. I need your help."

"For?"

"Vengeance," she answered. "Yil spies killed my mother."

She was Shan's responsibility; he would do what he must. To have any chance at achieving her vengeance, Ahk would have to get to Yil Island. He couldn't do it by himself though. He'd need their help.

"We might as well save the island while we're getting you your vengeance," Shan joked. It sounded no saner coming from him than when Joh said it. "To do that, we must intercept the mad queen, who will no doubt be protected by an entire army of Corrupt."

He looked from Ahk to Wex to Joh. They were exhausted to the very core of their carapaces. What a pathetic mob to lead on a mission to save the world.

Ahk made a choked noise that might have been a laugh.

"Let's go steal that skerry," Shan said. "We'll head leeward, assuming we get airborne, and stop at the first town to steal healthier transportation and stock up on supplies. You." He poked a claw at Joh. "You go first. If anyone attempts to stop us, tell them to go away." He pointed at Wex. "Find whatever serviceable weapons you can. You're the muscle here." He faced Ahk. *And you listen for danger. Warn us if anyone plans something.* He bent an antenna at the two distracted dulls. *Them included. I'm not yet sure we can trust them.*

"We can." Reaching out a craft claw, Ahk touched his shoulder. "You're not who I thought you were. And you're not who you think you are either."

What does that mean?

She didn't say and he didn't ask.

AHK TAY KYM

What is happening to the youth of today?
They disrespect their elders; they disobey their mothers. They ignore their queen. They riot in the streets, inflamed with wild notions of justice, equality, and worse yet, individualism.
Their morals are decaying.
What is to become of them?
— Soak Rhat Heez, bright philosopher

After finding a piece of burning wood left from Shan's fire, Ahk followed the others through the tunnels beneath the ancient temple. Faded carvings decorated cracked and compacted clay bricks, the walls sagging. In a few thousand years this once holy place would fall in on itself. The air changed as they ascended from the bowels of the earth, the smoke clearing the farther they got from the cells.

Pleasure squirmed her wing stumps, ran shivers through her limbs as she strove to hear the thoughts of anyone awaiting them. Those following behind kept up an incessant stream of worry, doubt, insecurity. Except Wex, who's strangely focussed mind flitted from question to question, picking them apart. Each time she reached a dead end, a recursive argument, or a satisfactory conclusion, she moved to the next, the previous question becoming unimportant.

She doesn't care about the answers.

Had Wex got any pleasure at all from the process, Ahk would have thought it her talent. Instead, it seemed like an unhealthy compulsion.

There's no happiness to be found in questions.

There didn't seem to be much in answers either.

THE STORM BENEATH THE WORLD

Not that the others were happy in their thoughts. It seemed unfair that listening in to everyone's misery gave her so much pleasure. Were they not in danger, she'd laugh. Shan, the most beautiful ashkaro she'd ever seen, nephew to the queen and born into a wealthy family, was the most insecure. What did Ahk think about him? Did she hate him for damaging her? On and on, constant worries over the opinions of others. He spent so much time concerned about what others thought of him he had no time to think about himself.

Ahk tried to block their thoughts and focus on the hall ahead. The volume faded a bit but not enough to make a difference. Maybe with practice she could learn to selectively listen.

She staggered, suddenly weak. *I'm so tired.*

Though she couldn't remember the last time she slept, the exhaustion felt more mental than physical.

Seeing the end of the tunnel ahead, she slowed. Night had fallen while they were locked away. With Alatash gone, the sky was an ink swirl punctuated by the occasional phosphorescent fauna flitting through the air.

Stopping within the temple entrance, Ahk searched for other thoughts and found nothing.

Shan staggered forward, antennae straining. "The way is clear? We can get to the skerry?"

While she couldn't hear his words, he thought them as he spoke. Realizing she might be less alone than she feared, she wanted to fall to the dirt and scream thanks to the gods above.

Ahk shook her head. "I don't know. If there's anyone out there, they're too far away." She peered into the dark toward where the skerry had been tied down. Careful to keep her voice low, she asked, "Can anyone see anything?"

Wex's antennae strained toward the distant skerry. "I smell the beast; it's not good. Shan's right, it's dying. There are guards there as well. At least four."

While the others huddled together, arguing about what they should do, Ahk stared toward the skerry. She thought she made out its dim shape but wasn't sure if she imagined it. *I wonder if I could hear its thoughts.*

For that matter, what about other creatures? Once she'd slept, would she hear what tramea and rafak were thinking? The Redemption said the gods provided the ashkaro with animals for sustenance and to use as needed. It was generally agreed that while some creatures were smart enough to be trained, they weren't sentient. Joh said Queen Yil commanded islands. Insane as the claim sounded, he believed it. She'd even caught flashes of memory of his conversation with the other dull they'd brought out of the desert school. Those were a tangle of emotions, guilt and anger.

While one might give a trained tramea an order, or direct a skerry by applying physical pressures, the animals didn't understand what the words meant. Training wasn't real communication but rather teaching something to react in a predictable manner to a given stimulus, whether it was words or prods with a sharpened stick. Commanding an island without having first trained it to react was different. The colossal beast would have to understand the queen's intent. What happened next was a mystery. Did Queen Yil command islands like Joh made suggestions, leaving them no choice? Or did the island choose to obey?

Ahk struggled to imagine what an island, so old the ashkaro living on it had grown from mindless insects to a thriving civilization, might think about. Was it aware of the tiny lives existing on its back?

Are we like those parasitic gnats always trying to drink from your eyes?

Maybe diving into the storm and shedding the weight of ashkaro civilization would be a relief to the island. If it dove deep enough, the raging hell of Kratosh might scrape away eights of thousands of years of accumulated life and dirt. Everything they ever built would be gone, as if they never existed.

She felt small and helpless. Even Queen Nysh, the centre of all life on the island, would be swept away by raging fires. The island would rise from the storm renewed, ready to begin again.

She'd read about archaeologists digging into the soil to unearth old ruins. There were reports of massive layers of ash hidden deep in the dirt heaped upon the island's back. Her teacher said it was due to raging forest fires. She wasn't sure she believed that anymore.

It's happened before.

Thinking about the firestorm of Kratosh, Ahk glanced at Shan. Distracted, he didn't notice. All four of them had rare talents, but only his seemed like it might be linked to one of the gods. Was there more to his talent than simply making fire? She'd worry he was a servant of Katlipok except he never thought about it. Of course, he could be a servant and not know.

I'm being silly.

The Queen of the Storm would never pick a pretty male like Shan. The thought was ridiculous.

"We're all tired," said Wex. "I'm not sure we can defeat four soldiers." She darted a nervous look at Ahk as if worried the bright heard her thoughts and added, "I can't kill them all."

"Whoa, whoa, whoa," Shan said. "Let's remember we're all on the same side. Those are loyal soldiers, members of the Queen's Claw. We can't kill everyone just because they're in our way."

"What are you suggesting?" demanded Joh. "That we give ourselves up?"

Wex hissed, interrupting whatever Shan was about to say. "Everyone back into the hall!"

The four students retreated in an awkward tangle of limbs.

Wex crept to the entrance, antennae perked and testing the air. "There's at least one of the Queen's Wing patrolling the school grounds on a tramea."

The thoughts of the others were fading, as if they walked away from Ahk.

What if this was a temporary aberration instead of the sudden development of a new talent? What if she lost this and was once again alone?

Please, no, Ahk prayed to the gods who abandoned their creations.

"I'm really tired," she said. "It's getting harder to hear you. If I lose this…If the talent never comes back…" She couldn't speak it aloud.

Joh reached a craft claw toward her, touched a shoulder as if afraid she'd hit him. She watched his mandibles and antennae move, heard his dim thought.

"You won't," he said. "You lost your talent and then developed a new one. Have you ever heard of that? There must be a reason."

Was he right? What happened to her was unheard of.

The gods want me to have my vengeance.

Joh's antennae twitched in frustration. "We're going into the jungle. We're heading leeward until we find somewhere with a skerry. Then we're flying to Yil Island." He looked from student to student, forcing them to make eye contact. "We're going to save the island. Follow me."

Keeping low and quiet, everyone obediently shuffled off across the field toward the jungle. Surprised, Ahk followed. It wasn't until they were well into the mad tangle of foliage, Shan complaining about how dirty everything was, that Ahk realized the others had obeyed the little dull without a moment's hesitation. All conversation had abruptly stopped, and they'd set off without question.

He didn't leave them a choice.

The scary part was that no one acted as if motivated by compulsion. Rather, it had seemed perfectly natural that everyone unanimously decided to leave at the same time. It was insidious.

By telling them what to decide, he makes it their decision and so of course it feels natural.

The other three students perked up, looking back the way they came.

"They've seen us," Wex said.

Joh scowled at the clear path left as they blundered through the foliage. "Run!"

They ran.

JOH

She who wanders far from the hive will never discover her true self.

—Ancient Proverb

When everyone bolted at top speed, disappearing into the trees, Joh realized he'd accidentally barked an order. With a groan, he staggered after them. As the smallest of the group, he was also the slowest. Even Ahk, carapace malformed and hideous, moved faster, though not by much. Exhaustion dragged him down as if the gods had poured water into his carapace and filled his limbs. His thoughts moved like thick mud. More than anything, he wanted to lie down and sleep. Between what happened beneath the temple and then getting everyone moving, he had nothing left. Never had he made so many suggestions in such a short period of time.

Once again, he learned something the teachers should have taught him or at least let him experiment enough to learn: The more someone resisted his suggestions, the more pushing them cost. That soldier who was able to ignore him—and he worried what that meant—had all but spent his reserves.

He stumbled over a root in the soil.

I can't believe Ahk almost told Wex.

He'd have to talk to Ahk about that at some point. Or maybe he should admit his crime before Wex learned the truth. The thought hurt more than expected. She was quite literally his first and only friend. He didn't want to lose her.

Then you probably should have left it up to her to decide if she liked you, idiot!

THE STORM BENEATH THE WORLD

Ahead, Ahk slowed. Joh pushed himself faster, trying to catch up. She looked as tired as he felt, each step an effort. Her malformed carapace made gritty grinding noises. Soldiers crashed through the jungle in pursuit. Still distant, they were gaining ground.

"Tell the others to slow down and wait for us," Ahk shouted as he caught up.

Without him and Ahk slowing them, they might escape.

Sacrifice yourself to save Wex.

Surely that would redeem his crime.

If I get caught, they'll have no chance of saving the island.

They might not even try. Shan, pretty, shallow, and self-serving, would decide it was too dangerous. More than likely, he'd turn around and head back to Kaylamnel to turn himself in. Wex wouldn't try to stop him. She might argue, but in the end, he was a five-name bright, and she was a two-name dull.

He glanced at Ahk to see if she agreed with his analysis of the situation. She made no sign she'd heard his thoughts.

Wex will go on alone because it's the right thing to do.

She'd die.

He couldn't allow that.

Joh shouted, "Wait for us!" into the jungle.

Something in him broke and he staggered to his femorotibial joints, raptorial claws sinking into the damp earth. Even utterly drained he found it difficult to comprehend how different the windward side was from where he grew up.

Ahk sagged against him when he stood, and he struggled to keep her upright.

"Your thoughts are gone!" she yelled into his face. "I can't hear anything!"

Before he had a chance to question her, Wex and Shan returned, looking guilty for having abandoned them. Joh wanted to explain it was his fault but was too tired.

Wex faced him, antennae betraying pent tension. "I've been driving myself crazy, going around in circles. Did you tell me I had to be your friend?"

Joh's heart crumbled. He wanted to lie or beg forgiveness. She'd leave him now or kill him to free herself from the compulsion.

"Yes, but don't worry about it. We'll talk later." Even as the words slipped out, he felt the blurred smear of pleasure and exhaustion. With that last suggestion, he felt emptied.

Wex's antennae relaxed. "They're coming," she said, gripping her single stab stick.

Two soldiers broke from the trees, slowing to a stop when they spotted their prey. Bright females, one carried four stab sticks, the other holding a spear and shortbow with an arrow nocked but not yet drawn. In the dark, they were barbed shapes of nightmare, robbed of detail and all the more terrifying.

"Shan," said Wex. "Burn them."

Shan gestured his craft claws at the two warriors, throwing a few stuttering sparks into the air. In the momentary light, Joh caught a few details. Scarred veterans, carapaces dotted with long-healed wounds, they wore the uniforms of the Queen's Claw, damp from the sprint through the jungle.

Antennae straightening in surprise, the soldiers spread out. They moved with a flawless and deadly grace sending a flutter through Joh's heart. It seemed cruel of the gods to write an appreciation for dangerous females into the blood of every male.

"Stop," he said. "Return to the school and tell the headmistress you couldn't find us."

They ignored him. Seeing Ahk's charred white carapace, they discounted her too. One gave Shan a long, appraising look, an antenna bending toward him in invitation as if she might bed him here in the jungle. Then, both focussed on Wex, the only armed female.

"Chynn wants the male dull," said one of the soldiers. "Unconscious."

"If he doesn't put up a fight, maybe we'll bring back the pretty one too," said the other.

Wex stepped between Joh and the brights. "Joh is my friend. You can't have him."

One of the soldiers snorted in disdain. "Stupid dull. You can't stop us."

THE STORM BENEATH THE WORLD

WEX JEL

Every female gives her life for what she believes. Every male gives his life for what he believes. Sometimes ashkaro believe in nothing, and so they give their lives to nothing.

But to surrender who you are and to live without believing in something is more terrible than dying – even more terrible than dying young.

—The Redemption

Joh told me to be his friend.

A moment of rage and then her anger was snuffed like a candle tossed in water. Learning the truth changed nothing. Joh was her friend. Yes, he betrayed that friendship by telling her they were friends, but it was easy to understand why he had. A dull runt, suddenly alone, he would have found the school terrifying. Had he not made his suggestion, she wouldn't have given him a second thought. It hurt to admit, but even afterward she saw him as a stupid dull. Knowing he was so much more only came after spending months together. Having already picked at the questions as to why they were friends, she knew the answer: He wasn't what she first thought. Knowing what he was *supposed* to be, she'd underestimated him. Despite the imbalance of power, not once had he abused it. Instead, he tried to make her cadre leader and supported her at every turn.

He may have told her to like him, but he never told her to love him. She knew that in her blood just as she knew he loved her.

It was all right, she wasn't worried; they'd talk about it later.

Clutching her single stab stick, Wex faced the two Queen's Claw.

THE STORM BENEATH THE WORLD

One main eye watched each soldier, tracking their movement in the dark, her antennae testing the air. Ahk and Joh leaned against each other for support, both ready to collapse. Ahk looked up, one eye sliding to track the bright with the shortbow.

Can you read my thoughts?

Ahk shoved Joh away, spilling the little dull to the damp earth, and threw herself at the bright with the bow. Wex acted without thought, attacking the other soldier. Ducking low and thrusting with her lone stab stick, she hoped to catch her enemy unprepared. The bright danced nimbly away, batting aside Wex's attack with ease. Her carapace rang with eight or more solid *thock* sounds as the soldier pummelled her with the blunt sides of her sticks.

Wex retreated, pain pulsing through her. It happened so fast, the blows landing like a roll of thunder, Wex hadn't seen an opening.

By all the gods of Alatash she was tired.

The soldier's antennae took on a mocking angle. "Come now dull. You can do better than that!" Four stab sticks spinning in intricate patterns meant to distract and dazzle, she skittered forward.

Wex bent a main eye in Ahk's direction in time to see her take an arrow in the thorax. Ahk wobbled two more steps toward her opponent and crumpled. The distraction cost Wex, brutal blows landing on the joint of her front left leg, splintering the carapace at the joint. She retreated, limping.

Shan, an ill-defined shape in Wex's secondary eyes, screamed and hurled himself at the soldier who wounded Ahk.

The bright warrior that Wex faced followed in a low prowl. "Let's even the odds, make this sporting." She tossed a stab stick to Wex.

The soldier followed the thrown weapon with an attack. One of her stab sticks swung low, aiming to take out Wex's remaining front leg. Another stabbed straight toward one of her main eyes seeking to blind. The third snapped out at the claw holding Wex's single stick.

All three weapons engaged in an attack, the soldier was exposed for a fraction of an instant.

Joy screamed through Wex's carapace. The gods of Alatash shone their light upon her soul and she knew her talent for the gift it was. She lifted the undamaged front leg just enough that the attack passed beneath. Turning her head a few degrees, the stab at her eye slid off her carapace, leaving a long groove. With a raptorial claw she caught the stick swung at her weapon and dragged the bright closer and off balance. Exactly as she'd seen, the opening appeared, promised utter bliss. Wex's stab stick followed the path drawn in her mind's eye.

Euphoria.

Rapture.

No word could encompass what she felt as the warrior died. Seeing the weakness in another's defences felt good. Knowing what she must do to take advantage of it felt better.

Nothing touched the rapturous moment of the kill.

The gods made her a murderer.

They made her *want* to kill.

They made killing her path to salvation.

"Drop your weapon or the pretty one dies."

The glory of the kill had been a distraction. Shan lay helpless beneath the other soldier. She held a spear pressed against his throat, her bow nocked and aimed at Wex. At this range it would be impossible for a skilled archer to miss.

Wex judged the distance. *It's too far.*

"We're going to quietly wait here until the others catch up," the Queen's Claw said, voice calm. One main eye watched Wex while the other studied Ahk, making sure she was down. Her secondary eyes focussed on Shan and Joh, the lesser threats. "Then, you're going back to your cells. Bound and gagged this time. Maybe broken." She pushed her spear against Shan's throat, gouging the softer carapace there.

Shan whimpered in fear.

"Put your weapons down," Joh ordered the bright.

She ignored him.

Shan hadn't been able to make fire. Ahk had stopped babbling everyone's thoughts. That last order for them to wait must have spent the last of Joh's power.

He's too tired. We all are.

Maybe she still had a little left.

"Fine," Joh said.

The archer was moving before he finished that single word.

Antennae straining, talent searching for an opening, Wex saw it all.

Limbs tensing to drive her spear down, killing Shan, the warrior's thorax twisted to bring the shortbow to bear on Wex's only friend. She saw in Joh the intent to tackle the bright female. A male, he hadn't started moving yet.

Too slow.

There was a reason males didn't fight females.

Save Joh.

Nothing else mattered.

The Queen's Claw, a veteran of battle, moved with the speed of a striking rafak. Her thorax reversed its motion, the tip of the brutal arrow glinting in the dark. Even as the soldier drew a bead on Wex, the spear spun in the bright's other claws, blunt end clipping Shan's head and then whipping around to intercept Joh's clumsy attack.

Wex screamed, threw her only weapon, and launched herself at the warrior.

Pain, as something slammed into her head, one main eye suddenly blind.

The distant thrum of a bow string, a low note of death, the now freed claw already reaching for another arrow with unerring precision.

The swung spear impacted with Joh's head dropping him. The instant contact was made, a claw released the haft, drawing a sheathed stab stick, spinning it so the point would intercept Wex's mad lunge.

Wex saw the choice she must make: Twist her torso and save herself or kill the warrior and save Joh.

One working eye, thoughts fracturing like a clay tile smashed to the floor, Wex found the hole in the warrior's defences.

She tackled the Queen's Claw, felt the stab stick breach her carapace and drive deep into her thorax. With a raptorial claw she caught the wrist holding the arrow, twisting it until it broke. One craft claw tore at the bright's eyes while the other plucked the arrow from her failing grip. Wex's weight bore them to the ground and that moment she lived for.

Alatash above sundered the clouds, split her wide and filled her with the joyous light of the gods. They loved her and she was what they made her. There could be no greater pleasure. She was death and in death

she found her redemption.
>	*My friend. My love.*
>	Joh would live.
>	Nothing else mattered.

THE STORM BENEATH THE WORLD

THE STORM BENEATH THE WORLD

SHAN WYN VAL NUL NYSH

Grieve not for the fallen for like the river of days all life is endless.

To live is to die is to be reborn again, each time closer to that final perfection, our moment of redemption.

—The Redemption

A wet gagging sound woke Shan.

What? What happened?

Face down, crushed to the damp mud of the jungle, blood trickled into his mouth. Swallowing reflexively, he gagged again, coughing. His wings felt like they'd been bent to breaking. Everything hurt.

Blood?

It was dark, the jungle air humid. Night insects hummed and buzzed. The distant call of an arachn echoed through the trees. The sound was the deep rumble of a full-grown hunter.

I saw one in the Nysh City Zoo.

Squat and low, it had been an armour-plated monstrosity, all rage and hunger and blood blue eyes. One of the pouncing breeds of arachn, the zookeepers had broken four of its eight legs to slow it. It still sent shivers of revulsion when it lunged toward the bars trying to grab Shan so it could suck the meat from his carapace. His mother had laughed at him when he hid behind her.

Shan tried to move, couldn't.

He remembered the spear, held against his throat. Was the blood his? Was he bleeding out in the muck?

Scared the bright was still nearby, maybe standing ready to finish him, he whispered a soft, "I surrender."

Someone groaned nearby.

"Joh? Was that you?"

Another groan. "I think so. She hit me in the head. It's…Oh. Oh no." Joh sobbed, a heart-rending sound of misery. "No, no, no."

Am I damaged? Am I dying?

He couldn't ask.

Joh rose unsteadily and moved closer. "No, Wex, no."

Wex? Not me?

Relief flooded Shan.

"Joh? I can't move."

The runt dull ignored him.

Shan wriggled, struggling to find purchase in the mud. He discovered a partially buried tree root and used it to leverage himself somewhat upright. Between the dark and the mud splashed across his main eyes, he saw little detail. His head ached where he'd been so rudely struck. Reaching up he found a dent in the carapace between his antennae. A groan of horror slipped out.

Getting his stronger raptorial arms involved, he was able to push himself into an awkward sitting position. A dead female, devoid of all colour in the absence of light, lay across his lower abdomen, pinning his rearmost legs. One main eye stared glassily past him as if something interesting stood beyond his shoulder. An arrow jutted from her thorax.

Shan pushed her off and searched himself for more wounds. Finding only dirt and shallow gouges he could later buff out, he sighed with relief. Joh, antennae sagging in grief, wings hanging loose and dejected, stood over another heaped shape in the dark.

Shan coughed mud. Another crumpled form, a murky grey where everything else was shades of black, looked like it might be Ahk. She lay still.

"Wex?" he asked. "Ahk?"

"Wex is dead." Joh's voice came flat and hard in the dark. "Ahk will live."

"The soldiers?"

"Wex killed them both."

"A dull killed two Queen's Claw?"

That was impossible, even for a Corrupt!

Joh didn't move, didn't answer.

Shan said, "I'll check on Ahk," and staggered to where she lay.

Crouching at her side, he found her dazed but alive. One eye swung to focus on him, slid past as if she'd eaten too many fenrick leaves. She made a clumsy attempt to stand but only managed to splash more mud on him. For the first time, he didn't mind.

If only Mother could see me now.

Would she be proud? Probably not.

"You're going to be all right," he said.

The errant eye slid back toward him and Ahk punched him lightly on the shoulder.

"Right," he said, bending an antenna to show he was being funny, "you can't hear me."

Can you hear my thoughts?

She didn't react.

"Come on," he said, offering her an arm. "Let's get you up."

Once he had her upright, they leaned against one another, exhausted mind and soul and body.

Shan gave her a gentle nudge. "I'm utterly fatigued and covered in filth. I bet I could pass for a dull fieldclaw."

One eye watched him, showing no sign she heard or understood. The other found Joh. She sagged against Shan and he struggled to keep her standing. "Are there more coming?" she bellowed.

"There will be if you keep shouting."

When she continued to stare blankly at him, he shook his head. "Not yet."

But there would be. Headmistress Chynn would have tramea patrolling the sky come first light. The bedraggled skerry would be pressed into service too. Queen's Claw would search the jungle for tracks and have no trouble tracing their mad blunder through the foliage.

Joh remained at Wex's side, keening in grief and loss. A stab stick jutted from her thorax, a claw's length of arrow sticking from one ruined eye. It must have punched through her skull, and Shan shuddered to think about the damage on the far side.

Shan looked from Ahk to Joh. As the only bright here, any

decision would fall to him. More than anything, he wanted to lie down in the dirt and sleep, but there was an arachn out there and he was too pretty to die.

And I promised Ahk I'd help her save the island and get her vengeance.

A cracked laugh escaped him, though no one reacted.

Mother constantly mocked him for wanting to see romantic plays at that gorgeous old theatre in the heart of Nysh City. It was always the females who saved the day, rescuing the desperate but exceptionally gorgeous male from his evil captors. Later, of course, once the hero brought him back to her estates, he'd show his gratitude. Those were some of Shan's favourite scenes. Once, as a child, he complained to his mother that there were never any male heroes. He told her that when he grew up, he was going to write a play about a male who saved the day. 'You go right ahead,' she'd said, laughing. 'Just don't be too disappointed when no one comes.'

That had been the death of his first dream, though many other dreams died over the following years.

It's time to show the world that a male can be the hero.

It was as if the gods planned this for him from the beginning. A five-name fallen from grace. Corrupt. Obviously, this play was a tragedy, and the tragedies were always the best. The fact he loved Ahk despite her horrible scars spoke volumes of his depth of character. Joh would be the plucky sidekick. Shan darted an eye in the dull's direction. Perhaps plucky was the wrong word.

I'm going to save Nysh Island.

Happily, the dim-witted dull had already supplied the hollowed carapace of a plan. Shan would have to fill the rest with life to make it real. They'd head leeward and take the first skerry they found. Assuming they were suitably recovered, Joh could suggest the owner lend it to them.

"We have to get moving," Shan said, gesturing toward the trees with an antenna so Ahk would understand.

Both main eyes still on Wex, Joh said, "She sacrificed herself to save me."

The dumb little dull was clearly deranged from loss.

"We have to go," Shan tried again.

Joh ignored him.

After making sure Ahk could stand on her own, Shan moved to the dull's side, gently reaching out with a comforting antenna. "She would have wanted us to continue." They always said that in the plays. Though it was annoying how many times a male character had to die to motivate the female hero into action.

"Joh," Shan said, wondering if this was the first time he spoke the dull's name. He searched for the right words. *Nothing has changed?* Oh, gods above no, that was all wrong. In the end he settled for the direct approach. "Queen Yil is coming. She's going to kill everyone on the island." A flash of inspiration. "You were right." Shan spun the runt until he faced him. "I can't do this without you."

Something changed in the dull's antennae, a twitch of rigid rage.

"*We* can't do this without you," Shan amended.

Joh turned a single eye in Ahk's direction, and she nodded. Maybe her talent for hearing thought was returning, or perhaps she guessed what Shan was doing.

"Why?" Joh demanded. "Why would I help save any of you brights. The whole lot of you can burn in Kratosh."

Shan had no answer to that. The runt grew up in the desert, probably had no concept of civilization. He didn't know what they were fighting for because he'd never seen it.

Ahk moved to Shan's side, entwined a craft arm around one of his. It was a strange move, intimate and yet distant. "You gave Wex no choice but to be your friend."

Joh's antennae bent away in shame. "She died because I was afraid of being alone." Without another word, he set off into the jungle.

Still holding his arm, Ahk pulled Shan into motion. They followed the silent dull.

What just happened? Did he decide to help us?

He turned an eye toward Ahk, but she ignored him.

JOH

What kind of cruel gods make happiness a trap?
What sick mind decided that doing the one *thing you're* really *good at would leave you a hollowed and broken shell?*

—Anonymous

You gave her no choice but to be your friend.
Numb with loss Joh walked for hours without seeing, his antennae and secondary eyes scanning for danger, checking the terrain ahead so he didn't trip. Damp leaves painted him in cool dew. Water dripped from the canopy above in a soft and pattering rain. His walking claws sank into the sodden dirt with every step, the indentations left behind filling with water. A few days ago, he would have stopped to marvel at the moisture. This was what he'd imagined Alatash to be like, a city of warmth and rain where you could drink by tilting your head back and opening your mandibles. And here it was, on the island he'd lived on all his life. The priests talked about the differences between the windward and leeward sides, but they left too much out.

If they were honest, no dull would remain in the desert.
He wanted to cry for the terrible injustice, but it was only a distraction.

You gave her no choice.
Wex was a two-name, daughter of a shift-manager, and he was a one-name runt. The only reason she'd been willing to speak with him was because he told her to be his friend.

She sacrificed herself to save him because that was the kind of friend she was.

THE STORM BENEATH THE WORLD

Ahk caught up to Joh, walked alongside him. "I suppose the question now is, what kind of friend are you?"

"If you constantly read everyone's thoughts, you'll fall to the lure in no time." He turned an eye in her direction. "Without your antennae, I can't tell when you're using your talent. Do you still feel the lure?"

Robbed of expression, she didn't react. "Listening to you two—hearing your pain and his doubt—gives me such incredible pleasure." She stumbled over an exposed root. "It's the only way I can communicate. If my choice is between living a long life alone and having friends I can communicate with and dying much sooner, I'll choose the latter."

Shan followed, fussing over his carapace.

"We are not friends," Joh said.

"Because brights and dulls can't be friends?" She laughed, loud and forced. "Shan doesn't think of me as a bright anymore. Neither did the guards or the headmistress." Ahk lifted an arm, scraped away flaked carapace with a craft claw. "Neither do you."

They walked on in silence. She was right. Like Shan, she was less of a bright the moment she discovered her talent. Now, scarred and mutilated, whatever her carapace once looked like no longer mattered.

"Is this all it takes to change what we are?" Ahk asked. "If we splash Shan with mud is he suddenly a dull? If we paint and shellack your exoskeleton in the finest salon until you gleam, are you a bright?"

No, it's in my blood.

"And yet here I am, blood unchanged, bright no longer. If we aren't our outward appearance, what are we?" She didn't wait for him to respond. "It's what's within. And for the first time, I know what's inside all of you. I know Shan's deepest secrets just as I know yours. Guess what?"

This time she did wait.

"He's secretly a dull inside?" Joh asked, antennae showing his sarcasm.

She snorted an awkward laugh. "No, he's bright all the way through. He's afraid."

"He should be. We're going to die."

"Strangely, that's not what he's afraid of. Don't get me wrong."

She touched Joh. Such contact between ashkaro was rare between two so socially separated. Maybe she was making sure she had his attention. "He's insecure. He's afraid of what everyone thinks of him. You, the lowly dull, doesn't give a rafak's fart what the five-name bright thinks, but he's terrified you don't like him."

"I *don't* like him."

"He's scared you think he's stupid."

"He's an idiot."

"More than anything he's terrified of being alone."

Joh had no quick answer to that. Wex was gone.

I am alone.

"You're only alone if you turn your back on us. You suggested to Shan that taking care of me was the only honourable course of action."

Back on safer ground, Joh said, "I knew that otherwise he wouldn't."

"Liar. You thought you needed him. What you don't know is that he'd already decided he had to help me. He desperately wants to be a good ashkaro. He wants to be brave. He wants to be a hero."

"He isn't."

"Unlike me," Ahk said, touching Joh again, "you don't *know* that."

They separated to go around a large puddle. Behind them, buffing his carapace with wet leaves he'd plucked from a tree, Shan stumbled into it, cursing.

Unlike Shan, I'm not stupid. You're manipulating me toward something. Spit it out.

Ahk didn't react.

"Not reading my thoughts now?" he asked. "Or not willing to answer?"

Again, she failed to respond.

Getting her attention, Joh repeated his questions.

"You were right," she answered. "I can't constantly read everyone's thoughts. No matter how desperate I might be for connection, it's a terrible breach of etiquette." She poked him below his lower shoulder. "Though less egregious than forcing folks to like you."

Do you like me? The thought slipped out.

Ahk's wings stumps shuddered and squirmed. "You're standoffish and distant."

That's not a no.

"It's not a yes," she said. "And I hear you thinking that you don't know how else to be, that growing up in a shack in the desert with your father left you ill-prepared for friends."

"I should tell you to never read my thoughts again."

"I'm surprised you haven't tried."

"Give it time."

Ahk turned both main eyes on Joh. "You're going to need my help to stop the Mad Queen. You're going to need Shan's help too."

"What makes you think I'm not going to flee to the nearest Corrupt island?"

"Because you swore you would earn Wex's friendship."

"She's dead."

Ahk didn't answer. She didn't have to.

Wex's death didn't free him from his promise.

"It's funny," Joh said. "Shan's afraid he won't live up to the expectations of others. I'm afraid I will. We're both going to die because of what others think."

They walked on in silence, Joh wondering if Shan's insecurities made him more likeable or less. On the one claw it was nice to know there was a real ashkaro within that pretty carapace, someone with doubts and questions who muddled through life much the same as the lowest dull. On the other claw, the vapid idiot had everything given to him and squandered it on pointless worry. For the most part, females were unaware Joh existed. They either failed to notice him or treated him like a servant. Only Wex had been different and only then because he told her they were friends. Had he not made that suggestion, she would have treated him the same as the others.

"You do your friend a disservice," Ahk said.

Stay out of my thoughts.

Cocking her head to one side, she gave him an appraising look. "That's interesting. I heard that thought but it carried no compulsion."

"Stay out of my—"

She slapped one of Joh's craft claws, interrupting him. "I don't know if that would work, but please don't. We are a hive of three. If I lose you…" She looked away.

A hive of three.

He'd been a hive of one until he met Wex.

"If you're going to listen to my every thought, can you at least occasionally pretend I have some privacy?"

She stared off into the trees like she hadn't heard.

"Thanks."

"You're welcome."

They walked on, following the path of least resistance, always heading in a vaguely leeward direction. Sometimes they ran into foliage too thick to pass through and went around. The jungle teemed with life. Carapaced wrigglies crawled in the muck. Long, segmented creatures slithered along branches or fled into holes tunnelled in the damp earth. Juvenile rafak darted through the trees chasing prey, snapping it out of the air and devouring it whole. They passed trees webbed thick in slug-white strands, hollowed animal carapaces hanging trapped, the arachn nowhere to be seen.

"Thank you for trying to distract me," Joh mumbled.

"Purely self-serving," Ahk answered. "Your pain is too much to bear."

Burnt carapace or no, Ahk was still a bright from a good family. Yet here she was, worried about Joh, doing what she could to ease his pain. Maybe she was right and what was inside the carapace mattered more than the shell. It hit him then that all the ashkaro he never bothered getting to know each had inner lives he never knew. Zyr and Bin, his fellow students, both now dead. The teachers, Rel and Fel Shyn, also slain by Yil assassins. Raht, the headmistress, brutally tortured on her own dining room table. Kris Kork, the spy. Joh had thought he was using the mimic, but Kris had his own reasons for going along with Joh's plans.

Their deaths slid off my carapace because I never bothered to get to know them.

But they'd each been someone real. He'd seen their colours and judged them, but Ahk was right; they were so much more than that.

I never knew who they were inside.

Though Joh had remained distant and aloof, they'd never been mean or cruel. He remembered Wex's worried looks when he shied from group conversations or took his meals alone.

THE STORM BENEATH THE WORLD

Did you ever worry about her?

No, he hadn't. Instead, he'd fretted over his own guilt. Over and over, he promised he'd earn her forgiveness, but not once had he seriously considered freeing her from the compulsion.

And you think Shan is an empty shell?

He wouldn't run away. No longer would he set himself apart. The Mad Queen attacked his home and there could be but one answer.

A hive of three.

The most pathetic hive he could imagine, but that's what they were.

Three doomed children.

Even if they stopped Yil and saved Nysh Island, there could be no happily ever after like in the Redemption's parables and morality tales. No one survived the lure.

For Queen Nysh Na Kan Oh Rok An-Rah.

For the students and teachers who died at both schools.

For every bright and dull who called this queendom home.

For Wex Jel, my only— He felt Ahk's presence at his side, sensed the lingering stench of charred exoskeleton. *For Wex Jel, my friend.*

One eye followed Shan while the other slid to look at Ahk. She gave him a sharp nod of agreement.

For my two new friends.

When Alatash fell below the windward horizon, the sounds of the jungle changed, taking on an altogether more sinister timbre. Everything that had squeaked and chittered throughout the day fell silent. The smaller rafak disappeared, hiding from the predators of the night. Things writhed through the branches above the three young ashkaro.

Finding a clearing, Joh and Ahk stopped to wait for Shan.

"Do you get the feeling something is going to reach down and snatch you off the ground?" Shan asked when he reached them.

"I didn't," said Joh. "Until a second ago."

"We'll camp here," the bright decided, gesturing at the clearing.

As if they hadn't stopped here for exactly those reasons.

"Have a lot of jungle survival experience, do you?" Joh asked, regretting his sarcasm.

"Mother took me hunting sometimes."

Surprised, Joh felt a flash of guilt. "That's unusual, isn't it? Very progressive of her."

"My job was to oversee the dulls setting up the camp."

"Ah."

"I learned a lot though."

"Such as?"

"Always travel with a slow-moving dull in case something decides to chase you."

With no camp to set, the three huddled for warmth.

"Should we take turns staying awake?" Joh asked.

"Good idea," Shan answered. "You're first." A moment later, he was asleep.

Joh woke to find the other two had collected fat grubs and left them on a long leaf. They'd also laid out several stalks that leaked fluid from the snapped ends. Tattered shreds of dream fell apart like an arachn web in a storm. He'd been walking from town to town, telling every ashkaro he met to be his friend and to be friends to all other ashkaro. All alone, he'd brought about the moment of Redemption when the gods returned to their abandoned children.

Stupid dream.

Ahk, resting nearby, said, "I liked it."

"Don't worry about falling asleep," Shan said, somehow sounding magnanimous, as if it fell on him to forgive the dull. "Neither of us woke up once the whole night." He nodded an antenna toward the stalks. "One of the things I did learn was that you can suck the water from those. It's less dangerous than drinking from a puddle. Mother said puddles are stagnant." He looked uncertain, like he wanted to say more or apologise. "The grubs aren't bad either. Not spiced, of course. Could never get them this fresh in Nysh City." He made a show of examining their surroundings, said, "I'm going to look for tracks," and marched from the clearing.

Joh ate the grubs without tasting them. A few months ago, this would have been an unimaginable feast. Plump grubs. Clean, crisp water that didn't leave a gritty film in his mouth. How could he take pleasure in anything now that Wex was gone?

THE STORM BENEATH THE WORLD

"Give it time," Ahk said.

"I'm not Shan. I can't simply let the terrible things I've done slide off my carapace."

Ahk stood motionless and unreadable. "First, stop comparing yourself to him. Second, neither of us hates him more than he hates himself."

Shan returned as Joh sucked the last of the moisture from the second stalk. His posture wavered between pleased and smug. "I found a path. Looks like a hunting trail used by the locals. Should lead to a town. Let's go!"

The bright set a fast pace, Joh and Ahk following.

A bright town? Joh had never seen one up close, couldn't imagine what it might look like. There'd been a settlement not far from the shack he shared with his father, but there'd been less than eight brights living there, all of them disgraced in one way or another, and none with more than three names.

You're trying not to think about Wex.

It felt like he'd be spending the rest of his life trying not to think about his friend.

Luckily, it's not likely to be all that long.

An hour later they stepped from the jungle, blinking in the bright light of Alatash. Joh stared in shock. In the valley below, clay brick homes surrounded a lake so big hundreds of ashkaro could walk into it and not rub wings. On the far side, a river wound its way north. Boats, large enough for one or two ashkaro, skimmed the lake, brightly coloured sails catching the wind. As far as he could see, they served no purpose other than going dangerously fast, the females riding them leaning far out over the water to maintain balance. A slim arrow of a vessel caught a gust, skipped across the surface like one of those tiny arachn who walked on the murky water at the bottom of the well. The bright piloting the little craft turned too fast, and it tipped, spilling her into the lake. Sounds of laughter echoed up from below as the other sailors mocked their friend.

A larger vessel sat at the docks located at the mouth of the river. Well-dressed dulls, cleaner than any Joh had ever seen, hustled back and forth, loading barrels, and unloading crates.

"Probably taking fresh fish to Nysh City," Shan said, standing at his side. "I know this restaurant where they fry them in fat and serve them with honey wine."

Though Joh knew the words, when strung together in such a sentence they became near meaningless. He'd never seen, much less tasted fish. Honey, wine, and restaurants were mythical things.

Those houses located closest to the lake were the largest, many several times bigger than even Headmistress Raht's home. Farther back were structures of only one or two stories, though still palatially spacious. Beyond those, a maze of cobblestone streets lined with smaller single-story structures. Nowhere did he see a single wood shack.

"Where do the dulls live?" Joh asked. "Do they walk here to work?"

Shan gave him an odd look. "Those little hovels on the outskirts, that's where the dulls live."

Hovels?

Even the smallest and crudest was large enough to be comprised of several rooms. Each one had a chimney, a stout front door, windows with glass, and a lush garden.

Not far from the docks was a clearing surrounded by pylons. A permanent staircase constructed of wood and brick stood at the centre. A wide disembarking platform sat at the top of the stairs, a moored skerry nestled against it.

"There's our ride!" Ahk shouted at them. Then, "Sorry," when she saw them flinch.

"Come," said Shan, once again taking the lead. "See the flag mounted over the steerage?" he asked. "That's a private skerry. I know the family. There'll be a crew of two or three retired Queen's Wing. Joh, you'll have to deal with them. Shouldn't be a problem, right? Just tell them to take us to Yil."

"Right," said Joh. "Only a few highly trained killers. No problem."

"Good. If we're lucky, they're provisioned for a long journey. By all the gods of Alatash, I can't remember the last time I saw a fully stocked bar or slept in a real hammock."

Shan stopped, turned to face the others. "You two look awful."

"Thanks," said Ahk, showing no hint of pain.

THE STORM BENEATH THE WORLD

"Sorry. I mean you'll draw attention. Hold on."

The bright searched through the underbrush until he found a few clawfuls of damp leaves. Returning, he scrubbed at Joh, tutting the entire time. Joh suffered the treatment, uncomfortable at the proximity. Not since he was a baby had someone paid such attention to his exoskeleton. A five-name bright cleaning a runt dull was unheard of. Shan doing so with no hint of shame or self-consciousness was nothing short of a miracle.

Antennae bent in concentration, Shan worked on a scuff in Joh's carapace, buffing it out. Happy with his efforts, he backed away to admire his work, head tilting this way and that to check the play of light.

Seeing something in the set of Joh's antennae, Shan said, "If we're going to save the world, I don't think any of that matters."

"I think I misjudged—"

"Anyway, Shan added, one antenna hinting at humour. "What does a dumb dull runt know about carapace maintenance."

"Ah. Right."

Shan turned on Ahk. Nothing would minimize the horrendous damage she'd suffered. "Umm… Follow me. Joh, you deal with anyone I can't talk us past. Otherwise, save your strength. Without you, we're doomed."

Ahk nudged Joh. "I think that was a compliment."

Once again Joh and Ahk followed the bright male. Shan walked different now. He strutted, carapace gleaming in the light. In the jungle he'd been another Corrupt fleeing for his life. Here, he *belonged*.

Their entrance into town did not go unnoticed. Shan drew the eyes and antennae of every female, many calling tawdry promises of affection from their boats. Even the attention of the males lingered in appreciation and more than a little jealousy. Ahk drew an altogether different kind of regard. Seeing Shan, many would step politely aside to allow him to pass on the narrow path. When they looked past him and saw Ahk, they hastily retreated in fear and disgust.

Disease, some hissed. Abomination. Blasphemy.

Don't listen, thought Joh. *Save your strength for later.*

Ahk gave him that maddeningly expressionless look and said nothing.

THE STORM BENEATH THE WORLD

No one noticed Joh. He could have been invisible.

Entering the town, they followed a winding clay brick street. There was no sand anywhere, each brick polished to a gleam. Botanical gardens lined the road, trees laden with fruit, bushes trimmed to look like rearing rafak or posing tramea. Bright children played in yards or chased each other through the narrow lanes between estates. Gardeners, all flawlessly clean dulls, stopped to watch, leaning against their hoes and shovels. Everything spoke of permanence and care and an eye for beauty and colour.

Wex would have loved this.

Had some of the bricks from Brickworks #7 made their way here?

Shan led them straight to the landing area. A Queen's Claw, armed and armoured in wood and bone, stood sentry at the bottom of the steps. A second bright female chatted with her. Spotting Shan, they stopped talking to stare.

"Greetings," he said, bowing to the two females. "I am Shan Wyn Val Nul Nysh." Noting the family crest on the older female's vest, the same as the flag on the skerry, he added, "Quyn family?"

Seeing Ahk, the soldier rested her craft and raptorial claws on her weapons as if expecting attack.

"I am Vhen Dyns Quyn," she answered, with a bow of her own, "the family matriarch."

"A pleasure," he said, in a way that suggested the pleasure was mostly hers. "May I ask where this skerry is bound?"

"Once we've rounded up the children, we're heading for Nysh City."

"You're well-supplied?"

Vhen looked shocked at the blunt question. "Of course. We're in Nysh City for a day before we continue north to the family cottages on the windward edge."

Joh wanted to laugh. Here was a three-name bright, family matriarch, owner of at least one skerry and cottages, getting defensive about her wealth. Shan had a way of making everyone feel shabby and poor.

"Joh?" said Shan. "Now would be a good time."

"Right. Vhen Dyns Quyn, you should give us transportation."

"Why of course," answered the female, directing her response to Shan. "I'd be happy to give the queen's nephew a ride."

"Perhaps a little more specific," suggested Shan.

"Lend us your skerry and the crew. You want to stay here for a few more days."

"I was thinking how nice this town is," Vhen agreed, still addressing Shan. "The children love racing on the lake."

"We'll be back before you know we're gone," Shan promised.

The Queen's Claw watched the conversation in silent amazement. Being of lower caste than Shan and Vhen, speaking her opinion would have been a terrible breach of etiquette.

"I'll call the crew down and explain."

"No need," said Joh.

"Your dull really is quite rude," the matriarch told Shan.

"Yes, I'll talk to him about that."

"It would be best," Joh added, "if you didn't tell anyone about this."

Vhen huffed. "Bossy little thing, isn't he?"

"Quite," agreed Shan. "What is the skerry's name?"

Vhen turned a main eye up to the skerry. "This is *A State of Slow Decay*. He's been in my family for generations."

"I promise we'll take care of him" Shan swore. "Shall we?" he asked Joh and Ahk.

Once again taking the lead, he headed up the stairs. Joh stepped aside, allowing Ahk to go next.

When Shan was out of hearing range, he faced Vhen. "From now on you will treat all males and dulls as equals. In fact, you will make equality your life's work." She stared at him in appalled shock. "And you," he said to the guard, "will never speak of any of this."

"So very rude," muttered Vhen as Joh followed his friends up the steps. "As if I would ever treat anyone as anything less than equal."

The guard said nothing.

A few minutes later, after suggesting to the crew that they obey whatever orders Shan gave them, they left the village behind. Disgusted by the malformed white, the crew avoided the three youths.

Joh leaned heavily against the front rail, exhausted from using his talent so often in such a short time. Ahk stood to his left, Shan on her far side. Lush greenery passed by below as the skerry built speed and altitude. Unlike the Yil skerry, this one was healthy and well-cared for. It climbed faster, the world falling away beneath them. Yet no matter how high it got Joh saw no sign of the island's edge. Nor could he see the desert, which lay several days in their future.

A rafak, skimming the tops of the trees, matched pace with them.

Is that you, Kris?

The creature ducked into the foliage, disappearing.

"How far are we from the leeward edge?" Joh asked.

"More than a week," Shan answered. "Less than two."

He tried to imagine flying over endless storm, no ground below, and shuddered.

"And how far is Yil?"

Shan gave a helpless shrug. "It used to be many months away. I heard it's getting closer. Maybe a month? Two?"

"How will we find it?" Joh asked.

"It's an island. How can we miss?"

Ahk turned a main eye toward Joh. "My mother flew with the Queen's Wing. She commanded battle skerry, flew missions to feral islands and fought pirates. She told me that after a couple of days travel, Nysh Island disappears. The scale is beyond comprehension. With no island in sight, you can't tell how high you are. You'll be coasting along, and everyone starts feeling faint because the air is too thin, or every breath begins to burn because you've unwittingly lost altitude. You're alone in the nothing with only Alatash to guide you. They lost skerry in the river of days all the time. A crew would go out on patrol and never come back."

Shan stared out over the sprawling forests. "If Ahk is right, how can we possibly find another island? Are we making a mistake?"

"I don't think we have anything to worry about," Joh said. "Izi's luck will guide us. If we fail, she dies with everyone else."

"That would be brilliant," Shan said, "if I hadn't overheard one of the doctors say Izi wasn't going to survive the night. With two barbed hunting arrows deep in her guts, she was probably dead before we left."

Joh hadn't heard that. Was he wrong about the power of her

talent? "But you don't know that she's dead."

"I guess not," admitted Shan.

Standing in the middle, Ahk placed a craft claw on Shan and Joh's upper shoulders. "It doesn't matter. Even if we knew for sure Izi was dead, we'd still have to try."

Wex would never give up.

She sacrificed herself to save a single friend; how could Joh do any less for an entire island?

AHK TAY KYM

The older generations claim we are as we always have been, as the gods made us. They say the self is not to be found in selfishness, but in service to queen and Redemption.

They have half the truth. Selfishness is not the path to self. Likewise, our deepest past remains with us. But hive has many meanings. There's the hive you were born into, your family, your town, your queendom, your island.

And then there's the hive you choose.

If you want to find yourself, find your hive.

—Anonymous

They flew south and windward, the crew following Joh's suggestions as if it were the most natural thing in the world for brights to obey a runt dull. Days passed, the ground below fading from verdant green to a thousand shades of brown. The others spoke of the change in the air, how they missed the damp of the jungles, and she felt none of it.

Shorn and alone; she remembered that foul dull's words.

A Slow and Gentle Descent into Dark was long gone by now, the skerry and its cargo of corpses having burned to nothing in the storm beneath the world.

She tried not to think of her mother's soul suffering for all eternity in the fires of Kratosh.

The nights were the worst, sleep its own nightmare.

Trapped in her unfeeling carapace, the dark stole the world. Ahk was an insignificant gnat of consciousness. She craved connection and found only oblivion.

THE STORM BENEATH THE WORLD

I will hold on long enough to avenge you, she told the memory of her mother.

The truth was, she'd lost so much more than a parent. The vengeance she once craved now seemed like a pale mockery.

The entirety of the Yil Queendom must have been poisoned by the Mad Queen; there could be no other explanation for their willingness to follow such insanity. Another queen would rise to take her place. Perhaps the new queen couldn't send Nysh into the storm, but there'd still be war. Many would die.

If killing Queen Yil wasn't enough, what then?

Ahk saw the answer, handed to her by the gods: If she could get Joh close enough to the Mad Queen, he could tell her to send her own island into the storm.

Kill them all.

True vengeance, brutal and bloody and utterly complete.

For you, Mother. For Queen Nysh and all the island.

Death was in the details, but she had time.

Decision made, Ahk fought the urge to haunt Shan and Joh's dreams. It was bad enough listening to their thoughts during the day. At night, their minds fell to chaos. Flashes of imagery, moments of unspoken contemplation painted thick in the regret of hindsight.

Over and over Joh replayed Wex's last moments. He begged and pleaded with her killer. He threw himself into the path of the attack that killed her. And each time she died anyway.

He's torturing himself.

Shan dreamed of being the first male god, concubine to the Queen of the Storm. Together they burned the clouds from the sky to expose the dead city of the gods. With seamless transition he dreamed they travelled to a Corrupt island and found someone with the talent to heal Ahk. She stood with him, once again whole, and his guilt faded. Then, she blackened and melted, layers of exoskeleton sloughing away to leave her malformed and sickly white. The guilt returned with crushing force. In every dream sparks danced around him and the air stank of burnt meat.

Leave them alone.

Much as she needed the connection, it was still an invasion.

THE STORM BENEATH THE WORLD

Shorn and alone, she slept.

And dreamed.

She was a retired captain of the Queen's Wing serving a wealthy family. Flying high above the queendom she looked down upon the beauty of the island below. Lush jungles and rolling fields of healthy crops. There was something comforting in understanding how small you were. Up here, even queens ceased to matter. All was hive. All was belonging, each ashkaro part of a greater whole.

Ahk wrapped herself in the dream until it splintered apart, became scattered remnants sinking toward endless uncaring black.

Fear and confusion, *No! No!* and then the dream was gone.

She found another dream, crawled into it like it were her own. She walked her mother's plantation feeling the damp wind feather her antennae, basking in the rich scent of life. The mother of her dream wasn't the mother the Yil spies sent to the storm, and she'd never seen this estate, but it didn't matter. The dream supplied the escape she craved, and she fled to it.

The ground became swamp, and she sank. The fields died and browned, insects falling dead from the air. The world felt flipped, the sky above a raging inferno and still the mud swallowed her whole. The world shrank until she was alone, a soul screaming in terror as it disintegrated.

I've felt that before!

Caught in the drowning dream, she struggled to remember.

Watching the soldier die back in the dungeon.

She recalled the way the last sparks of consciousness clung desperately to existence, as if becoming nothing was the most terrifying fate imaginable.

Ahk woke with a start. Euphoria filled her to bursting and she basked in the bliss until understanding returned: she'd been using her talent in her sleep, escaping to the dreams of the crew. She reached out, searching for their thoughts, and found only the tiniest dwindling motes.

They're dying.

Someone was stalking from room to room, murdering the crew.

Rolling out of her hammock, Ahk crashed awkwardly to the floor. Had she made noise? She couldn't know.

Where was the killer?

THE STORM BENEATH THE WORLD

She found Joh and Shan still sleeping. Closer, she found a raging storm of tortured thought. It was a dull male begging for scraps in Yil city. It twisted itself to serve males and females alike, becoming their foulest craving. It was a bright female lording her power over her helpless family. It was a student in a school for the Corrupt and it was a spy and an assassin, lurking in the shadows, waiting for the order to strike. It hated itself more than it loved its queen. It sought redemption in service and loathed what it did in that service.

It stood outside her bedroom door.

Service is salvation, it thought. *Kill the heretics. Earn your salvation.*

HERE WE GO AGAIN!

I sat down to write The Acknowledgements and then it turned into the Acknowledge Mints, and I knew I was goofing off.

And so, instead, I'm going to babble a bit. I might accidentally thank a few people. Who knows?!

I wrote *The Storm Beneath the World* back in 2018. It went through the usual beta-read and editing process and then I sent it to my agent, Paul Lucas, at Janklow & Nesbit. He loved the book and spent a year and a half shopping it to publishers. We got some lovely feedback, but in the end the book was a little odd and no one quite knew how to sell it. This is the story of my life. The first book of every series I write has been shopped to publishers and rejected. Some have gone on to win awards, land in the finals of the SPFBO, and sell rather well. But there's still that little twitch of depression when word comes back that all the publishers worth submitting to have passed on your beloved book baby. Each time, it kicks the shit out of my self-confidence for a few months and I wonder if I've written a shitty book. The fact my agent loved it doesn't help. The fact my beta-readers loved it doesn't help. The amazing early reviews don't help. The fact this has happened so many times before doesn't help.

Each time, I need to claw my way out the far side.

What makes it funny is how excited I am to send my agent a new book each time. Those weeks and months of "Maybe this is the one!" Right now, Paul is making notes on *The Driftland Dragons #1*, a middle-grade fantasy I wrote for my daughter. Once we're happy it's as slick as it can be, he'll start shopping it. This being something out of my typical wheelhouse, it's particularly exciting.

THE STORM BENEATH THE WORLD

I sent the first draft of DUST OF THE DEAD to my First Reader, Carrie Chi Lough (thank you!), a couple days ago. Once I hear back from Carrie and make any needed changes, I'll fire it off to the awesome folks on my Patreon (thank you!) who help with beta-reading. Once I'm happy the book is the absolute best I am capable of producing, it'll go off to Paul and the cycle will continue.

There is something masochistic here. The entire process, from that first *Ooh, I have an idea for a book* moment, through the world/character building, the months of writing and editing, and then all the waiting while it's in publisher limbo is kinda unhealthy. At least for me. I think some (most?) writers are better at dealing with it.

And yet I fucking love it.

I don't want to do anything else. The thought I might someday have to is so much more awful than the waiting.

So, if you're one of those crazy people who buys my books, thank you! And if you're one of those even crazier people who reads them, thank you!

I love writing books, but a big part of that is knowing there are a few folks out there enjoying them. Your letters, emails, messages, tweets, and whatever else are all MASSIVELY appreciated. I started writing for *me*, because I had an idea for a story (*Ghosts of Tomorrow*) and wanted to know if I could tell it.

I keep writing for *you*.

Mike Fletcher
Feb 5th, 2024

Printed in Great Britain
by Amazon

06965593-572b-4830-a8fb-f08a3ab39778R01